In the Valley of Dying Stars

H. Grant Llewellyn

*Front cover is a detail from The Garden of Earthly Delights
by Hieronymous Bosch*

Also by: H. Grant Llewellyn

- As Wind In Dry Grass (2010) TheCall Co. Ltd.

For *M,* as always

There are no eyes here
In this valley of dying stars
In this hollow valley
This broken jaw of our lost kingdoms

T.S. Elliot: The Hollow Men

Prologue

Four years ago, the world was a recognizable place. Its seven billion inhabitants prosecuted their lives in typically mindless fashion, just as they had been doing for some five or six thousand years. There was no reason to believe 2013 would be different; but never forget that 'two things are infinite; the universe and human stupidity.' [1]

It began just before Christmas when hundreds of transport trucks carrying food to the cities exploded en route. A terrorist organization - or organizations - had carefully plotted the sabotage and over a period of a few days installed time bombs in over five hundred cargo vehicles. They exploded on highways, at unloading docks, in truck stops and in city traffic. Within twenty-four hours of the first explosion, food supplies in the major cities were gone and the population began to riot. As the chaos spread, numerous unaffiliated anti-government groups and terrorist organizations that had waited years for this golden opportunity, poured their best efforts into the mix and within a week, The United States was brought shuddering to its knees.

Almost a million citizens died in the first ten days.

The government might have regained some vestige of control had not a twisted, most unnatural permutation of nature, intervened to create a perfect storm. A mutating virus, released from a military lab (whether deliberately or by accident will never be known) quickly spread through the population, killing over two hundred and fifty million in the United States alone. It took flight from JFK to Bangkok and London and soon enough, the old world was no more.

In its place remained a desolate, transfigured no-man's land, where friend and foe be the same man separated only by a few hours and a modest change in circumstance; where the weak and the incapable - and the unwilling - were consumed like krill by a monstrous whale; where to be female was a burden and a curse, a temple of fear where no twentieth century American woman ever imagined herself

5

to be a congregant; where there were no children; where gangs of heavily armed men declared themselves dictators of tiny fiefdoms and ruled their enthralled populations with an iron fist; where packs of feral dogs as many as a hundred strong roamed the deserted cities leaving behind nothing living when they passed; where the stench of decaying human flesh rides the wind...

And yet, as real as the present situation was for most of the survivors, it retained a surrealistic aura, not so much like a dream or nightmare from which one does not immediately wake, but more like a hypnotized state where one is seated in a comfortable chair hallucinating from drink or fever. In a dream, one usually has a sense of the absurdity even when confronting it. One knows intrinsically that it is a dream and though terrors or great pleasures may linger for a moment or an hour after waking, eventually the dream is lost and soon enough not even its residue remains.

But this! What was this?

What Albert and the others had witnessed in the years following the Great Catastrophe, was neither imagined terrors nor simple death; it was not even the orchestrated mass death of war. It belied concentration camps and gas chambers, carpet bombing and nuclear blasts.

The bodies of the dead lay in heaps or strewn across the land for years after the disease outbreak. Pyres of burning dead roared night and day and those remaining could do nothing but feed the flames. The stench of burning human flesh and the sight of bodies was a permanent scar on the landscape of every mind still functioning; cities in ruins, cannibal gangs; perpetual insomnia; the whole Pandora's box of tribulations loosed upon the innocent and the guilty in equal parts and without discrimination; the coming of hell to earth.

In the once-great United States of America, an economic calamity in the year 2007 started the process that ended in this avoidable cataclysm.

In order to stave off what they believed to be an economic Armageddon from which recovery would be nearly impossible, the government took twenty years future earnings of the country's workers and pledged it to a coterie of Wall Street banksters, investment "experts" and other assorted criminals who had in fact had deliberately and with malice aforethought, created the doomsday scenario in the first place. The crack of doom thundered from the maw of Hell, itself: The whole of civilization would be sucked into the vortex of these corrupted and putrescent financial institutions if they were allowed to fail. They had to be propped up, supported with more money and then more and more. But, surprise of all surprises, this money was to be borrowed from the Federal Reserve, which was owned by these very same banksters caterwauling doom and perdition should they lose their billion dollar bonuses.

If we go down, they were quick to offer, you shall come with us.

So a shuffling, sycophantic government of slime-covered wretches sucking the jism of the Federal Reserve for their very existence, then agreed to repay the Federal Reserve all the money they had just borrowed from the Federal Reserve to give to the Federal Reserve in the first place so the Federal Reserve and its coterie of sneering conmen and blood-suckers would not default on society.

"We're doing God's work," the pus-sucking Necromancers claimed, indignant at any criticism from the masses with their torches and pitchforks. Except there were few masses, few pitch forks, few torches. Imbecilic super-communists and an assortment of the lunatic fringe had a cookout in front of the Stock Exchange in New York and went potty on the steps of Oakland City Hall, but alas, nobody cared. Certainly not the taxi drivers and carpenters and waitresses and shoe salesmen who were informed that they had to pay the money back to the banksters that the government had given the banksters because they had borrowed that money from the banksters who needed their money back. They were much too busy trying to pay their own bills and support Lord Blankfein and the gang downtown, to protest anything. I mean, you gotta sleep sometime.

Yes, children this is really how it went.

The amount will never be known, for the caper was pulled off under a program of secrecy and obfuscation, outright lies, deception, payoffs and probably not a few murders mafia style that was protected by a veil of National Security. It was a calumny so monstrous in mien and proportion that it was literally unbelievable. Not a one of the thieving, baby-raping, scum sucking, filthy slugs who profited from this grand deception was ever charged, investigated or even questioned about what happened.

Ever fearing reprisals from a discontent public, the government of the United States under the guise of omnipotent National Security, began to tighten the restraints on public life. New agencies formed, with ominous names such as, Family Relocation Camps" and "Fusion Centers." Eventually they grew to comprise almost a million employees spread over ten thousand different locations among two thousand separate agencies consuming unknown and unaccounted for billions and ostensibly reporting only to each other.

Warrantless wiretapping, arrests and detention, the torture of suspects, extra-legal assassinations at home and abroad, random searches of commuters on subway trains and buses where those without the right "papers" were detained for questioning - sometimes for days - video surveillance of almost every public street and quarters and widespread recording of conversations between private citizens; campaigns to encourage citizens to spy on each other and report anything "suspicious" (which included talking, whispering, using cash, carrying a backpack, talking on a mobile telephone, texting, taking pictures, wearing hooded garments, supporting certain political candidates, referring to the U.S. Constitution and attaching certain bumper stickers to personal vehicles), to name just a few - became the order of the day.

Terrorists continued to stuff bombs into their underwear and board airplanes unchallenged except for an alert passenger; Islamist jihadists well protected against criticism or scrutiny right inside the U.S. Military murdered U.S. soldiers on U.S. military bases inside the continental U.S., and government contractors were paid $800 for a toilette seat and $1 million to ship two 19-cent washers to a Texas army base.

There were billions available for any scheme no matter how ludicrous, ineffective or counter-productive so long as the words "terrorism" or "security" were attached.

CEOs from Goldman Sachs squirreled away, at public expense, such treasure as had never been seen before, then went on to run the U.S. Treasury and influence, if not outright control, all financial legislation thereof. Once they had arranged the laws and loopholes in their favor, they returned to the company to take advantage of everything they had created. Miscreants from Monsanto moved on to head up the Department of Agriculture, craft the next generation of laws and then returned to take up the helm of the company that was attempting to control the food supply of the entire planet. Disgraced execs from the drug industry's highest echelons moved over to run the Food and Drug Administration and swam back in a sea of bogus cancer treatments, questionable vaccines and murderous medications having assured the public that "charlatans" selling bee pollen and extract of petunia would be prosecuted to the hilt. Washington inside lawyers went to Justice and former oil company executives took over the Environment portfolio. And former government managers of emergency services found themselves miraculously running companies that sold emergency equipment back to the government!

Trillions for the banks; hundreds of billions for electioneering by the putrescent filth that occupied both chambers of the congress, but nothing for the man about to lose his home; nothing for the medically uninsured; nothing for the tens of millions of jobless wandering the streets. Trillions to rebuild Iraq but not a dime for Detroit or the abysmal Louisiana school system or the crumbling sewers poisoning the drinking water.

And for those who dared object there was the slow but persistent suppression of free speech through multitudinous layers of bogus hate legislation, Internet policing, onerous punitive taxes and the banning of certain words.

"If you see something, say something," they urged from the bully pulpit of Washington. Just make damn sure not to say anything we don't want to hear.

Police forces across the country encouraged a campaign of brutality against the citizenry that could not possibly have any other purpose than to remind the saps who was in charge. The Gestapo would have been proud.

Handicapped children were assaulted; women were pounded into the ground for sleeping in the wrong place; eyes were gouged out; innocents were gunned down, occasionally murdered outright and witnesses arrested. Victims of police attacks were charged with assaulting police while they remained unconscious in intensive care. This included an eighty-five year old WWII veteran who made the mistake of confronting a police officer who had ordered his car towed. The old man placed a hand on the police officer's shoulder. The brave officer picked up the frail old fellow and slammed him head first into the pavement, crushing his vertebrae. These grotesque freaks along with private security guards and campus police-pigs, blasted mace into the faces of unarmed students sitting silent and unresisting on a sidewalk protesting – guess what?: Police Brutality! But they took it a lot farther than that and the complicity of their civilian overlords was apparent and undeniable. How else could an Albuquerque school district get away with having a 14-year-old student arrested and jailed for burping in class? Or how about the California securi-

9

ty guard who broke the arm on a 16-year-old girl for spilling crumbs on the floor, calling her 'nappy head' all the while? A 12-year-old in New York was arrested and taken out of school in handcuffs for writing, "I love my friends…" on a desk. County officials in Virginia charged a couple with Class 3 misdemeanors and forced them into court – because their children were late for school. When recounted these stories appeared unbelievable – literally. So skeptics would invest a few moments research on the Internet and find not only that every one of the above occurred exactly as described, but that newspapers and television archives from one end of the country to the other were full of similar incidents. Fear and a concomitant hatred of police swooned the nation prompting one snarling blue-bellied cacique to ironically remark that it appeared as though people had declared war on the constabulary. It seemed as though it could only be a matter of time before someone took it into his own hands to reply to some of these syphilitic sacks of porcine excrement waddling around with guns and badges. But the sad truth was simple: The egregious behavior of police departments went unanswered virtually everywhere.

But that wasn't the half of it. The American Nation by 2013 was rent from stem to stern. No aspect of life escaped the swelling malignancy of fascism, corporate greed and malfeasance, political chicanery and suppression of public will. Private gardens came under the scrutiny of the Department of Agriculture; herbalists were tormented by the Food and Drug Administration for making tea; those who dared sell raw milk were the subject of multimillion dollar undercover operations and jailed; people were forced to purchase the products of large corporations and forbidden from trading foodstuffs amongst themselves lest they cause injury. Commercial hamburger crawling with E.coli and imported melons and lettuce teaming with listeria and salmonella left a string of corpses across the country. So, in response, the government immediately banned the sale of homemade cookies at school functions and arrested anyone caught selling lemonade from a Radio Flyer. Police inspectors were assigned to Kindergarten lunchrooms to make sure everyone ate the same deep-fried ptomaine chicken. Family barbecues were raided and the participants strip-searched and sent to county jail.

Conglomerates with gross revenues far in excess of the GNP of two thirds of the world, prohibited American farmers from growing anything but prescribed genetically-modified crops by bankrupting anyone who dared harvest his own beans. After the courts declared corporations to be human beings, there was nowhere left to appeal.

American life had been annexed by a government that had long since lost any sense of purpose other than the preservation and expansion of its own power.

The 'government' by the year 2013, in partnership with the banking industry, was the largest and most powerful criminal organization ever conceived by men.

Each day, it added clusters of security legislation and enforcement teams, passing egregiously unconstitutional laws in the middle of the night whose only purpose was to protect the criminals and the gangsters and political miscreants from the people they supposedly served. But who would protect the people from them?

Indeed, it seemed so powerful and so omnipresent that resistance was futile and the overwhelming majority of the population acceded to whatever was demanded of them, with an alacrity that would shame a sheep in the slaughterhouse. They dutifully turned in their neighbors, sent their sons into the meat grinder of pointless wars (pointless unless you were Halliburton and made billions from the adventures); consumed the dross they were given and complained of nothing but the increasing price of cable television and the persistent failure of the Chicago Cubs. The question ringing in the minds of millions of Americans: Who won Dancing With the Stars, last night?

But, double, double toil and trouble;[2] a rage was in fact brewing among the cognoscenti. Conspiracy theorists, subversive militias, oath keepers, sovereign citizens, survivalists, religious lunatics, anarchists and psychopathic vegetarians had one thing in common: They wanted out. And no matter how the authorities tried to uncover them and suppress them and eliminate them, they could not. With every subterfuge, entrapment and frame-up at their disposal, the anti movement grew. The bedlamites marching around in the woods playing soldier and the demented loudmouths broadcasting their paranoid lunacy across the Internet were not the problem and the government knew it. The quiet man was their greatest fear; the man they could not identify. They knew the majority of U.S. soldiers would fire on their fellow citizens if ordered to do so, but what of those who would not? Who were they? Where were they? How could they be identified?

Concentration camps were established in every region of the country to handle the expected trainloads of saboteurs. They knew one group of psychopaths or another would manage to pull off something of a magnitude so terrible and at once magnificent in its horror that it would alter the balance of the universe.

Presidents of countries and companies were united in their calls for a New World Order.

But the New World *Dis*order they ended up with, was nothing like they envisaged. Soon, it would blow back on them in ways they had never imagined.

Part One

But as for the cowardly, the faithless, the detestable, as for murderers, the sexually immoral, sorcerers, idolaters, and all liars, their portion will be in the lake that burns with fire...

Revelations: 21, 8

Chapter One

Lake of Fire

Albert Smythe held his breath for a moment and then exhaled slowly. He breathed at a steady pace until his entire body was vibrating at one simple, clear frequency. He watched through the riflescope as the chubby colonel opened his mouth wide to laugh, his head tilted back. Albert slowly filled his lungs and became still...

The 30.06 bullet left the barrel at Mach 3 and traveled 1000 yards in about a second-and-a-half. It dove into the cave of the colonel's mouth like a smart cruise missile and then exited through the back of his head. Sullied now with blood and brain matter but undeterred, it carried on half way across the base before it smacked into one of the few remaining ash trees left in Southern Indiana. (There it remained for twenty-seven years until a woodcutter named Mikol discovered it and put it in his pocket.) All this before said colonel's body had stopped bouncing on the ground.

The crack of the shot breaking the sound barrier followed quickly on the heels of the vanished bullet and the half dozen subordinates who had been kissing the colonel's ass, left their beloved leader in the dirt and bolted for shelter.

Albert watched the scene through his scope until the personnel on the base had shifted into gear and were preparing to mount a search and destroy mission back down the trajectory of the bullet. The helicopter started to rock as the blades whopped the air and Albert could see the pilot and the copilot rapidly getting the machine ready for takeoff. The side gunner appeared and Albert sighted on him but did not pull the trigger because the metal insect had started to wobble off the ground and a miss might further identify his location without giving him a kill in exchange.

He slowly and carefully bagged the rifle and climbed the few feet down to the ground from the bough of the old oak he had used as a nest.

His escape route was well planned and he turned west and folded into the dense brush and trees that over the last few years had crept back up against the grain field. Once upon a time, this field, like millions of others had danced and cheered in the summer breeze but now it lay fallow, unturned, overgrown and silent. He passed over it without leaving a trace.

He walked a calm but steady pace, relentlessly increasing the distance between himself and the kill zone.

By the time they arrived at his nest, he had plunged almost a mile into the forest and they found nothing, not even an expended shell casing for their efforts.

The helicopter made ever widening circles in a great spiral from the supposed origin of the shot and several teams had started beating the woods in a futile attempt to locate the shooter. They searched for an hour in all the directions of the compass but nary a trace would be located. Just as in the previous eighteen killings, they hadn't a clue who was targeting them or how to catch him. How could he tell who was who when all insignias had been removed and saluting and other tokens of rank were forbidden? Who was painting the victims for the shooter? It was well understood that the mysterious assassin only shot senior officers. The joke among the enlisted men was, "did he take requests?"

Posting to the forward base established at Provost in this, the fourth year of 'The Catastrophe,' as it came to be called, was now considered a punishment. The Provost Legion had the highest desertion rate among the bases south of Indianapolis from the Illinois border all the way across to what used to be Cincinnati in what used to be Ohio. The distemper was exacerbated by the fact that Provost was a hub in the transportation of men and materials throughout southern Indiana and Kentucky and so could not be abandoned.

The woods around Provost had become Albert Smythe's home over this time. The original public lands comprised around two hundred thousand acres but the private lands added another two hundred and fifty thousand to the sum and now that there was no distinction, the vast concourse of limestone cliffs, sandstone canyons, sink holes, hidden caves and underground rivers was an almost impenetrable hideout, for outlaws like Albert.

It was also the home base of numerous armed gangs, packs of wild dogs and the ruins of a few communes - it was exaggeration to call them towns - where the naïve and the moronic had been massacred and their meager possessions divided among the conquerors.

Albert knew the seven hundred square miles probably better than anyone. He had traversed the area from French Lick to Rome, both ghost towns now and could walk in blind darkness through the woods on his directional instinct alone and come out within yards of his destination. There was no one who could track him and the few who had tried had not returned.

This included two women from one of the rag-tag special operations units the army had cobbled together. Albert did not discriminate on the basis of gender. The younger of the two had been moderately attractive. He had considered trying to recruit her, maybe induce her to desert and join him. But then he had found them glued together and he shot them where they lay. They died without fear or knowledge, burrowing into each other's struggling flesh. It was a kindness. They had come out here looking for him and they had succeeded. He dare not imagine what they might have done to him.

They were adequately equipped and he stripped them of everything including their clothing, which he burned in place before moving the bodies. Their GPS tracking devices and all electronic equipment went onto the fire next. It took a while for him to locate the subcutaneous transmitters but he eventually found them - under each left breast - little wormlike scars that had not completely healed. He excised the devices and examined them with a magnifying glass before smashing them. Then he collected their weapons and ammunition in a blanket and set it aside. He dragged the older woman to a dolomite cliff and rolled her into a deep crevice. He dragged the younger one a quarter of a mile into the woods and left her for the dogs.

Albert hauled the blanket roll of weapons about a mile into the woods and hid it loosely under some brush. Then he returned to the kill zone and sat down to wait.

The search helicopter found the burn site where he had disposed of their clothing about a day later. That had been the last triangulated location of the transmission from their microchips, but they located neither body, which meant that he had extracted the only transmitters hidden in their flesh. The search team did not even attempt to look for the guns, which meant they had not put tracking devices on those yet. Eventually they must figure that one out. Albert marveled at their incompetence. He could have killed them all. But it was more important to let them go, to send them home empty-handed. The day would come when he would want to lure them into an ambush, but today was not that day.

Albert sat down to catch his breath. He had been churning through the woods for the better part of an hour and hypoglycemia was turning him into Gumby.

He removed a small container from his jacket and slowly ate the contents over a period of about fifteen minutes, sipping some water and breathing slowly. After the sugar fugue subsided, he remained where he was, watching the woods for almost an hour before he decided to move again.

He had to walk almost sixty-five miles back through the woods to his own home base and a lot could happen before he arrived. It was safer to move during daylight because their night vision equipment didn't function as well and in this thinly populated forbidden zone, any heat signature would be taken out without notice. Occasionally he came across a deer or a feral domestic beast that had been blown to pieces by a drone missile, reminding him that the criteria for pulling a trigger or loosing a bomb was now zero. If you saw it, you killed it. Period.

Even the pretense of civilian authority was gone and individual military units tended to commandeer an area and claim it as their own. They continued to liaise with some central command but were generally left to manage their sectors as they saw fit. The military had annexed virtually all of the known stocks of preserved food, bottled water, medicines, fuel and just about anything else they deemed a vital necessity. Their soldiers were fed, housed, and cared for much differently from the mass of the population which had been originally quarantined in any one of about one hundred "Family Relocation Camps" the federal government had established in the first decade of the 21st Century, directly in anticipation of coming national disasters.

Now the dispossessed congregated in empty towns, camped in gypsy parks, scrabbled for tradable items and lined up obediently and quietly for the food distributions managed by their military masters. The military had quickly realized the importance of maintaining control of the food supply and hoarders were shot without trial. Gardens were strictly controlled and a significant portion of fresh produce ended up at the officers' mess. Once the military had euthanized anyone that might present opposition, they turned the majority of the population loose to provide slave labor for the various outland control units. In exchange for an MRE or a chocolate bar, the sheeple would work somewhere between eight and twelve hours a day, mostly collecting the dead for burial, but also helping repair living quarters for their masters and keeping the commander's dogs groomed and exercised.

The Council of Governors,[3] a coterie of ten political hacks who could be counted upon to enforce the Draconian rules of martial law continued to officially manage each of the ten sectors into which the country had been divided; but the military was in control. They had the guns. And the food. And just about everything else.

Indiana was in Sector 3, which included Wisconsin and Minnesota, Illinois, Michigan and Ohio. Michigan's long association with citizen militia groups through the 1990s right up to the moment of catastrophe in 2013 had resulted in a particularly brutal occupation by marines and private contractors. After what was left of the militia movement had been taken to the Beech Grove detention facility outside of Indianapolis where they were water-boarded, electrocuted and burned with blow torches before being gassed and cremated, Sector Three became a kind of internal rendition clearing house for dissidents from around the country. Rumors, mostly unsubstantiated, but nonetheless persistent, circulated in American Free Forces units that more than twenty five thousand civilians had been murdered at Beech Grove alone by Homeland Security and FEMA in the four years since the first transport truck had exploded on a bridge going into Manhattan. Indiana had become one of the centers of resistance and while a modicum of peace, order and government prevailed in many parts of the country, here it was total war. The Spanish Deguello had sounded and mercy was neither expected nor extended. Almost everyone carried a suicide capsule in the event of capture. Informants and traitors were burned alive along with captured soldiers and videos of the events were sent to their respective unit commanders.

Albert considered all of this as he wound his way through the woods, as wary of running into militia as he was of government men. For the last year, he had managed to stay out of communication with anyone on either side. Once considered by the authorities to be the leader of a widespread resistance movement, his name eventually faded and rumors circulated that he had been captured and killed. No one had linked him to the assassinations. Yet. And that's the way he wanted it to stay.

He had been crossing and re-crossing the new wilderness, memorizing the landscape, learning his craft and preparing for the all-out battle he knew must eventually come to this part of the country - if not the whole country.

Albert could have made this journey back to his camp in his sleep, though he never took the same trail twice. Some internal homing device had activated in his brain and he could tell by the vegetation, the slope of the land and sometimes the wild dog population where he was, to within a few hundred yards.

There was a small dog pack following him now and he tried to keep in their shadow as much as possible. There would be drones and helicopters looking for him, and the dogs provided a decent cover. If he could appear to be just another member of the pack, the searchers might pass on by.

He'd seen this particular group last week on his way in to kill the colonel. It was led by an unusually intelligent Rottweiler who seemed to understand that Albert was much more of a danger to the dog pack than the reverse. At 31 inches at the shoulder and weighing around 170 pounds, it was the largest Rottweiler he'd ever seen. It managed the pack with a force and brutality that was mesmerizing. He'd come upon them in conflict with a second pack that was venturing west and had wandered into the Rott's territory. The Rottweiler had killed three opponents in less than two minutes. He grabbed a particularly aggressive pit bull by the neck and snapped it's spine with two or three violent shakes.

Albert took out his .45 auto and pulled the slide. No dog, no matter how big or strong or insane would stand up to the slug from that weapon but Albert wanted nothing more than to pass from his territory and leave the pack be.

It reminded him of his German shepherd, Ludwig who had been shot right in front of his eyes by a uniformed psychopath in the early days of the catastrophe. The dog had been his constant companion since he was a few weeks old and Albert missed him still. He had poured kerosene down the cop's throat and then tossed in a match. He watched him burn to death, never taking his eyes off the writhing, screaming figure until his last fetid breath passed into the night air.

Even now, he could work up a rage over the incident and the memory was often enough to make him pull the trigger on some hapless guard or auxiliary constable assigned as an overseer among the new order slaves. Albert killed policemen, soldiers, elected officials, spokespersons - anybody, in fact who assumed a position of authority or power, except those he believed had been elected by common consent. And he killed without remorse or regret or even very much thought. When he found them, he killed them. Once he killed them, they were gone and he could go find another one. He would keep killing them until there were no more leaders and no more subalterns to carry out their orders. He was not restricted to the official enemy as far as it went. He had killed three militia leaders in the last sixteen months among the dozens of regulars that had fallen to his rifle or his knife.

The first errant militia commander was an ex-soldier who had deserted the National Guard about six months into the catastrophe after his unit ended up in a fire fight with farmers who were refusing to go to an internment camp 'for their own good'. This soldier had watched his brave comrades turn automatic weapons on eighteen men, ranging in age from about sixteen to seventy. Several stood unarmed and others sported ancient double-barreled shot guns with No. 5 shot - particularly good against rabbits but somewhat ineffective against Kevlar designed to withstand an armor piercing AK round at point blank range. "For your own good," were the last words these men heard before the Guard unit opened fire. So this errant soldier deserted and found the Indiana Liberty Militia unit near Provost. And for a short time, it worked.

Adam Rickhauser was brave. He was eager. He was determined. But like most revolutionaries who start out full of idealism and righteousness, the original objectives soon became subordinate to his personal ambitions. In a matter of a few months, with his superior military knowledge and training and his forceful personality, he usurped the existing leadership and took control of the militia unit that had hitherto acted against the military and in defense of the civilian population and turned it into a private enterprise. And once he discovered how willing the ordinary man was to obey in exchange for some apparitional security, any sense of self-restraint he might have possessed at the beginning was completely abandoned. Soon he decided that all able-bodied men between sixteen and sixty had to perform a stint in the unit if they wanted to remain within the boundaries of what he considered to be his zone of control and all women were required to obey anything they were ordered to do. Obey or take your chances out there, he told them. But then he decided no one could leave lest they take intelligence about his operations with them. In short order, he had a small feudal kingdom maintained by a coterie of eager overseers and supported by several hundred slaves whose only hope was escape - which was unlikely, death, which was always available or promotion into the ranks of the slaver.

How did he manage it, you might ask, but the answer is before you in pages and pages of history. There is a man born in every generation who cannot organize or lead on his own and in fact seldom has such ambition. But he will, in exchange for the illusion of prestige or the deviant thrill of wielding some small authority, gladly embrace the ambitions of another no matter what or wherefore. He is susceptible to uniforms and flattery, his eyes veritably glisten at the sight of his treasured symbols, whether they be the gun or the whip or the hangman's noose and he keeps the equipment clean and shiny and always at the ready. You may see him polishing the apparatus of his small province until his face looks back from every surface. In the soporific monotony of peacetime, he most often joins the police force where he can at least torment with impunity those unfortunate citizens within his reach. And it is most certainly from among this sorry lot, that most conscienceless enforcers are later recruited. He presents himself to anyone who will command him, eager to obey, eager to enforce another's code for he has none of his own save his dark pleasures, purchased cheap with promises of immunity and the praise of his masters. And he rounds up his fellows and puts them on the trains and when they arrive at their destination, his twin unloads them and herds them into the gas chambers, all in the name of peace and tranquility.

The militia commander deposed by Rickhauser had an understanding with Albert they both respected; they ignored each other. Albert traded with them occasionally and they had spent some time together socially in the evenings, but for the most part, they eschewed each other's company. This changed abruptly one day when Albert came out of the woods to find the old commander dead and Rickhauser standing in his place.

"Natural causes," they said and in a way that was true. It was quite natural now to kill anyone who got in your way and those who could not defend what they laid claim to were eliminated without any sentimentality whatsoever. Death- killing, at least - was no longer the purview of an anti-social element ostracized from normal life or the fanciful subject of academia and theatre; it had resumed its original role as arbiter. The word murder had been removed from the lexicon. There was no longer any such thing as an "illegal killing." Homo sapiens had reverted to his savage state of ten thousand years ago but taken with him as much weaponry from the twenty first century as he could carry.

"You're Smythe," Rickhauser said, eyeing him.

Albert did not respond and this made Rickhauser grin.

"You should join us," Rickhauser added. Then he left, followed by his eager supplicants.

In the intervening months he had little contact with the group until he arrived at their last known rendezvous looking to trade some venison jerky for a can opener. He still could not believe that among the hundreds of utensils he had managed to secure for his own survival, he had neglected to include a can opener.

This particular morning he was bartering with a woman named Corina who had long, straggly, mouse-brown hair and light, watery eyes. She invited him into her drab tent to negotiate further, but he declined. He could smell her across the table and he wasn't that desperate yet.

In the middle of their conversation, two men approached him, both wearing the flashes of the Indiana Liberty Militia. They were carrying AR15s with full clips and for a moment, Albert thought he recognized one of them.

"Ain't seen you around here in a while," the man said. Albert couldn't place him. He nodded and turned back to Corina to show her the jerky he was offering in exchange for the can opener.

"You wanna come along with us," the other man said to Albert's back.

22

Albert turned again and looked at him, astonished, but not showing it.

"Why would I do that?" Albert asked.

"Everybody here has to do their bit. The commander wants everyone signed up."

This time the man showed his impatience and took Albert's arm to move him along.

"Okay, just let me put this stuff away," Albert said agreeably and returned the jerky to a pouch on his side. The man removed his hand and Albert smiled and stepped towards him. All he could do was widen his gaze as Albert's blade struck him in the throat and ripped out his trachea. The man tumbled, blood spraying like a burst hydrant. The other man did not have time to react and Albert slashed him twice across the face, first opening his nose right to the bone and then hacking through his left eye and cheekbone. He could not even scream as Albert twisted the blade breaking off a section of the bony orbit before he plunged it into the brain.

Through all of this, Corina's expression barely changed. She handed him the can opener and he wiped the dripping blood from his eyes and mouth before he retrieved the venison from his pocket.

"Thanks," he said.

She nodded, the glint of an unborn smile in her eyes.

Now he had to make a run for it. It would take only a few minutes before they came looking for the two guards. The obvious route was east through the light bush towards a heavy rock ridge a mile away and he gathered the two AR 15 rifles and the Beretta side arms from his victims before setting out. The fifteen shot pistols were top quality and worth taking, though he didn't much like the 9 mm ammunition. It was a very good short range machine gun bullet, badly suited to its other employment and vastly inferior to both the .40 caliber, popularized by Glock and its death-certain cousin, the mighty .45 auto that he preferred above all. But two Berettas were worth their weight in gold, these days - literally.

He made sure his trail was discoverable if not too obvious as he headed towards the far bluff, locally known as Eastman's Ridge after the teenager, Roger Eastman who had killed himself there. He had explored the area many times and knew there was a narrows between limestone rock shoulders that was used by hikers in the old days and deer and dogs since. He'd give them the choice: Go back to your trailers or follow me and die. He was half way there when he heard the siren indicating someone had found the two dead men.

Panting and wheezing by the time he reached his destination, he sat down and caught his breath. He drank some water. They would travel in a group of at least half a dozen, he guessed, moving relatively slowly because they had to clear every possible ambush along the way. It would give him the time he needed.

He had to climb the last seventy feet to the top of the ridge and it was hard going over the crumbling limestone. He used the few tough little trees as grips where he could but his boots repeatedly slipped off the holds or broke loose rock from the face. Ten feet from the top he rested, sweat dripping from his face and stinging his eyes. He reached for a scrub cedar but it pulled out as soon as he put weight on it and he had to grip the face of the rock, spider-like, until the cascade of dirt and loose rubble exhausted itself and the rock face stabilized. Without looking, he found another crevice and inched his way up until his arms crested the bare, weathered hump and he was able to swing his body over the top. He lay on the ground panting, nearly passed out.

Albert Smythe was not a young man. He was now fifty-two years old and while he was in excellent shape under the circumstances, the kind of exertion he just went through, taxed him to the limit. When he finally sat up, his head was spinning and felt swollen.

He scouted the ridge a few dozen yards in each direction until he found a nest that gave him a clear view of the opening in the woods where he expected them to appear. When he sighted the rifle, his eyes swam and he couldn't focus at first. He closed his eyes and worked on his breathing. Perhaps ten minutes passed before he opened them and his head was clear. He was still sweating profusely and the rivulets crawled down his sides. There was nothing to do now but wait.

He was surprised to see Rickhauser actually leading the column as they emerged from the tree line and Albert studied him in the scope. He was either really arrogant or really stupid. Albert now had the opportunity to behead this little posse on the first shot. The idiot didn't really have the respect of his men, after all, Albert surmised, or he wouldn't strut out front like a turkey at a shooting match to prove himself. One by one, they emerged from the tree line until eleven men were crouched in a close pack scanning the bluff. What he wouldn't give for a mortar about now.

24

The commander waited a few more minutes and then leaving the modest shelter of a few boulders and one dead tree, he walked out into the open to study the ground. Albert continued to watch, aghast at the stupidity. He heard the murmur of their voices though he couldn't make out the words. Within a few minutes, Rickhauser had found the trail marks Albert left for him and, once again out front, led them directly into his line of sight.

"I don't believe this," he muttered.

They were fourteen hundred yards out, beyond Albert's capability as a marksman. Over the years, he had managed to obtain a reasonable skill, but he just didn't have the talent a real shooter needs. Wind, humidity, elevation, parallax...all must be analyzed as one and the perfect moment chosen. With his 30.06, he could shoot five-inch groups at a thousand yards and after that, he just couldn't seem to make it happen. By ordinary standards it was remarkable shooting; by the standards of real snipers, he was not even in the same universe.

Two of the men lit cigarettes and the commander stopped and tilted his canteen, taking a long draught. They were still too far out. There was no way he could guarantee a strike at that distance and a miss would do nothing more than jerk them out of their dream state.

"Come on assholes," he muttered. "Come to Jesus."

He counted to ten, slowly and then unable to resist the urge any longer, Albert filled his lungs and gently squeezed the trigger. A few seconds later, the bullet went straight through Rickhauser's chest and into another man's leg. The troop scattered like birds, several turning around to run back to the tree line and others crashing into each other as they dove for shelter behind the crumbling outcrops and boulders. The next two shots missed and it gave them enough presence to return fire.

They had no idea where he was but it was a safe bet that he was in front of them so they sprayed the cliff edge with automatic fire until a cloud of dust hung between the two adversaries. Albert raised his eye to the scope again and zeroed in on a large bearded man trying to hide behind a rock half his size. Albert's bullet deflected slightly off the boulder and crashed right into the man's head, tearing a trough through his face. He pitched back and the mass firing started again. Albert waited it out and sure enough the firing stopped. A man emerged from behind the dead tree and started to run back to the woods. Albert led him carefully, trying to compute the elevation and bullet drop and wind and then pulled the trigger just as the man entered the shadow of the trees.

The others started firing again, but it was sporadic and disorganized. They had no idea what to do next. Albert knew he was no von Clausewitz but he had begun to learn some basic field tactics after almost four years fighting regular army from behind dead trees and rocks. This group seemed incapable of even instinctive self-defense. He lowered his rifle.

Through binoculars, he watched the remaining half dozen men cowering behind inadequate defenses. The man with the bullet in his leg had crawled back to the tree line and pulled himself to safety.

Albert bagged the rifle and picked up his spent casings. In a few moments, he had moved far enough back from the cliff that he could stand up without being seen. He walked across the rubble plain and vanished into the next set of woods.

He thought of Rickhauser now, as he walked, steadily lengthening the distance between himself and the confused soldiers scrambling around trying to find the shooter who had plagued them now for sixteen months straight. Except for the tentative inveigling of a small dog pack easily routed with a shot to the air, he was alone. He did not expect to be followed. They weren't up to it - yet. He knew that would change. It had to. There had been numerous reports of rebel organizations making nice with each other intending a concerted mass attack against the Provost Legion. The rumors were too many and too consistent to be disregarded and the army had to know as much about the situation as anyone. They would in all probability attempt to preempt any coordinated effort by hunting down and eliminating any group or individual that might take part. They would come after him, just not today.

He sat down on a log and listened carefully for a few moments before taking out his water bottle and opening a small purse of dried meat and fruit that he carried with him. He still had a long way to go and did not expect to make it back to sanctuary this day. He contemplated finding a suitable camp for the night and continuing in the morning. One real danger was the dogs. Another problem was his visibility to night glasses from drones or pickets. He would have to stay put and he could not make a fire. He chewed slowly and decided to spend the night.

First, he looked for a large fallen log, preferably one overgrown with moss and leaves. He cleared the ground under and beside it and lay in a cross-thatched nest of supple green limbs. He covered that with more leaves. The sticks would keep him off the ground and the leaves provided some insulation. He would sleep, fitfully, hunkered up close to the tree - underneath it if possible - to confuse the night cameras. He slept with the 1911 firmly in his grip and lying across his chest.

Albert had not slept through the night even one time in four years. That probably accounted for his being alive. He could not count the number of times he had awakened just soon enough to save himself. He slept in twenty-minute bursts, a light sleep that serves only to rest the eyes and not the brain, which most craves it. He did not move in those twenty minutes. He did not snore. His breathing was slow and quiet. All this he had trained himself to do knowing that he could not lose a single fight. He could not surrender. He could not be captured. He must never be surprised. He had to win every contest or die. He did not take prisoners. If his adversaries surrendered, he would allow them to emerge from hiding and then he would gun them down. He spared no one. He had killed heavily armed, well-trained Special Forces operatives and he had blown the head off a sixteen-year-old girl who had surprised him in a poorly constructed ambush. That incident had burned itself into his brain. Her partners, two older men had tried to run. He followed one to a stream bank and drowned him, watching him struggle and suffocate in the clear water. The other, he gutted with his Emerson knife as the man crouched behind some rocks and left him to be eaten live by dogs. When he returned to the scene, he realized that she was a teenager, probably no older than sixteen and why or how she ended up with those two was anybody's guess. He knew she had tried to kill him and would have done so without thought or conscience. Yet the sight of her wasted limbs and sunken chest with its withered, deflated breasts sickened him to the core and for the first time in many months, he questioned the value of his own survival.

Albert had not started out life as a killer or in fact as anything very unusual at all. He was so mundane and boring a character that people often didn't recognize him the second time they met. And they never remembered his name. He had been a truck driver for twenty years and retired early to a small piece of land where he built a solitary life, caring for a few animals and tinkering in his shop. He had no talents or abilities that he knew of and had never played a musical instrument or written a poem. He had been inadequate at all sports and completely useless in social situations. He had managed two relationships with women in all his life. One was a homeless woman who deserted him without warning and the other was a woman he had met during the early days of the catastrophe. Maureen Grogan. He had thought of her consciously or unconsciously every day since she had disappeared, leaving him a touching, if somewhat dramatic letter. It seemed to cut his last ties with the human race. Remembering her emerging from the shower, hair slicked back like an otter, skin smelling of soap, eyes like cracked puries...he yearned. He didn't realize how disconnected he had become until he killed that girl.

He had survived, but at what price? Should he have sacrificed himself to that young woman? Would that have improved the state of things? When he looked at her, he felt as if he were falling and the image would not go away no matter how he justified it. He was now so covered with violent death that it would not wash off.

He recalled his brief acquaintance with the old Jew, Nathan Hammergold who owned a delicatessen in New York where he often stopped to eat after a delivery. Albert had been curious about the old man who had survived a concentration camp during WWII, coming to America in 1945. He was ninety-six years old when he died. Albert had once asked him about surviving for so long and Hammergold had tried to explain to him that sometimes it wasn't worth it. "Sure, I survived," he said. "So what? They say the best of us went up in smoke." That's when he referred to some old rabbi who had asked the question that now hung in Albert's mind.

If I am only for myself, what am I?[4]

After the killing of that girl, Albert vanished into the deepening wilderness all around and reverted to the solitary existence he had enjoyed before the catastrophe. Wearing Indian-style knee-high moccasins that he had crafted himself, he left no trail wherever he went. His clothing was a soft, felt-like flannel or deer hide, which made no sound when it scraped a branch. His face was almost black with ingrained dirt; his scent a mixture of earth and trees, wild fruits, deer musk and forest air. He could wait in a deer stand for days until the unwitting prey wandered under the limbs that held him to partake of the apples or dried fruit he had placed in its path. When that gentle head bowed to the ground, he leapt straight down onto the back, try-

28

ing to break it with the first blow. This did not always happen and occasionally the deer tried to run. He would cling to the struggling, terrified animal as it fought to escape him, the knife pushing into the throat until the telltale spurt of blood shot out over the forest floor and the beast collapsed. It lifted its head to look at him and died. They always did that. He thanked the deer.

In those months, all through the second winter into the early spring, he never saw another human being or fired a shot. He perfected certain skills including the ability to hit a target at twenty feet with his knife. He could hit a six-inch spot nine times in ten. It wasn't good enough, he knew, but it kept him busy throughout the early part of that long winter. He traipsed from one end of the woodland to the other and back again. He circled through fields and forest over hundreds of square miles, looking for nothing whatsoever and finding it everywhere. He began to recognize the abstruse changes in terrain that allowed him to know where he was at almost any moment. Few would notice for instance the subtle shift in proportion of walnut to maple south of the Emit River, the dark, fruit bearing *Juglans nigra* prospering in the modest flood plain below the waterway and crowding out the maples which clung to the rocks and tougher bedding of the north side of the stream. The Emit flowed underground for large portions of its traverse but Albert knew which side of the river he was on just by looking at the trees. And the transformation of orphan boulders from sandstone to limestone that indicated the irregular fault-line that separated a hundred million years of geologic shifting, told him when he was within three miles of his lair. The squirrels prospered where the oaks were plentiful and the dog packs few. The wide strips of scrub cedar indicated where fine farmland had once rippled the landscape and he could tell when he had changed counties by the shift from corn stalk to soy, what few remnants remained, and the gradual transformation of the soils from forest earth to a rusted, iron-bearing clay.

There was a large colony of black and white rabbits near the west end of the old National Forest boundary that stretched for almost ten miles, likely the result of feral pets escaping or being released after the great calamity and breeding with the local drab population. Their territory never changed and its boundaries declared his position relative to the hundred and twenty foot radio repeater at Norman's Trace. And the Rott had carved out a strict territory of about twenty square miles with easily recognized boundaries that he patrolled with

29

a dedicated regularity; always glad to tell strangers when they had trespassed and more than willing to correct their navigation. Albert could tell from a distant landmark how far he was from any destination within a thirty-mile radius by eyesight alone.

***

Chapter Two

It was Year Two, The Ides of March (by his guess), when he made a discovery that changed his life for the balance of his years and would have consequences generations after his bones had been nibbled to dust by the mice and his name was almost lost to memory.

Pursued by a gathering nimbus from the south, he headed towards the shelter of the rock face along the divide that separated sandstone boulder fields from limestone bluffs. He scrabbled down a washout and found himself tracking along a dried streambed, one that clearly would overflow in a flash flood.

His senses caught a flicker of lightning far off and the deep and menacing follow of thunder. The first fat drops struck with determined force.

Within a hundred feet of his descent point he discovered a deep gash in the wall of the cliff about five feet from the ground. It would do. He climbed up and fell against the back wall. It was not quite dark yet and he saw that this was merely the opening to a passageway that seemed to vanish into nothing.

The beam from his flashlight exploded against the walls, dark, dripping stone that glistened back at him with a shiny innocence. He moved cautiously, expecting any of a number of animal attacks but save for a disgruntled copperhead and a few outraged mice, the corridor was surprisingly empty. It was fifty feet long and burrowed deep into the rock but it was clearly not man made.

The beam of his light seemed to fall into space as he approached the last five feet. He crept to the edge and looked down. A natural stone walkway descended from the edge of the corridor in a long sweeping curl to the bottom of a cavern that could be no less than a hundred feet in diameter and at least half that high. And at the bottom, the Emit River emerged from a ground swell, passed along the side of the great cavern and descended underground once again, leaving behind a swirling pool of black, icy water.

Albert new instantly what he had discovered and it awakened in him a sense of purpose that had been disintegrating all winter. He had re-discovered the Gannet Cave system, a karst architecture undermining vast swathes of southern Indiana, a hidden labyrinth where no light ever penetrated, where blind fish swam invisible waters through a baleen of stalactite and stalagmite webbing that had not been disturbed for ten thousand years. It was invisible, impenetrable and, virtually, indestructible. No drone missile could pierce its armor; no infrared probe would reveal it.

He sat down on the edge and played his flashlight all around, in awe of the magnitude of the room and then it struck him. Where were the bats?

Vanished, that's all. Like the bees before them, the great clouds of cave bats had disappeared, almost overnight. White Nose Syndrome, they called it. A fungus, maybe; a bacterium or a virus or a click of the evolutionary clock. No one knew; no one cared excepting a few eggheads and scat collectors. The fruit bats were okay, they didn't inhabit caves but half a dozen other species did. They spent the winters back in the darkest corners of the limestone caves where temperatures never varied and bore their young. But now they were gone. Insects and mice had cleaned the cave thoroughly of almost all the guano and now there was nothing to indicate they had ever been here.

The analogy wasn't lost on him as he descended the flowstone walkway to the cave floor past the fat, melted-looking columns of calcium carbonate. The caramel draperies had almost reached the floor in several places and he had to break them off to get through. While large sections of the cave were simple, unadorned rock, the dripstone formations had almost occluded the grand hallway of the cavern. The beam from his flashlight snagged in a cataleptic rain of soda straws, turning them on like a chandelier. There were numerous rock shelves, some six feet high and as deep that appeared free of the drip and large sections of rock wall was iced caramel over a foot thick and growing. The stream running along one side murmured constantly and he thought he saw a small fingerling dart out of sight. The stream ran to a pool about ten feet in diameter where it turned slowly and splashed over one edge and disappeared back into the earth.

"Hail," he shouted.

It had been almost a year since he had "gone native" and the sound of his own voice flying back at him after it hit the far wall startled him as much as if it had been a stranger's. He had not spoken to another human being in all that time. The discovery of the cave was the first moment that he'd felt some sense of excitement or hope in almost twelve months of solitary roaming. He didn't know why it pleased him so much, but it was as if he was waking from his own troubled hibernation with a raw appetite. Here was a sanctuary, a dark, cool refuge, part confessional, part asylum where he could build once again a tiny life for himself amidst the chaos and murder that stalked the earth with such relentless greed.

In the halcyon days before the catastrophe he had constructed for himself a fantastic habitat including a log residence hewn from his own woods with a fireplace of stacked fieldstone collected by his own hand. He had poured his entire life and fortune into the creation of a biosphere where he could exist in cheerful solitude, tinkering with small inventions, eating the food he reclaimed himself from the land and observing the earth from a safe distance. He asked for nothing and offered nothing. Even as the country seemed to be hurtling itself into destruction through the manipulations and deceits of the governing class and their bankster accomplices, he had created for himself an underground shelter where he might survive anything - at least for a while. Survive at all costs. That was the point, wasn't it? I will survive. I will eat when starvation ravages the world; I will warm before a flame whilst the ice gauntlet grips all else. But when those times had really come, he discovered that there was no satisfaction in such success. It both surprised him and in a way disgusted him. He had become like a child breathlessly wanting to show a meager creation to a parent in exchange for praise.

He wanted someone to know what he was doing. He wanted someone to see it and remark on it and acknowledge it. This was not a part of him long hidden and suddenly revealed by circumstance; this was a part of him that had never before existed. This was new. He had changed. What we see as change in most is merely the revelation of true character through the abrasions of time and experience. Men do not change; they hide among the forests of their own self-delusions until age or wisdom or just plain fatigue permits them to appear as they really are. But Albert had changed and he found it hard to believe.

His wondrous and somewhat maniacal creation, his underground survival bunker remained undisturbed on the land that he once claimed as his own. He had not been back to visit it for several months but he thought of it now, trying to inventory his memory for useful materials. It was a long walk - about sixty-eight miles back to his land on the outskirts of Provost and anything he wanted would have to be carried back sixty-eight miles through the hinterland. There were no more private vehicles operating, the occupation forces having laid claim to any and all fuels, however held or discovered. Soon after, they enacted a punishment of immediate death for anyone found possessing them "illegally." It would be a long, tortuous journey back and forth as he relocated the contents of his shelter and various stash points to this fine, new home.

He moved with some caution, still uncertain if he was as alone as he appeared to be, lancing a hidden shelf with a flashlight beam or kicking aside a teetering stalagmite to make way. He crouched down over the stream and let the light play against the reflective bed. There was no question now; he could see small fish, perhaps four inches long darting through the jewels of water, immune to light but doubly sensitive to sound. The plunk of a stone hitting the surface scattered them. He wet his hand and tasted the water, tentatively, trying to discern its contents, whether it carried a faint odor of sulfur or the taint of dead flesh. But it was essentially neutral and he scooped a handful into his mouth and spit it out. He stood up and glanced around the room one more time and then caught a deep shadow at the far end. As he approached it become clear that this was a passageway into yet another cavern, equal if not larger in all aspects to the primary one he had discovered. There was less calcification here, the formations isolated to a few corners and only one wall was encased in a thick layer of flowstone which seemed to emanate from a crack along the edge of the ceiling. The cave was enormous, more than a hundred and fifty feet across and at least seventy-five feet from floor to ceiling. The stream was not evident here, but further passages and deep crevices told him that there was a lot yet to be explored. He had expected to find some animal life here, a wolf or a dog pack or even a black bear. But there was nothing; not even, it seemed, the remnants of previous ownership. It was possible that it simply hadn't been discovered for a long time by either man or beast, as unlikely as that was.

In their endless quest for food, the canine race traveled wherever the nose led them and their ability to cover wide swathes of territory and hear and smell over large areas made it hard to believe that a nest like this would be missed. Finally he found part of what he was a looking for: A debris pile of small animal bones and a swath of fur. Here was the skull of a raccoon; here was the femur of a small deer; and here, the bones of a dead pup curled against a rock face and already succumbing to permanent embalming in the calcium drip.

The storm raged all day and half into the night before it decided to move on. He went back down the passageway to the slash-like entrance and shone his flashlight into the formerly dry streambed. It seethed with water that came within a foot of the ledge. That explained a lot, he realized. The mammals would all have discerned immediately that the cave was subject to flooding and would have avoided it.

He remained on the ledge until light and watched the floodwater lower almost as quickly as it had risen. When it had reduced enough, he climbed down and waded along the bed until he found a suitable place to climb the wall. It was not steep and the rain had washed away a lot of loose material so he found handholds and hoisted himself back up the face in a few moments. That was a year ago. Or was it? Time was no longer a linear quantity, a comforting and recognizable delusion that maintained worldly order. How long had it been? He tried to recall.

Okay, December 2013 the shit hits the fan and then all winter fighting and then all summer 2014 fighting and running and then...the girl...you killed that girl winter 2014 and then the cave, 2015, spring...March, maybe and then the summer killing and then the winter 2015 in the cave...the cave, you're in the cave and then spring 2016 just killing them and running and collecting and then the winter 2016 back in the cave with all the books and the stuff...all the stuff...all the stuff...and then...now...spring...2017...the melt is over...it's summer now, 2017...four years...killing time again...kill them all...

He was right back where he started; he had just killed a relatively high ranking officer and he was on his way back home.

He opened his eyes and remained still, tucked under the log, not even breathing more than was necessary.

Something had awakened him. It was a movement, too furtive to be a deer; deer are silent and so attuned to the vibrations of the air that they know when to stay and when to run; they don't hide; they don't move stealthily through the woods. They know. Something had made the noise, something trying very hard not to make a noise. There is only one animal that has to concentrate so hard on not making a noise.

He pulled the hammer back, muffling the sound against his clothing and closed his eyes, trying to locate the direction. There it was again. A tentative movement, a boot compressing a stick or sliding off a stone, or an arm letting a branch go too quickly.

Okay. Okay. They know you're here. They know you're around here. They are trying to triangulate. There's got to be more than one. They always travel in packs.

There it was again. Same place. One man.

It's not them. One man. One... He turned his head slowly in the direction of the sound, certain now where it was coming from. Whoever it was didn't know how to move silently through the woods, but was trying. But was he being followed or was he just lost and terrified? He waited and sure enough the individual moved again, sloppily. He waited.

The sounds coming from his right side were constant now. The individual had decided it was okay to make noise. Albert watched his right flank and within a few minutes he saw a man wearing a military uniform trying to push his way through the underbrush. He was alone. With movements only a forest animal would detect, Albert rolled out from under the log and began crawling towards the man fighting his way through the bramble and Thornberry and devil's stick that filled the matrices between the trees of southern Indiana forest.

The soldier was tired, he could tell and probably lost beyond redemption. He had a sidearm but it was holstered and he bore no other insignia of unit or rank. Albert leveled the .45 at CBM and started to squeeze the trigger. He could almost hear the spring stretching in the action when he slowly released the hammer, deciding he better find out what he could before he killed the intruder. He deliberately cracked a branch and waited for a response. The man stopped and was looking around frantically. Albert rose slowly and the man turned to look at him, his eyes darting back and forth. Deserter, Albert decided. REMF trying to get away.

"You looking for something?" Albert asked him. The man couldn't speak. He just stared. Albert frowned.

"I'm going to give you some instructions," Albert said, pausing to allow the message to sink in. "You best do what I say. I won't give you no second chance, understand?"

The man nodded and raised his hands high up in surrender.

"Take the pistol out and throw it over here," Albert said. The man's hand was shaking as he retrieved the army-issue Beretta from its holster and held it out towards Albert.

"Just toss it," Albert said. The pistol landed a few feet from Albert and he let it lay, watching the intruder carefully. He may have been garbed in army fatigues, but this was no combat soldier shivering in front of him. He was terrified and seemed almost relieved to have been "captured" if that wasn't too much of a stretch of the word.

"What are you doing out here?" Albert asked him, but the man didn't answer; he just stared at Albert with terror-laced eyes. "If you don't start talking to me I am going to kill you," Albert said calmly.

"No," the fellow managed and his arms shot straight up again in surrender.

Albert took a few steps, picked up the sidearm and tucked it into his belt.

"One more time and that's a lot more than I usually do," Albert said. "Are you alone?"

"Can I put my arms down?" he asked.

Albert nodded.

"I'm AWOL, just trying to get the hell back to Missouri," the man said. "Alone. Ya. Alone," he sputtered. "Ain't nobody follering me that I know of..."

Albert believed him. This guy could have been followed by a herd of buffalo and he wouldn't know it.

"AWOL from where?" Albert asked.

"Provost Legion," the man answered.

"Put your hands on your head and come this way," Albert said.

He directed him back towards his rough camp sight and gestured for him to sit down on the log. He did and seemed relieved to be sitting as well.

"Who are you?" Albert asked.

"Sergeant Lonny Pickens, 426-39-8457," he recited automatically.

Albert studied him for a few minutes without speaking. Pickens fidgeted and coughed a few times.

"I ain't lookin for no trouble," he said. "Just let me be going. You can keep the gun," he said hopefully.

Albert just looked at him until Lonny Pickens eyes wavered. "I guess you kin do perty well what ever you want," he conceded.

After another moment's silence Pickens asked, "Ain't you cold? Been freezing my arse off all night. Would've made a fire but I got no matches. I ran off so quickly I didn't have time...I-"

His voice petered out and he hung his head and closed his eyes. "Honest to God, mister, I'm not looking for trouble." And then he was silent. Albert watched him closely.

"How come you run off?" Albert asked him.

"I just couldn't stand it any more," Pickens said. "I was just reserve, you know, weekends. I went in for the extra money and such and then when all this happened...well, you know what happened and then I got deployed and I haven't been home since. Haven't heard from anyone. It's like that for most. They hate it down here, all except Griggson's boys, of course. They'll do anything the colonel says and everybody hates them too...but...ah shit, I don't know. I just couldn't take it, that's all..."

Albert continued to watch him but he was pretty sure that Pickens was as harmless as he appeared. "

You're a long way from Missouri," he said.

"I know it," Pickens nodded

The younger man had hit the road with no food or water, no supplies of any kind in fact, other than a pistol that he probably couldn't use worth a damn.

"What you figure on eating between now and then?" Albert asked him and Pickens shrugged and looked lost. He was shivering involuntarily.

He said, "You ain't got matches either, huh?"

Albert poked his thumb at the sky.

"Drones can see a fire through a Charleston fog."

Pickens looked up quickly at this and shook his head.

"Not around here, they can't. Provost only has two drones and they're both out for parts. Haven't been flying for more than a week. I aught to know; that was my job."

Albert accepted this information without showing any surprise.

"What's wrong with 'em?" he asked casually and Pickens took it as an opportunity to talk about something he knew instead of fighting for words and ideas in the realm of survival where he was clearly at a disadvantage.

"You got to keep them tuned pretty high and when the board went out on the big one, the one they call Freda, well, they called Indianapolis for parts but they ain't got a lot to go around you know and so they were stuck with the little one and they broke it on the refueling pad when a HUMVEE knocked into it. That's them all over, you better believe it. They are like a dog fuckin a football. I tried to tell 'em but they told me to keep sending 'em up and..well, you see what I mean, huh?"

Albert studied the ground. "You used to run them?"

Gaining confidence now, Pickens gestured and smiled for the first time. "Oh ya, I run 'em and the computers too. They gimme that job because I know those things pretty well. I ran my own IT until this bullshit came down and I was doing pretty good, you know. When they heard I was handy with that they just told me to keep it running and I did as long as I could. I just got tired of it all, you know what I mean? They are all just out for themselves now. They're not doing anything for the country I can see. I figured I'd just go home and..." He let the sentence dangle and went silent. "Guess there isn't much to go home to, is there?" he said after a while.

"Probably not," Albert agreed.

Albert couldn't quite shrug off the ominous sense of being watched by the eye in the sky but further questioning had convinced him that Pickens was who he claimed to be; no small feat in these times. Machines do break and the more sophisticated they are, the more attention they need and the more likely they are to malfunction. Shovels don't break down very often.

Albert took out the small purse of dried meat and fruit and offered it to Pickens who accepted it with alacrity and closed his eyes with the first few bites.

"How long have you been out here?" Albert asked him.

"Five days," he said.

"I been drinking off the plants and such...there's water every-where around here, but I haven't had much to eat. "

"How did you expect to get to Missouri without food?"

Pickens nodded and chewed slowly on a piece of jerky. "Well, you know...just figure it out as I go along, I guess. Shoot something...I dunno."

He handed the pouch back to Albert who indicated he could keep it for a while.

"Thanks," he said, already somewhat rejuvenated. "See, I was out with this crew over towards Highway 61 snooping for a broad-caster. I just run the locator," he explained, somewhat defensively Albert thought. "The spectrum analyzer," he added.

Albert shrugged; pretending not to know what Pickens was talk-ing about.

"It picks up the signals and you can get a pretty good bead on a pirate station that way...Anyhow, the HUMVEE hit a small IED, nothing too bad, but it was enough to turn the vehicle over and every-one got bounced around pretty good, knocked out...you know. I crawled out and just started running. Couldn't have told you what suddenly made me do it. I wasn't planning it...just sort of happened."

Albert watched the other man chewing the bits of jerky and dried apple. The man lifted his hand to scratch behind his neck, prob-ably just a nervous gesture, but it exposed a small scar on the wrist that Albert hadn't seen up to now.

"Are you wired?" he asked him. If Pickens lied, he'd kill him where he sat and probably Pickens figured this out because he blanched and held out his arm, pulling back the sleeve so Albert could get a better look.

"This? It's an ID chip, that's all. It's not a tracker."

"How do I know that?"

"Hell, they don't do everyone like that...only the guys who go out deep, you know the Special Forces and so forth. Why would they wanna track a nobody like me?"

"You seem to know a lot about the computers and such," Albert said with a frown. "Maybe they want to keep an eye on you...in case you run off."

This made Pickens blanche again and Albert watched the fear creep over his face like an invisible stain. Albert felt sorry for Pick-ens, sorry for the young man's fear and his confusion but he couldn't

40

see a way out of killing him now. He didn't have to scare him first. Just wait until he wasn't looking...

"I don't know," Albert said slowly, shaking his head and tightening his lips together in a concentrated frown.

"They aren't going to chance losing a helicopter chasing me around," he said.

He looked hopefully at Albert who gave nothing away.

"Don't you think they would've got me by now if they could?" he said.

That was not an argument from Albert's viewpoint. They could be tracking him to see where he went or who he ended up meeting. They might have let him escape just to follow him around.

"Honest, mister...I just want to go home to Missouri," he said. I don't want trouble."

Albert played the ground with a twig and thought about the possibilities.

"See, I figure you must be a spy of some sort," he said. "You're here to find out stuff and then report it. Maybe you're a painter."

"No way," Pickens denied emphatically. "I ain't nobody. Honest to God. Do I have a laser on me? Come on, check. "

"Better grab some zees," Albert told him. "Come dawn I'm moving and you're coming with me."

"Where we going?" Pickens asked, fear laced through his voice, but Albert was already feigning sleep.

In short order he snorted and snuffled like a winter bear and let the pistol drop out of his hand. Pickens didn't try for the gun or even move from the log where he sat, arms dangling between his legs. It wasn't a very good test of Pickens' intentions, Albert knew. It didn't really mean anything but it made him consider whether killing him was really necessary. Pickens just sat there ignoring every opportunity to escape or engage his captor - exactly like someone trying to prove how trustworthy he really was.

Pickens leaned his head on his arms and was more in a trance than asleep when first light broke. He was shivering and Albert could hear his teeth chattering. After a paltry breakfast of water, dried fruit and jerky and a salt tablet, he took them west through the woods along a fairly obvious deer trail, Pickens following about twenty five feet behind. To Pickens, who had no idea where he was going or where he was, the hours stretched on, every step a claim against his mental state and his stamina. He was young, but in spite of everything the world had become, he had not hardened up very much and didn't seem even remotely capable of looking after himself. Albert would have covered more than twice the distance had he been alone and it occurred to him that at this pace, they would run out of food long before they hit the Hayworth Rendezvous.

After about six hours of steady walking they came to a seasonal tributary of the Emit River that normally flowed only from April to June and then died off until the October rains. Then it would bubble for another month and vanish again. Albert was no longer certain what month it was, but the last vestiges of snow were gone, the trees were in full leaf and most of the trails were already overgrown with bramble and Ninebark, Buttonbush and Elderberry. It was too late for morels but the chicken of the woods hadn't appeared yet so he figured it had to be June. Not a good time for rabbit, either. The water was cold and clean, at least.

He took the rabbit anyway. Sometimes in summer you might find a worm in a rabbit's neck but the fears of tularemia are overstated and severe cooking kills just about anything. And the truth is a rabbit can get sick any time of year. Albert's cooking these days was not very sophisticated beyond a wood fire and spit. In fact it was strictly B.C.: Burnt to a Crisp, but it cured most ills. Pickens watched Albert clean the cottontail with some trepidation. Albert had killed the rabbit with a knife throw from about fifteen feet, something that would not have unduly impressed a seasoned woodsman but to a city born and bred computer geek wandering around lost it had an element of the exotic and the terrifying all at once.

"You ain't gonna start playing the banjo, are ya?" Pickens said with a grin but the joke fell flat.

Albert collected a few sticks, scraped out a hole in the ground and set a fire with a low flame. He fed it for half an hour until the coal bed was pulsing evenly and then he hung speared sections of the quartered bunny over the bed. In short order the smell filled the small clearing, hemmed in as it was with cedar and overgrown sassafras.

"Sure smells good," Pickens said. Albert nodded.

"Not much use except to kill the hunger," he said. "Got no fat in it. Better off with a possum."

Pickens shook his head slowly. "Don't known if I could eat a possum," he said. "The way they look and all..."

"Hell, what part of Missouri you from, boy?"

It took a long hour to cook the rabbit during which not much was said. Pickens tried to make conversation a few times, but Albert rebuffed him. Finally Albert stood up and handed Pickens a stick with a hindquarter on it.

"You go ahead," Albert said, "I'll be right back."

Pickens almost didn't hear him he was so absorbed in cooling off the steaming joint. Albert slipped into the woods.

Pickens gnawed through the leg stripping every sliver of meat from the bone before he tossed it onto the coals. It was only then he realized that Albert had not returned.

He looked around, listening and then stood up. He wandered the perimeter of the clearing and called out "Hey," several times. After a few more minutes he sat down and tried waiting some more. Hunger pulled him back to the fire and he took another piece and worked on it slowly, constantly looking around like a wary beast stealing another's kill. He sat in silence for another hour after that until the coals had burned completely down and the sense of foreboding that had plagued him since he ran from the overturned vehicle, returned with a vengeance.

He had refrained from eating the remaining skewers of meat but in a sudden flash of anger he grabbed them one after another and tore into them, viciously, never thinking he might save them for later. Several times he stood up and shouted: "Hey, what's going on?" He tried pushing his way into the woods but he was afraid to leave the campsite and lose his way back. He fell into a despondent mood and sat for another hour before he allowed himself to accept that Albert was not going to return. Pickens was right back where he started.

He rose slowly and started walking in the direction he thought Albert had gone. He found the vague indications of passage including a broken stem and an overturned rock. It allowed him the faintest hope that he might find his guide. But within ten minutes he found his pistol hanging from a branch and he knew with a depressing certainty that he was on his own again.

"Fucking asshole!" he shouted.

His voice fell dead against the foliage and increased his sense of confinement. He pulled the slide back and made sure the weapon was loaded and then holstered it. He had no idea where he was going or what to do next. He knew that Missouri was west of Indiana but he had no sense of direction in the woods. The trail that he had followed for a while had disappeared and he found himself trapped in a copse of unwelcoming nettles and various thorn bushes and in no time he was scratched and bleeding. He worked his way out towards a clearing and sat down against a tree. He bowed his head and sat there for a long time.

It was almost night when he decided to move again but got no further than a fallen log before the quick darkness overtook him. He had no blankets, no bedroll, no food...nothing. The various nocturnal travelers heard his quiet sobbing, but they didn't understand. Pity had never been part of their lexicon.

He made it until morning, by alternately falling into a dismal sleep for a few moments and waking in a panic, blind, cold and terrified. He moved in what he thought was a westerly direction, stopping wherever he found it to slurp down a few drops of water. He walked that second day until about noon when hunger derailed him and he flopped down and stared into the dappled foliage.

It takes a long time to die of starvation. The mouth would dry out and become caked or coated with thick material. His lips would become parched and cracked. His tongue would swell, and might crack. His eyes would recede back into their orbits and his cheeks would become hollow. The lining of his nose might crack and cause his nose to bleed. His skin would hang loose on his body and become dry and scaly. His urine would become highly concentrated, leading to burning of the bladder. The lining of his stomach would dry out and he would experience dry heaves and vomiting. His body temperature would become very high. His brain cells would dry out, and the thick secretions that would result could plug his lungs and cause death. At some point within five days to three weeks his major organs, including his lung...heart...brain, would give out and he would die. [6]

Several times he prodded himself to continue but gave up every time. He had no strength to keep going. He had entered the hunger phase when mania takes the mind for a ride on the Ferris wheel. He couldn't stop thinking about food and the more he thought about it the more crazed he became. It would take another day at least before his craving subsided and he no longer fantasized about eating. That was a long day from now.

He lay down on the damp, cool ground and stared up at the light filtering between the leaves. Something walked across his face but he paid it no mind. He took the pistol out and pulled the hammer back and then placed it against his temple. At that moment a bird landed in a branch high above him. It seemed to be flapping in slow motion. He smiled and watched it until it flew off. Time passed, but he had no sense of it any longer. It was a gentle breeze, that's all, a comforting earthly exhalation cooling his face and hypnotizing him into a prede-ceased state where he could drift unimpeded by discomfort or fear. The last thing he thought of before he blacked out was the day he walked along a pond's edge with his father and skipped stones. It was a cool, pleasant, fall afternoon and the old man was smiling to him-self. He always wondered what his father had been smiling about that day...

*

"Here," Albert said, allowing some water to trickle into Pickens' mouth. He smacked his lips and stared bleakly up at him. His hearing was affected by the hunger and Albert's voice seemed stretched. For his part, Albert wondered if he'd left him too long. Perhaps Pickens had passed the point of no return, his body so dehydrated and stripped of energy that he couldn't even process the fluids and nutrients for recovery.

Albert had been watching him from no farther than a hundred feet the entire three and a half days that Pickens had wandered. He had to make sure that he wasn't communicating - inadvertently or otherwise - with his base at Provost and that they weren't monitoring him without his knowledge. It takes nothing to track someone through satellite GPS technology. People had been attaching transmitters to their dogs for years and by the end of the first decade of the 21st Cen-tury, tracking technology had become so advanced that a chip could be placed inside a human body without the individual even knowing and its signal picked up from the other side of the world through satel-lite relays. And that was only the tracking technology of public rec-ord. What the military or the spy services or intelligence gathering outfits might have that the public knew nothing about would probably defy belief.

All Albert knew was that if he could imagine it, so could some-one else and someone else again could build it. And as he considered himself a man of only modest intelligence and imagination, he was forced to conclude that the enemy was preternaturally omnipotent.

"Why'd you come back?" Pickens croaked hoarsely after an hour of sipping water and chewing on dried berries.

"I never left," Albert said. "I was watching to see if you would call in."

Pickens closed his eyes and breathed slowly. Tears sprouted and rolled down his cheeks.

"You're wasting water," Albert told him.

Albert dug a shallow pit and got a fire going while Pickens lay on the ground, sucking on a wet rag and carefully chewing the hard, dried nuggets of fruit and jerky.

Albert wasn't sure he would make it but he had decided to help him rather than leave him to die or kill him out of caution. A year ago, Pickens' uniform would have been his death warrant but Albert thought of the dead teenager every time he contemplated pulling the trigger on someone.

He mounded dirt and loose rock around the rim of the pit and this allowed him to encourage a slightly larger flame. Pickens was shivering and the night was coming in cold. Albert glanced at the young man occasionally to make sure he was still breathing while he arranged a campsite for them that might have some comfort as well as offer a modicum of protection. He replenished Pickens' rag several times until he could swallow mouthfuls without choking.

While Pickens rested and the fire rolled quietly against the walls of the pit, Albert took some of the trail mix and dumped it into a small pan of water. He stirred slowly until the solution reached a gentle boil at which point he began to drop in more material. The worms twisted violently a few times before death and the ants struck for the sides managing a few strokes before they were boiled. He tore the wings and head off a dozen grasshoppers, moths and a dozen skippers and cloudwings he'd scooped from some wild marsh marigolds and then took the flower petals as well. It all went into the grayish mass. He let the stew simmer until it was reduced to a thick paste that he spooned onto a small metal dish.

Pickens choked on the first spoonful. "Too hot," he said.

Albert allowed it to cool off a bit and then tried again. Pickens managed to eat about three ounces before he began to cough. Albert poured him a cup of water and held it for him.

"Give it a while," Albert said.

"What in hell's name is that stuff?" Pickens asked.

"It's bugs, mostly," Albert told him.

Even in his withered state, Pickens was able to look horrified. "You mean-?" he started to say. But he didn't finish the sentence. He lay back and closed his eyes.

"Jesus H. Kee-rist," he sighed.

***

Chapter Three

It took Pickens almost two days to recover enough strength to start moving again. Albert was surprised because the man had not really gone that long without food. Either he had a particularly weak constitution or he was suffering from something else. On the morning of the third day, they ate a bowl of warm bug paste, licking the container clean.

"Remind me to ask you for the recipe," Pickens joked, his face already losing the sardonic sneer of a skull and filling out with fat and muscle.

"Do you know how to use this?" Albert asked, handing back the Beretta.

Pickens nodded and took the pistol. He pulled the slide, positioned himself in a shooter's squat and fired three rounds into a tree a hundred feet away. Albert went over and checked out the target. The bullets had landed within an inch of each other, and two had overlapped slightly.

"I grew up with guns," Pickens said. "My father and I use to shoot all the time. He was quite a hand."

Pickens pulled the clip, ejected the last bullet and caught it before it hit the ground. He cleaned it off, pushed it back into the throat of the magazine and then reinserted the clip before holstering it.

"Locked and loaded," Albert said.

Pickens shook his head. "Not me. I like to think before I speak."

They headed into the woods, Albert cutting a fair pace, but Pickens was able to keep up. They stopped every few hours and drank some water, but they were out of food. They would need something soon if they were going to keep going at this speed. Albert wasn't too concerned. Sooner or later a pack would pick up their trail and start to follow them. He'd eaten a lot of dogs in the last year or so and as the old Miami he had traveled with for a while had shown him, the younger ones, the pups, tasted better but the older ones, dark and stringy and beef-like had more fat and other nutrients to offer. It had been much harder to eat his first dog than his first cupful of fried worms and grasshoppers. His stomach and seized as the first lumps dropped but by the fourth or fifth dog, he had ceased to even think about it. The dogs ran free and scavenged what many would never have touched. They ran themselves like a private herd and death neither frightened them nor even appeared to interest them much. When one of their own dropped, he was immediately torn to pieces. In fact, a slight limp could be a signal for the others to turn on a pack mate. The one drawback to eating dogs was the fact that they also consumed feces. They ate dog shit, cat shit, human shit - anything that could be forced down the gullet. It was probably why they were so successful, but Albert could never quite forget the saying, "You are what you eat," and it came back to him at the most inauspicious moments.

Pickens was running out of gas after about seven hours and Albert knew they'd have to stop for the night. They had made about ten miles, respectable enough under the circumstances but it was still taking too long. The Hayworth Rendezvous, where Albert was to meet with certain people, was still eighteen miles away. It would make him a day and a half late. Time wasn't what it used to be, of course and arrangements were subject to the verities of a world without clocks and without real deadlines. But this was one meeting he did not want to miss. Pickens plopped down and breathed heavily. Albert watched him.

"What kinda sick are you, anyway?" Albert asked.

Pickens closed his eyes and breathed slowly. "I don't know...never used to be," he said.

Albert watched him as Pickens slumped and fell into a heavy sleep. He decided to leave him and look for food, but at the same time he had to stay close in case a pack found them. It didn't look like Pickens would awaken soon enough to save himself and the dogs would kill him within seconds. They go for the throat and that was if you were lucky. Otherwise they might rip your abdomen open or tear an arm to pieces and you could watch yourself bleed to death while they rendered you into bloody slaw. They can tear your gut open and run with the intestine until it snaps - while you watch.

Hunting is about patience, surely, but it is also about luck. Any hunter who disclaims luck is probably a fisherman. There is more skill and less luck in fly-fishing for a trout then there is looking for a deer. He would have to stroll farther into the woods if he wanted to find one now. With everything grown in so thick and plenty of fresh water, they wouldn't be wandering much. He knelt down at one point scribing a circle around their camp and found deer scat but it was old and dry. In the end, it was back to filet of grasshopper.

"Bugs again?" Pickens complained and then laughed as an hour later Albert handed him his share of gray paste.

"Mmmmm mmmm," he said.

Albert shrugged and swallowed a mouthful. He made a face and expelled a grasshopper leg between his teeth.

"Better when the locusts fly," he said. "More meat on 'em."

They kept the fire low, in spite of Pickens' assurance that the Provost Legion's eye-in-the-sky was not currently operating. It was actually safer to build a small, enclosed fire at night than it was in daylight. Smoke was a dead giveaway for miles around while a properly sheltered flame can be hidden from anyone outside of a much smaller radius. Albert let it die out and they sat in almost total darkness. The single, extended high-pitched howl of a coyote calling its brethren was the only sound for a while. Both remembered, that not so long ago the nights were filled with sirens and air horns and chattering jake- brakes. Jets streaked past followed by rolling thunder and sometimes what passed for music among teenagers impinged on a pleasant evening. And the sky seemed to have changed, as well. Perhaps the dousing of all those billions of bulbs and search lights and neon advertising signs had revealed stars and other objects no one had seen for three hundred years. Or maybe the stars really were brighter.

"This reminds me of when me and my dad used to go deer hunting," Pickens said. "Three or four times we never even got one but we stayed out the whole week," he added.

Albert was not interested in reminiscing and he did not answer. Just the way some drunks always end up crying in their beer there are people who feel they have to comment on everything, including silence. They were afraid of silence; they might have to hear their own thoughts. It wasn't that Albert didn't think about the past - he did so often - but it was just that: Thinking. Thinking is something you do in silence. After a few moments Pickens got the message and stopped chattering.

They woke before dawn in a gray mist that condensed readily on anything it touched. This would slow them down even further, Albert thought as he pushed through fresh trail to the Southwest.

"Aren't you supposed to use a machete or something?" Pickens asked as he caught a branch swinging back at him.

"Waste of time," Albert said. "And energy."

The rain started about ten o'clock and by noon both men were soaked. They had to stop and dry off. Albert knew very well the consequences of even a mild illness in these times. It wasn't just the absence of doctors and medicine; who would feed you if you couldn't look after yourself? He kept the fire as small as possible and tried to use dry debris for fuel in an effort to keep the smoke signal to a minimum. He knew the risks. But the chance of getting caught won out against the near certainty of illness.

"Take off your boots," he told Pickens who was standing as close to the fire as he could holding his hands over the meager flames.

"Didn't they teach you nothing in the army? Your feet are what carry you around or haven't you noticed?"

During the American Civil War more men died from sepsis than from bullets. During the Vietnam War there were more casualties from jungle rot, malaria, snakebites, and Agent Orange then all the dead from bullets. In these times a case of foot rot or an illness - any kind you want to name - could be a death sentence. [5]

"You're on your own out here," Albert told him. "You show up at a settlement or a rendezvous coughing and sneezing they are as like to kill you and burn your body as they are to ask your name."

It took them a full hour to dry off, Albert becoming more and more agitated as smoke curled up through the canopy. When they finally got going again, it was almost three o'clock but fortunately the days had begun to stretch and it would be light enough to travel for at least another five hours. Albert was just not sure that Pickens would last that long.

They stopped again around six o'clock near a stream that was still running high. As they emerged from the trail into a small clearing by the bank, Albert caught sight of a large snapping turtle sunning himself on a gravel bank.

Fortunately they had come upon him from behind and while turtles have superb vision they can't hear worth a damn. He was a big one; at least twenty-five pounds and Albert could already taste the chewy, beef-like meat and the aroma of a thick porridge. He motioned Pickens to stop and then indicated a large oak. Pickens got the cue and very quietly moved in behind the trunk and out of sight.

Albert meanwhile had moved a few feet closer to the turtle who was fortunately still unaware of the situation. They can move quickly enough when aroused and if he got to the water, that would be it; one for the turtle, zero for the hungry bushwhacker. They can see and they can sense ground movement. Whether they are lying in wait on the bottom of a pond waiting for an unsuspecting bluegill or tucked into the grass anticipating a nice black snake supper or perhaps a mouse soufflé - sans soufflé - they are not to be trifled with. If they can't get away, they will fight. They will turn and hiss and those jaws will open, daring you to make a move. One this size could take two fingers off in one bite, its thousand pounds per square inch vice quite enough to crack just about any bone in the human body. It always reminded Albert of a dinosaur, something left over from the Mesozoic with its heavy, studded carapace and that weaponized tail - it was like a cross between an Ankylosaurus and an armored personnel carrier.

He was five feet away when it alerted and turned on him with a fierce rapidity, it's tail slashing the grass.

"Shit," he cursed.

You can't take them from the front. He took a stick about three quarters of an inch thick and jabbed the beast. It grabbed the branch and crushed it and spit it out. It advanced towards him in that determined, belligerent, brave, rolling gait and he backed up a few feet. He found another stick, this time about two inches thick. The turtle's jaws clamped down on it and held it but it could not break through. It gave Albert the few seconds he needed to step behind and grab the tail. The beast swirled in a rage, dropping the stick and trying to twist itself around to get at him, but they both knew it was over now.

Pickens came out from behind the tree and admired the captive. The big snapper had settled down a bit and just hung upside down knowing it was over.

"I've never eaten a turtle," he said, his hesitation evident.

"That's up to you," Albert replied. "Stand back," he said.

Albert laid the turtle down on its belly and kneeled against the shell to prevent it from escaping. He jabbed a stick at the beast until it stretched its head out and grabbed it between those herculean jaws. Albert pulled the head out as far as he could and then took his knife and pressed down on the back of the neck. The blood spurted and flowed and the turtle struggled savagely as Albert calmly sawed its head off. The severed head continued to bear down on the stick, the jaws opening and closing repeatedly. Its legs thrashed the ground trying to swim while the blood poured into the dirt.

Albert stood up and the headless carapace started walking away.

"Jesus Christ," Pickens yelled.

Albert glanced at him and shrugged.

"It always happens like that," he said as they watched the carcass twist and claw at the ground. "I seen a dog grab a snapper head been lying on the ground for maybe three four hours and the damn thing near tore its ear off. I don't understand it, but that's the way it is."

The cleaning and butchering was no less appetizing with globs of pustulated fat and guts that stank beyond anything normally encountered in dead animals.

Mis-cut a buck and you can kiss the meat goodbye - if you dare. Glands lay hidden under the back legs producing foul substances so powerful that merely touching the knife against them and dragging it across the rest of the muscle would render it inedible. And an otherwise edible sheep can be ruined in exactly the same way. But they were like Channel No. 5 compared to turtle guts.

"Jesus," Pickens said again.

Albert sliced the pale, almost white meat from the legs and around the back and began chopping it into small pieces. He ordered Pickens to bring some Queen Anne's lace he'd spotted near the bank and he recovered a clot of hen-of-the woods hiding under a rotting log. In his small pan there was no way to get a proper soup boiling but the combination of wild plants and turtle meat simmered with some deer jerky and dried fruit was soon gone to the last drop.

"Say thank you," Albert said, licking the gravy from his fingers.

Pickens looked puzzled and shrugged.

"OK, thanks," he replied.

"Not to me," Albert said. "That turtle saved your life."

The sudden infusion of protein put them both into a post-prandial near-comatose state and they hardly moved for almost two hours. It was reckless behavior and Albert woke with a start, shocked by his own laxity. He nudged Pickens with his boot and the younger man came to but remained nearly hypnotized for a few minutes.

"Best sleep I've had in a month," he said.

Albert finished cinching his pack and indicated it was time to start moving again.

"We're just lucky dogs didn't catch the scent of that cooking," he said.

The point was made and Pickens shook himself awake and stood up.

"We going to travel at night?" he asked.

"Full moon," Albert replied tersely and disappeared into the undergrowth.

They slogged through the thick matrix of bramble and Johnson grass, sloughing off the hungry grope of leaf-heavy branches of Sassafras and wild raspberry and Devil's Stick. The moon shone brilliant and cool in a near-black sky and it was surprising how much of the light managed to find its way through the foliage and illuminate the ground. They were following a deer path, very narrow and seldom used, but used enough that a lot of second growth had been trampled, easing their passage.

One good meal did not bring them back to full strength and Pickens was starting to flounder by midnight. Then his stomach cramped violently and he went off trail and hung over a log for quite a while. Now he faced dehydration because of the diarrhea and profuse sweating and they would be slowed again.

Albert resigned himself to the circumstances and built a small campsite and started a few twigs, allowing them to burn to coals before he set the pan of water. When Pickens emerged from the bush he was drawn and unsteady.

"I don't know what the hell happened to me, man," he said. "Must've been that turtle but you seem okay."

He sat down and held his head, elbows propped on his knees.

"You'll be alright," Albert told him. "Might not have cooked that turtle enough," he admitted.

The thought that he had been eating raw, something whose smell was so overpowering it could make you retch, brought a loud regurgitant belch from Pickens who just managed to fall back out of the campsite before he began heaving. There wasn't much to heave, however and he returned weaker than before, his eyes and mouth watering.

"Hold on," Albert told him, unable to hide his irritation completely.

He had stripped a raspberry plant of its leaves and they were simmering in the pan.

"This'll help," he said.

Pickens sat glumly for the next half hour while Albert brewed the potion.

"What the hell's this now?" Pickens demanded, warily.

"Just drink it and shut up," Albert said.

By the time Pickens' stomach had calmed down and his bowels had stopped convulsing, it was three a.m. and both men were too tired to continue.

Albert allowed him about six hours of sleep and then woke him with a fresh mug of last night's brew. Pickens' face soured as he sipped it, but he was clearly improving.

"We have to make it today," Albert informed him. "If we get separated, just keep heading southwest. You know how to figure that out, right?"

Pickens looked at Albert, his eyes widening with apprehension.

"Why should we get separated?"

"Because I'm not waiting for you any longer," Albert said. "I gotta be somewhere."

Pickens stood up and finished the cup of tea.

"You got a watch on, right?"

"Ya..."

"Here, give it to me."

Pickens removed the watch and handed it to Albert who looked at it and handed it back.

"Not a digital, asshole," he said shaking his head derisively. "Just keep up, okay?"

By late evening Albert knew they were closing in on the Hayworth Rendezvous.

The ground was freshly trampled, broken stems and branches still showing green. They had left the trail several hours before and traveled due west for a while before turning due south until they crossed the "highway." Pickens had fallen behind periodically and Albert had adjusted his speed to give him time to catch up but he had refused to stop. He wanted to be inside the camp by dark.

He waited now for Pickens to appear, having lost sight of him half an hour before. Presently he heard the crashing of a clumsy city boy trying to find his way through the woods. When he showed, Albert saw that he was exhausted and probably couldn't make it another mile. Fortunately they had less than half that distance to cover.

The Hayworth was a moveable feast, of sorts, trying to keep distance between itself and the Provost Legion and at the same time encourage outlanders, as they called themselves these days, to visit and trade. Word of the present location had circulated for several weeks and it would prove to be the largest gathering of its kind so far. Hayworth, the mid-level systems manager who had initiated the first get-together almost three years prior was dead and had not been replaced with any new central command figure. Albert had known Hayworth briefly in the beginning. His management skills were all he had after the Catastrophe and he put them to use organizing wanderers into traders who would roam the land collecting whatever they could and returning to this moving marketplace to exchange their haul with others. Hayworth had no illusions about creating a new society, or even establishing some kind of peaceful coexistence among the disparate groups. He just couldn't help organizing people and getting them to do things - even useless things - so that ennui could not encourage the release of the devilment hiding in one and all. Albert had liked him, well enough, but he knew instinctively that Hayworth wouldn't last. And he was right. The rather small, portly man was jumped by marauders of an evening shortly after the third gathering and partially eaten before they were caught by a militia group and hung. It was still called the Hayworth and would be for some years. It had been many months since the last rendezvous and Albert expected a lot of pent up emotions to come loose. Very loose. Even from half a mile he thought he could hear the shouting and laughter.

"How much farther?" Pickens gasped, falling to the ground.

Once again they had failed to find any quick solutions for food and having no time to stop and hunt properly, they had been eating wild berries and insects all day. Albert marveled at how quickly men adapt as he watched Pickens snatch a caterpillar from a tree, tear off the head and pop it directly into his mouth.

Half an hour later Pickens wanted to rush the camp where he could smell roasting meat and clearly hear the voices. Some of them were women. Maybe there were whores. He licked his dry lips thinking about them.

But Albert held back. It was true that the Legion was not concerned too much about traders but they were always on the lookout for any form of firearm or gathering of militia groups. Possession of a firearm of any kind held the same penalty as possession of gasoline or diesel fuel without Legion approval: A rope and a stool. They no longer wasted bullets on executions.

It was no secret that the military had recruited hundreds of wayward travellers as agents and sent them out to report back on everything from settlement activity to secret farms. You could never tell if the man you were talking to was an agent or not. You could know someone really well and still be fooled.

Fortunately communication between Provost or any military establishment and free roaming spies was limited and difficult. There was no telephone service left anywhere and there was no convenient way to charge batteries or transmit data electronically. Every time a line went up the militias took it down. The military still had some satellite COM in place but that was threatened by a dearth of personnel to maintain and operate ground equipment. The renegade militias were in fact better off than the military in some ways because they had collected and stored old short wave and CB radio equipment before everything went to hell. They had been preparing for years, burying guns and ammunition, hiding generators and fuel supplies and food and medical equipment. The military had never considered the possibility that it would be reduced to less than a tenth of its nominal size and that they might be pressed for supplies for an extended period. Or if it had occurred to some, they had been ignored.

The spies wandering the outlands now often had to report in person or get to secure locations before transmitting their information which gave the object of their betrayals time to react.

There were supposed to be pickets every few hundred feet four hundred yards out and an inner ring at two hundred yards opposite the spaces but Albert and Pickens walked right into the camp without being challenged by anyone. When they breached the north border, Albert saw why. Blazing fires licked the night and shining, drunk faces appeared to be flying around on their own.

There had to be a thousand people gathered here, the largest non-military group he had seen in years. Tents, lean-tos and blankets propped with sticks occupied every spare piece of flat ground and the roar and laughter of acute alcohol poisoning filled the night air. They passed five groups hovered around fires spitted with dogs of various sizes and a sixth with a brace of cats turning slowly over the flames. The two newcomers barely occasioned a glance from the huddled groups and that was more to throw a warning. As they proceeded, the grounds area grew until it looked like an army bivouac with rows of tents and several areas sectioned off for toilettes. That didn't stop drunks from pissing where they stood, several not even bothering to drop their trousers first. The women, even the drunks were a little more aware and they would squat, pants down and then use a handful of leaves or grass as toilette paper.

People caromed off each other and several trees and in the space of five minutes they saw five fist fights, one of which appeared to leave one man dead, his head slit open against the rocks of a fire pit. This provoked another round of shouting and someone was stabbed in the arm.

"Should have killed him," Albert observed. "Now he's going to die slow and hard."

They got the come-on from both men and women as they traversed a corridor of tents and hastily erected shelters and Pickens stared dolefully at women who would have sent him running in other times. Albert stopped and turned to him. Pickens knew this was the end of the road and the emotion swelled in his face.

"Thank you," he said, holding his hand out. Albert looked at the hand and back at Pickens' face and nodded almost imperceptibly.

"Sure," he said. He knew the younger man wouldn't last long - a week maybe, if he was lucky. He stifled the impulse to dispense some fortune cookie wisdom and turned away.

Albert moved slowly along the edges of the camp, staring discreetly at different revelers but not finding who he was looking for.

"Hey," a female voice hailed him.

He stopped and looked at the shadow moving beyond the penumbra of the nearest fire.

"Not interested," he said. She melted away.

He followed the sound of someone beating metal drums with an uncontrolled savagery and found himself on the edges of a great circle of worshippers, all mesmerized by a black man with several pails of different sizes and materials striking out a rhythm so powerful it stopped everyone who heard it.

58

He had seen these kids in New York years ago occupying street corners and banging out insane rhythms for the tourists on plastic pails, tin cans and garbage lids. This "kid" was about twenty-five and his skin clung to his bones without strength or even life. In New York he was not unique and had to fight for every tip; here he was almost without competition and no one had anything to give. Albert smiled when he thought of his times in New York. It was the only city he ever enjoyed. He had seen musicians playing Charlie Parker on street corners unable to get a gig who would have put ninety percent of the working musicians to shame. He had heard the Tchaikovsky violin concerto in the subway and he had seen a woman leap out in front of a taxi and then he'd seen the driver ask the cop if she had insurance.

"I ain't payin for this," the driver shouted as the medics spirited her dead body away.

The drummer stopped, exhausted and the huge circle of observers, perhaps two hundred people, broke up and wandered away without leaving him anything at all. He sat, leaning over his drums, a glazed look of desperation shining in the firelight.

Albert walked over and the drummer looked up at him hopefully.

"Pretty good," Albert said. "Ain't heard that in a while."

The drummer acknowledged the compliment and then shrugged.

"Not good enough, I guess," he said.

Albert placed a shiny, round object on the pail and the drummer picked it up. It glinted in the light. He looked at Albert as if to make sure he was really standing there. Then his shock gave way to a scowl and he tensed, as if preparing for a fight.

"This what it looks like?" he asked.

Albert nodded.

"Well what the hell do you want?" the drummer demanded.

"I'm looking for somebody," Albert replied. "I thought maybe you could check around for me, you being so well known around here."

The drummer held the coin up to the light again and stared at it in mild disbelief.

Albert continued: "Nobody will think twice about you wandering around here."

"People been killed for a whole lot less than this," the drummer said.

Albert agreed. "I'd appreciate if you'd keep it to your-self...where you got it, I mean."

The drummer looked at him earnestly and pocketed the coin.

"And who should I say is calling?" the drummer asked.

"Just tell him the meeting is on," Albert said. "Then come look-ing for me."

Albert told him the name of the man he was looking for and watched him disappear into the darkness, wondering if he would keep his word.

A silver round was a valuable item, so valuable that any number of people would gladly slit your throat to get it. In the old world it was worth about forty dollars. In this world - who knew? He'd have to find someone to trade with, someone who could break the piece down into its constituent parts of canned food, ammunition or other, more tradable goods. There was no money in circulation, to speak of. Only genuine gold and silver coins were worth anything. Ten thou-sand dollars in U.S. Treasury notes wouldn't buy you a cup of tea made with a dog's ear. But a single silver coin could be bartered for life itself. The problem was finding a fence. If you approached the wrong man, you could guarantee you'd be dead within a few mo-ments and stripped of everything. If the assailant happened to believe you had more than one, he would be determined to find your stash. And that was with silver. A gold eagle, worth say, $1800 before the Catastrophe might as well be radioactive unless you knew where to take it.

Albert was betting the drummer knew his way around better than most. It had been the same in the old days when he was a trucker. A black owner operator had to be twice as good and twice as smart as anyone just to stay even. They were the toughest men he'd ever known. It was obvious the drummer hadn't eaten properly in a while, but he was still alive.

***

Chapter Four

Small fires sputtered in between tents and shacks and every-where, men and women sat huddled together, mostly silent, poking a stick at the coals or staring into nowhere. A few chatted, meaningless drivel for the most part. Albert walked past, catching fragments here and there. The desolation was punctuated intermittent-ly by savage screams and the unforgettable sound of human flesh coming in contact with a tree branch at high velocity or the childlike grunt and shriek of a blade opening up the bowels.

There weren't many rules here. Well, better said, there were new rules and they were self-enforced. The only universally accepted principal at a rendezvous was that there would be no cannibalism. If someone died, their body could be burnt or buried or left to rot in the woods, the killer being responsible for disposal. Anyone caught eating human flesh was burned alive. Without that prohibition, the rendez-vous could turn into a smorgasbord in five minutes flat. You want to eat people? Be my guest. Just don't do it at a rendezvous.

Albert wasn't going anywhere in particular. He wandered slow-ly among the comatose and the ebullient, careful not to become in-volved in any way with what they were doing.

He watched two men with clubs fighting in a ring composed of maybe fifty others, their eyes stuck on the spectacle of blood and murder. The prize was a package of cigarettes, still in the wrapping, a bottle of beer and a live chicken in a wooden cage. The hen watched calmly, squeezed on both sides by the steel mesh and unable to move. There was only one outcome for her.

The fight was sponsored by a known gold trader who went by the name of Dazzling Daz, a very tall, lean fellow with the narrow, elongated head of premature birth and a pair of women's diamond earrings that hung down almost to the level of his mouth. Daz had fifteen accomplices, more or less, who guarded him and obeyed him in return for a steady supply of food and drink and even the occasional bauble. He had a high-pitched voice, incongruous with his physical size but somehow appropriate to his somewhat effeminate gestures. He was rumored to have a significant stash of coin somewhere and he readily traded for precious metals with anyone, anywhere at any time.

His preferred method of execution for those who betrayed him, was slow strangulation. One of his minions caught holding out could expect to be suspended from a gibbet, his toes just touching the ground. There he would dance, sometimes for hours until his strength gave out and he settled into the wire noose and choked himself to death. Daz would watch the proceedings along with everyone in the band, sipping wine and smoking cigarettes that he had distributed for the occasion. He claimed he took the idea from Hitler and modified it a bit to suit a world without movie cameras. He wouldn't get to watch it over and over again, but he could draw it out and make a night of it. Why his men never got together and killed him and shared out his stash was not very difficult to understand. They were followers. They needed someone to direct them and they knew it. Without Daz they would squander whatever wealth they managed to obtain and soon be just another platoon of zombies among the thousands wandering the wastelands. Daz picked his men carefully, making sure that no one with any self-respect or enterprise was ever admitted to the ranks.

Never underestimate the allure of petty authority: A comfortable, secure position somewhere in the middle, something with limited, specific responsibilities and duties, something that didn't require creative thinking or diplomacy. You get your orders, you perform your tasks, you receive your emolument. You sleep just fine, thank you. It's amazing what a man will do for 'a little bit of colored ribbon.' [7]

Like any mob boss, Daz kept his "friends" very close and his wealth very much hidden. There was no heir to the throne, here. Daz might encourage one for a while and then another and then set them upon each other and consign them both to the burn pile without a thought. He would die some day along with the secret location of his stash - believed to number almost five thousand gold and silver coins and bars. He couldn't take it with him, but he made damn sure that no one else was going to have it either.

The two men in the ring stood apart, chests heaving, eyes racing in the firelight. There was plenty of wagering going on among the spectators, small items like a few cigarettes or a couple of 9 mm rounds. Maybe someone had a pre-1965 quarter or dime and was willing to chance it. [8]

Daz was offering three to one on the smaller man.

His opponent was bigger, but older and all the emotion had drained from his face. His arm dropped, not actually broken but probably too painful to move. Daz looked on, incensed, as they closed again, his champion, now with only one arm to swing the club. He parried a furious attack from the smaller man whose desperation shone through like a light in a fog. The one armed man tried a wild swing and missed, throwing himself wide open for a split second. His opponent gritted his teeth and swung the bat with tremendous force against the one-armed man's head, splitting his skull with the blow. There was loud cheer from the crowd as the man toppled, dead before he landed. The smaller man stood over him, gasping for breath, his face streaked with a filthy mixture of sweat and probably tears. He tossed the bat to the ground and went to claim his prize.

Daz glared at him and everyone froze for a moment, wondering if the trader would renege. He had not only lost the prize, but a fair number of bets, as well. He looked away and the man took his beer and cigarettes and chicken and left.

Albert watched Daz paying off the bettors clearly resentful of the loss. Daz didn't often lose. But he had to pay out if he wanted to stay in business. Two men took the loser by the legs and dragged him off the grounds to the edge of the woods.

"Dog meat," one said.

Daz caught sight of Albert as he moved around the edge of the makeshift arena and he grinned and called his name. This caused half a dozen people nearby to freeze in their tracks and stare at him. Albert pretended not to notice and went over to where Daz was seated, drawing on a cigarette and sipping from a clay mug.

"We all heard you were dead," Daz said, his face open in a smile.

"I heard that too," Albert replied. "Was kinda hoping to stay that way, but I never had no luck."

The men laughed and Daz indicated a stump beside him. Albert shoved it up against a stack of MREs and sat down.

"Don't trust me, huh?" Daz prodded him.

"Oh, I trust you all right," he said. "I trust you to be yourself."

This brought another big smile from Dazzling Daz who pulled a mug out from a black hole somewhere and poured some amber fluid into it. Albert sniffed at it for a while and then handed it back. Daz shook his head and took a draught from the mug.

"Satisfied?" he said.

"Thanks," Albert said and allowed a few CCs of the precious liquid to coat his tongue. He kept it there for a full minute, allowing the alcohol to burn and sink in, draining it of all brilliance and power before consigning it to the trash heap of the human stomach.

"There's a man who can appreciate a drink," Daz said, looking around.

"Been a while, that's for sure," Albert said.

They sat in silence until Daz decided he was hungry and he instructed one of the men to open an MRE and get it ready for him.

"How about you?" Daz asked, but Albert shook his head.

"Just ate," he said.

The men looked at him, astonished and even Daz was surprised. Who would turn down a meal these days?

"Suit yourself," he shrugged.

One of the men tore open the puce plastic wrapper of an MRE and extracted all the ingredients for a beef dinner. The smell of the meat when he opened the vacuum-sealed pouch hit Albert like a wall but he showed no sign.

"Wha'd'you think of our little show?" Daz asked after a few moments.

"Disgusting, I'd say," Albert replied. "Sooner or later this kinda thing is going to come back on you," he added. "But you know that."

Daz nodded, "ya," and shrugged. "So where the hell have you been," he asked.

"No place, mostly," Albert said. "Layin low for a while."

"I must admit I never expected to see the great Albert Smythe again, not after that attack on Foreman's Mills.

"That was a humdinger," a voice came from the darkness. Albert thought he recognized it but gave no sign.

"HP Slim said he saw you take it in the gut. Swore on it."

"Well, I can understand that," Albert said. But he offered no more information and they knew enough not to probe further.

Albert finished the drink and stood up. Rather than soothe him, the brief taste of brandy had ignited in him a howling desire for more; not just the booze but also the company. Just sitting around having a drink and talking shit. It was a deep craving and he was sorry he had awakened it. But he had accomplished what he intended. It wouldn't take an hour for everyone in the camp to know he was here. If that didn't smoke out Jubal Case, nothing would.

So Albert had a man searching for Case and Case would soon have men searching for Albert. Albert and Case had never met and Albert wanted a look at him before they sat down and shared a pipe.

They were both known by reputation but having heard the stories told about himself, Albert believed none of it. Albert had ripped the heart out of Col. Herbert at Foreman's Mills and eaten it while it was still beating like some sort of Olmec priest. He had killed more people than had been counted in Makepeace County before the Catastrophe. He had hidden in a basement all through the Foreman's Mills fight and then run into the woods to fake his death. He had been burned, shot, beaten to death, hung, buried alive and recruited by the Provost Legion, brainwashed and turned back out to paint rebels for helicopter attacks; he had developed a taste for human flesh. He was a fascist vegetarian who killed anyone caught eating meat. He was really a woman. He was a communist. He was CIA; FBI; BATFE; Homeland Security; Army Intelligence. He was an alien. He was a robot. He was an alien robot vegetarian...

He doubled back through the woods and checked to make sure his equipment was where he had stashed it. It was all there, untouched and presumably undiscovered. He looked at the full moon and carefully inventoried his person.

He carried a small five-shot .22 Magnum revolver in his pocket. It was small enough to go undetected with a visual scan giving him enough time to get it out. At close range it was devastating. A gut shot from that revolver was a death sentence. It wasn't called a belly gun without reason. He always packed a shoulder holster .45 with four clips. He wore an Emerson knife under his collar and against his back. The lining of his jacket was razor wire and there were four hard, carbon fiber knives sewn into the sleeves. He carried something for them to find so they would think he had been disarmed and something they would miss, even if they used a metal scanner. In a flash, he had killed a man with a knuckle punch straight to the temple. He had strangled many with that very wire now lying across his shoulder. He had twisted a carbon fiber blade in the guts of more than he could remember.

So, part of his reputation, the part that claimed he was a killer, a savage killer, a remorseless and fiendish killer, was not exaggerated. In fact, they didn't know the half of it. Albert had committed sins he couldn't even think about. Albert had gouged out a soldier's eyes who had murdered an old couple he felt were moving too slowly - and then turned him loose in dog country. Albert carried images around in his brain that would have driven an ordinary man completely mad.

And yet, Albert was an ordinary man. Was. Used to be. Albert was once an ordinary man and then a government out of control, a government he had always supported and vouched for, a government he had paid for, showed up on his property, on his land, land he had bought and paid for by their rules, land he claimed and occupied, land where he intended to live out his life without any interference with or from the outside world...his life, his land...and they had murdered his animals and taken his property and abrogated the agreements that he had lived by and labored by for all his years. All for his own good, they said.

And so, Albert had transformed himself from a nonentity, a man without remarkable features and no special talents, a man with ordinary intelligence and less than ideal physical strength and size, a man without ambition of any kind with respect to his fellow man - into a bloody scourge the likes of which had not been seen in living memory. He was not feared without cause. They just didn't know the reality of it. Whatever they were capable of in their vulgar, greedy pursuit of authority, Albert was capable of ten-fold in his pursuit of revenge. If they thought they could terrorize to keep control, well, it had never been proved but there was a story that three soldiers trapped in an abandoned house and out of reach of assistance, had exchanged fire with him for ten hours and then committed mass suicide rather than be taken. Was it true or not? Albert never responded.

He watched the trail to the rendezvous for an hour before he ventured back into the camp. The shouting and fighting and laughter had not diminished and perhaps had even jumped a level. He moved carefully among the crowds, keeping close to the drunks and revelers, moving away if anyone noticed him, traveling for a while with a group of teenagers who were shouting: Fuck! Fuck! Fuck! Fuck!, over and over again, their faces lit in a mesmerized ecstasy. Albert moved with them until they seemed to vanish into the night, the last of them blinking out at the edge of a bonfire. Their voices carried back for a few moments and then they were gone.

He followed a wandering group of mixed drunks towards a large bonfire that beckoned from a depression surrounded by trees with all their lower branches stripped. A dozen naked people gyrated and screamed as they circled the fire while another hundred or so watched, their eyes lit with firelight but empty nonetheless. A couple fell to the ground copulating. The woman rose to all fours and began howling while the man mounted her from behind. A young woman, no more than twenty stood before the surging flames and raised her hands. Everyone stopped dancing and watched her as she tilted her head and began to scream obscenities at the sky. The crowd began to chant: Do it! Do it!, swaying back and forth in unison, the big wave a hundred years of Monday night football had taught them. "Do it," they shouted, voices barking out the phrase louder and louder until the girl seemed to fall into a trance. She pitched forward right onto the flames and began immediately to scream. The crowd cheered her on: "Burn! Burn!" as she scrambled among the blazing logs trying to push herself upright. Her hair flamed and Albert caught a glimpse of her face just before she gratefully fell into unconsciousness and lay herself down on the coals. The smell of her burning flesh passed over them and the crowd grew silent for a moment and then began to disintegrate, leaving the copulating pair alone before the flames, grunting and gasping, their faces blank.

Albert joined another platoon of zombies and drifted with them towards a collection of huts and makeshift tents fanning out octopus-like from a rocky clearing. He was about to peel away when he spotted the drummer moving towards the outcrop, obviously searching for someone. His eyes scanned the crowds and Albert managed to hide among a group of men dragging a large dead dog down one of the pathways.

Following the drummer were two men, well dressed in military style fatigues and openly carrying rifles. Concealed handguns, knives and various other instruments were common among any group but few carried long guns openly for fear of being targeted. If you found yourself caught in a Legion raid, it was a simple thing to ditch a handgun or plant it on a rival. Those carrying long guns just stood out too clearly and were most often killed by advance sniper teams before the raid even commenced. One of the men followed Drummer Man, while the other started searching the alleyways. Bad move, Albert observed. A few minutes later he saw a woman, well vested and with long hair hanging down from under a peaked cap. She was either carrying or had three tits, and she moved with a studied grace.

For another hour, he wandered around the campsite, occasionally looking inside a tent or joining a cluster of half-starved, empty-eyed spooks watching a dog or a spit of rats turning over a fire. He spotted one other suitor among the crowds clearly looking for someone.

He decided to follow the woman and eventually, she showed evidence of frustration and stopped, looking around, unsure of where to go next. He saw her lift her collar and speak into it, something she should not have done so openly.

"Bang," Albert whispered.

She turned quickly after that and started back towards the tent city fanning out from the rock clearing. She stopped several times, mimicking Albert's methods, hiding briefly in a crowd and watching her back trail for followers or disappearing behind a shelter and reappearing a few moments later on her own path. She was making sure that no one was following her, but Albert wasn't impressed. She was unnatural and anyone, trained or otherwise would have picked her out in a minute. If this was the kind of talent Jubal Case was bringing to the meet, things did not look promising.

And then he lost her. He had taken his eyes off her for a split second, just enough time to get around an old man stalled in the path, vomiting onto the grass. When he looked up, the woman was gone.

He dodged behind a moving crowd and flowed with it for a few minutes, trying to catch a glimpse of her again but she was gone. He peeled off the crowd and walked down a tent alley where small fires burned in front of every a shelter.

"What ever you're looking for, we got it," a man's voice called to him.

Albert could see him back of the tent, a large canopy of plastic, probably a hay tarp from the old days, draped over several branches and propped up with poles cut from cedar. His senses doubly aware and his confidence stung badly by the woman, he moved on without responding.

Before he had gone a dozen feet he was accosted again, this time by a woman.

"My girls are clean," she said. "Boys too if you want. Both. Whatever..."

He swung wide of the next assemblage of plastic sheets and blankets and tin roofing, leaving the reach of the meager fires and allowing the soft woods night to cover him.

He watched for a while as men and women transacted in the alleyways and then disappeared into the tents. Several times he heard screams and shouts and a man would be ejected and on one occasion he watched a bouncer shove a patron so hard his head bounced off a tree and cracked like melon. The bounced patted him down, removed a pocketknife and a few bits of change and dragged the body off the trail and into the woods.

He waited in the shadows for another hour before he moved, hoping the woman or Case would come looking for him again; but the only activity that transpired before him was the repeating, desultory process of flesh exchange.

When he emerged from cover the moon had fallen and taken the shining silvery light with it. Drab shadows were all that remained. Albert took a few steps and felt the air vibrate around him before he caught a peripheral movement. He dove and rolled before the club made contact and had his Emerson out by the time he had righted himself. The figure came at him and Albert crouched, preparing to sacrifice his arm for a chance to kill his attacker. He saw the man's face for a second and then his skull fractured with a loud crack and he hit the ground.

*

Albert came to slowly, blood caked on the side of his temple and his skull pounding like an oil derrick. He could see but he could not hear quite properly yet. As he came round, he realized he was lying on a cot, still clothed and without any manacles or restraints. His .45 was still under his arm and the Emerson had been laid on the table beside the cot. A hurricane lamp hissed quietly. There was even a glass of water and several small white tablets beside the knife. When he tried to sit up, the room spun and he immediately retched, though nothing came out of his near-empty stomach. He lay back and closed his eyes and began to count backwards from fifty. When he reached thirty-seven, he stopped and opened his eyes again. He was not drugged but he was sure he had a fractured skull. The pain was so severe when he moved his head he had to clamp his teeth together to prevent his moan from escaping.

It wasn't long before he heard voices and the door to the shelter opened, allowing a sudden burst of brilliant light into the room. He fell back as it pierced his eyes and sent pain shooting back through his cranium. Two men entered, one of them quite a bit taller with a baseball cap covering a bald pate. Beside him an older man, one who peered at him owl-like from behind a pair of glasses and shined a small flashlight into his eyes. He straightened up and nodded at the taller man.

"He's fine," he said, and left.

Jubal Case sat down on a stump beside Albert and folded his arms.

"Hurts, don't it?" he said.

Albert blinked, a mordant sense of *déjà vu* taking him back to another tent where an army deserter was him helping recover from a bullet wound and had said exactly the same thing.

"Sure as hell," Albert croaked, but his voice had no strength.

"That's all right," Case soothed him. "You just heal up a bit and we'll get together later."

"I'm ready now," Albert said, gritting his teeth.

Case couldn't help grinning.

"Ain't supposed to sleep with a head wound anyway," Case admitted.

Albert managed to sit up but the room continued to spin wildly.

"That's for you," Case said, indicating the ibuprofen tablets.

"Suit yourself," he shrugged when Albert declined.

"Are you Jubal Case?" he asked finally.

"Who wants to know?" Case replied.

"Albert Smythe," Albert said evenly, "but you know that."

Case nodded.

"I just wanted to hear you say it, is all. Pleased to meet you, Albert. Been hoping we'd get together for some time now..."

***

70

Chapter Five

They had moved him from the rendezvous about five miles north to a camp set up in a limestone quarry.

Most of Indiana was limestone, Salem limestone as it was officially known and quarries were abundant. Huge man-made canyons with perfectly sheer walls and occasionally pools of clear spring water dotted the landscape from Bloomington to Bedford but also far beyond. This particular quarry was fifty feet deep and dry. A bore tunnel had been dug into the side opening a cavern almost the size of a football stadium. Limestone was part of the same calcium carbonate chemistry that lined the walls of Albert's hideout but in this case the stone was clean and pure - the best in the country at one time.

Now the great hall was the temporary headquarters of Jubal Case's army, a battalion size collection of deserters, wanderers, killers, spies and criminals looking for an opportunity to loot.

As he ventured outside for the first time since his "capture," Albert was dismayed by the character and condition of the men and women. Case had been on top of the Provost Legion's hit list, considered to be a genuine threat to the thousand heavily armed and trained soldiers - which included a helicopter unit, drone battery and special forces company composed of a twenty or so SEALS, RANGERS and MARSOC collected from the leftovers after the first plague. The Provost Legion could not be defeated, or even seriously harmed by this group.

He began to wonder why Case even bothered. There was no way these people, even if they were trained and motivated would stand a chance against the Legion. For a paranoid moment, Albert wondered if he'd fallen for it. Perhaps Case was just the bait and those who crowded around him were being set up. That's how he'd do it. You ain't that important, he told himself. They think you're dead anyway.

He had stayed out of the fierce sunlight for another two days after his first encounter with Case but now the sun felt good as it penetrated his clothing and warmed his face. The headaches had diminished but they were still present and he was waiting for the ibuprofen to kick in. Why were these guys all lying around out in the open like this? There was something wrong-

"Hey," a familiar voice greeted him. Albert turned and Lonny Pickens stood a few feet away, not sure if he should greet him or not.

"I didn't know," Lonny said, a little wonder in his voice.

Albert grunted.

"I guess I-" Lonny sputtered.

"Forget it," Albert told him. "What are you doing here?"

"They were watching us from when we entered the rendezvous. They weren't taking no chances so they picked me up. 'Course I didn't put up any fight to speak of."

It almost sounded like an apology. He glanced momentarily at Albert while he spoke.

"I didn't know who you were till they told me. Honest to God."

Lonny offered Albert a pouch of tobacco and some hand cut squares of paper but Albert shook his head. He didn't need to be worried about tobacco when he was in the field. He'd seen it kill men just because they couldn't get their minds off it. Made them do stupid things like burn grass and toilette paper when they were hiding. He wouldn't travel with a smoker and if he'd known he might have left Pickens to die.

Lonny sat on a rock ledge and started to roll one.

"I almost couldn't b'leev it when they told me," he said. "We - the Legion - we thought you were dead. Everybody thought you were dead."

Albert nodded. "Ya? Who did they think was shooting their officers?"

Lonny shook his head slowly.

"Couldn't figure it out because HP Slim told everyone he seen you take it in the gut. Nobody survives being gut-shot these days...so...we just figured, I guess," he said, concentrating lighting the rough cigarette. The smoke blew back in his eyes making him tear up.

72

HP Slim had disappeared shortly after Foreman's Mills. Now Albert knew why.

"Seen HP around?" he asked, trying to sound casual.

"He ain't around," Pickens said, uncomfortably.

Albert watched him smoke.

"Legion?"

Pickens nodded. "It was pretty bad," Pickens said. "He swore you were dead right up to when they opened him up for the dogs."

That's not what he had supposed at all. He had believed Slim was a turncoat and had been brought in from the cold after the fight. He'd seen him run. He'd seen it with his own eyes. It was difficult to put it together. Everyone had been sure at one point that HP was a painter, sent in by the Legion. And yet here was Pickens declaring he'd seen him tortured to death by that very same Legion.

Pickens seemed to know what Albert was thinking and he exhaled slowly.

"They thought he was doubling back on them," Pickens said. "Nobody ever really trusts a traitor, do they?" he asked pointedly.

Albert didn't answer.

Pickens flicked the cigarette and looked dolefully at him. "There just ain't no way to prove yourself," he said.

Albert found Jubal Case sitting under a sun-shelter, conversing with three other men. They watched him walk up and their conversation stopped.

"How's the head?" Jubal asked.

"It hurts," he said. "I'll get over it."

Jubal stared hard at him for a moment and then turned to the men beside him. He introduced them, first names only and then told them they were speaking to Albert Smythe. Two of the men showed surprise but the third just nodded, a hint of a smile on his face.

"Do I know you?" Albert asked him.

"He's the one give you that headache," Case said.

Albert extended his hand and they looked at each other briefly.

"Pleasure," Albert said.

Case handed out glasses and removed a half drunk bottle of vodka from behind his chair. He dolloped a bit into each glass and feigned a toast before shooting it back. The others sipped theirs a little cautiously and Albert merely held his in his lap.

"Anybody want to start?" Case said after a few moments silence.

The man identified as Freddy appeared ready to speak and eyes turned on him.

"I ain't heard nothing to bring back with me," he said. "Unless you fellows have some sort of plan, I guess I'm going to have to decline."

Albert was loath to speak but he forced the conversation his way.

"I got something to say," he informed them.

"What are you doing out here in the open like this?"

Case looked around. "There's a fellow here -

"-Ya, I know him, Lonny Pickens," Albert interrupted. "Claims he's some super secret computer guy run off from the Legion to join the circus. Well what if he's full of shit?"

"We been out here for almost a week," Case said and we've heard back from our people -

"What people?" Albert demanded.

"We have a few inside; they know Lonny."

"They know him as what?" Freddy asked. "I'm with mister Smythe here. I don't believe a word of it."

"Then why aren't we dead?" Maxwell, the other man said.

"Because they are waiting until we all get here and then-." Freddy offered.

Albert was looking at Brent, the man who had clubbed him back at the rendezvous. He knew why they'd done it that way. If they had tried to "persuade" him to come along, he'd have killed them on the spot. Albert's reputation preceded him and he did little to modify it. It was known that Albert had a serious case of oppositional defiance disorder and he came and went on his own terms. Period. Always. He was still embarrassed at having fallen for the ruse with the woman wearing the ball cap and he had been trying to find her since he came to. He wanted to meet her. He wanted to shake her hand, sort of. The so-called meeting at the rendezvous had been a setup all along and he should have known it. There was no way Case would announce his travel plans like that. You're slipping buddy. Your days are numbered.

Case stood up and motioned Brent and Albert to follow him. He left the other two with the bottle of vodka and that seemed fine with them.

"We had to know," Case said after they had walked a few yards.

"I know," Albert replied.

"You being dead and all..." Brent drawled.

The sun blazed down on them and shone blindly off the white, stone walls.

"I still don't get how you know it's me," Albert said.

Case glanced at him and Albert waited for the answer.

"There's a few here recognize you," Case said.

"And," Brent added, "I was at Foreman's Mills. I was in that first rush when everything went to hell and you drew them off. When we brought you in the other night I seen the track across your gut where the bullet skimmed you," Brent explained.

Albert said nothing, but he would never forget that day.

A platoon of maybe fifty Legion soldiers under a lieutenant had occupied the old stone building at Foreman's Mills for about a week when rumors came down that they were preparing to set up a transfer point for captured "insurgents." Everyone knew by then what that meant: A one-way trip to Beach Grove and the crematorium.

Beach Grove was a FEMA operated concentration camp - there was no other way to describe it - where dissidents had been incarcerated from the first days of the Catastrophe. Tens of thousands had been murdered there by UN troops and private contractors, specifically detailed for the job because of their inherent lack of empathy with the American citizens they had been ordered "to serve and protect."

Captured rebels would be questioned at Foreman's Mills then trucked to Beach Grove where specialists would reduce them to gibbering, bloody revenants before throwing them - often still alive - into the ovens. Designed by a Chinese multinational corporation with plans lifted right from the archives of A.J. Topf & Sohne, the original architects at Auschwitz, these new and improved combustion chambers could dispose of a human body in eighteen minutes. The belt, replete with manacles to hold down the shrieking victims, moved at a constant pace, corpses and sacrifices entering at one end and smoking, empty chain mail conveyor belt exiting at the other. Once a week, the ashbin was emptied using a giant forklift truck. For most if not all the men involved in that attack, it was a better way to die than the alternatives. You could surrender and be murdered after torture, kill yourself, or die fighting.

The attack had originally been set up by "General Herbert," (everyone called him Herbie) an affable military fantasist with a lifetime subscription to Soldier of Fortune magazine, a spanking uniform he'd designed himself and enough charisma to pull in about seventy five followers.

The plan had been to assault the building on three sides. The back being a solid wall of limestone with no doors and all the windows bricked up that looked onto an empty courtyard with a river running behind it, would require no attention. Many had argued against a full assault, knowing that the troops inside were heavily armed and well stocked. But Herbert insisted they could breach the front doors while cover fire enfiladed the windows on the flanks. They had two RPGs taken from a depot near Madison and on the signal from Herbert the rockets were shot through the front. The explosions shook the building and only sporadic defensive fire was returned, convincing everyone that they had dealt a significant blow to the garrison.

Herbert ordered the assault and about seventy-five men and women, variously armed and none carrying more than thirty rounds headed straight for the maw. At three hundred feet the 50 caliber machine guns hidden on the roof and in the attic of the building opened up, slaughtering dozens in a matter of minutes. The rest pulled back behind cover and took pot shots at the barricaded soldiers until the walls of the mill courtyard exploded and a fully armed Abrams tank lunged towards the rebel line, its machine guns chattering and shells walloping into the trees.

Albert stood up and started firing when a stray caught him in the side. He grabbed his stomach and fell forward. The last thing he saw was HP Slim running. The thirty-minute battle had left a hundred and twenty five militiamen dead. The army had no casualties at all. Herbert had died in the first wave, cut in half by a 50 caliber. About forty men and women, most badly wounded managed to crawl away. Eighteen of those died over the next week. The Legion and its spies had arranged the entire operation in advance.

It was precisely this kind of fiasco that had since kept Albert away from any of the organized groups, even though some were quite competent and just as determined as he.

He'd ended up fighting with Herbie's idiots brigade because he wanted that captain supposedly in charge of this new transfer unit. But it only takes one sleeper to compromise an organization and there was simply no way to convincingly verify anything people claimed about themselves or anyone else. That sleeper had been HP Slim, who had been vetted a hundred times and had planted his share of IEDs to prove it. Then karma blew back on him and his new masters fed him to the dogs - literally.

The presumption had been in the militia movement for years, that every unit no matter how carefully vetted, had been infiltrated by informers or federal agents and the "conspirators" tried to act accordingly. In the early days after the 1995 Oklahoma City bombing, these were the guys who egged others on and called for violent attacks, entrapped idiots with ebullient encouragement and fake explosives and occasionally assisted in the murder of innocent civilians to cover their own tracks. But they were easy to spot and the FBI and BATFE and Homeland Security and only God knows how many other clandestine organizations had to change their tactics. They smartened up and by the 2005 subway bombing in London, the militant groups, whether they were Pure Islamist or Pure Idiots, White/Black/Hispanic/LGBTQ Nationalists, Neurotics or Assholes, Anarchists or Arachnids, had all been completely and totally compromised and they couldn't tell the players apart. Bribery, extortion and departmental promotion allowed the government forced entry into every aspect of every organization in the country.

So when the first roundups of U.S. subversive groups began shortly after New Years Day, 2013, (i.e. anyone who wasn't down on all fours when the jackboots started goose- stepping) the government knew the whereabouts and plans, hideouts and ammunition depots, breakfast preferences and toilette paper consumption of 99 per cent of the known disorganizations in the country. They all went down hard, the militias especially so. Within six months their leaders were all executed and those unresponsive to reeducation or resistant to becoming rats for the system were sent to Beach Grove.

It had been sporadic guerilla warfare since then, an assassination here or an IED in the roadway there. A few suicide attackers had attempted to breach the gates at Provost with vehicles, bicycles and horses and none had gotten ten feet inside. There had been talk about something big happening, something coordinated, but so far it was all just talk. When Albert had heard of Case's recruitment efforts, he sent a message back through the underground that he'd like to meet. Case must have figured it was a setup as Albert was supposedly long dead and hadn't been spotted in almost two years; hence the elaborate ruse to get him to the rendezvous and then lead him astray so Brent could bonk him on the head.

Speaking of his head. It was throbbing like a whale's heart.

"Come on," Case said and led the way into the mouth of the access tunnel.

Dim, oil lamps cast enough light to keep you from smashing into walls but the ceiling vanished in soft blackness after only a few feet. Tables had been set up, a few chairs, even an old sofa stood against one wall. Several guards patrolled with M16s or some equivalent. Case ushered them deeper into the cave and finally stopped at a small round table with a hurricane lamp. A woman emerged from the darkness and Albert recognized her as the bait he had taken a few evenings ago at the rendezvous. Her hair was tied up in a bun and she wore no cap but he knew her instantly. She looked at him and a brief smile chased across her mouth and vanished. Case saw the interaction and couldn't help a grin, either.

"Albert, this is Greta...I think you've met."

Albert and Greta continued looking at each other, simple appraising looks without enmity or favor.

"Don't feel bad, man," Brent chimed in. "She's a pro..."

Albert looked at him inquiringly.

"CIA, Homeland...whatever you want," Case said.

"Ya. Well fuck you," Albert said to her, adding, almost as an afterthought: "No offence."

She shrugged and took a chair at the table, resting her arms in her lap. By the way she sat, Albert knew her hand was on a pistol grip under her clothes. She watched him, a little cold now, and then placed both hands on the table.

"Okay?" she asked.

Albert sat down, trying to find a place where his back wasn't open to the world, but the table had been placed in position for that very reason. No one had any apparent advantage here.

"Let's get over it," Case said, business like. But before he could begin, Albert commandeered the floor.

"What the fuck is she doing here?" he demanded.

"You say she's connected all the way up and...what, her conscience got the better of her? Tell me why I shouldn't blow her fucking brains out right here?

"Well, first because then you'd be splattered yourself," Case admonished. "We let you keep your guns because-"

When he heard this, Albert froze in a controlled fury, not trusting himself to speak right away. He rose and pushed the chair away. Several of the guards had moved in closer and unshouldered their weapons.

"You're the first one I'm going to kill," Albert said, looking straight at Greta. "And a few more before those monkey's get me," he added. "And you fucking well know I can do it, too."

Case and the others watched Albert carefully, aware that the slightest movement could set him off. He was known for it.

"Albert-" Case started to say.

"You *let me* keep my guns?" Albert interrupted.

"A sign of good faith for Chrissakes," Brent interjected. "We didn't have to let you wake up. What the fuck's a matter with you? You want out, just go. Get the fuck outta here."

Greta had been watching him without blinking, her face calm, almost disinterested.

"You'd let me walk outta here, would ya?" Albert said. "If that's true you're even stupider than I thought."

"You're the one with the bump on the head," Greta said quietly.

She had seen the look in Albert's eyes many times and she knew he was on the verge. Something had to give or there would be some kind of a bloodbath. The two guards were joined by two more, and they all held weapons on Albert.

"Should have acted when you had the chance," Greta said. "Now we've got you again."

Albert nodded slowly in agreement and looked around.

"Well, you know what happens next, then," he said.

Case stood up and waved off the guards.

"Let him be," Case ordered. "If he wants to leave here, you let him go. Whatever this asshole is, he's no traitor."

Case sat down again and the guards reluctantly moved away. Albert could see they still had their weapons presented and regardless of Case's instructions, they'd kill him in a breath.

"Get them monkey's off my back or somebody here is going to die," Albert said.

Case shook his head.

"Back off," he ordered. "I'm not kidding. I guarantee you he will not do anything if you just back off."

They disappeared into the darkness, out of reach of the meager lamplight but Albert was certain they were still holding on him.

He knew he was acting irrationally, but now he had to save face. It was Greta who seemed to get it.

"I understand your doubts," she said. "I'd be exactly the same. I might have even done something about it by now."

"So?" Albert replied.

"So nothing," she said. "I don't have any solutions for you. I guess it's up to you whether you want to take the chance. I mean you can always kill me later," she said wryly. "Unless I kill you first, of course."

"How did she come to be here?" Albert asked.

Brad answered with an earnestness that made Albert's stomach clench.

"She helped us set an IED that blew up a Humvee with seven of her own guys in it," he said.

Albert nodded. "I see, but how did you find her? Where did she come from?"

Brad's mouth seemed to freeze and then he shook his head derisively.

"Man, what more do you want?"

"How did you meet her?" Albert demanded again.

"Look, she's okay," Case interjected. "We've checked her out."

There was an uncomfortable few moments before Albert sat down again. The headache had come on gangbusters. Case took over the sit-down again, acting as if nothing had happened and the others were grateful for the opportunity to move on.

"It's hard to know where to begin," he said leaning forward, his arms on the table.

"We all know what's been going on in our own little corners for the last few years but there is a bigger picture and we've got an opportunity if you want to call it that to get somewhere...do something about it...shit...I don't even know what that means.

"Everybody's got his own agenda, I understand that and I'm not here trying to unite the tribes or anything. You can all go do whatever the hell you want...you and everybody else. It's just that as long as the military and the leftover politicians are in charge, things are going to be like they are. And I don't know anybody who wants that except them."

Albert cast a glance at Greta and she looked back at him without any doubt or hesitation. That was the first moment he noticed that she was quite a pretty woman. Her features were thin from malnutrition and her skin had tightened a bit, but she had all the symmetry and intelligence associated with female allure. At least you're not quite dead yet. She smiled again, seeming to know what he was thinking. But of course she did. She knew because she was trained to know. He looked away.

"It's not just us." Case continued. " Everyone wants these bastards dead or run off. There are guys dealing with Indianapolis, St. Louis, Atlanta...I mean you name it. The thing is we can't do anything about them. But we can take care of things down here."

"I don't get it, Albert said. "What's changed? Last time I threw in with a bunch of assholes, present company included, it was a worm festival. Who is supposed to be running things this time?"

Brad nodded and pursed his lips.

"Case here ain't no General Herbert," he said.

"May be so," Albert shrugged. "You wanna find out the hard way? Shit. I've killed more of those bastards myself than any of your goddamn group gropes ever accomplished."

"We're aware of that Brad said. "That's why you're here."

"I'm not bossing anybody around," Albert said. "I'm no leader and I'm no follower. I'm about the worst thing an organized group can have. I don't obey orders. Anybody's orders. Ever. Does not play well with others. Runs with scissors, get it?"

"We get it," Case said. "We figured you might have something to say or maybe you want to know what we're doing so you can...do whatever the hell it is you do..."

"Or maybe you just want to keep me out of the picture in case I screw up another one of your fiascoes."

A teenager appeared out of the darkness and went over to Case and whispered in his ear.

"Good," Case said.

No one spoke for a few minutes. They heard footsteps coming towards them and two men appeared out of the gloom, one of them hobbling with a cane and the other, much younger, wearing camouflage.

"Who's this?" Albert sneered. "Father Time and Captain America?"

The newcomers had arrived from Indianapolis just that morning, a mere hundred and fifteen miles away but after a two and a half week journey. Case introduced everyone and typically, they both stared hard at Albert.

"It's an honor," the younger man named Curtis said as he reached over the table and extended a hand.

"Sit down," Albert told him.

Case said, "Curtis is a liaison officer with the Indianapolis Third Regiment. "Leslie is commander of the Vermillion County Volunteers."

Albert stared at Curtis for a few seconds and looked at Case.

"That's right," Case said. "He's the one Indianapolis Army Group has sent out to try and make contact with us...you know, negotiate."

"Don't tell me," Albert said caustically. "He's really a double agent and our dearest friend."

"That's right," Curtis said. "I'm taking a hellofa chance here for you people."

Curtis blushed hard and tried to stare down Albert but there was no way to win. There was nothing he could do or say that would convince Albert that he was anything but a plant. Albert felt his chest getting tight and the mild claustrophobia he had developed after spending too much time in his own underground bunker, was lapping against the shores of his self-confidence.

"I think I've had enough," Albert said, standing up.

Case and the others looked at him unhappily.

"Tell your guys not to miss if they try anything," Albert said cheerfully.

He took a last look at Greta and pulled his trigger finger.

"You specially," he smiled.

It took a few minutes for his eyes to adjust when back outside. The sun was directly overhead and he took off his wristwatch and set it to twelve o'clock. Now it would be a useful compass again, at least until it ran down. It was a self-winding watch but three or four days on a table would run it out.

It took him a few minutes to get orientated and then he headed across the great expanse of sheered limestone to the tent city at the far end. The same people were lounging around or sleeping when he got back to the hospital tent where he'd first awakened.

His cot was now occupied by a woman coughing violently. She leaned over to vomit into a bucket. The nurse or whatever she was didn't seem to notice and kept measuring something on a table with a teaspoon. His pack was where he'd left it and it appeared untouched, but he would check it carefully, remove the contents and burn it as soon as he was clear of the quarry.

The patient opened glassy eyes and stared at him blankly. He stayed as far from her as possible as he gathered his things. The nurse finished what she was doing and turned around with a cup of some colored liquid. Albert glanced in her direction and straightened up as she came towards him. Her face was greyish with fatigue but it was the purple scar running from her eye to her chin that made him take a second look.

She looked right at him and then switched her attention to the woman on the cot.

"How's your head, Albert?" Maureen Grogan said, as she brushed past.

***

Chapter Six

...water hissing against the plastic shower curtain ... running down her and sliding over her. And her hands feeling the surface of her own skin, the back of her neck or her belly or her thighs, hands roaming around at will. ...naked feet on the floor, the gentle slap and suck of flesh against the polished wood and a slight vibration in the air as she stopped. Then another door opened and closed...the vibration in the room as she entered, her hair still wet and streaked back like an otter.

She sat down on the sofa and ran her hands over the leather.

...when she crossed her legs and a slip of white ankle and calve flashed it hit his heart like a stone. She reached over to pick up the coffee cup and the cords in her neck stretched languidly.

He knew it was coming but still he flinched when she touched his arm. He turned to her and they embraced, trying to find some way to fit into the contours and crevices of unfamiliar bodies. He felt the pressure of her breasts against his chest and heard his own breathing. And then:

Dear Albert, Forgive me for not waiting to say goodbye to you in person...

"It's nothing special," she said, keeping her profile to him. "Everybody's got a story."

They were sitting on a stone ledge outside of the hospital tent. He nodded and stared at the ground. It was true. It was like former inmates of a concentration camp getting together for a reunion. What could anyone say? Hi. My name's Joe and I watched UN soldiers rape my mother and sister to death. Hi. My name's Louise and I ate my baby brother after he died last year.

"Jubal found me in a slave train near Evansville."

"A what?" Albert said. There was a strange smile on his face, almost a grin of discordance.

"A slave train."

"What the hell is a slave train?"

"What do you think?"

"I don't know what to think. Do you mean black people?"

"Jesus Albert...People. Women, mostly."

"Mostly?"

"Oh, I see it's worse if-" But she could see by his expression that he didn't really understand what she meant.

"Jubal and Brent and about ten men attacked the train outside of Evansville when it stopped for a transfer...not a real train, like a choo-choo train...just a string of wagons and horses and they thought it was carrying food or something. When they opened the containers, they found us, about thirty of us. We were being taken to a military installation somewhere in Kentucky."

Albert looked around the quarry, unable to meet her gaze for a moment.

"Case's men killed everybody that didn't get away," she said. "I didn't have anywhere to go, so here I am."

Albert stayed his hand but it seemed magnetized by her shoulders. He wanted to put his hands on her but the idea seemed disgusting and alluring at the same time.

"What are you going to do? They said you-" But when she looked at him she saw that he was not going to join them. "Oh," she said.

Albert didn't know what to do. He hadn't been this confused in years, not since he accidentally killed - *accidently my ass - that young girl. You killed her. Period. It was no accident.*

"Are you leaving then?" she asked.

He was afraid to answer.

"I haven't decided," he offered, half to see how she reacted. She looked into the distance for a moment and then thought better of it and said nothing. He was disappointed.

She returned to her patient and he remained sitting on the ledge, trying to sort himself out. The thing about fantasies is they're all yours. Everyone does what they're supposed to do. Everything's perfect. And then you are foolish enough to try and make it happen and people just don't cooperate. They don't want what you want. Go back to dreamland. Don't get distracted. He couldn't tell if she was glad to see him or not. Maybe she had a boyfriend or something. If he stayed around hoping she was going to fall into his arms...well, he wasn't that stupid.

I can pretend all I want. Get out. Get the hell out of here.

He must have spent several hours alone on the ledge because when he came back to the present, his watch said after three p.m. although he had no memory of the time passing. Some sort of incident around the hospital tent had fetched him from his reverie. He saw two men emerge carrying a stretcher with the now-dead woman, her mouth lolling open as her head fell sideways.

"Thought you'd be gone by now," Case said, coming up beside him.

Case glanced over at the hospital tent and smiled to himself. This annoyed Albert and he frowned at him.

"I haven't changed my mind," Albert said.

"Take your time," Case replied. He left and walked past the hospital tent without looking inside.

Albert waited to see if she was going to come out and then lost patience and walked over. She was writing at a desk. She looked up at him and then went back to work. He watched her and then sat in a hard-back chair against the tent wall.

"Were you a school teacher?" he asked her.

"How did you guess?" she said, smiling. She still only showed him her left profile.

"I just figured," he replied. "The way you write."

This time she looked at him full on and he saw the scar, a dark purple worm crawling from near her right eye right down to her chin.

"I know that was...cowardly," she said. Albert shrugged and looked away from her.

"You don't owe me anything. You didn't then, either."

He hadn't exactly rescued her. She was being detained in her own home by men who had commandeered it for their operations against the UN forces roving the countryside in the first days of 2013. They had abused her to some degree but even she admitted it wasn't really forced; unless withholding food that they were in no way re-

86

quired to share with her constitutes force. Whatever they were, they hadn't raped her.

But she went along with him after a firefight at the farm had left them dead or on the run. He had taken her back to his cabin outside Provost that had somehow, miraculously to that point, evaded destruction.

He had his own power, then, and hot water, refrigeration...privacy. He had hoped she would stay, but she disappeared, leaving him a brief note. He had read the note so many times the paper had finally worn out and he burned it. And then she faded into a pleasant memory, something he recalled at will on long marches or periods of almost total immobility in a sniper's nest. And now, here she was again.

"I thought I could do something. I didn't want to just live off another man," she said.

His headache was back full force and she sounded a bit like she was talking under water.

"You got anything for this?" he asked, holding his head. He saw her rise and retrieve some more ibuprofen tablets and water. He threw them back and gulped.

"Jesus," he said.

"You probably could use another night here...before you head out into the woods," she said. "It's up to you, but I'd recommend it."

Around six o'clock Case's men started passing out MREs and it was the first time all day some of the layabouts had moved. Albert walked beside Maureen, hesitant and still unconvinced that anything around here was what it appeared to be. But he couldn't bring himself to leave. She had this gravitational hold on him.

Albert wasn't used to standing in lines any more or doing anything in fact, that he hadn't personally decided to do. She pulled his coat sleeve as he tried to walk to the front and he moved obediently back in beside her.

"Steady boy," she said.

The line moved quickly and in five minutes they were passing the setup tables where Case and Brad were handing out military MREs.

"Beef Stroganoff, or chicken and rice?" Case asked him. Albert frowned at Case's flickering smile.

"What the hell is so damn funny?" he demanded, and Case allowed the smile off the leash.

"Enjoy your meal," he said.

Following her across the quarry floor, Albert had a sudden urge to run. It was like every warning signal he had developed in the last years went off at once. There could be nothing here for him. She was locked into the "community" thing and he wouldn't piss on this fraternity of fuckups if they were on fire. And besides that, after a few weeks - if it even took that long - the sex would wear off and they'd be left with each other and nothing to say except I told you so. It wasn't her fault. He just knew himself well enough to realize that human relationships were not only not his strong point - he was borderline incapable. For a while as a child they thought he had Asperger's Syndrome but a decided willingness to behave like they expected, made them back off. What they didn't realize and he had only realized himself of late, was that he really didn't know what to do. He imitated what he saw other people do and judged the response. If he got approval he knew it was the right thing. If not, well, he'd learn a new routine. Otherwise, the only fact Albert was sure of was this: He would kill every cop and soldier, would-be politician and hired thug that he found until they finally managed to kill him. That was it. That's Albert Smythe. Killer Extraordinaire.

She had a small three-man nylon tent put together with aluminum poles. It had a canopy out front shading two chairs and a small table with an oil lamp and five gallon clear plastic jug of water. Inside there was a narrow army cot with a sleeping bag. She reappeared from one corner with two tin plates, a fork and a spoon.

"It ain't much but it's mine," she tried to joke.

He just nodded, embarrassed now to be there, already trying to find a way to extricate himself.

Asshole. Asshole. Asshole.

"Pardon?" she said.

He looked up and shrugged. "I didn't say anything."

She indicated one of the chairs and they sat opposite each other busying themselves for a few minutes with the MREs, taking out the packets, placing the entre into the heat pouch, securing the sugar packets aside. She kept turning away from him, offering him only her left profile.

"I used to think about you all the time," she said. "I'd remember that wonderful cabin of yours and the shower...my god, can you imagine a hot shower! It's been years."

"Well, I'm glad you enjoyed yourself," he said stiffly.

"I didn't mean-"

He stood up, leaving the meal uneaten.

"This is stupid," he said.

It wasn't worth trying to make it back to the rendezvous and thence to his stash where he'd left his rifle and certain other valuables, such as binoculars, ammunition, a small medical kit and extra food. He would spend the night and leave first thing in the morning. He hated to admit that when she had suggested he stay, he thought it meant something particular. And when she suggested they eat at her tent, his heart began to pound wildly with anticipation. He was remembering her body from before, the texture of the skin on her thighs and the heavy softness of her breasts. He imagined he saw the muscles working in her arms and legs right through her clothing.

"Asshole," he spat out loud.

He saw Brent and Case approaching him and he stopped and waited.

"Where are you headed?" Case asked.

"Looking for a place to crash," he told him.

There was a few moments silence as they studied each other and Case nodded once and looked away.

"Over at the distribution table they'll find you something," he said.

There was more silence and then Brad decided to leave. He nodded at Albert who returned the gesture and walked off.

"I'll walk you over," Case said.

"I'm alright," Albert replied automatically.

"Jesus Christ," Case breathed. "What the hell is the matter with you?"

Albert looked at him, confused and then stiffened up angrily.

"You brought me here, remember?"

"Ya, ya. I brought you here because I thought...we could use your experience. I've got a collection of idiots, drunks and fools who think they are going to take on the U.S. Army and capture the flag. I was hoping you could...I don't know."

They had started walking and Albert said nothing.

"Look, I know your reputation-"

"I wouldn't go by that if I were you."

"Right," Case laughed. "Me too. What I'm saying here is that in spite of your activities, I don't think you know what's really happening."

Albert looked at him sideways and shrugged.

"So?"

"So maybe if you knew..."

"What? I'd quit my evil ways and join your band of merry maggots?"

They had reached the distribution area and a gaunt man of about forty got up from a chair and came over.

"You got a couple blankets or something for this guy?" Case asked.

The man turned without speaking and began rummaging around a pile of garments, coats, blankets and just about any textile product that had been scrounged up. There were stacks of canteens, binoculars hanging on a wall, mess kits, gas masks, and just about anything else that people had contributed. Albert surveyed the rest of the contingent and showed no sign but almost spat. This wasn't even a make believe army. This wasn't anything. It was just a bunch of aimless, half-starved, mentally destroyed zombies who happened to be in the same place at the same time. Case couldn't be serious. There was no way to teach these people what had to be learned. There wasn't one in ten who could hold a conversation never mind plan a strategic move against the most powerful enemy in human history. It amazed him over and over again that people thought that because the army was corrupt, that it was filled with bullies and psychopaths, that probably anyone with a conscience had been weeded out, that they were bad people with an unjust cause - basically a criminal gang - that it made them somehow vulnerable to the good guys. What had mutated out of the American Army of the early post-Iraq era was a merciless, highly skilled, doubly motivated, well-supplied, killing machine. Even the pretense of limitations that used to be placed on soldiers, at least for public show, was gone. There were no limitations. They answered only to the next level boss. Motivated? They were now motivated by self-preservation and by greed. And there were no restrictions. He'd been witness to one mass suicide; he'd not do it again.

"I think I know what you're thinking," Case said, handing him a couple of wool blankets and a pillowcase stuffed with a few rags.

"Then you know what my answer is," Albert said.

90

"Will you come to this meeting with me right now?" Case asked, earnestly. Albert was caught by the remark somehow. He felt himself slipping. He looked at Case as if he were mad.

"A meeting...a meeting," he repeated like it was some kind of magic incantation.

He started to rattle with laughter. Tears filled his eyes and he couldn't breathe. The laughter was an almost silent wheeze. He thought he would loose his footing. It rose in pitch, higher and louder, spreading out in a vast bloat of the bitterest irony. And then it burst. Albert's eyes were brim with tears and bloody red from the exertion. His stomach muscles ached. He hadn't laughed like that in so many years it was beyond memory.

Case looked away, waiting until he had fully expelled the demon.

"Sure," he said, finally. "I'll go to a meeting. I haven't been to a meeting for a while now." He started to laugh again.

"Is there going to be a tray of jelly rolls? I'd like a lemon or maybe a bear claw..."

He started to laugh again but it ended abruptly. It just emptied out of him like a broken vessel. It rushed and splashed and then...nothing; just an empty, cracked container.

THE MEETING

They were back in the great hall sitting once again around a table, Albert subdued and introspective and several of the others discomfited by the formality of the gathering. Case no less than the others, was unsure of himself and he stared vacantly into the gloom for a few moments. It was all the same people from the first meeting, but now there were two others present, including Maxwell and Freddy, the two soldiers who had greeted Albert when he first emerged from unconsciousness. This time there were no guards. Albert looked up once at Greta who studiously avoided eye contact and once at Curtis, the uniformed liaison officer from "the government" ostensibly there under a flag of truce in order to negotiate some sort of....what? Surrender? Agreement?

Case took a breath and cleared his throat.

"We have to make a decision," he began. "There's a window open right now and we either take it or...I dunno, maybe we just fight it out until everyone's dead, I guess."

91

"Who elected you?" Albert interrupted.

All heads turned his way and he kept his eyes on Case who didn't disguise his displeasure.

"It just sort of ended up that way," he said pointedly. "You going to put me on your list now?"

"Get on with it," Brad said, as unhappy with Albert's behavior as Case.

"I'm going to turn the floor over to Curtis here because he can tell you better than I can what is happening out there."

Curtis appeared eager to speak and he stood up as if addressing a roomful of officers at a briefing. Albert imagined a bullet breaking in the door of that white, shaved temple and drilling a borehole right through his brain before it smacked into a wall somewhere.

"Things are bad," Curtis said.

"They're bad for you - us - and they're bad for them. I guess I could say us there too. Everything's breaking down. There are no parts for the equipment and we're running out of fuel. It's getting to the point where it costs more fuel to escort a tanker than what gets delivered. We've - they, they've - been living off storage. Nothing new is getting made. Depletion of reserves. It's like the end of the hourglass on a million different things. The out-posts, like Provost and Glamor and Crutchfield are getting stretched. They're supposed to be out on S&D but they can't afford to do it. What this means is that they can't expect any help from Indianapolis. We - They - have their own problems. It's kind of like every man for himself. I think you can see where I'm going with this..."

He paused and looked around, just like he'd been trained to do. When his eyes linked with Albert's he blinked. The refulgent contempt was overpowering.

"I know what you're saying," Albert said.

Now everyone exchanged looks before focusing on him.

"What we need to do is gather everyone we can into one army, so to speak. Each district gets itself together and then when we're all set and in one place, a large concentrated force aimed at each army outpost...you and cunt-lips here send the coordinates to Indianapolis and they send in the drones. Oh, and maybe the helicopters and then they follow it up with tanks, Humvees, APCs, whatever for mop up. This way in one operation you can wipe out the entire American Free Forces all the way from LaGrange to Perry. Good plan. I might have come up with it myself if I was a government sucking psycho. As it is, I'm just your run of the mill private enterprise psycho, so all I can say is, 'Count me out,' and if you morons really buy this shit, you will get exactly what you deserve."

Brad jumped to his feet, glaring wildly at Albert in a challenge he instantly regretted. Albert didn't move, hardly looked at him while Case calmed him down and made him sit.

"You're wrong about me, Mister Smythe," Curtis said, his twenty five year old face jittering with a mixture of terror and outrage.

Albert was looking at Greta who had honed her eyes in on him and sealed them over with a reflective sheen.

"Such language," she said sweetly. "Can't a girl change her mind?"

It was meant to arouse Albert's latent impulsive stupidity, which was well documented, but he had her in place now. There was no doubt in his mind at all that she was a spy and they were now officially locked in the dance.

"Sorry," Albert apologized. "I meant to say cunt brain. I just happened to be looking at your ass when I was speaking."

"You don't know anything about these people," Brad managed to say, his voice pleading with Albert to 'be reasonable.'

"You don't either," Albert said.

"The difference between you and me is that I'm not fooling myself. You're right about Jughead here; he might very well think he's on our side - whatever side that is - at least until things start to go south. But this shit-covered succubus is nothing more than an IED with tits. She is here to commit mass murder and don't try and work your way around it. She'd burn a regiment of her own kind - again, whatever the hell that is - to prove her loyalty to you, just so she can kill you too. If you do not take this bitch out, she's going to bring you down."

He stood up.

"If I see anybody - and I mean any body - once I leave this quarry, I will kill that person in a bad way. And then I will come back here," he said.

He walked into the gloom and then emerged a few moments later into the semi-darkness outside.

No one saw him leave the quarry.

*

It had been three days since he left and he was as certain as he could be that no one had followed him. Even Greta, as good as she might be, would not be able to out-woods him. And she probably knew it.

She would track him for a while until she found the haversack standing out in the open on a rock outcrop. Her jaw would drop for a second. She'd curse and fall in behind cover. But she wasn't in any danger from him at that point. He had found the locator she had sewed into his pack and dropped the whole package eleven miles north of the quarry. He didn't smile thinking about it. It wasn't a victory. It was a sad lesson in reality.

She would contact her people, whoever they were and tell them she was blown. Smythe had proof she was a plant. She needed extraction. Then she'd start to think about it.

She tore through woods heedless of the whipping branches and the rock traps and the tree roots that tripped her. She moved nonstop for a full hour getting maybe three miles until she was out of breath and bleeding from whip marks and stumbles.

She sat down, took out her combat knife and held it up to the flame of a lighter she carried, a sort of mini blowtorch that could survive complete submersion and a fall from an airplane. "Congratulations Greta" it said. She removed her dirty remnants of a bra. The cold air excited her nipples and she couldn't help a small laugh. She felt under her left breast, her fingers moving slowly, passing back and forth, pressing until she found what she was looking for. She could just see the depression her finger had left. She drew the point of the knife across the mark and blood surged out and ran down her side. Tears sprouted as she dug around with the combat knife, but she never uttered a sound. After almost a full minute the knife stopped against the small transmitter they had implanted in her. It was deep and she trembled from the pain of self-excavation. When she managed to lever one end of the device into view, she gripped it between thumb and forefinger and pulled. There was no holding it back this time and she wailed like a banshee as the extra inch and a half of stainless steel wire that had been deliberately wrapped around muscle tissue to make extraction excruciating and difficult if not impossible, tore out strips of her living flesh. Blood seeped and flowed over her belly and the sudden electrified pain overtook her. She tossed the bloody device and her satellite phone into the woods. She ripped up the bra and fastened a sort of compress around the wound to try and keep pressure on it, put her shirt back on and started to run again. Her vision blurred as she weakened from blood loss.

She had gone perhaps a half-mile from the site of her surgery when the missile slammed into the exact location. It had homed in on her transmitter and probably struck the ground within a meter of where she had thrown it. The fireball mushroomed up, a perfect crimson flower of napalm and C4 and anything else they could cram into the warhead.

And cruising somewhere above it all, the drone that had been sent to find her.

*

Albert watched the entrance to the great hall for an hour, taking the glasses off every few minutes to prevent himself from falling into a hypnotic state where he ceased to see movement at all. He recognized all the players and marveled once again at the herd milling around in the open like buffalo waiting to be shot from a train. He thought he caught a glimpse of Maureen once, but he couldn't be sure. He wondered how long it would take. It had been three days and they were still ensconced in their bivouac pretending they were out of the cross hairs for a while. He dare not make a fire or do anything that might be spotted and contented himself with occasionally munching on the energy bars he had swiped from the commissary.

From his elevation he saw what a death trap a quarry could be. The walls were fifty feet high except where the ground sloped at the south end. But even that was a climb. The huge blocks of limestone left by the miners looked like toys from a giant two-year old. The blocks littered the area around the quarry and were stacked in other places like product, waiting to be picked up for delivery. It was an easy stone to work with. It fractured clean, holding the cement without protest. Split-face and squared it was one of the great building materials of all time. At fifteen hundred pounds a cubic yard it was a bitch to lift into place. But a good tractor could handle smaller blocks; let's say five hundred pounders, with ease. You could place them just where you wanted, knowing they'd be there a thousand...ten thousand years hence.

Of all the things in the world, that made him weep! He thought of the building he'd done, the fences, the barns...his cabin and he wept. He did not weep for the people he had killed. They deserved death. At least they had earned it. He wept for Ludwig, his grand German shepherd shot before his eyes by a psychopathic policeman. He wept for the family from Chicago he had given his property to. He saw once again the helicopter swooping down on them, electric machine guns chattering as it cut down the man and the little boy. He watched the F16 streak past and unload its slow-motion curtains of napalm, obliterating his place on earth. He wept for Ginny, the retarded woman he had tried to protect. He wept for the girl he had murdered.

He wept...until the first bullets slammed into the ground around the quarry.

It jerked him from his maudlin reverie and he watched through the binoculars as the two AH 64 Apaches twisted around and came in for a second pass.

There were already fifty dead from the first attack and Albert watched as the survivors raced for the open mouth of the bore tunnel. The helicopters lined up and came in one after the other, kicking up spurts of limestone dust as the bullets whacked the ground. Then they split and turned for a third time. Albert clamped his teeth hard as the last of the survivors made it to the shelter of the limestone cavern that had been carefully excavated by a peacetime aggregate company and then mapped perfectly by an army intelligence satellite to within six inches. The two attack helicopters charged the mouth of the tunnel at slightly converging angles, preceded by a thick hail of 30 mm. machine gun ammo vomiting out at 600 rounds a minute. Half a mile from the opening the Hellfires streaked from the armpits of the beasts and dove with unmatched precision right through the center of the opening. Before they peeled away, the machines released two more.

The explosions flared in the hall and from his perch he could see bodies flying in the air like the seedpods of a maple. They turned in slow motion and then slammed into the earth. Smoke poured from the opening and the dust rose slowly as the entrance collapsed, burying everyone inside.

Then they left; benign, beautiful, elegant, flashing their bellies at the target like a barracuda that had stolen the bait and got away.

It wouldn't be long before the cleanup crews arrived. They'd send in thirty soldiers under the umbrella of the choppers. They'd fan out across the three-football-fields area of smooth limestone and kick every single body that wasn't clearly a corpse. A bullet to the head would resolve any doubts. Why weren't they right behind the attack?

Albert scrambled down the slope of the south end and hit the ground at a good pace. There was nowhere to hide if they caught him but he had to know.

Several of the bodies called to him as he passed but he kept moving. They were dead one way or the other. He couldn't save anybody and he couldn't help anybody unless they wanted to die.

Smoke roiled out of the opening like a furnace and he couldn't even look inside never mind enter. He began turning over corpses, shifting them out of the way, levering them into piles as he searched for Maureen. He found Brad, his chest blown open, eyes still staring in confusion. Case's head lay all by itself against a rock wall. There were occasional moans and wails as consciousness returned briefly to the wounded.

A man watched him as he separated two women who had almost been fused by the impact of the missiles. Albert looked at the man and showed him the .45. The man blinked once and then closed his eyes. Albert pressed the barrel against the man's temple and pulled the trigger. Bits of blood and hair and skull blew back in his face. He spit out a small chunk of bone and stood up.

He found Maureen sitting, almost uninjured on a flat rock. Beside her lay two men who had caught a full burst from the machine guns. She looked at him as he approached and he wondered if she was so in shock she didn't recognize him. Her gaze wavered and she looked into her lap.

"I was over there," she said, pointing to a deep crevice in the wall where they had kept medical supplies. It was about the area of a house trailer and the neatly piled bandages and anything else that might assist the wounded was still in perfect order.

"Come on," he said. "You have to get out of here."

"I can't leave these people just lying there," she said.

Albert nodded and pursed his lips.

"These people are all dead," he said. "Anyone breathing when the cleanup crew arrives will be shot. Anyone who surrenders will be murdered on the spot or taken for interrogation, which means torture and then death. In your case you can expect to be raped to death...but they will revive you as many times as possible to keep it going."

"But I can't just leave them," she insisted.

"Okay," he said. "I'm not going to die with you, not here like this."

She stared at him a long moment, searching his face. They both turned when Pickens emerged from the smoking maw of the great hall, one arm dangling from a torn shoulder. Blood was oozing from his left side. They all looked at each other, unable to speak.

Others began to emerge from the hall in varying states of dismemberment. They walked or crawled, coughing and moaning. Eighteen people assembled themselves on the ground. Maureen immediately began taking them water and tried to stop the blood flow from the more serious wounds.

The womp, womp, womp of approaching helicopters got everyone's attention. They couldn't be more than five minutes out. Maureen was down on her knees trying to press against the rhythmic pumping of blood from a woman's chest. Albert took her arm and stood her up.

*

Greta pressed herself up against the trunk of a large oak and nestled between the exposed roots. It wasn't a hundred per cent effective but heat-seeking cameras would find it a little more difficult to locate her that way. She remained still, not out of caution but exhaustion. She had lost almost three pints of blood, about the limit of survivability without intervention. Her veins and arteries had constricted to keep her blood pressure high enough but had created a concomitant thirst. Her vision blurred suddenly and she lost feeling in her legs for a few minutes. The hole under her breast had stopped spewing blood but it continued to ooze and she knew that infection would kill her if she didn't do something.

Once again, she heated the knife, drawing the flame several inches up and down both sides of the blade until it was hot enough to sear skin on contact. Holding the breast out of the way with one hand, she pressed the knife into the wound forcing it deeply into the muscle tissue that had been ripped open when she extracted the wire. Her hand shook violently and tears shot from her face as she moved the blade around the hole. The smell of her own seared flesh filled her nostrils as the blood boiled and popped. The knife fell from her hand and she slowly collapsed to one side, thankfully oblivious.

The drone operator back at Indianapolis had been making slow circles around the target site, increasing the radius with each pass. The camera lens swiveled, dilated, contracted...zoomed over and over again. There was no way she could hide from him. He could read a newspaper from five miles up.

The drone hovered over the oak tree for a few seconds, the lens rotating and probing and then, the almost silent hunter moved on.

The operator turned confidently to his commanding officer and reported that there was no sign of life in a mile and a half radius of the target site.

"We had a signal on her and her phone," the corporal said. "I can't see how anyone could have survived that, sir."

The colonel grunted.

"She would have to damn near cut her own tit off to ditch that transmitter," the corporal laughed.

*

Grabbing what they could on the run, Albert and his two charges clambered up the south slope making it to the tree line with only a few minutes to spare.

They watched as the two helicopters slowly put down several hundred feet from the smoking mouth of the hall. The troops dismounted in typical fashion, fanning out expertly, covering each other against ambush...doing everything they had been taught to do.

The eighteen survivors had clumped together, several raising their hands as the platoon moved towards them. Five others went methodically through the bodies, occasionally firing a shot.

They dragged three of the women out of the group and forced marched them back to the helicopter. Before they got there, the automatic fire of M16s signaled what had happened to the others.

One of the women balked and tried to get away. The soldier threw her to the ground and then stomped on her back with his heel. Her screaming was inaudible under the canopy of sounds from the whirling blades. Then the soldier kicked her several times in the head until she stopped moving. The other women climbed into the helicopter without protest.

The birds climbed slowly, turned and shot forward. He watched them until they banked and disappeared.

It had taken twenty minutes from landing to egress.

Maureen cut the shreds of cloth from Perkins' arm exposing a mess of bloody hamburger that used to be his shoulder. He had fallen into shock and hardly seemed to notice. One machine gun bullet had severed the clavicle and the second had tumbled before it hit his scapula, splitting it almost in two. He was gaunt and pale from blood loss.

Albert watched from a few feet away as she tried to bathe the surrounding flesh with water from a canteen.

"There's no chance," he said, but she ignored him and he knew she wouldn't leave him now that she was out of immediate danger. The fact that they could hunt her down on a whim or she could starve to death or fall to a dog pack didn't matter. That was not now. Now was Lonny Pickens staring at the ground, blinking slowly, thinking it was night.

The first aid kit she had lifted contained everything needed to stabilize him until he could be attended to. She could even sew up what was left of his chest area and back. But Lonny needed a blood transfusion to survive. He'd lost four pints and his own marrow couldn't produce new blood fast enough, especially considering the wound.

"So what do you want to do?" he asked. "We can't give him a transfusion out here."

She lifted his dog tags and read the back. Lonny was 'B-.'

"I'm 'A' positive so that counts me out," she said. "What's your blood group?"

Albert shrugged. "I don't know. I don't think I've ever known," he said. "I know if you mix it up you're dead."

"Pickens is dead anyway," she said matter-of-factly.

She was rummaging around in the kit and pulled out a small metal box about two inches by four inches. She pried it open, revealing a syringe with three rubber tubes and a mounting post.

"You must be kidding," he said.

"Are you going to do it or not?" she asked him.

The two men lay beside each other on the ground, Albert's sleeve was rolled up past his elbow and Pickens was the same.

"The only problem with this is that there's no way to tell how much blood has been taken from the donor," she said. "I don't want to end up killing you, so as soon as you start to feel funny, you tell me."

Albert watched her face while she probed his forearm.

"Great veins," she said.

He felt the needle break his skin and the sensation of something entering his body. She moved over to Pickens and did the same. She had managed to pull the shreds of skin back over the wound and tape it up, but he needed surgery and convalescence to survive. All she could do was try to keep him alive as long as possible. It was the only reason she continued to live herself. How many times had she fondled one of the pistols imagining the crash of the slug through her head and the relief, the utter relief of total release.

Once the needles were inserted and taped in place, she turned the valve. Blood flowed out of Albert's arm through the clear plastic tubing and coursed its way like red lava down the other tube and into Pickens. If Albert's blood was the wrong type Pickens's immune system would charge in like a Mongol horde to wipe out the foreign cells and coupled with his weakened state, he'd be dead in hours. If chance had made them compatible he might survive.

Albert lost track of time and fell into a semi-conscious state, relaxed and light. He felt like he was floating...

*

Greta awakened when a caterpillar walked across her face and poked its head into her mouth for a look. She brushed it off and sat up, spitting and groaning. Searing, unceasing pain rushed across her chest like sheet lightning. There was no escaping it, no relief from it. What did she have? Take stock. She had water. She drank some. Her throat was swollen and she coughed up the first few gulps. Except for water and a few power bars, her Beretta 9mm., a combat knife, an aviator's watch, a butane mini-torch and a pocket full of hard candy, she had her training. An instructor, one eye missing, "still rolling around somewhere in Vietnam looking for me," he would joke, told them just before they were deployed what had happened "over there."

"We had located a little camp about five miles in-country. VC snipers, they said. I dunno. Maybe they were. Doesn't matter. We landed at the drop zone okay and managed to move in on them without missing a trick. I was no more than 10 feet away, watching them. They were laughing and eating...having a good old time. This one little slope puts his food bowl down and turns towards me. You guys are fucked, I say to myself. We go all in and in thirty seconds there are four dead VC. That's all it took. I am going through their stuff and I see the rice bowl. I pick up the rice bowl. It's not rice. It's bugs. Fried bugs. Centipedes, cockroaches, I dunno. Every kind of bug there was

and there was plenty of bugs in Vietnam, believe me. That's when it hit me. That's why we lost. You cannot defeat an enemy that can eat fried centipedes and smile while he's doing it and then ask for more."

She forced down the water and then broke half a power bar out of the package, saving the other half for a special occasion.

Greta was what they called a natural. You want warm and sexy, you get warm and sexy; you want ice maiden, she'll freeze the blood in your veins. She was completely bisexual - had been since puberty. She took to the work with an alacrity that even surprised those who'd been at it a long time. Where she'd come from, was anyone's guess. She appeared to have no family except the people she trained and worked with but she was not close to them, at least there was nothing personal between them. She was friendly enough, just enough to get by and no more.

She knew she had to rest, had to give her body a chance to build some blood cells if she was going to keep going. She could bear the pain and the hunger. But she couldn't bear losing. She didn't lose. She thought about what had happened and felt no rancor towards her superiors back in Indianapolis. She had seen them do it before. It was the call when someone became a liability, even a perceived liability. She bore them no grudge.

She was going to get better, fast, no matter what she had to do. Then she was going to track down Albert Smythe and cut his heads off - that's right, both of them - and deliver the trophies to Indianapolis. They'd be proud of her then. They'd let her back in. She drank some more water. It went down easier.

She watched a caterpillar pull itself up onto her leg...

*

By midnight, Lonny vibrated with fever, sweat glistening on his forehead in the moonlight and his teeth chattering like castanets. They covered him with the few blankets they had absconded with but it wasn't enough.

"We need a fire," she said.

Albert had recovered easily from the bleeding and was finishing off an MRE.

"Can't do it," he said.

He stood up. He took Pickens' Beretta out and checked the slide. It was loaded. He flicked the safety on.

"I know you can use this but don't unless you have to. Be sure. They could be half a mile from here and...you know what I mean?"

"Where are you going?"

"I can get down to the quarry and back before light. I'll see what I can scrounge up."

She nodded and looked away and then looked back at him.

"Thanks," she said.

"For what?" he snapped, his hostility evident. She didn't answer.

There was just enough moonlight now to guide him around the major obstacles and he moved rapidly down the slope into the quarry. The dead were already starting to stink. He stumbled twice and almost fell into the morass. Half way across he stopped and looked over the woman who had resisted the soldiers when they tried to get her into the helicopter. Her eyes were open, her back broken and her face crushed in. You're better off. He heard moaning from several quarters but no movement. He didn't stop to check them out. With the flashlight shielded, he scrounged around the medical area, filling a sack with anything that looked remotely useful. He stuffed in another couple of blankets. A voice called him from a corner as he left, looking for the food storage.

"Help," he called. "Help, please..."

Albert cursed and left the sack against a rock. He followed the man's cries until he located him propped against a stone wall in a puddle of blood, feces and urine. He blinked when the flashlight beam caught him.

"Please," he gasped. "You have to help me."

Albert bent down and looked closer. A piece of shrapnel was imbedded in his chest. How he had survived this long was anyone's guess. His left arm was broken and his legs seemed to be twisted incorrectly.

"Thank god," he gasped. "It's you!"

Albert felt his heart rate jump. "Who?"

"Albert Smythe. I'd recognize you anywhere," the man said and almost laughed. "You're going to help me, right?"

Albert looked into the man's eyes; pupils were dilated.

"Ya, of course," Albert said moving closer. "Just let me get you to lie back here so I can see better, okay?"

The man grimaced as Albert helped him lie back on the ground.

"My legs..." he said. "My legs."

"It's all right," Albert coaxed him. "Just let yourself relax...I'll figure out what to do."

He laid the man's head on the ground.

"My legs," the man gasped and then the Emerson slashed across his throat before the man could speak again. Blood shot past Albert's head and the man tried to look at him with his last seconds.

"I'm sorry," Albert said.

By the time he returned to Maureen and Pickens, dawn was breaking and he was ravenous. He dropped two large sacks on the ground and Maureen immediately began to sort through them.

"How's he doing?" Albert asked.

"He's alive," she said. She took the two new blankets and laid them on the semi-conscious man.

Albert had rescued two-dozen MREs along with bandages, ammunition and anything else he came across that seemed useful. They couldn't carry it all with them, but it might be of some value while Pickens shivered between life and death.

Albert plopped down and tore open an MRE. It was Swiss steak and mashed potatoes. He watched the steak come to life in the heater bag. She joined him, tearing one open herself and poured the sugar packet right into her mouth.

"Did anybody but us...?"

Albert shook his head.

"The only thing moving down there now are the worms and the crows," he said.

Albert became increasingly concerned about remaining so close to the quarry. They had to know some people got away - someone always gets away - and they'd come hunt them down. And then there was the dog pack. He'd seen evidence of their passage about two miles from the camp on a patrol. Three members of the pack had been torn to pieces and all that was left were a few flaps of skin and some head bones. And the maggots were taking care of those. One thing about the woods, he mused, it sure knows how to recycle. The problem was simple. The longer they stayed put, the greater their chance of being discovered by somebody. Eventually word of the massacre would get out and scavengers would start arriving to go through the detritus left behind. The attacking troops had grabbed every rifle or pistol they could see, but that couldn't be all of it. There was probably a millionaire's worth of junk down there, everything from guns and ammo to MREs to maybe a few gold coins.

"We have to move," he said.

Maureen had tended Pickens around the clock for two days and she was exhausted herself. But she wouldn't let him go. Every time he started to drift away, she brought him back somehow. His fever broke but he was semi-conscious and she had only been able to spoon liquids into him. He needed nourishment to survive. And the danger of infection was increasing geometrically.

"I won't leave him," she said. "I understand if you feel you have to."

Albert sat down and looked at them both.

"Suppose he wakes up. Suppose you get him conscious. What then?"

"Then we - I - look after him until he can travel."

"And when's that going to be?"

She didn't answer. She didn't care.

"Shit," Albert spat and walked to the edge of the cliff. Night was gathering for the third time here and he was anxious to get out.

Perhaps if he could get her away from him for a few moments he could...

"Shit," he said again.

Fucking asshole. Why couldn't he just get himself killed and be done with it?

She was wiping his forehead and fussing over him when he returned. She'd gone into some kind of trance or fantasy, herself. Some wraith had hold of her mind and she had linked her existence to this kid's life. If he died, who knows what she might do. It was obvious that something had happened to her and normal reasoning, pragmatic considerations no longer interfered with her thinking process. He was the one who had to make a decision. Not her. Hers was made: 'Til death do us part and maybe not even then. The right thing to do was leave them. Leave them everything but what he needed to get out of there and home and let them take care of themselves. He didn't owe either of them anything. Nada. Zero. Zilch. His duty was to...who? Himself? *No comment.* The world, maybe? *No.* How about revenge? *Sort of.* Mankind? *Don't make me laugh.* The viable individuals out there worth saving? You know, the ones who are willing to try and save themselves? *Maybe. To some extent.*

"I have an idea," he said. They allowed Pickens another night's rest during which she slept while he poured as much liquid down the throat of the wounded man as he could. When Pickens started wetting himself and fell out of the coma he woke her up. She bent over him and stared into his face.

"Can you hear me?"

He nodded but his face suddenly flexed with anguish. The pain in his arm and shoulder threatened to send him back to Never-Never Land.

"What-" he said, looking at her, but he couldn't finish the sentence. Either he couldn't remember what he was going to say or his system shut down. He closed his eyes and fell into a deep sleep.

In the few hours before daylight, they collected everything they had and put it into a sack, which he tied to Maureen's back. Then he slung a tumpline across her forehead and stood back.

"It's too much," she gasped.

He opened the sack and took out the water. It lessened the weight by thirty pounds, but she still couldn't keep her head forward. She'd never make it a hundred yards.

He reached in and removed another twenty-five pounds - of military grade so-called armor piercing 5.56 ammunition. The green tip cartridge wouldn't fit his rifles but as a trade item it was actually worth more than gold.

It went into the travois.

"Okay," she said. "I'll try it."

She hefted the pack and grimaced, but tried to look cheerful.

"Let's go," she said.

He lifted the end of the travois and Pickens groaned, but remained unconscious. Albert was suddenly furious. What was the point of risking two lives to save one? What was the point of spending all this energy on someone who probably wouldn't make it no matter what and if he did would be a cripple for life, a short life, at that?

***

Chapter Seven

We will say that they emerged, all three of them from the woods at Barrington Station, eleven days after leaving the cliff at the quarry.

Scouts escorted them to the village where they were greeted with a mixture of curiosity and trepidation. The sick man was bundled into the medical building and a charm of individuals of varying genders and races immediately began to torment him with cures and remedies he believed would be his end. Maureen collapsed on the ground. Albert could not unclench his hands from the poles of the travois at first and when he did, most of the skin of his palms remained. The whole story of that journey must wait until another time when there is some leisure to reflect on the "lesser" adventures of Albert Smythe. Suffice to say, that a lessor adventure of Albert Smythe is more than most mortal men could manage.

Now, a few days after their dramatic arrival Albert could hear Pickens screaming all the way across the town as the witch doctors, shamans and various quacks tried to put his scapula back together using piano wire, stainless steel hinge screws and duct tape. The shoulder was damaged beyond repair, that was certain; but they thought they could arrange for him to have a working arm from the elbow down. Part of the problem was Pickens himself, who had told them repeatedly that he was quite content to be shot and buried rather than subjected to any more of their tender care. They tried to keep him sedated with moonshine but the screaming pain he experienced from the shattered bones, which had already begun to knit incorrectly on their own, overcame anything they could provide. Albert couldn't figure out why infection hadn't already killed him. And how about that moonshine! How did anybody live to tell that tale?

Maureen had continued to stay by his side around the clock, taking her meals in the hospital tent and feeding Pickens with a spoon. Albert was certain she would have pre-chewed the food had it been necessary.

Albert had finally concluded that Maureen would probably not come back to the world. Why bother? He had told himself for the last week that she could get over it if Pickens lived but he doubted that now. If she had to give up Pickens as a life's work, she'd just latch onto something else. No, Maureen Grogan was lost and gone forever.

Albert shrugged it off after a few hours brooding and decided he would go back to doing what he did best. He wasn't completely recovered from their ordeal after the attack at the quarry but he couldn't stay around here for much longer.

He watched two men returning to the settlement from patrol looking tired but not indicating any signs of crisis. They glanced his way and acknowledged him with a brief nod as they headed for the dining hall. One thing for sure around here: The food was good.

Barrington Station had been a mail post on part of the old Centralia line out of Illinois and gained a moment of notoriety when in 1864, Abraham Lincoln made a brief stop during the election. Folks came to see him more from curiosity than political interest and he made no great impression on them other than the fact that his appearance had given them a few minutes worth of gossip and two drams of civic prestige. In any case, the next time Barrington Station got noticed was during the Great Depression when thousands of hobos riding the rails discovered an easy 'on' just outside of town where the tracks curved sharply and the train had to slow down. Then, with the slow death of the railroads over the next century, the town faded into a low-grade Mid-western somnambulance of unemployed farmers, meth cookers, eight-dollar factory workers and welfare recipients. The local grocery attributed fully forty percent of gross revenues to food stamps. Seventy per cent of the unmarried women between 14 and 21 were pregnant out of wedlock. (For those interested, the population was 97 percent white and two percent Latino.)

There was one last brief effort to salvage something in 2009 as the economy began its final momentous slide into oblivion, when the federal government, desperate to appear to be doing something, provided a grant to fix up the station house itself to its glory days of the 1900s. Rotten shingles slid from the rafters into huge dumpsters and were replaced with shiny plastic replicas of the original cedar shakes (guaranteed to last for a thousand years at least) and the fine Indiana limestone walls were cleaned and repointed. In deference to the new green energy policies guaranteed to save mankind from Arabs and global warming, the old windows with their rippled panes were replaced with new frames imported from China and fitted with the latest 'low e' glass. The old boardwalk was ripped up and replaced with fine treated lumber (guaranteed to last for God knows how long) and the parking lot was leveled and paved with sleek, new smoking asphalt divided up with very straight yellow lines to accommodate the hundreds of expected visitors.

Inside, counters were rebuilt, benches sanded and slathered with urethane. Walk in and the life size manikins greeted you with their frozen smiles. Mrs. Beardlsey, perpetually looking over the top of her spectacles, shoulders all puffed with cotton-wrapped sawdust; old Arnold Barlow who never smiled and moved his lips when he counted change; Lucinda French and her children, ever waiting for Mr. French to return from Memphis looking hopefully at the clock which read 2:30 p.m. An old baggage wagon replete with iron wheels and polished stanchions stood against the wall. The only thing missing from this diorama was an old "darky" to smile and shuffle. You could almost believe it was 1917 and the doughboys were heading to France, the Roaring Twenties were scheduled to arrive any minute and children respected their elders. Even now, it was swept and tidied and none of the letters on the sign welcoming tourists to visit "historic Barrington Station" were missing.

Albert sat down near the window so he could keep an eye on things and tried to imagine the times, but all he could feel was contempt for the inhabitants. He hated their naïveté, their self-satisfaction. But the thing he hated most about them was the mixture of faith and hope gleaming in all those fiberglass eyeballs.

He heard footsteps outside and then saw a woman carrying a corn broom step onto the platform and head for the door. She entered, head bowed and immediately began sweeping, carefully brushing out every corner. He watched her for a full ten minutes before she saw him and started.

"Jesus," she breathed. "You ain't supposed to be in here."

He frowned at her.

"We don't allow nobody in here except to clean," she said.

Haggard and sloppy looking, she was still in better shape than just about any civilians he'd seen on the road or at the rendezvous, for instance, but he wasn't entirely convinced she was in one piece mentally. He'd seen varying degrees of psychosis over and over again and her furtive glances and slightly schizoid mannerisms were telltale signs. But who was really all there anymore? No one was sane in the old sense of the word. How could they be?

"There's a tour at one o'clock every Sunday, but you got to sign up for it," she said.

He looked around the small room and smiled. Maybe she had been the tour guide, he thought and was just holding on by a thread. He stood up.

"Sorry," he said.

It was a short walk from the station to the town square, a desolate reminder of more recent times. Typical for its day, the center of town was occupied by a large limestone courthouse with a spire and a clock. Some of the more elaborate versions had thick white columns and broad lawns with canons and statues of soldiers. Barrington Station was a dressed down version with a WWII anti-aircraft gun turning green out front and a simple stone wall commemorating the dead from four wars. There hadn't been time to add the name of the girl who had been blown to pieces in Iraq before the world she had died to save had vanished down a toilette of perfidy and greed and outright criminal conspiracy.

All the windows of the old courthouse were broken and covered over with plywood or plastic and the lawn was trampled to mud. Every store around the square had been looted clean and turned into multiple family dwellings and then abandoned. Garbage was piled everywhere and the stink produced a fine tincture in the air. Here, in Barrington Station, the fires still burned four years after the beginning of the end and limping troops of empty-eyed citizens pulling farm wagons collected the dead and carted them to the pyres. Most - all - of the small residential streets were burnt out corridors and even now, four years later the smell of wet, burned lumber wafted on the air.

But the difference here began at the eastern spoke of that town center wheel which led past several empty gas stations and up to the 4-H grounds with its collection of barn-like buildings.

Horses stood tethered to rails or grazed along a fence line and a pair of Great Pyrenees staring fiercely as they patrolled. Past that, the beginning of what was actually two acres of garden and a field of hay ready for second cut slept peacefully in the summer afternoon. Tents and trailers were laid out in an orderly fashion, each small property marked off with yellow police tape. A man was leading a milk cow from the barn and she bellowed plaintively. He was followed by a woman leading another cow and then another. The cattle were turned out to a small corralled field where they immediately set to shearing the grass. A few days here had not cured Albert of his surprise at finding this apparently peaceful development. And the sight of a small heard of sheep running around a paddock seemed surrealistic, almost as unbelievable as the museum display at the station house.

In fact, until that moment when the woman told him to come back Sunday for a tour of the 600 square foot room, he had begun to think that some people or places might have managed to shake off the effects of mass hysteria and group insanity.

The current scene was a little deceptive in that there were almost fifty inhabitants living here and it seemed like a mere handful operated the place. Everyone else was well occupied. He'd seen that.

Their arrival had disrupted the usual routines somewhat but other than the fact that they had welcomed the three of them, he had been unable to find out much about what was really going on here. Riders came and went, meals were cooked and served, cauldrons of human waste were hauled away on flat wagons or burned in towering blackish plumes of wretched, acrid smoke. No work was asked or expected of him. No inquiries were made of his person or origins and no questions would be answered. And that was fine with Albert, for a while at least. So long as they looked after Maureen and Pickens he didn't much care what they thought of him. They didn't want him there. Fine. He didn't want to be there but he wanted a few questions answered before he left and his only problem was that he didn't know whom to ask. There was ad hoc leadership here and there and people deferred to one or another depending on what decision was up for grabs; but no one seemed to be in charge. But he didn't buy it.

A population of television-addicted sheeple with the attention span of a grasshopper and the work ethic of a three-toed sloth didn't suddenly develop Amish attitude because their welfare checks were late. Somebody was running this operation and he intended to find out who, before he left. He hadn't told them who he was and obviously neither Maureen nor Pickens would be that stupid. They wouldn't balk at a few friendly questions. He was no one to fear, right?

Maureen was sitting right where he'd left her when he had made his first visit to the invalid and his unfailing guardian angel since their arrival. She seemed happy to see him now as then and hugged him briefly, awkwardly and then pushed away from him when he didn't respond.

"How's he doing?" Albert asked her. "

"They think he's going to make it, believe it or not," she replied.

"Well you did save him, that's a fact," he said.

"It was you carried him for eleven days," she said. "You gave your blood!"

But Albert didn't bother to reply. She wanted him to be part of her great accomplishment, to "share," and he wasn't interested. He had carried Pickens hoping every minute of the time he would croak so they could leave him. It was only when he realized that his hopes of persuading her to come with him were, in a word, hopeless for the present that he switched modes and just kept walking without any purpose. He couldn't just leave them. He wouldn't just leave them. They just kept going west, eating what they could and feeding the comatose, wounded man on a grey slurry of insects and rainwater, half-cooked squirrel, a skunk, a nest of robins eggs...

Where were they going? There was nowhere to go. So they walked hoping they might find somewhere to leave him if nothing else.

"They don't care, you know," she said.

He looked hard at her for a few moments wondering why she wanted to play 'guess what I'm talking about.' He realized it was something to get him to come to her, a tedious and ineffectual manip- ulation that she probably wasn't even conscious of. This was the way people talked. This is social intercourse, Albert: Get used to it. But it infuriated him nonetheless.

"Okay," he sighed, "what are you talking about?"

"I'm talking about you," she said.

He felt his stomach seize and the sudden, furious racing of his pulse as the adrenalin squeezed his blood vessels.

"I'm telling you it's alright," she said, touching his arm.

He looked at her to see if she was playing with him or not but she appeared genuinely happy. Her face was lit with a weak, tentative joy.

She had told them who he was.

His discomfort multiplied by the second as he looked around the small hospital room and then moved back to the door.

"Albert!" she said, dismayed now.

He struck across the gravel driveway and hugged a barn wall. Walk...walk. You're just going for a walk...

It was a good, thick woods, undisturbed for years, overgrown with bramble and Walking Stick and nettles and raspberries.

He climbed a sycamore almost four feet across with huge branches and heavy foliage. Up about twenty feet he found a suitable perch. He carefully bent a few obstructing limbs out of the way until he had a fairly clear view of the entire town. He got as comfortable as he could and pulled out a purse of partially dried squirrel and berries. What could have possessed her? he wondered. He didn't believe she had turned him in out of venality. She didn't even realize she had turned him in. She had just lost her mind and no longer understood - if she ever had - that the old world was well and truly gone. There was no one and nothing to answer to except the self and the self, when seeking power is a shape shifter, appearing to be whatever the observer wants to see. She wanted to believe and so she acted like she believed and after a while she didn't know the difference. This is how people are caught.

*

Maureen sat down beside Pickens and watched him breathing. He had fallen into some sort of sleep after the last bout of pain and his eyelids jittered from dreams. But she was thinking of Albert and couldn't quite understand why he didn't believe her. She had spoken to Reverend Herkimer and he had seemed completely unfazed by the information.

Poor Albert, he was almost beyond redemption. He just couldn't believe any longer in basic human decency. No one ever tells the truth in Albert's world. Everyone is always out to do him harm. It wasn't hard to understand, of course, times being what they were and what he had been through, but how can things go on like that? Society - any society - was an arrangement of trust. No matter how many laws and safeguards and checks and balances you put into the system, in the end you had to trust. You had to trust that the majority of the people would abide by the social contract the vast majority of the time *because they wanted to*. Threats and prisons and fear are very ephemeral binding energies. People want to trust. They want to believe. Just give them half a chance and in no time you have two acres of gardens and milk cows and a helping hand when you need it.

Pickens stirred and opened his eyes. He looked at her without moving. She teaspooned some gruel into his mouth and he got it down without choking. He looked at her and half smiled but still didn't speak.

The door opened and sunlight slashed into the room, which had been kept dark in the belief that ominous, tomb-like conditions were conducive to healing the sick and injured.

Maureen rose and greeted Rev. Wolfgang Herkimer, whose great size always had the immediate effect of intimidating anyone he met. Swinging his ironclad hips towards her, he looked like a machine of some sort, maybe half human, half synthetic. What did they call it? Cyborg. A fat, stuffed-looking paw the size of a child's baseball mitt landed on her shoulder and he placed his broad, bearded face a few inches from hers.

"Your friend; how is he?" Herkimer asked, the tinges of a German accent still affecting his speech, though he'd come to the States thirty years previous as a ten-year old bringing with him one of the last cases of polio.

"He's going to live, thanks to you and your people," she said, covering his hand with her own."

He nodded vigorously. "Ya, ya," he said. "But it was you who saved him."

"Your people did incredible things under the circumstances," she said. "I still don't know why you put so much effort into a total stranger."

Herkimer studied her face and smiled.

"Well, they needed the practice," he laughed, and she relaxed for the first time in days. If Albert could only see...

"And your other friend, how is he?" he inquired.

She told him what had happened and he listened, nodding the whole time.

"Ya, ya..."

Herkimer shifted his huge weight in the steel lattice that kept his legs from buckling and grunted. Then he turned and swung towards the door, calling back to her: "See you tonight."

Herkimer struggled along the path towards a cluster of huts and trailers, stopping periodically to catch his breath and wipe sweat from his face with a handkerchief in an oddly European gesture.

His dwelling had been renovated to allow entrance and egress without any stairs and the doors were wider than normal. His six and a half feet of strudel and sausage had suffered in the first few years from a severe lack of food. His legs had shrunk to the point where the braces no longer fit. But since his arrival at Barrington Station, a healthy diet of buttermilk, farmer's cheese, organ meats and grain alcohol had restored him to his fully inflated self.

He opened the door and looked into the room before entering, sniffing like a curious but hesitant bull. It was a sparse room with little more than the chair, a bed a table and a few oil lamps. A counter held a stack of MREs. Satisfied, he headed straight for a broad stuffed chair and settled down in it slowly, his legs jutting out in front. He leaned forward and massaged his legs.

Albert placed the Emerson against the thick blubber of his throat and Herkimer froze, his eyes darting back and forth like cornered ferrets.

"Don't make me kill you, okay?" Albert said politely. "Please," he added.

Herkimer didn't move but he relaxed and nodded just enough to reply. Albert walked around front of him and deliberately sheathed the knife. He dragged a small coffee table over and sat down. They looked at each other for quite a while. Albert felt dwarfed by this giant who must easily top three hundred and fifty pounds. His sagging cheeks and grey-streaked hair made him look like an old mastiff. After a while he slowly began to massage his aching legs again.

"Hurts to walk anymore," he said. "Even to stand long is difficult."

Albert imagined the thud of a .45 smacking into that huge pannus, spilling over his lap.

"I figure you must be the guy to talk to around here," Albert said.

Herkimer shrugged.

"What is going on here?"

"People are living, that's all. What do you think?"

"I think maybe it's too good to be true," Albert said.

Herkimer nodded hugely, his whole round bulk bouncing. "Ya, ya...I know," he said. "What you think, I got everyone brain washed?"

"Something like that," Albert said. "If I look around am I going to find some thirteen year old girls all knocked up in a stable someplace?"

"You might," Herkimer laughed, "but not by me."

He looked at Albert sadly. "I can't even if I want to," he said.

Albert glanced at the crutches.

"You and your friends can leave any time. Nobody is here against the will," Herkimer said.

"You know who I am?" Albert asked.

"Ya, ya. Ve know. They are looking for you everywhere."

"Big reward, I expect."

Herkimer grimaced in pain as he massaged a particularly hard knot in his leg.

"I think they will be here by morning," he said.

"Who?"

"Caernarvon outpost in Beltrame, about twenty miles from here."

"How do you know?"

Herkimer looked owl-eyed at him.

"I have just been there speaking with them," he said.

"And you told them I'm here?"

"I told them I thought it might be you."

Albert's eyes narrowed automatically and he stood up.

"They will see your friend, the soldier and they will take him as well."

Albert almost smiled, though it was involuntary. It was just a reaction to Herkimer's brass.

"And now I am warning you of their coming," he said. "You understand, no?"

Albert sat down again.

"I guess I don't, really," he said.

Herkimer gestured at the counter.

"Please get me some water."

Albert saw the plastic jug in the corner with an old coffee mug beside it. He went over and pressed a little button on the spout allowing a few ounces of water to fall into the cup. He drank it back and then refilled it and brought it over to Herkimer.

"We are here because I cooperate with the authorities," he continued. "They come and we give them part of whatever we have."

"You're paying tribute to the army?"

Herkimer nodded, sipping the water.

"We cannot fight them. What's the point? So they come and take some vegetables and some breads...they like our breads very much. The women bake for them and we gave them wine. They have permitted four of our men to possess guns for hunting."

Albert nodded, beginning to understand.

"I must protect our community, no? But also I wish no one to fall into the hands of the army."

"You say tomorrow?" Albert asked, rising.

"Yes. They will send a small troop, perhaps six or seven in a Humvee and search everywhere. Our people will turn you and your friends over immediately if you stay; but we will not prevent you from leaving, either."

Albert stared at Herkimer whose small blue eyes watched him without wavering.

"If you do anything to attack them, we are finished. They will kill us all," Herkimer told him.

"The woman, Maureen, perhaps we can take her in and they will not notice. But you and the soldier are worse than the plague to us."

"Why didn't you just turn us in right away? Why go through all this?"

"If I had known, I probably would have but it was only after a few days the woman told us what happened."

"Now-"

"Now we must ask you to leave or surrender to the authorities unless you want to see us all destroyed. They will not hesitate. You known this."

"I don't see why you think you're going to get away with it anyway. They have a habit of eating their own."

"If they decide to punish us, then I will admit to hiding you...that way the others may escape."

"You're just a regular fucking Jesus, aren't you?" Albert scoffed.

"That is our constitution, you might say."

Albert stared at him, pondering the giant poured into the chair, hunched over his crippled legs.

"So why did you tell Maureen that it didn't matter?"

Herkimer looked up and sharpened his focus.

"This I did not say."

He tilted his head dog-like and seemed to reconsider something.

"I told her, for comfort sake, 'No stranger are you among us...but our son and our dearly beloved.' She must have misunderstood. I was speaking only of her." [9]

Albert flushed deeply with anxiety and closed his eyes and massaged his forehead. He was trying to compute the probabilities and they didn't appear favorable. The big man had returned this afternoon from his visit...twenty miles...a day's buggy ride...the army wouldn't have waited to send in a recon unit. The man was lying. He hadn't told them a damn thing. He could vanish in a matter of minutes if he had to, but Pickens and Maureen were heavy ballast. If he left them and a troop came around snooping, well, a secret among sixty people is no secret. Even if they hid Pickens someone would give him up and Maureen too. She wouldn't leave without Pickens and Pickens couldn't travel.

"Is it about time for one of their visits?" Albert asked.

Herkimer nodded.

"You didn't tell them anything...you didn't even go there."

Herkimer pursed his mouth and nodded.

"But you're about to, is that it?"

"Yes. After you have gone I will radio Beltrame and tell them you were here."

Albert had seen the antennae but there was no generator. He had assumed it was a leftover piece of equipment from the days of the cell phone. They must have a short wave radio hooked up to some kid on a bicycle or something. He remembered seeing a few solar panels on the roof of the hospital building. They must be charging batteries.

"You're lying again," Albert said. "You're not going to tell them anything."

Herkimer sat back in the chair. "I am just trying to save us," he said. "They will be here by morning. You must be gone."

Albert sat down again on the table.

"Why are you doing this?" he asked. "You took a hellofa chance not calling them when we first showed up? What gives?"

118

Herkimer closed his eyes.

"We all have a purpose, Mr. Smythe. My purpose is to see that people like you live to fight another day."

Albert remained there for a while after Herkimer's confessions. How was he going to lever Maureen and Pickens off their collective ass and still manage to move fast enough far enough to avoid a full-blown search mission?

He couldn't leave her behind. She was way past the point of no return on self-delusion. Traveling with someone you do not trust is more than dangerous; it's plain stupid. And he could no longer trust Maureen. Not because she was dishonest or sly but because she had turned religious. Her desires quickly became beliefs and those beliefs quickly transformed into dogma. No amount of evidence or reason would dissuade her from hearing only what she wanted to hear. She'd sell them all out on a promise. The Great Flying Spaghetti Monster will provide. Maybe he should shoot her.

When he got to the hospital she had taken a rare break and Pickens was sitting on the edge of the bed, holding his forehead with his good arm, the other one strapped tightly to his chest. He looked up when Albert came in and tried to grin, but it turned into a grimace.

"Shit," he breathed.

"Bad, huh?" Albert asked and Pickens just nodded.

"Can you travel?" he asked, knowing what the answer would be.

Maureen came into the hospital carrying a meal for Pickens and stopped short when she saw them together. Her eyes glanced off Albert's and focused on her charge.

"You shouldn't be up, yet," she scolded. Pickens looked at her.

*

It took them the rest of the day to get a mile away into the heavy forest that surrounded the town. Herkimer had seen to it that they had as much as they could carry and then left without saying a word.

Maureen quit arguing when Pickens stood up and the two men started walking out of the hospital. Albert had repeated to her Herkimer's comment that she could probably remain behind.

"He can't walk," she implored them. "He will die for nothing."

Pickens smiled at her. "You've done enough," he said. "Look after yourself."

Having her along was a mixed blessing. She looked after Pickens, which freed him up to scout and scavenge for food; but she was another mouth to feed and dangerously psychotic. She couldn't be counted on to do anything except look after Pickens no matter what was happening around them. He revisited the idea of killing her himself. Pickens might have protested but he would understand.

Now they must rest until Pickens could start moving again. They would be able to increase the travel time as he regained his strength if they didn't overdo it at the beginning. They had no fire and shared an MRE in silence. Albert ate his portion quickly and left them, Pickens lying back, panting, and Maureen fussing over him, though more for her own benefit than his.

From a new vantage point he swept the town with field glasses. Everything looked quiet but then he saw the Humvee arrive. It was fully outfitted with a .50 caliber machine-gun and the troops that emerged quickly and took up positions. Herkimer heaved his way towards them. The body language wasn't friendly. An argument ensued and three of the soldiers grabbed Herkimer, pinning his arms behind his back. Twenty or thirty residents had convened around the site and the remaining soldiers trained weapons on them all. Finally a ranking officer emerged followed by a civilian; Albert recognized him as one of the patrollers who had brought them in. Then Albert watched, his heart pounding ferociously, as the soldiers threw a rope over a tree limb and then attached the other end to the Humvee. Herkimer offered no resistance at all as they tied the noose around his neck. There seemed to be some discussions for a few moments. The officer gesticulated and then pointed to the civilian. The vehicle moved slowly forward, lifting Herkimer into the air, where he hung, jerking and twisting about five feet off the ground. Albert fell back against a tree and closed his eyes. Herkimer had known all along what was going to happen.

When he returned, Maureen and Pickens were sleeping peacefully; they hadn't even stirred with his approach. The Beretta had slipped from Pickens' hand onto the soft forest earth. Albert nudged her with his toe and she flashed awake, looking immediately for Pickens before she even determined what had roused her. Albert's fuse lit when he saw the anxious look in her eyes subside as Pickens came to. And then the rage broke in him and he grabbed her by the hair and jerked her to her feet. She screamed and he slapped her twice across the face

"Shut the fuck up," he said, his voice like a club.

She dangled at the end of his arm, unable to dislodge herself or even understand what had happened.

"Albert!" she squealed and he slapped her again.

Then he threw her down on the ground and stared at her.

Pickens watched the entire scene in disbelief, trying to fumble the pistol back but one look from Albert stayed his hand.

"Albert," she pleaded.

"Shut your fucking mouth," he spat at her again. "There's something I have to do. I'll be back by sunrise. Or not, understand? If I am not back by then it means I am not coming back. But if I do come back here and I find you two sunbathing, or having a tea party, or sleeping, or picking daisies, I'm going to leave you here. You are to spell each other in four-hour intervals. Four hours is enough to make the sleep worthwhile and short enough that the other person can stay awake. A person with the will, that is. You make a fire, you call out in your sleep, you do anything to attract anybody's attention I will leave you here. If you take a shit and forget to bury it, I will leave you here. Is there anything about what I just said that you don't understand?"

Tears had sprouted and ran down Maureen's cheeks.

"I'm sorry, really..."

"Shut up," his voice slammed her again. "I don't want to fucking hear it. There's a good man down there hanging from a tree to keep your worthless, fucking ass alive. For his sake I will try and do it as well. But I'm not him. One more stupid move, one mistake and I'll kill you myself."

A single torch burned about center of the village, casting angles of weak light against the barn board and metal siding. A few dogs barked intermittently. He saw the silhouettes behind makeshift curtains and got close enough to hear what was going on inside. It was some sort of group meeting, with more than twenty people gathered around a small table. He saw them clearly enough to distinguish individuals but half had their back to him. He tried angling himself a little better and saw what he was looking for.

The patroller was at the head of the crowd. The discussions went on for some time and Albert only caught some of it...cattle...guns...winter.

It was probably three o'clock in the morning when the group broke up. They were almost silent leaving the meeting and Albert had trouble distinguishing among them. He was afraid the patroller had slipped off before he could find him and he knew there was only this one chance to get him. By daylight he had to be ready to move again.

Then he saw a lone figure walking towards Herkimer's cabin and he followed him. The man looked around and then pushed open the door. Albert heard it click behind him. A match was struck and a lamp came to life. He heard the man moving around inside. He turned the door handle slowly and it opened. The door swung in slightly on its own. The man's back was to him while he washed himself from a bowl of cold water on the counter. Albert let the door close behind him as he stepped inside. The man's face was lathered up and his eyes were closed.

"Just a minute," he said, splashing water onto the counter.

He was younger than Herkimer and looked to be in pretty fair shape under the circumstances. He was taller than Albert by several inches and he did not wear glasses. When he turned, wiping his face with a towel, he saw Albert and straightened up. He had left his pistol on the chair out of reach.

"I thought you'd be long gone by now," he said.

"Just have one last thing to take care of," Albert replied.

The man smiled ironically and tossed the towel aside. Albert moved to Herkimer's big chair and lifted the military issue Beretta. It was exactly like the one Pickens carried.

"You want a beer?" the man asked.

Albert's eyes narrowed and he pulled the Emerson.

"Sure?" he asked again.

When Albert didn't reply, the patroller shrugged and took a mason jar of yellowish brown liquid down from a shelf and then sat down in Herkimer's chair as if he were talking to a neighbor.

"Why did you do it?" Albert asked.

His voice was calm but not too cold. Part of him really wanted to try and understand this man. Maybe if he understood more about him and people like him it would be easier to defeat them. He could kill more of them that way.

"Wolfie thought a great deal of you," he said, "but I guess you know that. Now."

Albert watched the patroller sip at what appeared to be a urine sample, smacking his lips.

"You should have some," he urged. "He was the one who showed us how to make it."

122

"You just going to sit there while I rip you open?" Albert asked.

"Wolfie knew what he was doing," the man said. "He knew the risks."

"So this whole fucking place is just a mirage like that railroad station with the psycho caretaker..."

"It's simple, Mr. Smythe. We got word back that Beltrame suspected we were hiding you. They were planning a big takedown that would have meant any number of casualties for us, so Rev. Herkimer told me to turn him in. The commander now thinks he's got me in his pocket."

Albert's face crinkled in disbelief. But the patroller didn't seem to be lying. Of course that's the mark of a great liar, but Albert wasn't looking for good news. He acted entirely on his instincts about the "truth," and if he didn't believe you, he shot you.

"Why would I believe a story like that?"

"Because you know it's true."

Albert stared hard at the patroller.

"If anything at all happens to me," the man continued, "they will tear this place apart. You want to take that chance, then you're right: I will just sit here while you do what you have to do."

"The man stood there and let them hang him...didn't even protest. I saw it."

"I know," he said, sadly. "I was there too. Is it really so hard to believe? Wolfie wasn't the first man to give his life for a cause. You would do the same. So would I."

"You think so, huh?"

"Can't be sure of anything, I guess. All I know is that everyone here is willing to die to keep you in the fight."

Albert slowly sheathed the knife.

"That's complete fucking insanity," he said.

"We manage to live here under the thumb of Beltrame outpost, but it's not living, really. They extort a great deal in exchange for their protection."

"So get yourself a fucking gun and fight back."

"We will fight when the time comes, when it makes sense."

"I see. Well what exactly are you waiting for?"

"They are starting to break down. We have heard that the entire cabinet, including the president has been executed. There is no civilian authority left and the various military units are fighting each other for control. And it can only get worse. Isolated units like Beltrame and your Provost Legion are basically unaffiliated at this point and we don't know where they are going to land. We don't know if we'll all end up in bed together or trying to slit each other's throat."

"We?"

"There are problems. I admit that."

"You mean like trying to get the white supremacist Nazi ass-holes over at Harrow to join up with the Niggers over at Witherton? Or how about the ten thousand little private armies with their kings and emperors all marching around pretending they're Attila the Hun? Soon as they get fed and fucked they'll either run or switch sides to whoever is winning. You can't organize these assholes. They can't even feed themselves, most of them."

"All noted and understood," he said. "The point is that something is coming and we are going to join in when it makes the most sense. Until then..."

"What? You suck cock and wait for me to do your killing for you?"

"Basically, yes." Albert couldn't help a laugh. "How do you know we won't end up on opposite sides?"

"I don't know," he said. "But I do know this: Everything is breaking down. They have no parts for their equipment. There's no one to repair things when they find parts. Ammunition is being used up. They've instituted what amounts to slavery in order to produce anything at all, from radishes to diesel fuel. They have special units going around the country - at least they did for a while - trying to shut down the nuclear power plants before one of them blows up. Do you know how many nuclear reactors there are in this country? We know of about a hundred and fifty. How many secret reactors are hidden away, God knows where? And what about the navy? You strip nine out of ten crewman off an aircraft carrier and don't replace any of them, how long before something catastrophic happens? What happens when a sub commander realizes he's on his own carrying around enough megatonage to not only start WWIII, but also end it? What about threats from overseas? What's happening in China and Russia? I could go on all night, Mr. Smythe and not cover the topic worth a damn. I do know that the way we are living now is pointless. Staying alive to serve our masters? I don't think so. And neither did Wolfgang and he wanted his death to have some meaning. He wanted you to keep at them in a way he could not."

124

Albert ejected the clip from the Beretta and popped the last shell. "Where are you getting your information?" he asked.

"There are deserters and renegades in every unit in the country. Some of them come to us...some of them disappear into the wilderness, but they all bring bits and pieces of information. We thought nine of ten people in the country had succumbed to the virus but it turns out it's worse than that. In places like New York and Los Angeles, it was ninety-nine out of a hundred. There is so much military hardware loose in the country right now that it wouldn't surprise me if one of these independent groups you speak of showed up with its own tanks and artillery. Maybe even worse than that. Think of a low yield cruise missile in the hands of some of the folks you mentioned. The military planned for the exigencies of social unrest. They imagined disorder and disease, panic, food shortages and subversion. But no one planned for this. There is no way to plan for this. And they are going to keep eating each other until they're all gone or someone triumphs. Someone will triumph. We want to influence that. We want to encourage these disparate units to destroy each other. We will have men in both camps. We will lie to anyone and commit any crimes necessary to destroy this monster. There is no way they will ever unite peacefully. We are prepared to do anything to see them destroyed, including sacrifice our own lives and the lives of anyone else."

Albert handed him back the clip and the pistol.

"Same ol' same ol'," he said.

"I thought you of all people would understand!"

"Really? What makes you think so? Herkimer was willing to give his own life for the cause as you call it and so am I. But I'm not willing to convince anyone else to do or not do anything. You guys never learn. Pretty soon you're going to be sitting in a big chair somewhere telling other people what to do and how to live and I'm going to have to slit your fucking throat. And believe me, I will do it."

He opened the door a crack and peered into the darkness. Then he slipped away.

***

Part Two

I know thy works, and where thou dwellest, even where Satan's seat is...

Revelations: 2, 13

Chapter One

Albert led Maureen and Pickens straight across the woodlands from Beltrame to one of the few encampments he knew of where they might survive – at least for a while. He had little hope for either of them. Pickens was in so much pain after the trip he returned to his near-comatose state, even before Albert left. Maureen had tried to talk to him but he pushed her away with indifference and silence. And not insignificant cruelty he would come to realize.

"There just isn't time for someone like you," he told her. "Gimme a call when you're all grown up."

The words had stung worse than the slap and she turned away from him in a rage.

Since then whenever he thought of her, he forced the image out of his head, but she was like a carnival pop-up; every time he smacked her down with a big hammer another 'she' jumped up and wiggled her tongue at him.

In two months he hadn't heard anything about them or returned to the settlement to enquire. Albert had dropped out of touch with even the heteromorphic society of the bush. Instead, he simply prosecuted his vocation.

Bullets sliced the air, found their mark and ripped the flesh of his adversaries. They fell. They toppled. They stumbled and crashed. He stalked them unrelentingly. He killed them while they ate and while the slept. He copied a Gurkha tactic of slicing one man's throat while he slept, but leaving the man beside him untouched. He came upon a platoon of raiders, about a dozen men and women who roamed the bush taking whatever they found. They left two on guard while the others found comfort in an abandoned barn. One sentry was asleep

127

when Albert cut his throat; the other dropped his rifle and ran. Albert blocked the barn at one end and lit it on fire. The shouting and screaming began within seconds and they burst from the unlocked end of the building, coughing and raging and he calmly shot them until his magazine was empty. The remaining five dispersed into the woods where they spread word of the murderer Albert Smythe.

He patrolled constantly, staying out for a week or longer before returning to his refuge for a few nights. Then he would choose a new direction and begin the hunt all over again.

On one occasion he emerged from the forest about fifty miles south of his camp and found himself on the outskirts of an impromptu settlement, this one with perhaps a hundred members. He had detected their sentries and moved around them to get a better look at the gathering. There were the usual ragged tents and a few primitive shelters and a fair mixture, it seemed of men and women. He did not see any children. They were clearly divided between the militia group and the citizenry, if they could be called that. At the edge of the encampment stood a doublewide trailer that had been dragged there with some considerable effort. This was apparently the militia headquarters. There were sentries outside and the shadows of movement behind the windows.

After a few moments a man stepped out smoking a cigarette. A few moments later another man was pushed through the door and stumbled down the trailer steps hitting the ground hard. His wrists were tied behind his back. The two guards lifted him and dragged him towards a cluster of tents and a large fire pit that seemed to be some kind of central gathering place. As Albert had expected, they shot him in the brain stem and he fell like a stunned beef. The commander walked away, followed by about half his men. The rest remained to oversee the removal of the body and its disposal.

Albert heard rustling in the bushes behind and allowed his hand to rest on the butt of the big Emerson. The noise stopped and then began again. Albert shifted his position under some overhanging branches and waited. In a few minutes a woman appeared with a small berry basket. Her face was scratched, filthy and roughed by weather. And her eyes were like cracked glass. She passed his position and he stepped in behind her and covered her mouth with his hand. He saw her eyes jam shut and she seemed to fall into a trance. He'd seen it in all herd animals. When wolves or dogs take down a

128

goat or sheep or a calf, the animal relaxes and lies back, it's eyes glazed. It doesn't seem to feel its throat or guts being ripped out in a bloody shower of snarling mayhem.

"I'm going to release you," he said, quietly. "When I do, you turn around slowly. If you say anything at all, I will cut your throat before the sound leaves your body, understand?"

She nodded and turned to him, her eyes open now and afraid.

"What is this?" he asked her, gesturing in the direction of the tents.

At first she didn't seem to understand the question and it reminded him of Ginny, the retarded girl he had tried to save from the initial onslaught that first winter.

"It ain't got a name far as I know," she croaked and then cleared her throat. "Who are you?"

"Just passing through," he answered. "You know they just executed a fellah about five minutes ago. Shot him in the head."

She sniffed and looked away again and he thought she might tear up for moment but it was just that cracked sheen in her eyes. This woman had no more tears.

"He disobeyed. That mister Mearsheimer, he don't allow that."

"Mearsheimer. The big guy with all the hair?"

"That's him and if he finds you here you are going to be next," she said, and then added almost as an afterthought, "and me right after you."

Albert looked into her basket. "Been picking berries?"

"No," she said. "I just hold out the basket and they jump right in."

He saw the smile crease her tortured skin and he allowed himself a brief grin.

"How many men does he have with him?" Albert asked.

"What you wanna know for?"

"Just curious."

"About twenty. The rest are just…like me. They do what they are told."

Albert thought for a moment and then seemed to come to a decision.

"I want you to keep on going the way you were."

"Don't worry. I won't say nothing, but you better get outta here, now," she warned him.

"You go ahead and tell 'em."

"Tell 'em what?" she asked.

"Tell 'em the truth. You saw a man in the woods poking around and he run off when he spotted you. You tell 'em he was moving west towards old Highway 19. You know where that is?"

"Course. I grew up here."

She looked at him for a long second or two and shrugged.

"It might get me off the hook if they find ya, anyways," she said.

"That's right."

Albert had not formulated a complete plan, yet, but he knew generally what he was going to do. As he expected, within ten minutes of the woman returning to the camp, a platoon of eight militiamen strung out in a ragged column, passed within fifty feet of his hiding place in a cedar copse. He waited until the last man had vanished into the trees and then started moving towards the trailer. The two guards were still posted outside and they seemed a little more alert than they had been. He suspected Mearsheimer was safely inside.

He figured the eight men would search for about an hour and then make their way back, empty-handed. He had lowered the odds a little but not enough for a direct attack. Instead he watched the trailer for about twenty minutes until the door opened and three men emerged. Mearsheimer stood in the doorway for a moment and then ducked back inside. The three set off for the far side of the encampment, laughing.

Albert was able to scramble around through the bramble to the back of the trailer where there was no sentry.

Albert set his pack down and removed a small incendiary grenade made from an eight-inch piece of pipe filled with a powdered mixture of nitro methane and ammonium nitrate and stuffed with a fused 12 gauge detonator. A byproduct of 1960s space research, it was soon discovered that when mixed with ammonium nitrate, that favorite of fertilizer bombers, nitro methane produced an explosive device more powerful than dynamite and capable of expanding at five thousand meters per second. This would undoubtedly blow the entire back of the trailer off, killing anyone who happened to be sitting there and ignite the fifty five gallon drum of diesel fuel that was being used to run the trailer furnace. He calculated that the entire trailer would be ablaze and out of control in three minutes. Long before that, of course, he would be repositioned and waiting for those who tried to escape the inferno.

He lit the ten minute fuse and moved quickly back through the brush to the edge of the dirt road. He crossed down a slope, out of sight line of the guards and then worked his way back up through the trees and scrub to a place barely three hundred feet from the trailer door. He saw a wisp of smoke rise from the end of the building and just had enough time to set up his rifle when the grenade exploded.

The concussion rocked the trees for fifty feet and the entire rear end and half the back wall of the trailer blew into the woods in thousands of flaming pieces. The fire was worse than he had anticipated because of a kerosene type heater that Mearsheimer had been using to keep himself warm while his slaves rattled around in threads and lived in tents and cedar lean-tos. The two men at the front of the building were thrown across the road. One of them crashed head first into a tree and his brains were leaking out his ear. The other man was on hands and knees, trying to regain enough equilibrium to stand. The mass of people stood still, watching the blaze from a distance unable to act in any way and clearly unwilling to do anything to save the occupant.

Albert drew a slow bead on the delirious guard and sent a round into his side. It knocked him down and he struggled only briefly, the bullet having found his heart.

It was no more than thirty seconds into the event when Mearsheimer struggled out of the burning trailer, his clothes and hair on fire. He was screaming and waving a pistol, firing blindly as he staggered off the steps and hit the ground.

His flaming body filled the scope on Albert's rifle, but he decided to let him burn.

Now the comatose masses came to life and began running, crawling into bushes and behind logs and scrambling into tents that provided no more protection than a butterfly's wing. Albert had to move again and he retraced his path north along the road until a point well below the trailer where he crossed and regained some higher ground.

There were probably half a dozen men left in the encampment. This included all their outlying sentries and the eight-man troop probably on its way back from the diversion. Twenty to one, he thought. He began moving towards the oncoming troop, guessing correctly that the men in the encampment wouldn't have any idea what to do. They would begin assaulting anyone within reach, probably killing civilians in their impotent rage.

He set up low, behind a rotting stump looking straight down the pathway. The first man to appear hesitated, a sixth sense telling him to be cautious but someone behind urged him on and he stepped out of the bush into a small clearing where the path would head west and south. Albert waited until he had passed and the men now pushed out of the woods in pairs and threes. He killed the front man of a triplet with a head shot and then led the last man as he tried to scramble back into the woods, hitting him high in the back and sending him sprawling. The third man in his trap dove for cover and began firing his automatic weapon in Albert's general direction. It took another minute before he was able to catch a glimpse of the man's head between the leaves and he fired, but missed.

Now the others were settling in, and automatic fire raked the trees around him. He lay down close to the stump and listened as the occasional bullet smacked into the rotting wood. But they had no idea what they were shooting at. After another few minutes the shooting stopped and Albert listened for their flanking movement. But it never came. They hadn't a clue where he was or what to do next. The only action they had ever seen, other than jerking off to Hollywood movies, had been against the pathetic, unarmed captives back at the encampment. Albert waited and after about ten minutes of silence, managed to slide his barrel between some leaves and survey the kill zone with his scope. They had run, leaving their dead comrades behind.

They would not come looking for him. Figuring into the equation their essential cowardice and ignorance of tactics, he reckoned they would set up a defensive perimeter, probably surrounding themselves with the unarmed prisoners for protection and wait for the attack they were certain would come next. They wouldn't even consider that it was just one man and should probably go flush him out.

Albert felt a sudden twist of anxiety thinking of the berry picker. He had probably signed her death warrant. Essentially leaderless, the group would likely splinter, following two or maybe even three separate alpha types. One would be the man who resented the old leadership and always believed he could do a better job. Another would be the reasonable man, not a coward, exactly, but one who was easily threatened. He would advocate abandoning the area, in effect running. If there were a third man, he would be inclined towards negotiations

132

and alliances, a man who didn't want to lose his goods, his chattels: A compromiser who would sell out anyone at any time and gathered like-thinking confederates who cared only for their own profit, however that happened to be defined at any given moment. And among this last group would likely be the smartest man, the one who would wait until the right moment before making his move and when he did, would slide into position without a sound, almost unnoticed.

He heard automatic fire back at the pit and wound his way back through the woods to the edges of the encampment where he came across fourteen bodies. They had all been shot at close range, berry lady among them. They were like camp victims everywhere; underweight, hollow-eyed, ragged and filthy. They looked better in death than they had in life, their faces relaxed for the first time in months, maybe even years.

He waited outside the perimeter, sleeping in ten-minute snatches until about three a.m. The moon had risen and fallen some and was now nesting in the tree line. And there were owls. He had seldom heard owls in the past but they were doing very well now that their habitat and their food source were prospering.

There weren't enough dogs and coyotes to keep the rodent populations down - whether rabbit, rat or raccoon - and there were no homicidal sport shooters or snarling farmers to assassinate the great birds. It would only take another ten years and the entire mid-west would revert to its early eighteenth century profile. Perhaps he would live to see it, to wander the country in a dream state listening to the animal life returning. Too bad the virus hadn't just killed everyone, he thought. *Including you? No, not me. Someone has to be left to appreciate it.*

He smiled in his sleep-state.

When he shook himself awake, the temperature had fallen to around forty degrees, enough to make it uncomfortable for the sentries. There were three men guarding the eastern edge of the settlement, about 150 yards apart. They possessed hand-held two-way radios and he could hear their clicking and light chatter as they checked up on each other. The man on the southern tip of the perimeter would call 'Tango One,' check. Then two and three would follow.

Ten minutes later they'd do it again. It was a completely useless and ineffective system that he breached with the first stroke. After Tango Three signed off, Albert pushed the Emerson into Tango-One's neck at the manubrium and severed the anterior jugular. The man was comatose in five seconds and dead in sixty. Albert laid him back on the ground and took his two-way, amazed at the almost comical uselessness of these armed bullies. Criminals are essentially bullies - lazy bullies. They will always choose the easy path and that is how you catch them. You show them an easy way and they can't help themselves. They will walk right into it every time.

Albert depressed the transmit switch twice. Tango-Two clicked back three times and Albert looked at the walkie-talkie with disgust.

"Tango-One, check," he said, and released the switch. He waited but no reply came back. The speaker clicked three times again and Albert felt a knot in his stomach. He clicked back twice and then depressed the send switch and repeated his call.

"Where you at, Jackson?" the voice came back.

Albert looked at the radio and back at the dead man on the ground.

"Jackson, you all right?" the voice said. He dropped the radio beside the dead man and melted back through the trees.

He'd gotten about a hundred feet when the first spray of .223 shredded the branches overhead. The lead snapped against the trees and leaves showered down. Then the firing came at his left flank. They had another man in the field and they were triangulating him. Bullets spattered like storm rain against the leaves and he heard several scream past his head at Mach 4 and smack into the wood.

The .223 was a terrible bullet that didn't impart a lot of energy when it hit - nothing like a .45 or a .308 round - but it often yawed on impact and didn't just make a hole. It turned human flesh into hamburger. Without immediate, high quality medical care, even an initially non-lethal wound could easily end up killing the victim by inflicting widespread, internal damage and inviting deep infection. It also allowed the shooter to carry almost twice the ammunition as someone with an AK47. Sure, the 7.62 X 39 was a relative powerhouse, but it was heavy and stable and didn't tumble quite as well. He felt panic rising in his stomach.

It was not the first time, but it had been a while since he'd screwed up this badly and he knew that he'd never survive a serious wound again or capture.

Think. Do something. Remember? Do something. Act. Don't sit there and be killed.

134

Their fire indicated three men were closing on him and would probably find him within a minute or two. They were tightening the circle. Someone had shown them some tactics. They would expect him to run directly away and when they were sure of his location, they'd just step up the pressure and track him down. He'd be able to avoid them for a while, but eventually they'd catch him. His only chance was to head directly at the nearest assailant, force him to react defensively for a moment until he could gain a better position. The lead rain was increasing and he had only a few seconds to make a decision when he rolled and began crawling towards the nearest shooter.

The man stopped to change magazines and Albert was able to gain another ten feet laterally. Albert could go no further without being seen. He had to wait until the man passed him and then perhaps he could shoot him from behind. They were talking on their radios again, calling for reinforcements. Another two or three automatic weapons and Albert wouldn't have a prayer. He caught a glimpse of his pursuer through the trees, a short man with a baseball cap and sunglasses.

He had stopped firing, as had the others and they were now pushing their way through the bush, stopping every minute or so to listen.

Albert led him for about twenty feet and when the man stopped, he pulled the trigger. The bullet deflected off a tree limb and the man dove for cover, spraying the forest all around Albert.

Jesus. Jesus.

He was already moving, circling to the front of the shooter. He believed the man would expect him to try and come in from behind and this time his guess was correct. The man with the baseball cap sprayed a wide swath of forest with his AR15 and ended up facing back in the direction from which he'd come. He snapped a double magazine out of the loading bay, flipped it and slammed the full one into the slot. Just as he set the bolt, Albert put three quick shots from his .45 into the man's torso. He died instantly, crumpling to the ground.

"Tango-One, say again....static...Tango-" came the dead man's radio.

Albert picked it up and squeezed the transmit button. "He's moving south," he said. Then he clicked the button on and off several times.

They fell for it this time and turned away from him. In a few minutes they'd meet up with the search team probably double timing it back and there'd be nine or ten of them on him. It was time to run.

Another month passed of similar incidents. The dead piled up and his reputation expanded and all the imaginative proclamations began again. He was a demon. He was a ghost. He was a robot. He was an alien…

It was months after he destroyed the Mearshimer settlement that he reconnected with American Free Forces.

On a clear morning Albert set up a sniper's nest at a sharp bend in the Old Provost Pike and waited for the patrol vehicle from the Legion that was expected before noon. This would be a fully up-armored and loaded Humvee, a fearsome death machine with a massive carapace invulnerable to small arms fire and capable of spraying finger-thick slugs at 600 rounds a minute in any direction. The men trapped inside carried all kinds of ordnance from side arms to semi-automatic grenade launchers. However, the top gunner had a weak spot – his head. Albert intended to shoot a hole right through his eyeball with a steel core 30.06 round designed for exactly that purpose. It was an easy shot, less than a hundred yards. That was well within Albert's proficiency and he knew he could make the target. He began regulating his breathing when he heard the clatter of the big diesel racing ahead of the machine, almost like a warning.

The green snout had just come into view when it lifted off the ground and turned on its side. Huge orange flames leavened with oily black smoke mobbed the still-sputtering carcass. The shock wave from the explosion rocked the seventy-foot maple tree where he was ensconced and he could feel the heat from the blast. Before the flames had a chance to subside, five guerillas attacked the prone vehicle from all sides. They directed their fire down the hatch and finally one got close enough to toss in a thermite grenade. The vehicle heaved one last time and more flames erupted, raising the temperature inside to almost four thousand degrees - just in case the shock waves or the shrapnel had missed someone.

It was an expertly placed IED and it was no concoction of black powder and fertilizer. This had been the work of a good block of C4, possibly even remotely detonated.

It unnerved him that he hadn't seen them laying out their ambush. He watched them through field glasses. They stood back while the flames slowly died and made one last check for bodies. There were none. That's when he recognized two men he'd fought with before.

He climbed down from the tree and walked out into the middle of the road. They didn't even seem interested and hardly looked in his direction. He stopped twenty feet away and watched the vehicle burning down.

"Nice job," he said.

One of the men grinned and came over to him.

"Think so?"

"I said it, didn't I?" Albert growled.

"Ya, that's him all right," a familiar voice came to him.

Pat Kingston came towards him grinning.

"We seen you up there hiding your ass in that tree," he said.

Albert shook his hand.

"Likewise," Albert lied.

Kingston looked at him sideways and smirked.

"Okay," he said.

How could you have missed them? What had happened? Just getting old? Tired? Time to quit?

"In case y'all don't know, this is the famous Albert Smythe, the guy you've all heard about. This man has been dead and reborn twice that I know of. I swear I seen him fly ten feet off the ground just from a beer fart carrying a baby goat. Dead or alive he's-"

"Shut up, Pat," Albert told him.

Another five men emerged from the bush, each carrying up-to-date rifles and well turned out in general. Several of them nodded.

"Where are you headed?" Kingston asked him.

"Ain't quite decided," Albert said.

"You're welcome to come along home with us if you want."

"Who is us, exactly?" Albert asked.

"Come on, I'll show you," he said.

That had been the beginning of his re-entry into the resistance, something he had stayed away from having watched amateurs kill themselves and their brethren all too often. But when they arrived at Camp Snowman, he found an entirely different situation. These men too had discovered the labyrinth of underground geodesic caverns that undercut hundreds of square miles. They had taken a page right out of the Taliban terrorist manual.

The caves had been explored, shored up where necessary and stocked with food, weapons, ammunition, medical supplies and just about anything else that might come in handy. More than a hundred men and women fit easily into the space and there was even a small cooking fire allowed at the very back. They were invisible to the damn drones as long as they stayed put and the depleted military units were not going to send out helicopters or special crews on a hunch. They didn't have the fuel, the men or the maintenance – just like the patroller had said.

"It sure as hell worked against us in Afghanistan; maybe now it can work in our favor," Kingston said

Kingston introduced Albert around and few failed to show some reaction. Some were astonished; a few were cynical and almost scoffed. Most held his gaze a moment too long and went back to work.

"Ain't had a real celebrity around here for a while," Kingston joked, but Albert didn't laugh.

Repeatedly scrape a knife across your dinner plate creating a series of spine-numbing screeches. That's how Albert felt about being recognized or noticed in this way.

"I'm not here to join up, Pat," he said.

"Oh hell, I know that. Just trying to make myself look good," he winked.

The camp was an assortment from various independent outfits operating, mostly unknown to each other, right across the country. There was a cluster of black soldiers sectioned off against one wall, looking decidedly uncomfortable. Albert had seen at least another dozen among the rest, but they seemed totally integrated.

Kingston took Albert over and introduced him. They eyed him but did not speak. When they were out of range Pat explained.

"They're new," he said.

"That doesn't sound too good."

"They're all right. We were watching them for a while. They put themselves together and have been hitting those Aryan Nation assholes over at Harrow. They left the Witherton crowd, you know about them?"

"Black something-or-others."

"Ya, well they're just another gang, now. So these guys deserted."

Albert shrugged. "This ain't a color war, is it?" he said.

"Don't nobody give a flying fuck what color you are around here," Kingston said. "Can you fight? Will you do what's got to be done? Until the others see that, they'll sit right there like a bunch of grapes."

Half of the company was former National Guard, men and women who had either deserted very early on in the crisis or had refused to march in the first place. That accounted for the efficiency of the IED attack, Albert realized. The other half was a typical mixed bag of wanderers, deserters, psychos, liars and opportunists. The difference here was simple. They performed in battle or they were out. Until they had been out on enough missions to satisfy all four of the command leaders, nobody even wanted to know their names. Not even the other black guys. They had all proved themselves and weren't about to squander the real, genuine and unqualified integration they had achieved for some "brother" still pumping ghetto jive and dissing whitey. If there had ever been a totally color-blind unit in the United States it was here in the American Free Forces. Play the race card here or the gender card or the short-man-complex card or the moron card, a bullet was all you could expect.

"That doesn't apply to someone like you, of course," he reassured Albert.

"No thanks," Albert replied.

"I'm sorry. I didn't mean that. I know there's nobody quite like you," Kingston said.

When Albert stopped to look at him, he burst out laughing.

"You got to learn to laugh at yourself, man. Loosen up."

The three other commanders were hanging over a map when Albert and Kingston walked up. Albert knew one of them, distantly but he couldn't place him.

The map was a fairly accurate field sketch of the Legion compound, including surrounding terrain for about a mile radius. This had been composed over a long period. The detail was sufficient for anything this bunch had in mind.

"Your first look at the whole forest, huh?" Kingston said.

Albert nodded. The compound was a rough rectangle running east to west, about twice as long as it was wide. Barracks, Quonsets and various other buildings were placed as accurately as possible. A web of paper strips with distances written on them crisscrossed the grounds. Entrances, hides and enfilades were all clearly marked. Albert hadn't known that the unit possessed four Abrams tanks along with two attack helicopters and two drones.

The drones were the problem and everybody knew it. As soon as things started, the drones would be feeding Intel back to the command center inside the compound and that would enable them to direct rocket fire, helicopters – tanks – whatever they had, right on top of the attacking forces. It takes three men to attack one in a well-defended position. In the civil war this number was as much a product of the equipment as it was good tactics. One man is firing; one man is re-loading; one man is changing position. It wasn't totally lost today, but three to one would not be near enough to breach the defense perimeter around the Legion.

"Besides, these guys are desperate. They know damn well what's going to happen to them if they lose," a commander named Morelli commented.

Deguello. Damn straight. No mercy: coming or going.

Albert listened to them planning the details for a while and then lost interest. They were supposedly going to coordinate six different companies at once. There were just over seven hundred shooters. A manpower ratio of 2:1. There were no medics or stretcher-bearers, no cooks or supply sergeants. This was a killers' only party. If you got hit and someone could help you, they might. But every man in the unit expected to die during the onslaught. Whether they could rout such a superior force depended on many factors. The Legion had known of the buildup for some time through its organization of spies and turncoats but many of them had been caught out as well. Their heads rotted on poles in every camp. The Legion didn't know exactly what to expect or when to expect it and that was in Free Forces favor. The Legion did not have the fuel to send its drones out on joyrides. The Legion was receiving no more assistance from Indianapolis, which was facing its own problems. But the Legion, even caught with its pants down was so much more powerful and capable than this rag-tag bunch, that even with complete surprise and great timing, the chances of success were slim to none.

"You're completely fucked," Albert said as they sipped real cof-fee in a dark corner of the cave.

"Ya...probably," Kingston replied. "You want in?"

"Sorry. I'm not into suicide. If I have to die I'm going to take someone with me. I'm not going to crash the guns or whatever the fuck you idiots are cooking up. Charge of the Light Brigade? No thanks."

"It's the drones, isn't it?" Kingston said.

"Of course it's the drones," Albert replied. "They have three hundred well-armed, incredibly trained, battle-proven soldiers who know they can't surrender. They will be able to see where every one of you fuckers is standing and be able to direct fire on you whenever they want! It's a dead end, Pat. Literally."

The coffee aroma filled his nostrils and he inhaled the steam coming from the cup.

"Where did you get this stuff?" he asked.

"You have to join my secret society to find out."

Pat took out cigarettes and lit one. He offered the pack to Albert but it was just a gesture.

"Maybe they won't fight," Kingston said. "Maybe they'll run."

Albert tilted his head.

"Well, I really hadn't thought of that. I suppose they could, but why would they? And where are they going to run to?"

"Regroup. Live to fight another day," Kingston suggested.

"There won't be another day," Albert said.

"Okay, suppose we take out the drones?" Kingston said.

Albert laughed for the first time in days.

"You're thinking of that Davy Crockett movie, the one where he sneaks outside of the Alamo to the Mexican lines and plugs the cannons or something. I saw that too when I was a kid. You are a fucking card, Kingston, that I will admit."

"Close, but not exactly," he said.

"You going to shoot the drones down with a ray gun or something? The fuckin things can read a newspaper five miles up."

"I know, I know. Listen to me. We got a guy who knows how to operate the drones. He knows the codes, the whole thing."

Albert stopped short and looked at Kingston as though smiling on a poor idiot.

"Right. And he's just waiting for the word from you."

"No, no, Kingston said. He's not on the inside. He's with us. We have to get him into the compound so he can send the drones back down on the Legion. Or send them off to Kingdom Come."

Albert had a sudden, uneasy feeling.

"Would this be a certain Sergeant Lonny Pickens?" Albert asked.

"How'd you know that?" Kingston replied.

At least Pickens had shown he could keep his mouth shut.

Lonny Pickens had been resting at the back of the cave when Albert arrived and he'd not noticed him. The unit had managed to second a small supply of combat morphine and the throbbing, shooting pain that had plagued him since the quarry attack was under control. His face had regained some of its natural contours. He strode towards Albert and Pat Kingston with a barely suppressed anxiety. He didn't know if he should acknowledge Albert or not.

Pat looked from one to the other as they met and waited to see some reaction.

"You know this guy?" Kingston asked.

"Never seen him before in my life," Pickens answered.

"It's all right, Lonny," Albert said.

Pickens was dumbstruck for a moment, relieved that he didn't have to maintain a difficult fiction, but equally unsure of Albert's reaction at seeing him here.

"I just can't seem to get rid of you," Albert said.

"No sir," Pickens croaked.

"Don't call me sir, you motherfucker," Albert said. "The only people who call me sir are cops and morons. I always shoot the first group. Which are you?"

A moment of difficult silence was broken by Kingston's laughter. Albert wasn't smiling, but there was no malice in his face. Pickens exhaled quietly.

As it turned out, the settlement where he'd left Pickens and Maureen after their escape from Barrington Station had been infiltrated and two weeks after their arrival it was raided. A helicopter with ten mercenaries of various form and content disembarked about three a.m. a mile from the camp. When they hit, no alarm sounded. The sentry on duty was the mole and he let them right in. It wasn't even a battle.

"They hardly fired a shot," Pickens said. "A couple of guys tried to do something and they were cut right down. Some of us got away. As for the rest…"

Albert couldn't bring himself to look at Pickens.

"They didn't take her," Pickens said quietly.

Now Albert had to look at Pickens face told him everything.

"I shot her," Pickens said.

Albert's heart was pounding and making him dizzy.

"She couldn't go through it again."

Albert nodded, stunned. He recalled the healed gash along her right cheek.

"She begged me," Pickens said. "I couldn't leave her...she was afraid. I had to-."

"I know," Albert nodded. "I know how it works. I guess after someone slashes your face open with a knife..."

Pickens looked long at Albert and then away. He seemed to be making a decision.

"What?" Albert said.

"She did that herself," Pickens said, "with a lid from a tin can."

Albert still didn't understand and Pickens stepped back, instinctively.

"She made herself ugly so they wouldn't take her again. She thought it would make her, you know...

"Safe?"

"Yes," Pickens said.

"She never told me a thing."

"Well she wanted to," Pickens told him, "she just couldn't find a way to do it."

Pickens didn't speak and he realized Albert was no longer present. He left him there and a few minutes later Albert disappeared into the woods.

He emerged three days later apparently no worse for wear. He never spoke of Maureen Grogan again, except perhaps in the howling depths of the savage nightmares that began to plague him. He never spoke of her, but the image of her face, shiny with tears, the jagged scar glaring red like a poison worm on her cheek while he berated her and then slapped her, hung before his inner eye until his last dying breath.

***

Chapter Two

Pat Kingston frowned and sat down on the ledge.

"I don't get it," he said.

"No big," Albert said gruffly. "I changed my mind, is all. You want me in or not? Just say the word and I'm gone."

Kingston looked into Albert's face for some explanation for the sudden change of heart, but none was forthcoming. Nor would there be.

"Come on," Kingston said.

They moved to the back of the cave where a small crevice he had not seen before seemed to glow. Kingston slipped between the walls of rock and Albert followed. They emerged in a second cavern, half the size of the first, heavily cloaked with flowstone and staggered with carbonate columns and loose geodes the size of watermelons.

The other three commanders, Vincent Morelli; a short, dough-faced older man named Roland Harding that Albert still couldn't place; and a Marine Staff-sergeant named Viola Ramsey were waiting. Pickens sat nearby. They were once again going over the attack plans for the Provost Legion, only now they had excluded everyone from the final discussions but themselves. If there was a leak, only a limited number of people could be responsible. The commanders, Pickens and now Albert as well would be forbidden from leaving the cave until the campaign began and each agreed to have no communication with anyone until then. They would remain right here in this ancillary cavern unable to communicate with anyone except each other. One word – even accidently; even 'hello' – would disqualify the commander immediately. He'd be isolated and probably shot. But that was not all. Only one man, Pat Kingston would know the whole plan. Morelli would not know the details of Harding's role and Harding would not know Ramsey's assignment.

Pat Kingston, for a man just thirty years old, had a self-control and a will unmatched among his cohorts. The term "natural leader" is often misused to describe the most successful; in this case, Pat was of one mind and people believed him. Pat was trusted. Pat Harding had watched the Provost Legion rape his mother to death. She was forty-eight years old and had lost a breast to cancer. He found his wife and two children hanging in a tree in his backyard, their genitals removed and stuffed into their mouths. That is why he was trusted not to betray the unit. Everyone had a story; but no one had a story quite like Pat Kingston's story.

"And you crazy fucktards all agreed?" Albert said.

"You're going to have to as well if you want to be part of this," Morelli told him.

Albert looked around the cavern.

"Don't worry," Kingston told him. "We have supplies in here for a month. I doubt if we will be here that long."

Albert looked from face to face and shook his head.

"Not me," he said.

Kingston looked dejected. The others shrugged and turned away.

"Me neither," Pickens informed them. He hobbled over and held his good arm up for Kingston to shake. There was a brief, reluctant goodbye and the one-armed bandit pushed   back through the cleft in the rock.

"What can I do to convince you?" Kingston asked Albert.

"Nothing that I can think of," Albert replied. "I'm not going to put myself in a jar like this for you or anyone else. I'm no good at strategy, anyway. From what I've seen of it, well, let's say it ain't worth a damn. Everything always goes wrong and men get killed because some asshole told 'em what to do. I am not that kind of an asshole."

"No, you're an entirely unique species all by yourself," Morelli said.

Kingston quickly intervened putting and end to that conversation by pushing Albert towards the entrance. He stopped and looked back at the others.

"I'll be right back," he told them. Already their eyes glowed with suspicion.

They left the cave and hugged the stone until they could slip into the woods.

Albert trusted Pat Kingston as much as he trusted anyone; but he put his hand into his pocket and cocked the hammer back on the .22 magnum he kept there for emergencies.

Please don't do this.

Kingston waited to make sure they weren't followed and then leaned against a tree.

"Put the piece away, Albert," he said. "I'm no different than you; if I was going to kill you, you'd never see it coming."

"Oh ya?"

"Ya. You don't want to fuck with me and I sure don't want to fuck with you."

Albert relaxed and leaned against a tree.

"This is probably better, anyway," Kingston said.

Albert listened, but more than half his attention was on the woods around him, checking for sounds or the sudden motion of a startled animal.

"Somebody's got to take out those drones," Kingston said. "And if we can't do that…well, you're right. We're dead."

"Let me get my back up against a wall or something, Pat. You're not even going to kiss me, are you?"

"This works out better," he repeated.

Albert snorted and eased his hand off the gun.

"You need to get numb-nuts inside the compound. Get him to the control center and let him do his thing."

"How am I supposed to do that?"

"That's your problem. But if you want to do something, that's what needs to be done. There's nobody else around who would stand a chance in hell of pulling it off. Shit," he grinned. "You ain't got but a quarter chance as it is."

The same idea had crossed Albert's mind earlier. He had studied their drawings and while he picked up new information, he also saw they had missed a soft spot in the perimeter defense that he had discovered during his own reconnaissance. He had mulled over various strategies to get inside the compound with the intention of setting off a series of explosives. If it did nothing else, it would rattle the bas-

146

tards. He had never considered the prospect of infiltrating the drone control center and taking it over.

"Have you discussed this with wonder boy?" Albert asked.

Kingston nodded.

"Ya. He understands."

"Exactly what does he understand?"

"That your chance of success is zero which is a whole lot better than your chances of survival."

His own death did not trouble Albert. He lived every moment of every day knowing that he was a marked man. If not a bullet or a knife, it would be a rocket or a baseball bat. He would trip and break a leg somewhere and that would be it; he would die, blithering and gangrenous talking to his piano teacher in Swahili. He'd sniff one day and that would permutate into pneumonia and that into lungworm and he'd die like a snake in a frying pan. He'd seen it many times. He was slowing down, getting tired quicker. He needed more sleep. He lost focus occasionally and wondered if he was going blind. One false move. One mistake. One misjudgment.

"You already had this worked out, didn't you?" Albert said.

Kingston didn't answer.

"You knew there's no way I'd go for that lockup. So what's your devious little mind cooked up, Pat? Now everybody saw me walk away so what's phase two?"

Kingston carefully and deliberately lit a cigarette and exhaled a brume of smoke.

"I figured you and Pickens could disappear...in a huff so to speak. I'll let my disappointment in you be known. Never in a million years would I have figured Albert Smythe was afraid of anything...you know the routine. Meanwhile, you take out those drones before we attack. Otherwise seven hundred men and women are going to be slaughtered."

Albert wasn't surprised by the plan; it was one he might have come up with himself. The only part he didn't like was the notion that he would suddenly have an entirely new reputation. He didn't revel in his position as "The Great Albert Smythe." But he had never imagined what it might be like to be considered a coward or worse, a turn-coat.

"It's a lot to ask," Kingston said. "I know that. Nobody's done more-"

"Save it, will ya?" Albert replied.

Kingston carefully put out the cigarette and tucked the butt away in his pocket.

"What's the timeline for this extravaganza?" Albert asked.

"You tell me; we can't hold it together for long. You know what will happen. People lose their edge, they have second thoughts…they desert. Someone talks."

"It could take me several days just to get back to my place. I'll need some things." Albert said.

"So that is a yes?"

"I guess. But you better have more for me than this fucking pep talk."

"How about instead of that Betty Crocker stuff you make, I give you some C4 and a bunch of detonators. How about a few real, U.S. army-issue hand grenades? How about night glasses that can see the stretch marks on your girlfriend's ass at three hundred yards."

Albert nodded. "Okay," he said, "but I get to keep anything I don't use."

Kingston laughed.

"Sure. You make it out of this alive, you can have just about anything you want."

About five miles from the cave in a small clearing surrounded by scrub cedar, Albert found the stash of weapons and explosives, just as Kingston had said. There was about 30 pounds of C4 in 1.25 pound blocks; twenty detonators; half a dozen hand grenades; an M16 with two hundred rounds in seven mags; an image intensifying night scope with infrared option; five gold eagles; and a crippled, half-asleep computer operator who probably wouldn't last two hours.

"Hi," Pickens yawned. "He said you'd come."

Albert didn't answer as he inventoried the material. He noted that there was no first aid kit. There was also a couple of good Alice-packs with frames and enough food and water for two men for three days. It was a message from Kingston. After three days either they wouldn't need anything or they'd be eating steak. After three days it would also be too late to save the American Free Forces Kingston Brigade, as it came to be called, from total annihilation. It was a twenty-hour march to Provost at full time. Ten minutes every hour they'd rest, have a drink of water…maybe chew on a power bar. Every four hours they'd add twenty minutes to the break but no more, lest their muscles cramp or they totally enervate from the depletion of re-

148

sources. It was a long, difficult, taxing march through heavy woods. They would have to avoid every short cut across open field and instead hug the rim of the woods all the way. Sometimes this would turn a twenty-minute walk into three hours.

"How exactly do you expect to make it?" Albert asked Pickens, who was sitting against a tree, eyes closed, trying to mentally suppress the throbbing pain in his shoulder.

"I dunno, really," he said quietly.

To Albert's way of thinking, it was a hopeful answer. No bravado, no extravagant promises. Pickens didn't really know how much he had left. Easier to lie down and die. Easier to forget about it.

"It'll probably kill ya," Albert said. "If you're lucky."

"Well. You are probably right," he said. "There's only one thing left I want to do, so we better get going before I chicken out."

*

Pat Kingston felt all eyes on him when he squeezed back into the cave. The other three stopped their discussions and waited for him to speak.

Kingston shook his head.

"What the hell does that mean?" Viola Ramsey demanded.

"You just let him walk," Morelli accused him.

"What was I supposed to do?"

"I always knew he was full of shit," Morelli said. "The Great Albert Smythe, my ass."

Kingston nodded, seeming to agree.

"Do you trust him?" the fourth man asked. Roldan Harding was the most contemplative among them, listening more than speaking, learning from everyone else's operations as much as from his own. Unlike Morelli who managed to irritate just about everybody, Harding was a quiet man with an extraordinary knowledge of tactics. His twenty-man platoon had the lowest mortality and the highest number of enemy scalps. Asked where he came by his knowledge, he just shrugged and said he'd read a lot of books.

"I'm pretty sure Albert Smythe is not going to flip on us, if that's what you mean," Kingston said.

It was not the absolute assertion they were expecting. Kingston seemed nervous about the entire business and didn't meet everyone's gaze.

"Somebody has to take out those drones," Morelli said. "How do you propose to do that?"

"If it concerns you, you will find out," Kingston replied.

*

Twenty hours into the trip, Pickens dropped to the ground, his mouth frothing. Albert pulled him into a copse of Sassafras and undid the Alice pack. He was breathing hard, but breathing at least. They were half-a-day behind from the frequent stops Pickens needed and now they were broaching on total mission failure.

He poured some water into Pickens' mouth, who choked and spat it out. His eyes opened.

"Fuck," he said.

"Ya," Albert agreed. "You need to keep drinking. You're getting dehydrated."

He took the canteen from Albert and tentatively gulped some water.

"You need food?" Albert asked.

Pickens nodded and Albert unwrapped a power bar for him. Pickens chewed it slowly, sipping water between bites.

"Where are we?" he asked.

Albert looked at him and then decided to tell him the truth.

"We should be there by now. It's another ten hours walk if we don't break down," he said.

He could see the discouragement take over Pickens' face.

"Jesus," he said. "I don't know…"

"Might as well try, huh?" Albert said gently.

"I didn't say I wasn't going to try, asshole," Pickens said, pushing himself upright. "I'm just telling you I don't think I'm going to make it. You listen to me and maybe I can help you out."

Albert strapped the Alice back onto him and they set out once again, pushing aside the clinging overgrowth that seemed to have returned to the woods ten-fold since the Catastrophe. He had to stay close to hear him because Pickens' voice was fading in and out.

"You have two options," he said. "You can take over the mobile control unit and direct the bird wherever you want or you can tap into its feed."

"You mean see what it sees?"

150

"Ya. The tap is easier and safer but you have to get hold of a dish and laptop with something like SkyGrabber. It's a program that milks the signal coming off the satellite. Two problems there. SkyGrabber doesn't work anymore because they started encoding the signals after a couple of retarded twelve-year-olds with a credit card milked the drone footage and sent it to the fucking Taliban. That was way back…few years ago. There's a way to unscramble the signal but you got to have the unscrambler. So if you can get me a satellite laptop, a dish, a box and a decent location, I might be able to get the pictures for you. Then you're going to have to get that information to…whoever."

"And how do we do that?"

"Fucked if I know; jump on a pogo stick."

"Can you show me what to do if I can find this stuff."

"Probably not…I'd say definitely not," Pickens said. He had to stop and close his eyes. He leaned against a tree.

"Just gimme a minute."

Albert drank some water until Pickens seemed to have recovered. The wounded man lurched past him and they were traveling once again.

"So you get into the command post and take over the stick. That was my job. Problem with that is, it would take a hundred men with rocket launchers to get through the security around it. Two of the tanks are parked in the defense perimeter. They've got the usual .50s and anti-personnel ordnance for the big barrel. There's a heavy machine gun behind sand bags every fifty yards. They've also got a box of grenades and launchers. They are way back at the east side of the compound so there's a kill zone two thousand feet deep around the launcher. The area is mined with Bouncing Betty, Blue Parrot, Claymore…you name it. The control room is armored to withstand just about anything short of a mortar or tank shell….Are you getting my drift, here?"

"They're really proud of this thing."

"You bet."

"What about a mortar attack?"

"Sure. Except the problem with range. The area for two miles around the base has been flattened or bulldozed or whatever. And they've got two helicopters – and the drones, don't forget – ready to spot and destroy. They can be airborne in fifteen minutes. The drone can launch in about the same time. But the range, man. That's the problem. The mortars are good for 3000 meters but you'd need a spotter, at least three or maybe four units to co-ordinate the attack...the chances of a direct hit your first time...you see what I mean? And one other thing: We don't have enough mortars."

"Could we hit it on the runway, somehow?"

"There is no runway. This is the latest baby. It launches right off the back of a vehicle."

"You ain't makin this easy," Albert said.

"Ya, I know. Except there's more. This is a next generation Reaper, not a Predator. This thing carries 14 Hellfires and two full-size gas-air bombs. It's laser guided and can spot anything, anywhere, night or day. It's got software now that blocks any foreign program from entering the guidance board. It's like a watch-dog that kills everything it doesn't recognize."

Albert finally stopped and put the pack down. He was breathing hard from the last two hours of non-stop marching. Pickens slid to the ground and closed his eyes.

"Gimme a minute," he exhaled.

There was no choice. He let Pickens sleep until dark. They had now been on the trail for more than 24 hours and they had less than two days to disable the drones before the Free Forces attack.

Pickens sat up and blinked.

"You let me sleep," he complained.

"Easier than burying you," Albert said. "You ready to go?"

A drink of water, a few bites of a sticky power bar and they were marching again. The soft, humid night, dragged on them.

"There's only one way in that I can think of," Pickens said. "There's a safety protocol in the event that every security barrier fails and the command center is breached. It's a kind of override, you might say. There's a second command room at the other end of the base. Two soldiers who do nothing else while they're on duty, man it. They sit there and they wait for a signal that tells them the control room has been compromised. That signal goes off the instant an unauthorized hand touches the joystick in the main command center. The joystick is programmed to accept only the operators it has been programmed to accept. It reads the identity chip in the operator's arm and clears the board for him. The wrong arm touches that stick and the signal goes off. That signal goes right to the doomsday. The two guys inside are likewise chip-authorized only."

152

"Jesus Christ," Albert said.

"They now have control of the drone. They confirm the destroy message with a code. If the new operator answers the code correctly, they can override and transfer control back to the main command center. If they get the wrong answer, they press a button and the thing explodes wherever it is."

"There's no way to take over either one, you're saying."

"That's right. Sort of."

"Okay, I'm listening," Albert said.

"We need to disrupt the line between them. Somehow we get a destroy signal to the guys in the booth that they think is real. The we confirm it by sending them the wrong code."

"I thought they had two drones."

"They do, but the other one is strictly surveillance and it was badly damaged when I was there. I doubt if they ever got it working again."

They had reached the edge of an old wheat field that had grown back in with various grasses, weeds and small bushes. It was two miles across or seven miles around. Albert decided they had to chance it.

They rousted partridge, quail and pheasant, flocking up in huge numbers, not seen since the last century. It was amazing what four years without the human scourge could do for a bio-system. There were pockets of soy, corn, wheat and some barley going to flower everywhere. They had to be non-GMO seeds, which were all designed to be sterile after one generation. Monsanto had lost. He thought he would never live to see it. It was such an amazing moment to be alive, he thought, as he marched deliberately to certain death.

By mid-morning they had reached the very outer perimeter of the Provost Legion, two football fields surrounded by a triple hump of razor wire, mines, motion detectors, surveillance cameras, searchlights and endless Humvee patrols. If you got past that, you faced hundreds of trained, tested troops that might have been hand-selected from the police departments around the country for their mindless brutality. Take the bloated miscreant who calmly sprayed mace into the faces of a dozen teenagers sitting on a sidewalk like he was misting his roses, and multiply him by thousands. These were the last holdouts, the hard core of military gangsterism. They swaggered around in their Pillsbury Dough-boy armor, the taste of blood and power – and now illimitable fear – caked in their mouths.

Each of the six buildings in the main cluster was a steel Quonset covered three-deep with sandbags and outfitted with full surveillance inside and out. A heavy machinegun guarded ever corner. Guards patrolled the outskirts on the inside of the wire as well as outside. Two Abrams battle tanks squatted near the entrance, barrels lowered. Two AH 64 Apache attack helicopters slept quietly, surrounded by sand bags and protected by a five-foot blast wall two-feet thick.

Pickens collapsed, nearly comatose and Albert let him lie.

It was hear that Albert had discovered a soft spot – not a failure, for sure - but a soft spot in the perimeter that would allow him to get a lot closer to the main fence without necessarily being spotted.

Unusually heavy spring rains had washed down this southwestern edge of the compound and eroded the positions of the mines. There were slight depressions wherever a mine had been buried. The earth just didn't have enough time to settle. So he could see his way through the field fairly accurately. There were two motion detectors covering the path he would take. But he was surprised to see that they were first generation technology. That's a few bucks you will wish you hadn't saved if I have anything to say about it. They only operated when the subject reached a certain speed. Add to that the fact that the operators, tired of reacting every time a grasshopper went past, had probably dialed back the sensitivity. If he went slowly enough, he wouldn't set them off. He could crawl right through them.

So now he's at the razor wire.

Okay, time consuming but no big deal. Snip, snip and like that. So I am lying there out in the open and the Humvee comes by. Bang, bang, you're dead. The patrols are regular enough. Get across the no-man's-land between the wire and the Quonset. Long run. A hundred feet. More surveillance cameras. Now what? Bang, bang you're dead.

They had little more than a day left.

Albert panned across the camp with his field glasses one more time. He could see movement in the compound but there was no building at the east end. There were gun emplacements and a heavy tank squatting in the center - all the paraphernalia of a heavily defended position but there didn't appear to be anything to defend. He saw the Reaper latched onto the launch vehicle. He saw the fuel depot; but no command center. Maybe they had moved the command center to one of the other buildings. But that didn't make sense. It would be less secure than out in the open surrounded by that bristling perimeter. He watched a couple of soldiers walk behind the tank. He waited, but they didn't remerge on the other side. A few moments passed and two different soldiers appeared.

"Christ. They've buried the fucking thing."

When he got back, Pickens was still asleep. He moaned constantly from the pain. He had stopped taking the morphine before they left because it clogged his brain. They had hidden themselves a few hundred feet into the woods and while Pickens slept, Albert laid out their arsenal. There were ten No. 8 blasting caps and a sophisticated remote detonator. There was plenty of wire. He checked the ammunition for the first time and discovered one clip had incendiaries and the rest were stuffed with green-tip penetrators. He'd get his chance to test that night scope in a few hours. But he still didn't have a plan. He hadn't figured out how to traverse that last hundred feet of no-man's-land that was under constant surveillance from two cameras. The sound of a cracking stick on the forest floor gave him barely a moment's pause from his thoughts before he resumed taking inventory as if nothing had happened. The adrenalin kicked in as he stood up and stretched. He wandered to the edge of their campsite looking for a place to urinate. The rustling continued, but whoever it was didn't care if he was heard.

Albert slipped into the bush and cut a wide arc aiming to come back in on the stalker's flank. He saw him pushing his way through the growth, trying to be as quiet as possible and not doing a very good job of it. He carried a weapon but he was not decked out for combat. Albert watched as he came out of the bush and looked over the stock of explosives laid out on the ground. Then he kneeled down beside Pickens and shook his shoulder. Albert moved closer, preparing to attack the man, when Pickens woke up.

"Lonny," the man said. "Are you all right?"

Pickens came to reluctantly. He sat up and the other man laid his rifle and a small pack on the ground and helped him sit up against a tree.

"You still alive?" Pickens said, forcing a grin.

"Ya, man. You don't look so shit-hot yourself. What the fuck, man…?"

"Ease up slowly, please," Albert ordered him. "Just stand up and back away."

Corporal Glen Favor did as he was told, his face taught with surprise and fear. He raised his arms and Albert went over and relieved him of his Beretta and his combat knife.

"You got anything else I should be worried about?" Albert asked.

"He's with us," Pickens croaked.

"Is that a fact?"

"You're Albert Smythe!" Favor said.

"Is that a fact," Albert said. "Who the fuck are you?"

"Leave him be," Pickens told him.

Albert gestured and the man sat down.

"Who are you?" Albert demanded again.

"Corporal Glen Favor, sir. 279-."

"Never mind that stuff. What are you doing up here?"

"Can I put my arms down, sir? They're starting to ache."

"He's all right, I tell you," Pickens said. "Leave him be."

Favor slowly lowered his arms but kept his hands on his knees.

"We expected you a while ago," he said.

"We were on vacation in the south of France and missed your call," Albert said.

"I got you the laptop," Favor said. It's in the pack."

Albert went over and opened the canvas bag. Inside was an army laptop in a brushed aluminum case. There was an extra battery and a few odds and ends he didn't recognize.

"I maybe can hack into the doom room computer."

"It's got a satellite hookup," Favor said. "Once you get in, you can send them the destruct code and then block the reply with more bull shit. That's the theory, anyway."

Albert put the equipment back.

"I can do it from right here," Pickens said. "Thing is, they got to believe its real on the outside, too."

"It isn't simple as it sounds," Favor said.

"They have video hookup with the main control room and a display showing them what's going on outside as well. There's lots of ways for them to confirm the blow order and they'll use them all. You wouldn't want to be the guy who blew up a Reaper by mistake. I mean that would be your last mistake."

Albert studied them both and frowned.

"Who are you?" he asked Favor again.

"I'm just a tech, that's all. I fix some stuff, reprogram a little bit if I have to. I'm not like Lonny here. I don't know how to run any of the shit or crack codes or that stuff."

"Aren't they going to miss this little computer of yours?"

"Eventually. I mean like if you wait too long, sure they will."

"How long is too long?"

"I'd say you better go tonight."

"Is that a fact?" Albert asked.

Favor nodded. "Kingston will be in position by midnight or so. Once they see your stuff going off, you've got maybe half an hour before Free Forces launch their attack – drones or no drones. They are not going to wait for daylight."

"Half an hour…"

"Maybe half an hour," Favor said. "That drone has to be airborne for Pickens to tap into the signal, but they don't want it airborne for too long. That's what I say. Once they see your stuff go off, you'll have thirty minutes maximum before the battle starts."

"Can you do your thing in half-an-hour?" Albert asked Pickens.

"I don't know," he said. "I sure fucking hope so."

Albert glanced at the explosives. He still didn't know how he would get inside the compound once he cleared the last of the razor wire. He explained his problem to Favor.

"I know where you're talking about," he said. "I will be monitoring the CCTV from twenty three hundred right up until oh six hundred. I will be the one watching you. Trouble is they have someone watching me, too. That's just the way it is these days. They're paranoid as all hell. If you give me a time…"

Over the next two or three hours, they established a time-line and sorted out the last details within their control. Favor said he would dial the motion detectors back far enough that Albert could keep moving – slowly.

Albert handed Favor back his pistol and his M16. There were no parting words.

**

Chapter Three

Albert tried to sleep but he knew it was a waste of time. The mind permits no leisure in the face of such portent. He closed his eyes, to be sure, and enjoyed the caress of the autumn breeze. A yellow sun tried hard to impart its warmth but the earth and all upon it could sense it pulling away, loosening its embrace. The trees were still full, though some color changes were now apparent. A golden maple glowed amongst a platoon of drab cedars or a shock of red oak leaves waved in the wind. As if the universe had stopped to take a breath, they waited inside that tabernacle of leaves and branches for the last light to wane that they might wreak a most unrepentant hell upon numerous souls unknowingly preparing their last supper.

Pickens had propped himself up as comfortably as possible, the computer in his lap. He slept, head tilted, mouth open, gasping for breath it seemed. The Beretta lay on the ground where it had dropped from his hand.

How he had managed to survive to this point defied everything Albert knew or believed. The man was sickly to begin with, severely wounded, barely healed and not well at that and incessant pain roiled beneath his skin.

Albert checked to make sure he was still breathing and then lay down again.

Neither would be alive twelve hours from now. This was a fact he knew and understood as clearly as anything in his life. He could not imagine himself being alive after this. He did not see himself walking around or talking or eating or fucking or anything at all. He wasn't the slightest perturbed by it. For Albert, like the overwhelming majority, life had ceased to be a long time ago. This inter-world state wherein they now dwelt only held them back from ultimate oblivion; not so much a purgatory where the finishing touches may be added to a soul of indeterminate destiny, as the anteroom of a final holocaust. He lived for vengeance, for hatred above all things. Hate had entered his blood stream, his cells, the protoplasm of his being. It was no longer rage; that had quickly burned itself out. Now was the time of hatred, of unmitigated, unrelenting, implacable hatred. It was a cold, barren ecstasy. He wandered this landscape a mere shadow whose quality froze the blood on approach. These were no longer men, he slaughtered. They were indistinguishable cells of a malignant volvox, dividing and multiplying, breeding, encircling and enveloping whatever it desired to feed upon. He would ride an atom bomb into this incubus conclave and happily enjoin his vapor to theirs just for the pleasure of knowing they would die.

Albert's job was to enter the compound and create enough confusion that the command post believed they were under attack. They would not consider the idea of sabotage from inside, at least not at first. After all, no one had ever breached the perimeter of the Provost Legion.

Carefully placed C4 explosives detonated in sequences duplicating a mortar attack would send them into full alert. Within minutes, the base would be controlled chaos. Within fifteen or twenty minutes, they would launch the Reaper, followed by an AH 64 Apache attack helicopter with its electric machine guns and missile contingent. Once the bird was airborne, Pickens would have to hack the signal between the bird and the command center, disrupt it somehow and trigger the destruct mode. He said it was like trying to grab hold of a lightning bolt with your bare hands and forcing it to hit the object of your choosing.

As he began to crawl down the slope towards the perimeter, Albert thought of seventeen hundred men and women hiding in the shadows, waiting to die. Like him, they weren't afraid; all they wanted was to go in a manner of their own choosing.

That little bastard better have those cameras off…

At dusk the solar powered camp lights kicked on. In a few minutes the various infrared and near-infrared lenses would click into place on dozens of cameras. The 500 kilowatt generator surged as dozens of pieces of equipment all over the base switched from solar. A spout of black diesel smoke identified the location. That was one of his prime targets. It wouldn't take much, if he could get up to it. The 500 KW set was hooked up to a 600 HP engine with a very vulnerable radiator. But the set had been buried, like the drone command center and four feet of reinforced concrete poured over the top. Likewise, the fuel tanks were buried and covered but there was always an opening, somewhere. You couldn't make diesel explode, but you could blow the tank and drain the fuel into the ground. He was hesitant about that because it would be more valuable than gold if the Free Forces managed to take over the camp.

Night slowly dyed the air and soon enough he was preparing his descent into the kill zone. The satchel of C4 was strapped to his back; he had the night scope. He had sharpened the Emerson and re-sharpened it and drew it slowly down the center of a blade of grass to be sure. The .45, as always, hugged his chest. He had two extra magazines. If he needed more than that he wouldn't need them. The little .22 magnum, pressed reassuringly against his leg. He left the M16 with Pickens who didn't seem that interested.

"What the hell am I going to do with that?" he said.

Albert left it anyway. He wanted to say something to him and Pickens could sense it.

"You're one hell of a man," he said finally. Pickens eyes seemed to shine in the twilight. He didn't reply.

"See ya," Albert said.

He and Favor had synchronized their watches and he checked his now as he lay flat against the earth. It was just after ten. The headlights of the patrolling Humvee appeared around the corner of the camp and headed in his direction. They had a fender-mounted searchlight that swept the kill zone constantly. The gunner kept his .50 caliber pointed at the wide, empty swath of ground. Their circuit took between five and seven minutes, but they were well trained and they mixed it up regularly. Intermittent reinforcement was the catchphrase. It was something all that obnoxious harassment of the citizenry by the TSA and Homeland Security and the Immigration Department had revealed. Check everyone, every time and people will get through. Mix it up though, make it so the bastards can't know if they are going to be taken out of the line for a search or not and you'll feel like a Portuguese pilchard fisherman off the Sardinian coast. Their time could vary by two or even three minutes. As they came opposite him, he began his crawl.

How slow is slow enough?

It was a matter of not jerking an arm or a leg or allowing yourself to be startled by a sound or a flash movement in your periphery; an unconscious gesture that would set off the motion detectors and ignite the sirens and alert the machineguns. He clawed at the dirt, reaching out like a man underwater and twisted his body slowly one way and then the other. A leg drew up, cocked and then pushed him gently forward. He brushed past the exposed tendrils of a mine and had to watch his left leg move past it so he didn't accidentally set it off. They had staggered the minefield but had unwittingly created a serpentine route all the way through. A few times he came close and had to squeeze himself between projections barely eighteen inches apart. The Humvee headlights probed around the corner and he lay as flat as he could against the ground, covered by the camouflage poncho. The searchlight tripped over him but kept moving and the vehicle carried on. This happened twenty times before he got to the razor wire, exhausted and cramped from the concentration and the controlled movements.

Concertina razor wire is one of the marvels of modern-day compound security. This was a classic construction; two uncoiled Slinkies of butchery, running parallel on the ground with a third on top in the crack between them. The rolls were intertwined so he couldn't just cut a few threads and pass through. He had to physically remove a section from each of the lower strings, wide enough to crawl through. Fortunately the top coil would hold the bottom coils in place, preventing them from snapping back and curling up or otherwise giving away his position. The eight-inch mini bolt cutters Kingston had supplied seemed just the tool. The high-tensile wire with its steel core made it immune to the soft, Chinese-steel jaws of ordinary pliers.

The Humvee came round the corner again and he pulled the poncho over his body and lay still. He'd see it move on through a crack. The light swept the grounds and then blinded him momentarily as it found that peephole under the poncho and hung there. The soldiers in the Humvee lingered for a long while, marking the spot. Albert imagined their conversation:

"That wasn't there before, I'm telling ya."

"You're outta your mind. It's just the light."

"I'm sure it was back farther."

"Okay, drill the fuckin black patch on the ground, wake the whole camp up, and turn on the freak show. When they ask you what happened, you tell them there's a big blob out there moving around and you tried to kill it."

The light lingered a few more seconds and carried on past him. He watched the Humvee turn and disappear.

Now all he had to do was snip away at the wire, remove the two sections, crawl through the hole without getting torn to pieces, replace the section facing the patrol vehicle, make it across 200 feet of open ground right in the path of the Humvee, quickly cut through a chain-link fence and put it back in place. He had five minutes.

He remained where he was, still as stone. Not two minutes passed before the Humvee reappeared. They had reversed the direction of their patrol and came around the corner at high speed. He heard the engine slow and stop and then the light skipped over the ground, shining in the razor wire like ice. It rolled over him and stopped and came back and sat there. Albert braced himself for the impact of the bullets. He'd been shot once and he knew how it felt. The wire might deflect some of the slugs coming his way. He'd have to run back across the minefield. He prepared for the leap, tightening his leg muscles, raising his elbows slightly off the ground for that big push. And then the light disappeared.

The engine started up and the Humvee moved on.

He was panting and sweating now, adrenalin squeezing him so tightly he thought his heart would burst.

Breathe, motherfucker...breathe...

He went to work with the bolt cutters, bending back each fresh end of gleaming wire. He had to enter his half-made tunnel to get to succeeding strands. He pushed his arms deeper. The strand's curled up and tried to retract. Only the top coil held them in place. He drew his arms back and nearly shouted when the razor barb caught the back of his hand, tearing open a furrow from wrist to knuckle. His hand was immediately drenched with blood. He thought of the pair of gloves he'd left with Pickens.

He dropped the pack and pulled open the flap with his good hand. He rummaged around until he found the duct tape and tried to pull it loose with his teeth. He gave up and felt around the roll with his thumb until it came to the tiny ridge that marked the end. His other hand was dripping blood and he had to keep it out of the way while he scratched at the edge of the tape with his broken thumbnail. Finally a tiny ear lifted and he was able get a full grip on the end with his teeth.

Once he began to wrap the wound, his body relaxed. He wrapped it around several times across the back and palm.

He put the pack back together, but now he couldn't strap it on. He would have to drag it the rest of the way. The bolt cutters were slippery with blood and dust and he dropped them several times as he twisted the steel-hardened wire. The first section of wire half unraveled on the ground and he had to drag it back and lay it in the coils. The second coil came easier and he had pushed it through when the Humvee lights appeared. The pack and the poncho were behind him and he was stuck halfway through the wire. The vehicle slowed but they didn't bother to sweep the field. They zeroed in on the poncho. It hadn't moved. They drove on.

Albert crawled backwards out of the hole, grabbed the pack but left the poncho where it lay. He was through the wire, standing straight up. He knitted the coil back together and started to run. He ran right into the camera. No alarm sounded. He was through the chain link fence and squatting down in the gravel behind one of the Quonsets when the Humvee came by. After a perfunctory sweep of no-man's-land, it drove on.

Albert fell back against the building and closed his eyes. His hand throbbed and blood continued to seep out from under the tape. He rested in one of the few blind spots in the camp, directly under the spy camera that had been focused on him a few moments ago. Favor must have pulled it off.

Albert had memorized every detail of the compound that he had garnered from Kingston's drawing back at the big cave and information he received from Favor in the few hours they had to talk. He was standing beside a Quonset used primarily for storage of personnel maintenance articles, food, uniforms and various medicines. It would be lightly guarded. He had to get inside and get a uniform before he began wandering around the compound. He moved slowly alongside the building until he could see the front. A single guard, as he had suspected, stood in the sandbagged entrance, thinking only about when his watch would come to an end.

Soon.

The storage shed was fairly isolated from the rest of the camp and he was able to get in behind the guard without being noticed. The man was wearing light body armor that covered most of his torso ruling out a kidney kill. He would still have to cover the man's mouth and drag him off balance, jabbing and slashing his throat. It was messy and noisier than he would have liked. It was a better death than many this man had no doubt handed out and more merciful than he deserved.

The large bay delivery doors were locked but the man door was open. Albert dragged the dead man into the room. The dead soldier was taller and broader than Albert; his uniform would not fit. In a few moments, however he was able to dress himself, at least to the degree where he could tolerate a passing glance. The big question now was how long it would be before they noticed that the guard was missing. He pushed the body into a corner and covered it up.

It was now a long, slow nonchalant walk across the pavement to the next Quonset, a huge tunnel-like structure outfitted as a barracks. It slept two hundred men. The stink from the latrines wafted from behind the building. Lights were on inside and he saw more than a hundred off-duty soldiers lounging around on bunks, playing cards or sleeping.

This would be the first explosion to try and kill as many of them as possible right off the bat and maybe even cave in the front of the building to keep them locked inside.

Sand bags, three deep had been placed against the walls of the building but only to a height of six feet. The roof was essentially very soft, weak steel bolted together in sections with the cheapest hardware the army could find at the time. He moved down alongside the building and saw two men coming towards him. He kept walking, head down.

"Hey, corporal," one of the men said.

Albert ignored him and the man called again.

"Are you ignoring me corporal?"

Albert stopped and turned.

"No sir...I uh..."

"Where are you going?"

"Uh, just to take a dump, sir."

The man approached Albert, with a determined stride. The other man stayed where he was.

"You're one of Captain Willoughby's men, aren't you?"

"Yes sir," Albert said. He had shifted the satchel and freed his hand up. He could probably get to the gun faster, but there was no way to muffle the shot. Maybe he could kill this man and hold him up, act like the man was sick and the other one would come over and then-

"What happened to your hand?"

"I cut it sir."

"Jesus Christ. Get out of here."

Albert turned and headed for the latrines. The two men continued on their way. What had he done to attract that Captain's attention? It wasn't the uniform or he would have said something…and then it struck him. He didn't have a reason. He didn't need a reason. He did it because he could. That's what they did.

They way they had blocked the Quonset up with sand bags made it relatively easy for Albert to get onto the roof. It was just a huge half circle of ribbed steel and he crawled along, flat as possible to about the halfway point. It would have to do. If he tried to get any closer to the front, he'd be spotted. The C4 had been packaged in small, 1.25-pound blocks and he figured it would take at least a dozen of them to seriously compromise the building. That would leave him with only twelve for everything else. Instead, he set five blocks in an X pattern and wired the detonators in series. It was a bit of a risk but he had been assured the switch could produce enough power to set them all off. He realized he could not collapse the building but he might set up a shock wave in that steel rib cage that would kill or disable many of the inhabitants. Crawling around back of the buildings proved easier than he had imagined. At the ordnance building he fastened another five blocks to the outer wall and moved on. The idiots had reinforced the roof with triple sand bags and left the back wall completely exposed. A decent shot could put an incendiary bullet right through that steel wall from a mile away, with the right rifle. That wasn't even an impressive shot. Hell. In 2009, a British Army sniper had killed a man at 2.5 kilometers: Two of them, in fact.

Albert had been lucky, so far, but he knew that was going to change. There were too many of them. And now the easy part was over.

He had to cross almost a hundred yards of open ground undiscovered to get up beside an Abrams tank parked alone but surrounded by wire and sand bags. A machinegun crew guarded front and back. Here he began to realize that the security around the camp was not just for subversives coming from outside; there were problems inside the compound as well. It seemed obvious now and he wondered why he hadn't seen it before. This wasn't a solid, united battalion. This was a collection of miscreants, men and some women who had made very bad choices and were coming to regret them. Some had signed on for survival, some for loot; all would perish and probably knew it. After what had taken place in the fifty miles radius of Provost Indiana over the last four years, no one involved could expect forgiveness. Their only hope was a quick death.

The tanks were being protected from elements within the compound. It made no difference to Albert. He wasn't here as a judge; he was here as an executioner. He could probably get right up to the rear machinegun undetected by moving along the chain link and keeping to the shadows. It was a risk, but he was running out of time. He had reached the limit of protection and now had to walk out in the open again.

He strode out from behind the last building, the satchel hanging off his shoulder like a purse. They saw him from a hundred feet and he could see them bristle like dogs.

"Hey, man," he called. "Don't be shootin' anybody, now."

One of the men got up holding his M16 while the other manned the .50 caliber.

"What do you want?" the man asked.

"Hey, man, don't be like that. We're all on the same side here, right?" Albert whined. "I got something here for yoose guys."

"Ya?" the soldier asked. His face hadn't changed and he held the rifle on Albert.

"Captain Willougby sent me over with this stuff," he said, taking the purse off his shoulder. He had been slowly approaching all the while and was now only a few feet from the gun.

"That's far enough," the man said. "What's Captain Willougby got to do with us?"

"Man, this fool don't know nothing," Albert grinned. "Can I just get a little closer into the light?"

He had his hand in the purse and was rummaging around. It distracted both men just long enough. Albert got the Emerson into the man's throat before he knew what had happened. Blood spurted and he tried to press down on his own carotid as he teetered backwards. Before he could react, Albert grabbed the other man and smashed his head against the heavy gun. The man tried to scream and Albert slammed his head down again. The bones of his forehead cracked and the man went limp. Albert smashed his head down one more time and threw him backwards into the gravel.

The fun's just starting...

Now the time constraints were narrowing by the minute. He figured they would discover the dead gunners within ten minutes at the most. He had to have the charges set. To disable the tank, he'd need a lot more C4 than the half dozen blocks he had molded into one. But he had brought along a tin funnel on legs just for this moment. He had attached four sticks to the funnel so that it could stand up on a flat surface, mouth up. He packed the C4 into it and pressed it tight. Then he placed the device as deep inside the caverns around the treads as he could reach. He set the charge and faded back.

He crossed the compound in the open once again and walked up to a guard slumped against a Humvee. There were five of them, parked together, heavy-duty versions with armor and protected gun nests. The guard reluctantly pushed himself upright and peered at Albert.

"Ya?" he said, belligerent not just because he was on duty, but also because his daydream had been interrupted.

"Captain Willoughby sent me down here to give you this," Albert said, walking into the penumbra from the overhead light.

"Captain who?"

Albert dragged the body between two vehicles and dropped it. Blood was still pumping from the slash in his throat and Albert could see his mouth working, trying to swallow. His eyes stared at Albert in disbelief.

His hand was throbbing and bleeding again. He removed the tape and redid the bandage, tighter. He had six grenades, three clips for his 1911 and his Emerson. The big bird rested on the launch rails, its signal beacon pulsing every few seconds.

There was no way to get anywhere near it or the helicopter. Even a suicide attack would have failed because they'd kill him before he got within grenade range and the bullets from his .45 wouldn't dent either machine at this distance. He was loath to mine the Humvees because they would be so valuable to a victorious Free Forces.

Then he had the idea of setting them up in the ground, like mines along a walkway between the barracks and the mess hall. It was also the shortest route to get to the ordnance shed from the barracks and from the communications Quonset that was otherwise out of his

167

reach. The C4 wouldn't have the concussive power it was capable of just lying on the ground or even buried slightly. Without some sort of container the explosion diffused too quickly. But set ten feet apart and wired independently, they would blow off some legs and create an acceptable panic once the show began.

He dropped the configured blocks on the ground and bent down to cover each with gravel as he went. He had just dropped the fourth cube when the officer who had accosted him earlier reappeared. He was heading straight for him with that deliberate, defiant stride. Albert bent down and pretended to be tying his shoe. The officer started around him and then stopped.

"What are you doing here, Corporal?" he demanded. "Captain Willoughby's troop is guarding the forward tank tonight, aren't they?" he said.

"Yes sir, I'm on my way-

"Stand up corporal."

"Yes sir, it's just my shoelace-."

Albert felt the hand gripping the shoulder of his jacket and yank him upright.

"Just what in the hell do you think-" the man sputtered, but he lost his breath and couldn't finish. He grunted and opened his mouth and Albert covered it with his hand and pushed him down, twisting the Emerson in his groin. The man's eyes bugged and the scream finally erupted from him when Albert jerked the knife straight up into his gut and sliced all the way to his rib cage. He didn't have time to get rid of the body. Instead, he placed the last two blocks of C4 under the dead man and ran back to the shadows. He walked along the chain link fifty yards or so, stopping when the patrolling Humvee passed.

He had direct line of sight to his first charges and the only thing holding him back now was fear and common sense. Once he pushed that switch, the war would have started.

"Okay," he said out loud. "Come and get it."

***

Chapter Four

He didn't know if it was just the moment of expectation or if life around the Provost Legion compound really had slowed almost to a standstill and then gone silent. It happened in the woods all the time. You are walking, your rhythms blend into the sounds around you, a highly charged outline glows at the edge of every leaf. A bird lands, folds its wings, tilts its head at you...the world holds its breath.

The charges atop the barracks exploded milliseconds apart, but to all appearances it was a single, massive, flaming irruption that shattered the ribbed steel arch and folded the metal in and down at such a speed and with such force that fifteen men lying on bunks below it were crushed where they lay. The shockwave slammed another dozen into the steel sides. A man flew backwards into the wall, his brain turned to jelly as he slid down to the floor. Others lay howling in the debris, backs broken, arms and legs twisted into strange configurations. Flames raced quickly across the plastic mattresses and nylon bedding. A woman ran screaming into the night, her hair ablaze.

Sirens and air horns blaring from every corner of the base soon eclipsed the howling of the damned. Flames from the burning building turned black and oily as plastic-based materials burned along with two-dozen human bodies, some of them still alive. Hydrogen Cyanide poured out of the conflagration, choking half a dozen soldiers pinned in a corner and finally killing them where they stood.

Compound lights blazed with sudden fierceness and the generator RPMs dove as the engine lugged, trying to catch up to the sudden demand. Within a few minutes several hundred soldiers were running for defensive positions, hauling helmets and rifles, struggling to strap on body armor.

From his vantage behind the corralled Humvees, Albert watched troops running for positions along the path he had just mined. The first group came upon the dead officer and they stopped, causing a sudden backup of oncoming troops. Someone checked the dead man for life signs and then flipped him over.

The explosion tore the body in half, showering blood and bone down on the scene. Albert hesitated a moment and then set off the other three charges, each one igniting with a flash and heaving bodies into the air. The knot of soldiers broke apart and fled in different directions leaving their wounded behind. At least a dozen were dead or dying in the gravel. They still had no idea where the attack was coming from and other than heading to their assigned defensive positions, they had not responded. Not a shot had been fired.

The Apache helicopter started to womp the air as the turbos whined. He watched the side gunner climb aboard even as the machine had started to leave the ground. With its electric M23 Chain Guns, its Hellfires and banks of Hydra70 rockets, the Apache was a fearsome killer, almost invulnerable to small-arms fire unless concentrated blasts of steel core ammo were directed at its most vital points from relatively close range. And even then, even the rotor, for example, once the favorite target of small arms, could withstand multiple hits. It was layered with redundant systems. Shoot out a hydraulic line here and another would take its place over there. But the GFAS (Ground Fire Acquisition System) had added such lethality to the big flying bug that even trying to shoot at it could result in almost instant death. Infrared detectors would immediately locate the position of the shooter and a fistful of missiles would be sent back down the path. Nothing can spare a helicopter from a direct RPG hit but the Apache was a most formidable opponent, nonetheless.

Albert was tempted to empty a clip of .45 hardball at the side gunner but it was the usual dilemma. Do you give your position away for a questionable target? He was still invisible and the longer he stayed that way, the better. The helicopter began to rise and spun on its axis. It banked and headed into the night. The red light on the Reaper was solid red now and he saw vapor coming from the engine as it prepared to launch.

Amid the chaos of panicked troops and enraged officers, he was able to slip from his hiding place and get closer to the ordnance shed. He had to be in direct line of sight for his switch to affect the detonators and it didn't take much to interrupt the signal. But even more than a new vantage point right now, he need a rifle and plenty of ammunition. From among the dead on the pathway he retrieved an M16 and was rifling the bodies for magazines when he spotted a SAW (Squad Automatic Weapon) poking its snout out from under a dead sergeant, its 100-round ammo box already attached. He collected as many of the 30-round clips as he could and got himself back into the shadows without being seen. The SAW could handle belt-fed or magazine ammunition and release it at one thousand rounds a minute for short periods. He had about two hundred and fifty rounds, but expected to find more as the night wore on. As it was, he could send a heavy swarm a thousand feet across the compound and have it arrive in a fairly good pattern.

A siren whelped as the Reaper readied for launch and he aimed the SAW high, hoping to pepper it at least, but the burst disappeared without hitting anything. He was too far away.

A commander had opened the ordnance shed and troops were grabbing magazines and ammo belts. It was slow going and a bottleneck was choking off the distribution.

So he pushed the detonator and watched as…nothing happened. He pulled the switch back, reset it and tried again. Nothing. It might be line of sight; it might be simple detonator failure. Whatever it was, he was unable to prevent the mass distribution of ammunition to the defenders, a fact that would have severe consequences later.

There was nothing he could do except try and get closer and maybe reset the detonators or find another way to blow the building.

He fired a long burst at the entrance and half a dozen waiting troops fell. The others dove and scattered.

The game had changed now. They knew someone was inside and massive efforts would now be directed to find him – or them.

Flares arched out of the compound and hung over the plain in front of the minefields. The roar of explosions and machinery was deafening as the Legion kicked into full defense mode. Albert aimed the switch at the tank just as it had begun to move. The explosion was contained by the heavy steel armor and that helped concentrate the already-shaped charge he'd placed in the axel wells.

Normally a small charge like that would do no more than temporarily disrupt the Abrams motion but this was different. The funnel-shaped charge drove straight down through the tread into the main axel, blowing the steel pads off on the way and disabling the cog. The tank lurched to a stop. A platoon appeared out of nowhere, it seemed and headed straight for him. They couldn't have seen him but they had figured out by now that charges had been set and they knew as much about it as he did. There were only so many locations he might be and retain line of sight to the beast.

He kneeled behind a pile of sand bags, aimed the SAW at the center of the group and fired. In a few seconds he ran through the one hundred rounds and left at least half a dozen dead or dying on the ground. They kept coming. He struck the empty box and slammed in one of his thirty-round M16 clips and kept firing, sweeping the on-coming wave. They were taking heavy losses and they stopped and fell back. They had spotted his muzzle flash and the slugs began to land all around him. It was no different from a hailstorm as lead and steel-core ammo raked his position.

As he hunkered down behind the sand barriers, he saw the Reaper launching in a blast of jet fuel and vapor. It would be airborne in seconds and reporting back to the operations room in minutes. The clock was ticking for Pickens.

Flares continued to arc, explode and float down over a battlefield where there was as yet, no battle. The second tank was rumbling up from the far end of the compound and it stopped a few hundred feet from the sandbagged entrance to the drone command center. Carrying forty shells and almost ten thousand rounds of machinegun ammunition, it was essentially unstoppable. Repeated hits with RPGs might set off reactive armor and expose inner tank armor to damage, but even broken down the tank became a bunker with a cannon. Deprived of most of the effective weapons available to the Legion, Free Forces soldiers might as well have been throwing rocks when it came to these lumbering battle beasts.

The double platoon that he'd fired on had regrouped and they were now broadening out for a flanking movement on his suspected position. He had four clips left for the SAW and six grenades. A diversion was his only hope of escape now. He rolled and crawled a hundred feet along the fence line until he was backed up against another building.

172

Around the corner a four-man team was coming towards him. They had to get a lot closer before he could risk a grenade. He pulled the pin and counted slowly, then tossed the grenade around the corner. It exploded almost immediately but was followed by a dense burst of automatic weapons fire. He had missed all four of them and they were heading his way now. He moved up the other side of the building approaching open ground where several hundred soldiers were still in motion. Five or six bodies lay where they'd fallen a few moments before.

He hugged the wall and waited for the crew to round the corner and come for him. At the first sign, he tossed another grenade. The explosion covered him for maybe ten seconds but it had once again missed its target. He threw himself down amidst the pile of dead. He tore the tape off his bleeding hand and rubbed his face and jacket with as much as he could squeeze out. Then he lay still. Around him he heard the clatter and shouting as the Legion forces got themselves under control. He could hear the officers barking orders over the din of incoming rounds and sirens.

Boots scraped the gravel. He was lifted, and rolled onto a stretcher. They didn't bother to check for life signs. He heard the command to take him and the others to a corner for burial. He'd lost the SAW and had only his .45 and the grenades left. He opened his eyes a crack and saw that he was being carried by two men, who themselves walked behind another two carrying a body and so forth. They didn't seem to be in any hurry. He couldn't decide whether to wait until they unloaded him or try to escape now. They were passing the motor pool again. He lay still.

The first incoming rounds aimed at the compound itself, were from a pair of 60 mm mortars that had been set up just outside the kill zone, past the wire. The first few finned shells and landed without causing much damage but they did reinstitute a mild panic in troops that hadn't seen much resistance for a while. Then the mortars doubled up, one lobbing shells into the compound in a random pattern while the other blasted a path through the minefield. Every time a mortar round hit the kill zone, it would set off one or two mines in geysers of rock and dust.

They swung their attack first east and then west, opening up as large an area as they could for crossing. More than three hundred men under Vince Morelli were set to breach the perimeter once they had a safe alleyway. The mortars continued to pave the way through the kill zone but heavy machineguns were setting up all along the perimeter fence and the heavily armored Humvees were tearing off on hunter-killer missions with full radio contact between them and the Reaper command. The Humvees would be apprised of everything the Reaper saw.

Albert felt himself being laid down in a line of other dead men. He glimpsed the streak of a flare heading outward and felt the concussion of a mortar round landing nearby. The stretcher-bearers dropped him hastily and he rolled sideways.

"Leave him, he won't mind," one of them said.

Albert crawled over the dead – there were almost forty bodies lying here – and headed back towards the center of the camp. He needed to pick up another weapon. The barrage of incoming mortar rounds had increased and combined with the thump of flares, the crack of rifle fire and the wallop of tank shells scudding into the ground.

A female rifleman was squatting by a Quonset, peering into the kill zone past the wire. She glanced at him and returned her eyes to the plain. Numerous mortar rounds had detonated the mines. She was speaking on a two-way and Albert realized she was directing internal mortar fire back at a location about a mile away in the scrub at the edge of the perimeter. He reached around her head and took her right ear in his hand. She struggled as he attempted to get his injured hand behind her other ear. She was screaming as he lifted her off the ground and twisted her neck as hard as he could. But his hand slipped and she almost escaped. She turned on him with the rifle and he batted it down before she could find the trigger. He pressed her against the fence and drove his knee into her groin. The pubic bone cracked and she shrieked in agony. He pulled back and drove the palm of his hand into her forehead as hard as he could. Her head snapped back and he punched her exposed throat twice. She was still alive when she hit the ground, gasping, her eyes crazed with terror and pain. He took out the Emerson and felt around the base of her throat and then guided the blade along his hand deep into her jugular notch. Blood spewed from her mouth. He took her M16 and the radio and found two more 30-round magazines in her combat vest.

Normally they would have held the second helicopter back for rescue or assistance or some unforeseen calamity but the intensity of the attack had unnerved them and they were starting to make bad decisions. The second helicopter rose from its landing pad amidst a hail of flashing lights and debris from mortar rounds. It was a hundred yards away. Albert leveled the rifle and emptied the clip into the side gunner. He slumped, still in his sling as the bird lifted off. As it spun around towards the attacking forces, Albert emptied another clip into the glass in front of the co pilot but to no avail. It clouded up but did not break. If he'd had another clip it might have.

The disabled tank was sending shell after shell over the wire into the trees beyond the perimeter and they landed in little orange explosions that sent branches tumbling in the air.

By the time the tank had zeroed on them, the mortar crew had moved. The advantage of the light mortar was evident as one man could run with it while the second man in the crew carried the ammunition and the third covered their traverse with rifle fire. They didn't have to move far to spoil the firing solutions of the tank crew or just about anyone else behind the fence.

But it was well past thirty minutes of combat since he'd blown the barracks in half and Albert was starting to doubt that Pickens could hack into the communications as he'd described. If he could intercept the transmissions, he could send bogus information to the doomsday crew in the second bunker, but if he couldn't, the bird would start reporting positions. Over the tree line he saw the streaks of Hellfires ramming into rifle positions. Plumes of orange flame lit the sky.

The concussion of a nearby mortar round knocked him down and slammed his head into the steel wall of the Quonset. He wasn't out, but he was seeing double and suddenly had to vomit. Then he realized he was deaf as well.

He slumped down and closed his eyes. A dozen troops passed his body without even looking at him. They were heading to the ordnance depot with stretchers, bent on replenishing their own mortar teams who had been bombarding the entire southern ridge. The second helicopter had joined the first in hunter-killer mode and he could hear the machine guns and the blast of Hellfires and Hydra 70s slicing through the forest.

Then sky above the perimeter lit up with a concentrated explosion at about 8000 feet. It was the Reaper.

Albert lay on the ground, the mayhem around him reaching a silent crescendo. He saw more boots running past.

The doomsday crew exited their command post and set the destruct charges. In a few seconds the ground shook violently as the earth absorbed the blast from a hundred pounds of C4 strategically placed around the bunker to ensure it's complete destruction. To the soldiers outside it was just another explosion at that point, but to the five-man crew inside the main Reaper command center, it was the stroke of doom. The steel doors clicked and banged as the automatic locks kicked in. Four men and one female officer inside tried frantically to open the doors but they knew the seal was virtually indestructible. The lights inside the room died suddenly and the five of them began to scream. The detonation contained by the four feet of reinforced concrete resulted in a shock wave that left no evidence that human life had ever existed in that burned out room. When the Free Forces detail inspected the underground communications center, they didn't even find a bloodstain.

At the sight of that Reaper explosion, a wild cheer erupted from the American Free Forces soldiers waiting back from their mortar crews under Vince Morelli and they began their advance, soon to be followed by Harding and Ramsey.

The Legion still had superior firepower, but without their technological nursemaid, they weren't entirely certain how to create a defense or fight a prolonged action. Years of relying on machines to do their thinking for them and make the decisions had drained them of basic skills that had made armies effective for thousands of years. Even as the terrorist attacks of 9/11 had shown them the danger of relying solely on electronic surveillance, they continued to invest their time and energy in automatic solutions. They actually believed that someday they would be able to fight wars from the living room with a joystick and a bottle of beer. Drones and surrogates would fight it out and may the best robot win. It never occurred to them that without fuel and replacement parts and evolving management that their prized proxies might become a liability rather than an advantage. They were conditioned to come up with firing solutions based on Intel from a bird at ten thousand feet. What were they going to do now?

At least Sitting Bull had taught them something and they kept their forces in one piece. But they had basically trapped themselves. The tank could make a run for it, perhaps, but where would it go? Once it ran out of fuel, the four-man crew would be stranded wherever they stopped. They ran anyway.

The tank swung its barrel forward and started a run for the opening. Hundreds of bullets were wasted on the beast as it crashed through the fence, over-ran the wire and headed due south. Without an RPG or some realistic tank killer, there was nothing they could do. It could hit 50 miles an hour and it soon outran any pursuers.

That didn't stop three fighters from Morelli's group from peeling off and jogging after it. The tank had a maximum range of about 250 miles, but at high speed that was significantly curtailed. And the gas turbine engines drank fuel at an astonishing rate. They correctly figured it would be dead within fifty miles. If the crew stayed with their machine for any length of time, Morelli's men would find them and kill them all. No one was going to escape.

The first black dots of Morelli's troops appeared in the south, outlined by the flares exploding every few minutes overhead.

A combined group under Roland Harding and Viola Ramsey, comprising more than a thousand guerilla troops from a dozen independent units were moving down from the north and east. They had reached the edge of the forest and barely two thousand feet of open space, mines and concertina wire separated them from the compound. Most of the defender's firepower was concentrated on their southern flank where they expected the main attack to come from.

Harding and Ramsey had other plans. Four machine-gunners set up on the edge of the woods and with a careful, deliberate precision, rained a hailstorm of lead and steel on the minefield. Geysers of dust and dirt exploded everywhere. They poured more than two thousand rounds into the ground. The opening was a hundred feet wide when the shooting stopped. Return fire was coming from the compound but the defenders were not prepared for the kind of rush that suddenly came their way.

Harding's troops had gotten hold of half a dozen still-functioning vehicles and enough fuel to turn them into rolling bombs. Gas pedals were jammed down, steering wheels tied in place and breaks released. The vehicles had been packed with glass jars of gasoline and detergent, a homemade napalm that was every bit as effective as the real thing at close quarters.

The drivers leapt from the vehicles after getting them started and rolled out of the way. Six flaming chariots bore down on the north fence, followed by Harding's six hundred troops. Two of the vehicles hit mines and exploded before they reached the chain link, but the remaining four made it right through, crashing into the fence and exploding on contact, showering burning, jellied gasoline on a few score defenders who broke and ran.

Once the defense started to collapse, Ramsey's sapper teams wound their way through the minefields on the north end arrived at the chain link fence without firing a shot. Every mine was marked with a white ribbon and while they quickly cut open the fence, a hundred men moved in silently behind them.

Albert still couldn't hear but his vision had cleared and he saw the troops breaking and running all around. Their only hope of escape was through the main entrance where the minefields had been terminated to permit a narrow corridor in and out of the compound.

More than two hundred of them began running for the front gate and a third managed to get past the guard posts when Kingston's troop opened up on them at close range. They fell like corn. Kingston had arranged a crescent of weapons of every sort two hundred feet from the main entrance and when the machineguns opened up, there was nowhere for the Legion troops to run except back to the compound en mass, where they collected in a defensive formation between two Quonsets.

Ramsey's troops on the north had pushed the rear defenders into the center of the compound where a major firefight was ongoing. They were not doing well and Ramsey saw almost half her men killed in five minutes. Harding's troops faired better and had cornered about seventy-five Legion soldiers where they were methodically shooting them down.

The Legion troops did not give up, though and fought back ferociously with a barrage of hand grenades that wiped out twenty-five of Harding's troops in one blow. Albert staggered into the open holding his ears, still unable to clear his head. He took out his .45 and fell back down against the wall of a Quonset and began throwing up again.

Morelli's men poured through the southern breach, wiping out a knot of about a hundred Legion troops hunkered in between the Quonsets. They now had effective control of the compound but there was still the problem of the Apaches. They would be communicating somehow with the Legion ground forces and would likely be coming this way at any moment.

Morelli took a dozen troops and they ran to the ordnance building. A score of Legion defenders met them with a .50 caliber and a

Humvee, killing everyone except Morelli and two female fighters. They had no way of getting inside the building. They would have to mount a full attack on the defenders and risk blowing the munitions in place. They needed an RPG if they were going to take on the Apaches or they could expect near annihilation.

Morelli tried contacting Harding and then Ramsey but either they were dead or their K-mart coms were down. He heard static and then Kingston's voice came through.

"We've got one of their Humvees, we're coming in," Kingston said.

Kingston's troops had blasted their way through the front gates leaving almost a hundred dead in their wake. They had commandeered a Humvee and were now blazing towards the ordnance shed. The tracers streaked into the knot of troops defending the building, sending bodies flying, but the Legion Humvee answered back with a burst of sustained fire that killed the gunner on Kingston's vehicle.

Then the stream of bullets dropped a few degrees and obliterated the driver and his shotgun. The Humvee was dead along with its crew. But the diversion had allowed Morelli and his two sappers to get around behind the ordnance building and they now moved cautiously forward, hugging the sand bags. The enemy gunner had his back to them. One of the women climbed aboard and pushed an automatic shotgun into the back of his helmet and pulled the trigger until his head was gone. She dropped a grenade into the hatch and jumped. An expulsion of fire and guts shot up from the vehicle.

The three sappers got into the building and found what they were looking for. It was like waking up in Aladdin's cave. Stacks and stacks of everything a killer could dream up, where there for the taking.

They were too late for the first run.

The Apache raced down the center of the compound at about a thousand feet emptying everything it had into the masses of men and women below. There was no distinction between friend and foe at this point. Body's jumped and jiggered with machinegun fire, arms and legs and heads flew into the air where they turned slowly in the eerie light of the flares. But the bird was out of ammunition and had expended all of its rockets and missiles at the troops in the southern forest. It had no choice but to peel away and disappear.

It's sister followed in quickly and took the same route, electric machine guns spitting wildly and rockets slamming into the ground lifting geysers of blood and bone and dirt.

But Morelli had a bead on this one and the RPG streaked into the flank of the machine, exploding with terrific force and knocking it off course. Black smoke poured from every opening and flames were visible in the gunner's bay. Even so, the machine did not crash. It was able to lift itself out of harm's way and streak north. The pilot would likely be able to set it down, even as damaged as it was. The crew would be grateful for it's ability to keep flying unless they were caught by Free Forces troops while making their way back to Indianapolis.

The battle was over but the fighting had not stopped. It continued for almost another hour, until the Legion troops had finally run out of ammunition. The last barrage of rifle fire from the attackers had no response. A sudden silence rolled over the compound.

Harding was the first to accept surrender. A hundred Legion troops emerged from behind burned vehicles, sandbags and piles of their dead, hands high. They had chosen between certain death and most likely death and they knew it. They had shown very little mercy in their rampages over the countryside and the realistic among them knew their chances of a pardon were slim to none, with the emphasis on none. But it is surprising what the tiniest illusion of hope can do to the a pragmatic mind.

Harding left half his detail in charge of the prisoners and took the remainder over to the disabled tank. The crew had not emerged. There was no way to get at them without heavy explosives and he wanted the beast intact if at all possible. Their communications and visual systems would show them exactly what was going on outside; they knew what had happened. He needed to get them to come out. He tapped on the tank, but there was no response. He banged the turret with a rock about ten times and then dropped it. Then the hatch opened and a pair of arms emerged. The crew was quickly extracted and joined their fellows in a ring guarded by Harding's survivors.

Ramsey's unit had left no one alive and they joined Harding in a hard silence. They had lost 70 percent of their unit.

They watched as Morelli marched another seventy prisoners into the group. Of the six hundred or so Legion troops, about four hundred and fifty had been killed. Of the seventeen hundred Free Forces troops, twelve hundred were dead and another two hundred wounded. It was a victory, but there was no way to see it as a triumph. There were no cheers and no laughter and no ease. The remaining three hundred Free Forces troops had surrounded the prisoners, disarmed them and they all sat now, hands on head. There were two conflicting waves of emotion meeting at that spot. Hate and Fear.

Pat Kingston finally arrived walking slowly. A path formed to let him through. He looked at the one hundred and seventy prisoners cowering up against the fence they had built for their own protection but his own expression revealed nothing. He walked among them and they looked at him fearfully, aware that their fate was in his hands. He seemed to be looking for someone, pushing some aside, yanking others out of the way. Finally he grabbed an older, stocky man with straw-colored hair and jerked him out front.

"You better know what you're doing, boy," the Legion commander said.

Kingston looked at him for a long time. The colonel's gaze never wavered.

"You just bought yourself a whole lot of grief," the man said.

Kingston frowned.

"So what do you want?" the colonel said after a moment. "Maybe I can fix things for you."

"I don't want anything I don't already have," Kingston said. "All I have wanted for the last three years is to watch you die and now I'm going to do it."

The colonel's bravado failed for a moment and he tried smiling.

"What's that going to do for you besides nothing?" he said. "I could help you people out."

Kingston nodded and smiled and the colonel looked hopeful.

But Kingston's hand came up so fast he didn't have time for it to register. The colonel screamed and bent over as Kingston ripped his ear right off its perch and held it in his hand. Blood squirted and ran in rivulets down the side of the man's head.

"You fucker!" he shouted and ran at him, but Kingston caught him with a palm thrust right into his nose. The cartilage split and blood began leaking from there as well. The colonel was already out of breath, but he stood his ground, raging, his chest heaving.

"Come on you fucker," he yelled again, one hand trying to wipe blood out of his mouth and the other held out in a feeble challenge.

Kingston walked up to him and stopped a foot away. He stared into the man's crazed eyes like a snake hypnotizing its victim.

Again his hand shot up so fast the old colonel didn't really see it. Kingston's gnarled thumb and fingers were clasped around the colonel's throat, slowly increasing the pressure with each passing second.

The man batted at Kingston's arms and tried to kick, landing one foot against Kingston's leg; but Kingston didn't budge. He stared right into the Colonel's face, squeezing his throat with every ounce of strength and all the hatred of the last years. The man's eyes bulged and spittle and blood dripped from his mouth. He made one last attempt, weaving back and forth to try and shake the grip, but Kingston never let go, never changed the expression on his face. Blood squirted from the colonel's tear ducts and ran down his cheeks and the vessels in his ears burst. He sagged but Kingston wouldn't let go. The man dropped to his knees and Kingston increased the pressure until his fingers and thumb met behind the colonel's trachea; then he ripped out his throat.

The heavy silence remained. Kingston looked at the flesh in his hand and dropped it. The crowd parted to let Kingston pass.

"Hey. What are we supposed to do with this bunch," Morelli called after him.

Kingston stopped and turned. He looked across the prisoner faces staring at him with a worshipful, pleading helplessness. Many were young and had been deployed almost immediately after call-up from the Guard. There were at least thirty women amongst them. Some of them had been nothing more than support staff, cooks, supply clerks and the like. They had all been armed when the fight was on but that was no more than self-preservation. Given half a chance the majority would run from the military that had enthralled them and never look back. They would disappear into the twilight civilization around them and try to make a life. Some would be tortured by memories; others would shrug it off; others would recall it with favor and plan to do it again. There was no way to tell one from the other. They were all just terrified, broken and defeated soldiers who had done the job they were ordered to do.

"I'm surprised you ask me that," Kingston said. "We're not interested in taking prisoners. What are we going to do with them? You want to be a jailer, Vince?"

182

"Well what the fuck," Morelli said. "We can't just let them walk, for Chrissakes."

"I never said we should," Kingston replied. "I don't run this show any more than you do. You make your own damn decision."

Morelli looked at Harding and Ramsey but their faces revealed nothing. The decision seemed to have devolved to him.

"There's something about having mercy on your enemies in the bible," a voice came from the crowd.

"Fuck the bible and God too," another replied.

Viola Ramsey, Staff-sergeant United States Marines had lived for sixteen years with honor, she believed. When she had deserted her Guard Unit, she knew she had broken the most important oath of her life. It superseded God, marriage and mortgage companies. Those who had remained made their choice as well. She had always been prepared for whatever consequences her desertion had wrought and she expected others to do the same. But she was still a woman and understood too well the disparity in fate's allocations. Men and women might be allies in battle but almost never in life.

"Separate out the women," she barked. No one moved and she turned to her troops. "Obey the order or I walk," she said.

The female prisoners immediately accreted into a tight knot and stood in front of her like schoolgirls. The relief on their faces was plain as the dirt and blood and tears.

"Line 'em up," Viola said.

A dozen of her soldiers ushered the women into a rough line.

"Over against that fence," she ordered and they marched them a hundred feet away.

They stood against the fence, terror starting to reignite in every face.

"Anyone who can't stomach it, step out," she ordered. Half a dozen men removed themselves from her troop and she took an M16 from one of them.

The women began to scream.

Their keening rose like flames out of their mouths and continued until the last bullet riddled form mixed its blood with the rest. Viola Ramsey allowed a single tear to run down her cheek as she walked away. She would have liked to explain to them that they were much better off than what had likely been planned for them.

Albert tried to stand again and was able to fight his way up the wall. He could see the throng standing around the northwest corner of the camp. The sky was lightening.

His hearing was coming back but there was a high-pitched ringing in his ears and he seemed to be off balance. He staggered towards the crowd, the .45 still in his hand. Blood dripped freely from his other hand once again and he didn't realize that bits of bone and blood and flesh were stuck to his face and hair and vomit had dried and hardened on his clothing.

The ground began to heave as he approached but he kept walking; it was like being drunk but without the knowledge of the cause. He really didn't know why the earth was rocking back and forth.

He saw the eyes turning towards him, looking like independent specters, disconnected from brains or body, trying to look through him. The gun slipped from his hand and he stopped and looked at it, but the earth was heaving and rocking and he couldn't focus on it to retrieve it.

The crowd was standing around a huge pyre with at least fifty bodies on it burning and stinking in an all-too-familiar way. Behind the warping haze of the flames he saw the rest lying on the ground...more than he could count. They had been shot where they stood. Several had died, their fingers still entwined in the chain link fence.

"Looks like we missed one," a voice came, but it was watery, the corners had been broken off all the words.

A man approached Albert with his arm extended. The gun stopped against his forehead. Albert rocked on the balls of his feet. His head tilted back and his mouth opened.

"Oh yes," he breathed. "Oh yes...please..."

***

Chapter Five

The Provost Legion compound was now in the hands of The Kingston Brigade of The American Free Forces, Central Command, Sector 3. The post was renamed Fort Margaret after Pat Kingston's mother and a wooden sign with crudely carved letters so described it at the entrance.

The flag of the former United States of America had been taken down and burnt, but not out of contempt. It could no longer stand, its progenitors and their descendants, politically and genetically having been essentially defamed, debased and erased from the book of life. It was ceremoniously folded and placed on a pyre where it was consumed and its ashes scattered to the four winds. Nothing had been devised to replace it.

The problems created by the destruction of central military authority were not limited to the Free Forces and the immediate civilian population.

Four distinct military command centers established themselves along the lines of the various arms of the service. The ranking officer of each determined that the only way to control the country and put an end to the chaos was the transfer all power to himself. This wasn't simply a case of Air Force Schwartz arguing with Navy Greenert, Army Thurman duking it out with Marine Amos.

The problem was, just as there was no central authority left in the country, there was little or no central authority left in the individual branches of the service, either. Each commander held his position by consent and that consent was tentative at best. This is not the military way, to say the least. Chain of command was drilled into the thick head of every soldier because a breakdown in the chain of

185

command resulted in total army disintegration almost immediately. The "bosses" knew it and lived in constant terror that the idiots who had signed up to obey them under false pretenses would realize there was nothing to stop them from going their own way.

In one case, a large contingent of Marines under an obscure but charismatic Lieutenant-Colonel had broken off contact with what remained of Amos's command and established an independent army in California. These renegades took with them, almost 70 percent of the troops, planes and land carriers such as Abrams battle tanks, APCs and Humvees that at one time was the Marine Corps. Now Amos and a few followers were isolated and vulnerable so they were actively seeking alliance with someone – anyone – who would restore the status quo. Not to be outdone, U.S. Army commanders had split three times and each Napoleonic general had taken with him, along with all his conventional equipment, enough nuclear weaponry to obliterate an entire state. The world would soon have proof that production of nuclear artillery shells had not been cancelled and the stockpile destroyed as the public record showed, but in fact, had been mass produced up to a 1.5 Kiloton level – the equivalent of a fifteen hundred tons of dynamite, but with the added virtue of massive, neutron radiation. They had a range of twenty eight miles and a kill zone of approximately one kilometer. There were believed to be fifteen such shells in existence of which one thousand two hundred and sixty eight had been accounted for.

The Air Force had retained control of the ICBMs in Wyoming, North Dakota and Montana, the bomber command and numerous other means and devices of dispensing mass-death from the air of a magnitude that even after 70 years acclimatization seemed bizarre, to say the least. The Air Force arsenal could eradicate all life on earth twelve times. The Russians had even more, including the largest bombs ever built.

The largest exploded nuclear weapon "Tsar Bomba was a 50-megaton monstrosity that exploded with the blast equivalent of fifty million tons of TNT in 1961 and created a kill zone of 60 kilometers. The Russians were said to have cracked the barrier to the construction of a one hundred megaton bomb

The U.S. Navy had failed utterly to keep control of its Trident submarines – all 19 of them – anyone of which could eliminate life in, say Europe or North America all by itself.

186

Nevertheless, there was one fleet that included two carriers, three submarines and a bevy of lesser craft. But their flat top aircraft had only enough jet fuel for one sortie and so they were being held back as a last resort or counter-punch. There were four other independent Navy groups, each with its own carriers and submarines, but they had one mutual problem: The submarine commanders began to realize that they were essentially invulnerable and undetectable and owed allegiance to no one. They could remain under water for years at a time (at least two-and-a-half times as long as the public had been told) and they carried enough nuclear missiles to destroy any city, any battle group, anywhere at any time.

They, in turn, were starting to face recurring mutinies and with their already depleted human resources, some of the boats were getting to the point where they would have to be abandoned. When that occurred, the question became both simpler and vastly more complicated all at once: Should we abandon the boat or should we destroy the world with Polaris missiles, first? No one was willing to compromise because compromise in this case became instant subjugation and as there was no society left imposing restrictions on behavior, the usual acquiescence was conspicuously absent from the average personality.

But, powerful, fearsome and almost indestructible as they were, these two arms of the service marched on fuel, not chicken-pot pie and as a result, they were marginalized in the battle for control of the world that would shortly ensue. They could defend themselves or align with some army group to share the spoils, but their efficacy depended entirely on steady supplies of petroleum products, which they did not have.

Now add to all that, units like the Legion that had been set up by Homeland Security and FEMA but were now thrown into chaos. Those that managed to escape total destruction were regrouping and aligning themselves with one organization or another, hoarding their munitions and trying to stay alive long enough to recreate some sort of viable counterforce to the citizen juggernaut that had usurped their power. The idea of "strange bedfellows" had never been stranger. Alliances were joined and sundered sometimes on the same day.

Albert slept for two days – they said. If he had dreamed, he couldn't remember. He woke like a man coming out of an anesthetic whose last remembrance was that blissful, penultimate moment before unconsciousness. No time seems to have elapsed but you are different. You closed your eyes; you open them and you are different. You feel pain that wasn't there before; or old pains are absent.

Or nothing; nothing in, nothing out.

He was lying on a cot. The ringing in his ears had stopped. His hand was bandaged properly. He flexed his fingers. He was wearing different clothes. His .45 was on the table beside him. He closed his eyes again and lay back.

In an ironic reversal of roles, it was Lonny Pickens who came through the door into the Quonset and sat down beside Albert's bed. He was grinning.

"I've almost paid you back now," he said.

When Albert tried to speak, his throat caught. Lonny handed him a glass of water and he sipped it until it was all gone.

"Something sweet," he croaked. "Got anything sweet?"

Lonny shook his head.

"Not me, but I'll get someone in here right off."

"Sit down," Albert said.

Lonny was not the man Albert had first encountered. One arm hung almost useless at his side and his face had taken on a permanent grimace from the unceasing pain of his poorly healed shoulder. His eyes were still fearful and childish. But he had done something almost unheard of and all thoughts and dreams of returning to Missouri to go squirrel hunting were long gone.

"You did it, huh?" Albert said.

Lonny nodded, but showed no pleasure or pride.

"It's not as big a deal as people think. It's just most people don't know how the computers work. I mean, shit, a bunch of kids hacked right into an FBI conference call back a few years ago. The fucking banks are supposed to have these unbreakable codes and people just walk in and help themselves to a million credit cards…It's bull shit."

"Ya…"

"I'll tell you what. They said you killed sixty-seven Legion troops by yourself."

Now it was Albert's turn to push away praise. It hardly seemed like a praiseworthy accomplishment except that they all needed killing.

"How many did we loose?"

"A lot," Pickens said. "A fuck of a lot. Almost eighty percent."

"Jesus," Albert closed his eyes. "Jesus…Jesus."

188

"I know," Pickens said.

"How about them?" Albert asked.

Pickens hesitated and then pursed his lips.

"A hundred percent," he said.

Well at least there was that.

Albert allowed Pickens to help him stand up and then he pushed him away.

"Fuck off, he said.

Pickens laughed.

"Sure, no problem."

They walked out into the daylight where the crews were piling bodies or burning bodies or collecting body parts.

In the immediate aftermath of the battle, corpse disposal was the most pressing problem. Legion troops were burned or buried in mass graves, but every single Free Forces soldier was retrieved and interred in a cemetery created in the no-man's-land on the north side.

Albert squinted in the bright sunlight and enjoyed the gentle warmth of the rays on his face.

As they walked through the camp, many eyes turned on them, an experience Albert had come to accept and disregard.

"Hey, Albert," a voice called out.

He kept walking.

"You're a regular hero," Lonny Pickens grinned.

"How long have I been down?" he asked.

"Two days and nights...this is the morning of the third day for you. I didn't know if you were ever going to wake up."

Albert considered the answer and shook his head.

"What the hell happened?" he asked.

"You come walking out from behind that building yonder and one of the boys stuck a barrel in your face. He was about two seconds away from pulling the trigger when I saw it was you."

"Oh," Albert said.

"So now I paid you back for one time; I still owe you one life."

Albert laughed but his face showed no humor.

"You want to eat something?"

"Where's Kingston?" Albert said.

"He's in the headquarters building with the others."

"Lot of graves," Albert said.

"Ya," Lonny answered.

Kingston's face relaxed when Lonny Pickens brought Albert into the room and he walked up to him, smiling.

"'Bout time you got outta bed," he chided him.

Viola nodded and smiled; Morelli glanced at him and then looked back at the tabletop map.

Kingston took Albert's hand and gripped it hard, his eyes almost welling up at the sight of him.

"What the hell's got into you?" Albert scowled.

"You two really done it," Kingston said.

"He's the one who did it," Albert protested. "All I did was kill a bunch of folks."

Albert suddenly had to sit down and they pulled up a chair for him.

"That's the second time I've slept around the clock," he mused. "Must be getting old."

Kingston lit a cigarette and inhaled deeply, holding it until his lungs had squeezed out every molecule of goodness and then let it go.

"You almost make me want to try that," Morelli scoffed.

"You don't want to start this habit," Kingston said. "They say it can kill ya."

Albert tore open an MRE that Pickens had laid on the table. The Salisbury steak began to swell and jump in the heat packet and the smell curled into nostrils.

"All I need's a beer," he said.

Pickens grinned and produced an aluminum can of Pabst Blue Ribbon beer. Albert looked at it and almost couldn't believe his eyes.

"Go on," Morelli said. "Been saving it for you."

Albert ate. Listening to the four of them preparing for the next attack. There was certain to be a counter-attack of some kind in very short order. They couldn't decide if the compound was a good defensive position to maintain or if it made them sitting ducks.

"What happened to the last bunch that owned this place?" Albert pointed out.

That was Viola Ramsey's view as well but Kingston and Morelli were loath to split the force into smaller units, which would have to be done if they were going to move back into the woods.

"They'll pick us off in little groups with those helicopters," Morelli said.

190

"They'll pick us off in a big group with helicopters and tanks," Harding observed.

"They're looking at us right now," Viola said. "They have to be. They know our strength and our position. They know what kind of gunnage we've got. At least if we spread out, they'll have to split their forces as well. It will take four or six helicopters instead of one or two. They'll have to detail a tank or an APC to every hunt."

"We're going to lose some people no matter what," Harding said. "I agree with Viola. We need to get the hell out of here right now."

"And abandon 25,000 gallons of diesel fuel?" Kingston demanded. "What about the food, the supplies we've taken here?"

"Take them with you," Albert said.

"And the fuel?"

"Leave it for them," he replied. "How many vehicles do we have?"

"Three Humvees and a triple axel that somehow survived. The tank can't be moved," Morelli said.

"You're welcome," Albert replied.

"Noted," Morelli said. "I'm just pointing out that leaving isn't as simple as it sounds.

Kingston sat down, frowning.

"I just can't see it," he said. All that fuel, the generator…the ammunition. Shit We lost twelve hundred good people taking this shithole and I don't feel much like leaving it."

"Scorched earth," Albert suggested.

"We need this stuff. We have nothing. We cannot walk away from supplies like this," Kingston said.

The point seemed to take with the others, at least temporarily and discussion turned to routine matters of patrols, watch and distribution of ammunition, food and beer. There was enough beer to give every man one can with 50 cans left over. Harding's group was assigned to distribute and Morelli's men took the first watch and patrol duty. Viola's group was to stand down.

It was later in the afternoon when a patrol came back with the news that an Abrams tank had been sighted fifteen miles out, heading directly for the compound. It could easily sit two miles out and methodically pound them into the mud if it was fully loaded. The only toy they had to stop it was an RPG7, the anti-personnel round – for the famous tank killer. The '7' wouldn't dent an up-armored Abrams equipped with exploding plates and who knows what else. They needed a special round: RPG 29. It was a two-part missile that was proven to penetrate Abrams armor at the turret, back and sides. A frontal shot was still questionable. The '29' round hit the tank twice: The initial impact detonated the explosive armor plates; the second missile following in behind, struck at the bruise and shot molten metal into the tank compartment, killing everyone inside or at least disabling the vehicle. Follow-up shots against tracks, turret joints and the underbelly would finish the beast like a brontosaurus brought down by a pack of raptors. But they didn't have any '29s.' The Legion had not requested them believing that anti-personnel grenades were what they needed against the insurgents.

"We do have another tank," Viola said.

"Can you operate it?" Kingston asked.

"Whatever they might say, I am a Marine; of course I can operate it."

They were about to find out if they could defend this position or not.

Two Humvees loaded with all the ammunition they could carry, including hundreds of M2 armor-piercing rounds in the utterly vain hope that they might have some effect, had set off to converge in a flanking attack on the behemoth. Each Humvee also included a two-man RPG team with half a dozen "7s". Albert and Pickens had joined them. Perhaps they could blow the explosive armor somehow and weaken the hardened regular indestructible steel and ceramic sandwich with enough repeated blows and then-...perhaps the tank would trip on a rock and turn over.

There was no cover against the tank inside the compound that could stand up to much. In a frenzy, hundreds of sandbags were taken from the buildings and laid down in a large berm facing south. But Kingston saw immediately that it was hopeless. The tank would blast through sandbags ten-deep without even knowing it.

"They will bring in Apaches very soon, you can bet on that," Morelli said. "We need to get the fuck out of here."

"Go," Kingston said. "Get everyone out of here. Take the north side; it's just over a mile to the tree line and there's still enough cover."

Morelli stared at him.

"You're staying?" he asked.

"Ya," Kingston said. "I feel like I led 1200 men to their death here and I can't leave."

"You're nuts!" Morelli shouted. "These men knew what they were doing and you damn well know it."

But Kingston had walked away. He was heading for the tank. Viola was standing beside it, looking at the ruined front cog and the split track.

"He sure did wreck it," she said. "Too bad."

Morelli and Harding had begun to assemble the last of the Kingston Brigade. A quick explanation was all that was needed. A few soldiers declined and stayed behind, probably feeling like Kingston that they weren't prepared to give this ground up. Not after what had happened. But the majority started running for the north-slope tree line, praying they could make it before the Apaches or a Reaper spotted them.

The compound that had been filled with the noise of machines and men only a few moments ago was suddenly quiet. Beer cans and burning bodies, were the only reminder left.

Kingston pulled the hatch closed as Viola directed him and she started the beast. It rumbled to life instantly and coughed out a great, black, belch of smoke. Everything inside was working and she deftly set it up for battle, instructing Kingston on the subtleties of ammunition loading and casing extraction.

"I figure we're probably dead either way," Viola said.

Kingston nodded.

"That's pretty much it anyhow," he replied.

Vision up to two- or three-hundred yards was good enough. After that, the camera work was pretty hazy. All she could do was swing the turret through about 180 degrees of arc and try to catch the incoming A2 before it caught her. The cramped quarters was already heating up.

He spotted it first on the horizon, about five miles out. It was heading straight for them but it wasn't alone. Two black specks flanking the beast had closed in and the three vehicles were racing towards the compound. Viola cranked the gun, set the firing solution and let one off, though it was way out of range.

"Maybe they'll get the point," she said.

Kingston watched them getting closer.

"Doesn't look like it," he said.

The three vehicles grew steadily in the viewfinder and the closer they got, the less things made sense. At three miles, Viola let off another round, which plopped down directly in the attacker's path sending up a spiral of smoke and dust. That's when the two Humvees closed in front of the tank. The men in the Humvees were waving their arms and shouting. The three passed into gun range and Viola set the cannon for a point-blank shot when Kingston stayed her hand.

"Fuck me," he said quietly.

"Right now?" Viola answered.

Five minutes later the two Humvees rolled through the southern breach, followed by the big Abrams M1A2 with its barrel pointed due south. Viola and Kingston climbed down onto the ground as the Humvees stopped. Albert poked his head out the top of one and glared at them.

"Jesus H. Christ," he said. "What the hell are you trying to do?"

The tank hatch opened and a man still in uniform climbed out. His face was bruised and bloody and he almost fell on the ground when he landed. He was followed by two of the three men who had set out after the tank when it made a run for it during the battle.

An astonished Pat Kingston gawked at them.

They pushed their prisoner towards him.

The three trackers had followed the tank's easy trail for a hundred and thirty miles. They had been running for two days when the came upon the tank, hidden under a limestone outcrop. Smoke from a small cooking fire led them to a campsite where the four crewmen were sitting around eating and talking like a scout troop.

"We made a mistake going in," one of the men reported. "They were able to get into defensive positions and we had ourselves a standoff for a while. Then Rafe went in behind them and drew them off. Me and Charlie took out three of them except for this guy here."

"Rafe?" Kingston inquired.

Charlie shook his head.

"So we had him drive us back when these jokers showed up and started firing at us."

"Lucky I didn't use the RPG, Albert said."

"Ya, I guess," the man answered.

He was staring at the prisoner, a man who could be twenty-five or forty-five; it was hard to tell these days. His eyes were fried and he looked around the camp, speechless. He couldn't avoid the stacks of burning bodies. But where were the soldiers?

"Where is everybody?" Charlie asked.

"I didn't do any shooting back there," the prisoner interrupted, suddenly. "You know that."

"Ya, I know that," Charlie said.

The man looked fearfully at Charlie and tears formed in his eyes.

"I was just a grunt," he said. "I never laid a hand on anyone. I never fired a round out of basic."

"Ya," Charlie said, taking the Marine combat knife out of its sheath.

"God. Please," the man whined.

The bones of his skullcap split like dry pine as Charlie slammed the knife down into his brain. He held the man up on the end of his knife and watched the light exit his eyes. Then he jerked the blade out of the man's head and he crumpled to the ground.

"Thanks for the ride, by the way," he said.

Over the next hours, the troops under Morelli and Harding made their way back down to the compound and Charlie and his partner in crime discovered the full extent of the slaughter. For many, the reality of their losses was just setting in. They couldn't help feeling happy to be alive. They had made it. And not one among them had anything to doubt about his performance. But once that initial elation wears off and the awful truth of friends and comrades slaughtered sets in, a different kind of feeling takes over.

The tank driver may have been the last actual KIA of this campaign but he was not the last victim. They had been seventeen hundred strong a day ago. Now they were barely three hundred and they had wounded to care for. They had won the ground and lost much of the reason for winning it.

"I don't see it that way," Kingston told them at a gathering a few hours later.

"I know what happened here just like you do. I've heard the talk about what's worth it and what isn't. I'm not here to try and convince anybody of anything. But I can tell you that every one of those men and women would do it again knowing full well what would happen and most of you would too.

"This ain't over yet, not by a long shot. I expect most of us won't see the day it comes to an end. The country we grew up in is long gone. The ideas of it are gone with it. There's nothing left except staying alive and killing the bastards who did this until we can figure this shit out and maybe have some other kind of life. No man here has been pressed into service. If you are here it's because you choose to be. If you follow my orders it is only because you choose to. I know that and you know it. Anybody here is free to go off and do whatever the hell he thinks is right and no one will say a word.

"You are saying what's the point? If we all get killed, what's the point? Well for me, the point is simple. I want revenge. I want these bastards dead. All of 'em. Every man and woman among 'em. I want them hanging on lampposts from here to the coast and back. I want to smell their bodies burning. I want them eradicated from the face of the earth. That's all I want. Now maybe that's not the right attitude to have, but if you run with me, that's the attitude you better have. Because I haven't even started to kill these fucking sons of bitches yet and I intend to keep killing them until they are all gone or I am dead."

***

Chapter Six

They waited for a counter attack that never came.

The discussions about whether to run or stand continued, but in the meanwhile, they remained in place.

They had two tanks and the Humvees and tens of thousands of rounds. It would take a superior land force to uproot them. A concerted air attack with Apaches or even cruise missiles would destroy them; but it was becoming more evident every day that fuel shortages were slowly crippling the monster military machines that had ruled the planet for almost a century. The government had stockpiled fuel and oil and the means of turning oil into fuel. Millions upon millions of gallons were barreled or pooled or waiting in tankers for distribution. But without a constant replenishment of supply, there could never be enough for unlimited action. And now, the various divisions were much more concerned about the enemy on their flank – huge consortiums of lethality just like themselves eager to destroy them. The fly bites of this ragged crowd were of no importance.

As word of the annihilation of the Provost Legion spread among Free Forces units and independents, hundreds of hitherto pacifist submissives and a whole new group of winning-side opportunists turned up trying to join the Kingston group.

By common consent, none was admitted. They were told to go and form their own militia units using whatever materials they could find. Requests for ammunition, weapons and explosives from the captured Provost Legion arsenal were summarily dismissed. For a short time, The Kingston Brigade found themselves ensconced inside the wire compound they had liberated at tremendous cost, defending themselves against the imprecations of hundreds of former zombies, cowards and turn-coats camped on their doorstep. So far there had been no deaths, but it was certainly only a matter of time before someone was killed. Now that the bad guys were gone, these Johnny-come-latelies felt entitled to some of the spoils.

Kingston was adamant and the others agreed.

He used a bullhorn to persuade the crowd to disperse and find their own way, but to no avail. Finally he ordered them to move back at least two miles from the compound or face forced removal by Brigade troops who were in no mood to be trifled with. The vast majority took the hint but a hard core of about thirty men and women camped just outside the old kill zone and refused to budge. They wanted guns, ammunition and admission to the corps.

"No fucking way," Morelli said angrily. "Who the fuck do you think you are?"

The gaunt spokesman for the outsiders colored at Morelli's discharge but wasn't put off.

"We want to join you. We want-"

"I don't give a flying fuck what you want," Morelli spat.

"Then give us guns and ammunition and let us make our own unit."

"I wouldn't give you the sweat off my balls," Roland Harding replied quietly. The remark startled everyone who knew him as the quiet listener, the man who always remained calm and eschewed provocative language.

"We're not leaving," the man said.

"You are interfering with a Free Forces forward battle unit," Viola explained. "There will be nothing to say if you get in the way, understand?"

"I understand. I-

"I don't think you do," Kingston said. "We don't know you. We don't trust you. Not a single one of you will be admitted to this brigade. If you attempt to enter the compound, you will be shot. If something happens here; a helicopter strike, for example, or a counter attack of some sort, we will consider you to be part of the enemy forces and you will all be shot."

Kingston's quiet, earnest tone seemed to be cutting through to the man.

He looked from one to the other, finally resting his eyes back on Viola Ramsey.

"There are seven women out there," he ventured.

Viola studied him for a moment, a small smile on her lips.

"If you are not at least two miles back from this encampment with the rest of your friends within two hours, I will lead a squad out to escort you there; if you resist I will personally shoot every single one of you. Is that clear?"

The man knew he had hit the limit and closed his mouth.

"Come on, Viola said, quietly. "I'll take you to the gate."

Albert watched the collection of lamentable fools trudging across the plain, stumbling over rocks and arguing with the air. They were nothing to him, but he felt a kind of pity. For whatever reason, they lacked the instinct for self-preservation. The best they could do was accrete other misfits like themselves into a clump, perhaps believing somehow that their combined gravity would give them spirit or power.

This new world had no room for those who needed looking after. And watching them he realized how ripe for the picking they were. Rejected here, they might very well turn up at the front door of a government unit and offer themselves for service. In exchange for some few crumbs and an identity, they would soon transmogrify into the next legion of automatons doing the bidding of some maniac in a stuffed chair. They wanted. They wanted everything. They wanted so badly it hurt. They wanted so badly they would take anything to get rid of that feeling of wanting.

"I know what you're thinking," Pickens said.

Albert hadn't heard him come across the gravel and he started, but didn't turn around.

"Ya? What's that?"

"We should get them back in here, offer them something just to keep them from joining the other side."

"Well, you're wrong about that," Albert replied. "I was thinking we aught to just kill them all and forget about it."

He left Pickens at the wire and started back towards the mess.

A patrol had shot a huge bull wandering loose in the north wooded area and pots of fresh, stewed meat simmered on a dozen wood fires. The smell drifted around the compound and men showed up periodically to look in the pots and make sure they weren't dreaming. The animal's hide was stretched out on the fence and its head was mounted on a gatepost.

The last bodies had been collected and interred and most graves were unmarked except for a limestone rock or a rough cross. The final count was thirteen hundred and twenty four KIA or dead from wounds; seventy five permanently crippled and out of commission and three hundred and fifty nine active duty remaining.

When Albert had finally gone to inspect the sixty seven corpses laid out in reasonably straight lines in the southeast corner of the camp, he did not expect to feel guilt or grief. The battle continued to flash in his mind and he saw them fall repeatedly. It was when he discovered Glen Favor's body among the dead that he felt a jolt. His gut tightened and pain shot across his chest. One of Favor's arms was gone and his left side was scorched black. Grenade or mortar. Maybe one of Albert's. Maybe not...

He called the detail over and two men arrived, their eyes burning from the smoke and stench of the pyres.

"He's one of ours," he said.

They nodded and called over another crew who rolled Favor into a stretcher and headed out to the burial site.

"Are you positive?" Pickens asked him that evening.

"Ya," Albert said.

"I guess he-"

"Don't say it," Albert interrupted him.

"I will say it," Pickens insisted. "He never expected to come out of this. I don't think he wanted to. He had too much on his conscience."

The next meeting among the commanders, Albert mentioned what had happened to Favor and the others accepted the news as one more piece of the tragic puzzle they had been assembling.

Kingston was the nominal head of the army and most decisions were run by him as a matter of course. But it wasn't a traditional military structure and he had no more authority than any man in the field. So far this was an army of citizens serving by choice. But at the same time, it was clear that leadership was necessary to keep some form of cohesion. Their power – their only power – resided in combined effort. Three hundred individuals cannot accomplish much. Three hundred individuals acting in concert at least had some possibility of success.

Kingston seemed strangely formal this particular evening and he put everyone on edge.

"I have something to say," he began and then stopped, as if he'd lost his way. No one spoke.

"I guess I have hit my limit," he said finally. "I never wanted this responsibility and now I know why."

"This wasn't anybody's fault," Morelli interrupted but Kingston shook his head.

"I know that. I don't know what else we could have done. I wish I – we – hadn't lost so many men. I never imagined..."

No one met his gaze.

"The thing is, I can't be the leader here anymore. Not after that. I don't have it in me but that isn't the whole problem. I realized after I saw that tank coming in on us that I made the wrong decision."

"What the hell-?"

"Let me finish, Vince. If that had been a real attack and we had stayed put, we'd all be dead for nothing. The right decision was to abandon the compound and run for cover. I can't take the chance that I'll fuck up like that again."

Viola nodded slightly. The others were expressionless.

"You were right Vince. You and Roland and Viola, you all made the right decision for three hundred and fifty other people. Me, I didn't act in their best interest."

"I stayed too, remember?" Viola piped up.

"I know that. And I regret it. I might have got you killed too, which would be a pretty big loss to this outfit. I don't think we got anyone else who knows as much about this stuff as you."

"Everybody out there trusts you," Morelli protested.

"They trust you, Vince. They trust all of us. That's the problem. I'm not the right guy anymore."

Everyone realized that persuasion was pointless. If Pat Kingston doubted himself, he was finished. He had to have a belief in his own authority. He had to believe he was right even when he was wrong because the only judge that matters is the last one. Was it a peculiarity of mankind or part of the genome of life itself? The elephant matriarch never questions her own authority; but, nor does she ever act out of personal ambition. The Alpha chimpanzee may be manipulative and cunning rather than physically powerful, but a crude democracy maintains his status. Only men put their own interests ahead of their fellows'.

No one was much surprised when Roland Harding assumed command. Viola didn't want it and Morelli was one to complete a task no matter what, but that task and only that task. Harding, in true Platonic fashion, neither sought nor avoided power but accepted duty as it was presented to him.

Over the coming weeks runners began to show up at the gates of the compound, which had been renamed again at Kingston's request. It was now called Fort Glen Favor. Someone asked if naming a fort after a traitor – even a 'good' traitor - was such a 'good' idea. Albert put him straight and the issue did not resurface.

They learned that tensions among various government agencies and military units had reached the point where shots had been fired. The Indianapolis regiments had been under siege by Michigan volunteers who formed a temporary alliance with a Chicago-area Brigade that had determined it was going to rule the Midwest. What the Michigan volunteers thought would happen to them after this situation was resolved, was never made clear. They had either bought a lie, or were pretending to until the moment arrived when they would turn on their newfound friends.

The question of who would resort to nuclear weapons first was answered in late September when Indianapolis forces deployed an upgraded mobile "Atomic Alice" type 280 mm cannon that could fire a 15 kiloton shell about 20 miles. Long believed to be extinct, the nuclear artillery shell had in fact undergone numerous transformations over the years and was still a significant element of the U.S. Army arsenal; so much for a ban on tactical weapons.

It is not clear what motivated the attack but some theorized a Masada complex deep within the corps. Indianapolis had fended off the larger Chicago group successfully, but severe fuel shortages had put them in a panic. A clot of about four hundred mixed regular and militia had been discovered, almost by accident and their position marked. To Indianapolis it seemed clear enough. They were nothing less than an advance unit and a full bore attack was on the way. So the great gun, hauled by two tractor-trailers – one front and one back – was set up in an abandoned grain field.

The shell airburst at two hundred and ninety feet about 3 A.M., it's shockwave felt ten miles away. The flattening, crimson pulse of the explosion lit the sky and incinerated everything in a half- mile radius of the blast. The fireball rose four hundred feet and lit the night for fifteen seconds. Every living thing within a one-and-a-half mile

202

radius died immediately or within two days from radiation poisoning. Fires raged two-and-half miles from the detonation.

Not to be outdone, the Chicago area group launched a single Pershing missile (also allegedly extinct) with a 200-kiloton payload that exploded over the Indianapolis Army Base, annihilating the Regiment and everything for a radius of a-mile-and-a-half. That explosion could be felt as far south as Fort Glen Favor and the spreading, flattening, roil of neutron radiation colored the sky for a week afterwards. Chicago conveniently failed to inform its militia allies about the pending strike and had them in a spearhead position three quarters of a mile away. They were vaporized along with everything else. The majority of the buildings in the city of Indianapolis, fourteen miles away were destroyed and radiation trickled down on an area of more than a thousand square miles.

That was the beginning.

Kingston agreed to attend the last general command meeting, which had been called the evening after the Indianapolis strike. Albert was asked to join them and by the time Pickens finally convinced him to come along, the conversation was well along.

Viola was the most knowledgeable among them and held the floor for a long time.

"What I am saying is this: It doesn't matter now if we go or stay," she explained. "If they go at each other for even a few days, there will be more problems than protecting a few thousand gallons of fuel."

"So it's your view that we disband?" Morelli said.

"It appears to be out of our league at this point," Harding said.

"There's no reason to stay," Viola said. "You can't keep that tank running for a week. It will break down before you can use it again, is my guess. You can't fix anything, you can't build anything and you can't defend yourself against air attack from nuclear weapons."

"Where the hell is everybody supposed to go?" Morelli demanded. "We just going to turn them out: Goodbye, have a nice life?"

"They can do whatever the hell they want," Kingston said. "That's the whole point,."

"Ya, bull shit," Morelli spat. "These guys need someone to tell 'em what to do and you fucking well know it."

"Well it's not going to be me," Kingston said.

"Ya, we know that," Morelli answered. "You've made that very clear."

The heavy silence hung in the air for a moment.

"You have the same rights as everybody else, Vince," Albert said reasonably. "If you want to stay and look after things, that's your choice. My opinion, for what it's worth is that this is over. We got what we wanted, now let's get out."

"Got what we wanted?" Morelli demanded incredulously. "What the fuck is that supposed to mean?"

"It means they're at each others' throats. It means we stand back and let them kill each other off. We let them do whatever the fuck they want and then we deal with what's left over."

The decision came easier than they had hoped.

The first great rumblings began the next evening. The earth seemed to tremble, the first whispers before a big quake but rather than manifest itself in a monumental concussion, it would fade and then begin again. It was almost a gentle shake as the 200- and 300-kiloton missiles were lobbed across the country. The spiraling, radioactive smoke tumbled and spread. Huge prolonged flashes of brilliant white light exploded the night, lifting the sky it seemed. The nights glowed; the days were caught in eclipse. Then came the one- and two-megaton deliveries. Stealth bombers were invisible to radar but not to the human eye at low levels and they hurled like shurikens across the sky, peeling away after their lethal larvae dropped from the belly. The lumbering rant of the sub-sonic B52 Stratofortress vibrated the air and the multiple streaks of its cruise missiles rent the sky. And then the huge ICBMs with MIRV warheads crashed back into the atmosphere and peeled off towards their respective targets and the sky pulsed crimson again. And then came the 3-and 4-megaton Trident missiles, arching beautifully out of the atmosphere to turn and begin the whirling dive back to earth along their perfect ballistic trajectory. A thousand feet above dear mother earth they burst in apparent silence. The light seared the eyes; the firestorm raged across miles of prairie and delivered whole mountains back to the sea. The screaming winds ripped the dead from their graves and the silent, sparkling, radioactive confetti, floated gently to the ground.

*

204

It was about twelve noon, yet the sky was dark, the sun almost obliterated by the floating ash. It felt cold, even for September.

It was a fifty-five mile walk back to his shelter. Two days if he was lucky.

Albert felt lucky.

***

Part Three

And the kings of the earth, and the great men, and the rich men, and the chief captains, and the mighty men, and every bondman, and every freeman, hid themselves in the dens and in the rocks of the mountains...

Revelations, 6:15

Chapter One

By his own rough calculations, it had been five years since Albert had spoken to another person. This in itself was not as much of a hardship for him as it might have been for some others. Reclusive by nature and certainly by habit, he had gone long stretches without indulging in more than the few perfunctory phrases necessary to commercial transactions. But he realized now that while he had not participated in the incessant murmur all around, he had been aware of it. He had heard other voices. He had heard other ideas. He had heard laughter and shouting. He had heard the banal monotony of idiot news broadcasters. He had occasionally watched a film, wherein people conversed. He had never been immersed in so much silence before. And silent it had been.

Only occasionally the tweet of a bird; dead, leafless trees might sing if the wind was hard enough but they could no longer whisper. Padded feet did not grace the earth except rarely and then vanished in a pheromone of dread. The sky was perpetually gray or brown and sunlight filtered through only with much effort. Occasionally the wind would clear a hole in the leaden weal and the bluest sky would shine through and sometimes even the sun! He would go and stand under it, close his eyes and lift his face to that brilliant patch and then it would just as quickly slam shut as if the warden had discovered an open cell door.

Five years it had been like that. Five years, during which he had not strayed more than two miles from his dwelling, the expanded cavern he had discovered by accident years before. He had moved everything he possessed from an underground bunker created before the

Catastrophe on his original homestead to this new, invulnerable hideout deep in the bowels of the earth. Here he would start again.

A honeycomb of karst cave formations undershot hundreds of square miles of southern Indiana and continued along the veins of limestone right into Missouri and beyond. Small entrances and deep protected ledges inhabited by forest creatures were many. Sinkholes often exposed the presence of hollowed out dens lined with calcium carbonate spikes or smoothed over with a salty caramel. But huge, echoing caverns like the one he had discovered with a perfect, hidden entrance, a constant water supply and access to even more empty spaces through a tentacle of corridors, was rare enough.

It took him fifty trips with travois to lug the food, the books, and the numerous materials that he had collected for his own comfort, across the abandoned farm fields and overgrown forests to this place. He had spent months stocking it with dried meat and preserved foods and MREs. He had transported his entire arsenal, including 7000 rounds of heavy ammunition and laid it all out carefully on shelves above the cool, damp rock. He had fashioned a hundred arrows for the recurve bow and could hit a target at 20 yards with respectable consistency. The hides of many deer and raccoon and coyote testified to his prowess. In fact, he had secured for himself a refuge few could imagine and even fewer had seen or ever would. His larder full, his powder, dry, his roof impregnable, he once again expected to wait out in peaceful solitude the days of fear and famine that had taken over the earth.

At destruction and famine you shall laugh: neither shall you be afraid of the beasts of the earth. [10]

And then came the grand battle plans of American Free Forces and he had joined them in the slaughter that unfolded and left eighty percent of their soldiers dead in exchange for control of a compound they almost immediately abandoned. Within days of their worthless victory, the cannibalistic destruction among government units and organizations mooted anything and everything they might have accomplished.

Every dream now ended with the flattening red pulse of the epistle of Bhagavad Gita. [11]

In the first few days after the nuclear battles ended, the consequences appeared to be localized. Each device described a concentrated zone of total annihilation with destruction in succeeding radii varying inversely with the distance. The firestorms might cause third degree burns at thousand yards and second degree burns at two thousand yards and blisters at two miles and so on. But within weeks, the sky turned gray and then brown and swooned as the uplifted ash and smoke from ten thousand volcano eruption equivalents, swole the lower atmosphere into a malignant canker.

That first winter, temperatures dropped to -40 degrees for three consecutive weeks; this in a land that had not seen a full winter's snow in seven years. Recapitulating Arctic Equinox, the thick, granular cloud cover reduced the days to a melancholy blue twilight and the nights to a blind darkness without a star-point to break the relief. The cloud-cover broke for a few weeks in spring and then closed up again. The forests below withered and the animal life vanished. The entire summer was bathed in gloom as fires burst into being, taking with them what the bombs had missed.

The second winter, the clouds thinned and a faint sun filtering through a haze of flashing particles and swirling dust, smiled weakly on those below. But this ended abruptly the following spring when a tumescent mass settled over the entire Midwest and did not budge for the next twelve months. The third winter was calm and blue skies returned for the better part of January. But the blanket crept in slowly once again and soon the earth was bathed in semi-darkness, the blazing forest fires shining through the haze and fog of ash. Even so, with each passing year, the cloud-cover thinned and dispersed more and more until the fifth winter when it was replaced by a semblance of vapor cloud as men recalled clouds, that precipitated the first full rains since the war. The rains began in late February and fell unceasingly for 60 days and nights, longer even than the trials of Noah.

The rivers crested, broke and rose ever higher. The old Emit, which was a trough about four-feet deep and a quarter mile wide disappeared in its lower plains under lakes sixteen feet deep that festered for months. The raceway below his cavern flowed and overflowed and water rushed down the hallway and splashed onto the floor where it climbed to two feet before it began to seep away. When it left, the cavern had been scoured.

Even then, the rains abated and the full sun blazing down through a new atmosphere, the land below was desert. Where forests had covered the round shoulders of rolling countryside for thousands of square miles, there now stood a stripped and skeletal province of burned-black columns, unvisited and unremembering of its own past.

So now it is late spring, the first spring in half a decade and the water no longer falls from the sky; instead it pools in a salmagundi of primeval mash home to creatures seen - and not seen before. Some are so small they are invisible. Some are large enough to hold in the hand where they wiggle and squirm, spitting out their proud new venom before plunging back into the evil drench. Soon they would make themselves known.

Albert felt the sun, weak and without confidence it seemed, but there, nonetheless. It pressed against his face. It warmed his eyelids.

He had not fired a weapon in several years, there having been no need for it. In the entire time of the earth's convalescence, he had taken only four deer, all by arrow. Two had been so malnourished as to be worthless. It had been mercy killing. Of the others, one was a 250-pound buck with strangely configured antlers he'd taken the third year. The rack stood on a stone mantle with the skullcap still attached. It would have been a 30-point buck by the old standards, a prize under just about any conditions. The tangle of antlers stemmed three inches in diameter from the base and intertwined and wrapped around each other and then turned outward again. As he dressed the animal, he discovered a second set of antlers had started to grow from the base of the skull.

The animal could just be a genetic freak, like a two-headed calf or Siamese twins. Or it could be something else, something much more ominous. There was no way to tell. The blood smelled and tasted normal. The gut was filled with some unusual material, including small pieces of wood and some undigested insect larvae. Perhaps the larvae had developed once he had eaten their host. He pulled out each organ and examined it closely, unable to discover anything unusual. The liver was a rich dark purple. The heart looked normal. If the animal had been contaminated by radioactivity, surely there would be some further indication. The meat smelled right. He sliced out the back straps and left the carcass hanging while he cooked them. Nothing unusual; nothing except a second set of antlers growing out of the back of the buck's enormous head.

Carefully stripped, the animal yielded almost 100 pounds of meat. Then there was the liver, the heart…the brains if he chose. If he didn't eat the meat, his supplies could run out before he had another opportunity. If he did, maybe he'd start glowing in the dark. In the end he decided it didn't matter.

210

The rifle felt heavy in his hands and he looked at it strangely, as if it were an unfamiliar device. He had spent an hour cleaning it and the bolt came back smooth and silent and when he slammed the shell into the throat of the barrel, it clicked and locked with a synchronous precision. There were four more rounds in the integrated box magazine and he had a pocketful in case he needed them. But it had occurred to him that maybe he was the last man on earth.

Janet Fillmore still wouldn't let you feel her tits.

The sound of his own laughter startled him. It ran between the charred trees and seemed to keep going until it faded. It didn't hit a wall and drop like a voice in the woods.

In spite of the scorching, the forest floor was in fact trying to come back. Tiny shoots sprung up around rocks and the remains of burned logs. He bent down and studied what appeared to be the track of a squirrel. The front feet were farther apart and displayed five toes or claws and the small mons. The hind feet were close together, but there was something wrong. At first he thought the far left appendage of the right foot had been inadvertently placed so that it appeared to be a fifth digit on the animal's left foot. But it wasn't; the squirrel, or whatever it was, had five digits on its rear feet.

He stood up and looked slowly around. There was nothing to indicate another living thing was anywhere near. Even the breeze had died.

After an hour of careful walking, he entered ground he hadn't seen for years. He did not come across another track but there was a decided increase in the bird population. He saw a full flight of what appeared to be starlings circling in a huge funnel to the south.

In another hour, he began to come across more growth. What had been a square mile of wheat in other times was a barren, static sea of dirt and ash except for patches, some the size of a football field that were producing shoots. Then he caught a column of smoke in the distance; not the expanding hammerhead of a forest fire but a single plume indicating a controlled burn of some sort. Perhaps even a cooking fire. He headed directly towards it and evidence of life began to appear everywhere in the form of death.

He came across skeletons. They were recent and many still had bits of flesh or fur attached, though they had been essentially stripped clean. The long bones were cracked open and the marrow sucked out. It was clearly evidence of a dog kill but the victims here were not just other dogs as was typical of wild packs. One heap of large bones was from a horse, probably a Belgian by the size of it. Somehow the beast had survived long enough to be killed and eaten by this canine gang.

Whatever had happened, the great nuclear holocaust that had been predicted and feared for 70 years had come and gone without destroying everything. Something had survived. Just like Albert had survived, others had survived. The column of smoke drew him onward.

He would find over time, as the remnants of human civilization began to emerge from shelter that even the nihilistic psychopaths in the old government had realized what they were doing and checked themselves before the last irrevocable act.

Over a few weeks the exchanges had stopped. This did not happen before such havoc as had never been seen was wreaked upon the earth. And in the subsequent years during which the ash had circulated and the lively little particles had settled, more died than had perished in the initial exchanges.

But not everyone and not everything was gone.

He came across trees that looked sick; their leaves curled as if infested with aphids and the chlorophyll anemic; bark was peeling; but the stanchions were alive. Their cells were multiplying. Undergrowth was starting to show, maybe for the first time in several years. The ferns were unraveling and some of the berry bushes were blooming.

Then he saw that the Emit River had changed course and had isolated a large section of farmland in a huge oxbow comprising thousands of acres. The "new" river had followed the path of a tectonic shift of some kind and created what was for all intents and purposes an island (excepting a thin land bridge at the north end). The river was almost a half-mile across in places and of unknown depth.

Further on, he came across footpaths used by both man and beast, and there it was.

A small human, probably a woman by the size of her footprint, was leading a horse. It was unshod. He bent down and studied the dirt for a while. The woman had a broken leg or some similar problem. She limped. The right footprints were all deeper and her gait was off. She led the horse with her left arm. She was probably left-handed. A man leads with his weak arm and keeps his gun hand free; a woman leads with her strong arm, to keep control.

She had stopped and mounted at a point where the trail started to climb and here he noticed that dogs had picked her up. The horse had bolted when they cleared the woods and was racing across the open ground.

Albert came to the edge of the woods and saw the distant bobbing of the rider. She was heading straight for the smoke. He heard the baying of dogs, but it was a call to arms, not a dinner bell. He lost the actual trail for a spell in the hard-packed earth but it was clear in which direction she'd gone.

There was a half-hour of silence after she disappeared over a rim, but he continued to follow the trail, fresh now with dog tracks and the galloping horse.

The first shot raced back across the open field and passed overhead. Four or five more followed in quick succession. There was nothing panicky in the retorts. They seemed to be considered, deliberate as if the shooter was counting between pulls of the trigger.

He came upon the first dead dog about a mile on. It was a skinny mongrel with orange hair. Another hundred yards and he found three more, each shot cleanly in the chest or head with a small caliber round; 5.56 probably, considering the crack from the shot. It had to have been a significant cartridge. Whoever she was, she knew how to shoot.

He could smell the smoke from her fire, now and the distinct odor of cooking meat.

She had parked herself in a grotto up against a limestone wall, the horse hobbled and grazing on the few leaves it could find and the woman turning a spit with a rodent of some kind stretched out almost the full length.

He watched her for a while until she stood up and disappeared into the woods - a little too casually.

He shifted position and tucked himself into a thatch of nettles that were leafless but so dense that they acted as camouflage. It didn't take long for her to break a twig coming back on his putative flank and he steadied his breathing and fell into an almost trance-like stillness. She brushed against something nearby and he held his breath. A few more minutes passed and she came into view, no more than ten feet from him. She poked around where he'd originally spied her and then crouched down to check the ground. Her eyes started to follow the scratchings of some kind of trail. When she looked up, she saw the barrel pointing out of the hedge.

Albert opened his mouth to speak but nothing emerged.

She was frozen in a crouch, staring at him as he pushed his way clear of the spikes and stood up in front of her.

He opened his mouth again and a kind of scratch came out.

She rose slowly and he shook his head, indicating the AR15.

"Down," he finally managed to croak.

"Better shoot," she said, holding her rifle pointed straight at him.

Albert watched her carefully and then lowered his own weapon and put the safety on.

"Talk," he said.

Albert was sitting against the rock wall and she was sitting opposite him. Neither had relinquished any weapons. One or the other of them should have been dead by now, and both appreciated it. Finally, he took the 30.06 and ejected all the rounds. He pulled the bolt and put everything in his pocket.

"What's the matter with your voice?" she asked. "You sick?"

Albert coughed out a single, hoarse laugh.

"No," he said. He cleared his throat loudly and tried again. "I haven't spoke to nobody in...I don't know...years...five years..."

She looked directly at him, her eyes cool and her hand still firmly on the trigger of the AR. She *was* left-handed.

"Where have you been, in a cave somewhere?" she said.

He indicated his water jug and she indicated he could drink some. He indicated the meat on the spit and she indicated he could take some of that.

He went to the fire and carefully sliced off a strip of roasting-

"Cat," she replied, sucking on a bone and throwing it back into the flames.

"I ain't had to eat a cat, so far," he said.

"Well, you just haven't been hungry enough," she said, wiping her hands on her pants.

He shrugged.

"Ain't et a human bean, neither," he said.

"Well, at least that's something we agree on," she answered. The AR was still across her lap, though she had stopped pointing it at him a while ago.

"What were you following me for?" she demanded. "Careful how you answer now."

Albert looked at the horse grazing a hundred feet away. He wanted to go and see the horse, to smell it and feel its heavy warmth under the skin but he imagined she'd probably kill him just for suggesting it. He knew he would in her place. A horse right now had a value that probably could not be exaggerated.

"I just started following your tracks," he said. "What happened to your leg?"

"My leg?" she spluttered. "What's wrong with my leg?"

"I don't know. I'm asking."

"How the hell-?"

They looked at each other over the fire for a moment.

"Nobody can track like that anymore," she said. "Who are you?"

"Nobody," he answered.

He laughed and she couldn't help it and joined in. She was afraid to relax but she wanted to. He had shown good faith so far. But then so had many others.

"Suppose I aks you a question or two now?" he suggested after a while. His voice was back and he had even started to remember some basic language skills.

"Such as...?"

"Who are you and where did you come from?"

She stared at him and looked away. Finally she took off the floppy hat she'd worn since they'd met and lay it on the ground beside her. Her hair was very dark and stringy and she had chopped the bangs out of her eyes with a knife at some point.

"I don't know," she said. "I don't think I'm going to answer any of your questions. I haven't killed you and you haven't killed me, but that doesn't make us friends."

The evening finally bloomed around them and the orange flames of the fire reflected off the wall behind him and shone against her face.

"I suppose you think you're going to stay here tonight," she said.

"I'll leave," he replied. "I ain't got far to go, anyways."

She studied him again and he could see her contemplating the coals.

"You are sure agreeable," she admitted.

"Well, I ain't looking for a fight or anything else for that matter. I guess I can't blame you for being skittish but you don't have to worry about me."

"Cuz you say so."

"That is all I can do," he said. "I'm going to get up now and leave and I don't want you following me to see if I'm back-tracking you or anything. You got my word. I'll know it if you do, so just stay put and I'll be on my way. And thanks for the cat."

"Valerie is my name," she said.

It stayed him and he fell back against the wall.

"Albert," he replied.

She looked at him for a long time, deciding whether to continue the conversation. Her instincts told her to shoot him where he sat and end the drama.

"You can stay a while if you want, I guess," she said.

"Well, I didn't want to travel back in the dark if I could avoid it," he admitted.

"Back to where? I've been all over around here and other than a few stragglers, I haven't seen anybody with an address."

"Well I've got a place...not far."

"Where you been holed up for five years?"

"That's right."

She tried to penetrate the darkness settling over them but all she could see was the point where the firelight touched his pupils and vice versa.

"What kind of place is it?"

He grinned but he couldn't tell if she saw.

"It's a big old cave," he said.

Her laughter was clear but it was tinted with desperation.

"Five years?" she said. "Ever since the war, the big war."

He poked the fire with a stick.

"What have you been doing?" he said.

"Just wandering around, mostly," she replied. "I started out in Charleston and just kept walking. I figure I must be somewhere in Missouri by now."

"Indiana, last time I looked."

"Well, Indiana then," she said. "It's pretty well all the same now, anyways."

"I wouldn't know," he said. "I haven't been outside of Indiana in about 20 years except to pick up a few things in Illinois."

"You haven't missed much," she said.

"I expect not."

216

"If you want to get going, you just leave," she said. "I won't follow you."

"Okay," he said, but didn't move.

After a few minutes she glared at him.

"What do you think's going to happen if you stay?" she said.

"I really don't know," he answered.

"What have you been doing for five years?" she asked.

"Reading, mostly," he said. "I have quite a library under the circumstances."

Valerie looked skeptically at him and snorted.

"Right," she said.

"Well," he said, standing up. "I think I will be going now."

She watched him gather his gun and pack and get ready for a trip back.

"Why don't you just relax," she said, awkwardly, laying the AR on the ground.

"I feel pretty relaxed as it is," he said.

"Well, then."

"Well what?"

"I-"

"You mean?-"

"It's up to you."

He laid everything back down on the dirt and walked around the fire to her side.

She didn't look at him. She was shaking - with fear - he surmised and maybe cold. It was cooling off quickly.

"You been raped, is that it?"

"Every living woman on this planet has been raped," she said.

"Well, I ain't no rapist," he replied. "I sure would like to feel a woman in my arms again but I ain't going to force anybody to do anything. That ain't my way."

"I figured that out," she said, turning towards him as he sat down beside her.

"You want to start just by holding hands?" he offered.

***

Chapter Two

Dawn was cold and gray but it was a normal cloud cover and blue sky and occasionally a slash of yellow sunlight broke through. They had remained in a kind of formal embrace all night, wrapped in the tattered blankets she carried, having fallen asleep after a few brief kisses. He could feel her bones under the clothing. The horse stood nearby, head drooping in discouragement. His ribs showed too.

They disengaged and he began to gather firewood. It was difficult to come by, most of the scattered limbs already burnt. But after half-an-hour of careful husbandry the flames leapt and caressed the old iron pot and water bubbled.

"I only got the one cup," she said, as she twisted bits of bark and some dried flower heads into a blue porcelain mug.

"How have you managed to keep that thing from breaking?" he asked.

"I don't know," she said. "I ask myself that every time I take it out."

"Eye of newt?" he asked, watching her work.

"I wish. This is just something I made up. It's not good for you or anything like that," she explained, cheerfully. "It's just for taste."

He wandered over to the horse. The big gelding, a Belgian/Quarter cross, was completely indifferent to his approach. He had expected at least some interest if not alarm, but the animal was too malnourished to give a damn. He rubbed his nose and blew gently into the horse's nostrils but it didn't budge.

"He's about had it," Valerie said. "I can't find anything for him to eat, not for a long time now. I figure I'll just have to eat him, instead."

"How long have you had him?"

"We did fine for more than a year. I could always find some leaves or something and a few times we even found a barn with some hay still in it. But the last few weeks..." she shook her head.

"I saw some pretty good pasture back towards my place," he said.

This provoked a palpable silence from her and he let it stand. The next move was hers.

"Okay."

In the hours since she'd shot them, the dog carcasses had been stripped clean. They passed the place where she'd got three of them and found two heads, three tails and some bloody hair.

"Where did you learn to shoot like that?" he asked her.

He was carrying the bulk of the horse's load himself while she led the sad beast on a halter without the bit. He followed them, listlessly, occasionally sighing or blowing in a cycle of despair and indifference.

"I figured it out pretty quickly once everything went to hell," she said. "The guy I was with had the gun and he died with the flu. After that it was pretty much use it or...you know..."

"Have you been wandering since then?"

"Pretty much. Nine or ten years now, I guess."

"How old are you?"

"How old do I look? Be careful now, I still got this rifle."

"I don't even know," he said. "We'll have to scrape some of the trail off you first to see."

She glared at him and then laughed lightly.

"You don't look so shit hot, yourself."

"Oh, I didn't say anything about how you look," he told her. "I don't think I have ever seen a more beautiful human being in my entire life."

As they crossed into the old wheat field, the horse suddenly raised his head and his ears twitched. The grazing was not two inches high yet, but the animal bent down and began tearing it up as fast as he could chew it and swallow. They hobbled him and lay the tack out on a rock while he wandered over about ten acres, yanking every green blade he came across. Unlike a cow, which can fill up and then re-digest for hours on end, a horse has to keep eating. He eats his fill, waits for it to digest and then he does it again. They spent the rest of the daylight hours following him around while he was sated for the first time in weeks. His spirit returned almost as soon as he finished his first course and he twitched his ears and nickered and stared at them when they came close. He was more aware of Albert now but he did not shy away. Valerie stroked his neck and he shrugged her off and returned to ripping up the sweet shoots.

At dusk they started again, the horse alert for the first time and its eyes receding back into its head. It would take a week of treatment to return him to health but there was more than enough pasture right here to do that.

They walked mostly in silence, the horse plodding obediently behind. They passed through the scorched pickets until moonrise and then Albert stopped and lay down the tack.

"You wait here," he said, quietly. "I'll be right back."

He was gone half-an-hour and when he returned, she was sitting where he'd left her, still holding the horse's lead with one hand and her rifle with the other.

"It looks okay," he said. "No way to get the critter in, though."

She shook her head slowly.

"I'm not leaving him," she said. "He's never left me."

The floor of the hallway leading into the cave was five feet off the ground. They needed a ramp.

"Come morning we could probably rig something up," he said.

"We'll be right here," she informed him. "If I leave him out here unprotected and some-"

"I get it."

He made several trips and brought out dry firewood and food and she gawked in amazement as he poured a few ounces of a clear fluid into a glass and told her to be careful.

The first taste made her cough violently and she spit it out.

"I told you to be careful," he said.

"What the heck is it?"

"It's my own special triple distilled, charcoal filtered creamed corn and niblet sour mash whiskey."

She tried again and managed to get a few drops down without retching.

"Keep going. After a while it will taste fine."

The horse snorted impatiently and scanned the surface of the wash with his nose looking for a blade of grass.

"He's still hungry," she said.

"Well, it's a full moon. It's about an hour back to the fields if you want."

She was tired and didn't want to get up. She had the look; her eyes were shiny and seemed like cracked glass. When she looked at you, she looked through you to somewhere else."

"Come with me to the Kasbah, honey."

He hoisted her to her feet and she teetered a bit before they started walking.

"I can't..."

When they got to the cave entrance she seemed to be sleepwalking. He tied the horse to a stump and then helped her up into the hallway. She was past resistance and followed him without complaint.

The fire he'd set a while ago was glowing and the walls of the cave reflected the soft light and caught in the carbonate straws. She was too tired to comment but her eyes took it in.

He led her to his cot and laid her down in it.

"I'm going to take him out for a late night snack," Albert said. "I'll see you in the morning."

She fought sleep while he pulled a few skins over her and then just seemed to give up and closed her eyes.

Albert unhitched Brutus, as she called him and climbed on bareback. The horse nickered and stomped at the unfamiliar weight and handling but in a few moments, Albert had him calm and they were retracing their path back to the fields. The animal seemed to sense what was happening and Albert had to restrain him from trotting off. The ground was too rugged for a shoeless animal and neither of them was familiar with this landscape to run it at night. The moonlight helped but it could create illusions just like the sun on a prairie.

Once they got to the old wheat field, the horse fought to get loose and it was all he could do to get the hobbles on his rear legs. In a few minutes he could hear the grass tearing as the hungry beast tucked in.

Albert found a comfortable place against a berm and lay back. He took out the flask of whiskey and his .45 and relaxed while the horse ate. Brutus just topped 17 hands and he was broad enough to look bigger than he was. Every few minutes he glanced over at Albert, twitched his ears and then went back to eating.

Albert took a long draught of the flask and then looked at it. The liquor burned all the way down and he closed his eyes. Then he took another gulp and experienced the rushing of his blood in his ears.

Even that was too much, he realized and he put the flask away.

A coyote yelped and Brutus looked around. Albert flicked the safety off the pistol.

He tried to imagine a way to keep a horse in the cave. A ramp of some sort would get him into the corridor and you could lead him around the walkway but how do you live with a fifteen hundred pound horse in the house?

"Nothing shits as much as a horse," he said out loud.

Brutus glanced at him.

"Ya, you. I'm talking about you," he said.

What if she decided to leave because the horse couldn't live in the house with them?

Me or the horse. Ya, right. Try that one out. Tell me how it went.

Brutus coughed loudly a few times and Albert stood up. He had over-eaten and he needed water.

He led him back towards the cave by a different route that took them up against a small exposed section of the Emit. Moonlight lay across it and the reflection of trees was indistinguishable from the real thing. Brutus lowered his head and began to suck the water. They both seemed to be caught in a moment when something startled the animal and he neighed ferociously and jerked back. It was all Albert could do to hold him from running off and he felt his shoulder nearly jump from the socket.

"Whoa...whoa..." he tried to soothe the animal but he was adamant and pulled Albert away from the stream.

"What the fuck?" Albert asked him, pulling the big head close with the harness.

Brutus jerked his head a few times to get away but finally gave up.

Albert mounted him carefully and they headed back to the cave with dawn an hour away. The sky was lightening and the air had suddenly cooled.

As they approached the wash, Brutus perked up again as if he knew he was going to see Valerie. Albert gave him a little slack and he trotted along the gravel bed.

At the entrance, he tied him up again and went inside. The fire was dead and the cave almost pitch-black, even though some daylight snuck down the corridor. She was still asleep. She looked like a sixty-year-old woman, her face creased and filthy.

Back outside he scavenged a few heavy trunks that hadn't been rotted or burned too severely and started laying in a ramp. Brutus watched attentively as though he knew somehow that it was for his benefit. It took about an hour and he had lashed six fairly stout logs together and filled in the cracks with mud and small stones from the wash until it was almost a smooth walkway. He'd have to add some crosspieces as well. Horses were funny about where they walked and what they stepped on. He had a horse once that came to an abrupt stop on a woods trail and could not be budged past it. Albert smacked the horse's rear, jerked on the bridle, pushed, coaxed and pleaded but the horse would not move. He finally noticed a black branch about an inch thick lying right across the path. The damn horse thought it was a snake and wouldn't budge until Albert stomped violently on the branch and then tossed it into the underbrush. The horse stared after the vanished snake and then calmly continued the walk.

Brutus resisted, but eventually he was able to coax him up the ramp into the stone corridor where he wrapped his eyes in cloth. Brutus calmed right down and followed him along until they got to the walkway where Albert paused to light a large heavy candle in a sconce. The smell of burning animal fat drifted around them.

Brutus slipped and neighed wickedly when his leg smacked against a stone knob but eventually Albert was able to lead him to the floor of the cave. Once he removed the blindfold, the animal stared around and began to walk quickly back and forth. He lowered his head to the running stream and poked it with his snout. The water splashed and he jerked his head back, sidestepped and then tried again. It took him five minutes to finally submerge his mouth in the cool water. Albert figured they would have to make the trip twice a day to allow Brutus to feed until something closer grew in.

While the horse investigated the shelter, Albert stoked the fire and put a two-gallon steel pot on to boil. In one corner near the stream, a depression had formed in the rock large enough for a sort of bathtub. The surface was rough and he had tried unsuccessfully to smooth it over by sanding it with stone. Finally he had managed to lay in a heavy rubber poncho as a liner. He dumped several buckets of water from the stream into the pool then set the hot water boiler to simmer while she slept.

He returned to his workbench and flicked on a small electric light that ran on a battery connected to a solar charger. The automobile headlamp blazed for several hours before it needed recharging and he was able to work on various projects, including a diary he had begun to keep the first year of incarceration. He had deliberately not reread more than a day or so of the previous scribblings each time he picked up the pencil, afraid of what he might have sounded like during the depth of those frozen, dead years. Now he was suddenly curious about it all for some reason. He flipped open the booklet at random and looked at the page.

Day 976. Cold. Always ~~codt~~ cold, these days. Saw the sun this morning but it covered up right away. Food for about 700 days left. No sign of animal life to speak of. A few birds, too far way to ~~shot.~~ shoot. Tried eating one of the blind fish but they are no good and have no meat on them. I might leave crumbs to see if there is a mouse. But if not, I need the crumbs. I am getting sick of this. I would rather be fighting than just sitting here waiting. Don't even known what I am waiting for any more. Three years now I have not seen another person. Am I it? Jesus Christ all mighty, I hope not. Could they really have killed everyone? No. it's just not possible. Someone will come by here and we will be friends. I hope every day I do not wake up. I will not " do it" *but I can hope I will not wake up. That is my right.*

He turned around and found her lying on his cot, looking at him. She sat up slowly and put her foot on the stone and shivered.

"It's fifty-five degrees just about all the time in here," he said. "For a while there it dropped a bit…" His voice trailed off. She heard Brutus behind her and he poked his head over the rim of the shelf and snorted at her.

"I got some real coffee if you'd like," he said, switching off the light.

The room fell into a soft darkness pushed back only slightly by the wavering candle- light.

He took her silence for a yes and poured a small amount of coffee into a cup and then added a teaspoon of sugar. She watched his approach and took the cup in a kind of dazed state. Her mouth was slightly open and her eyes were wide and searching his face. The suspicion he had seen in her previously was suddenly multiplied and she froze like an animal.

He backed away and poured himself a cup and sat on a crude chair made from tree branches and rope. She simply held the cup and looked at him. The steam spiraled slowly off the surface and entered her nostrils, startling her.

"I took Brutus there back to the pasture last night and he pretty well ate his fill, I'd say. He'll be all right till tonight, I expect. We'll have to keep after the shit or it will start to smell pretty bad in here, quick enough. I don't mind the smell of horse shit too much but too much horse shit, well that's different, if you know what I mean. Everything in moderation, they say. Except moderation, of course, you want plenty of that. Me, I'm kind of an extremist, I guess. Never could eat just one, you know what I mean? Don't you like coffee? I got some tea, if you'd rather. Ain't got no chocolate…do you want a bath?"

"A what?" she asked. She had heard him but she wanted to hear it again.

"A bath. I've made a little bath over there and I've got hot water here for you ready whenever you want. I don't mean to say you need a bath, unless of course you feel you need one. I'm just saying don't do it on my account…Jesus…"

She sipped the coffee mug and swallowed and then licked her lips.

"Can you turn that light on?" she asked.

"Sure," he said, grateful for something to do.

He flicked the little switch and the headlight blazed into the room, igniting the walls and shining on the water.

She stood up and walked slowly around, looking at everything closely and sometimes rubbing her hand over to check its texture or maybe just to be sure it was there.

"How did you do this?" she asked.

"I-." But what could he say?

"Were you joking?"

"Over there," he said. "I'll dump the hot water in and you can just lie there for a while if you like. I do that sometimes because...well, I don't know why exactly. It feels relaxing..."

He lugged the pot of water over to the bath and poured it in slowly. Steam rose in vertical clouds.

"I'll put some more on and you just say if you want it. Hot water doesn't go to waste around here, I'll tell ya. I mean the fire is on no matter what, so...and I've got plenty of water. It's been running pretty much like what you see there for about a million years, I figure."

They passed each other as she walked to the bath and avoided his eyes.

He filled the pot from the stream while she undressed and slithered down the rubber sides into the pit of the little pool.

Albert walked back, keeping his eyes on the pot.

She lay in the water for only a few minutes and then jumped up, horrified by the filth that was running off her.

"I had no idea..."

He came over and looked at her, trying not to add to her humiliation. She was so skinny her ribs were showing and her joints had swollen up. He had seen this before.

"Just take this," he said, handing her a blanket.

She stepped out and he bent down over the tub. He pulled a stone loose at the base and then peeled the rubber mat back. The water rushed out and raced down the slope of the cave floor to the stream where it was carried away within seconds.

"It's all right," he said, several times. "Don't you worry."

He replaced the "plug" and the mat and filled up the bowl again. She stood silently while he poured more hot water in. Then he took the blanket from her and she climbed back into the tub. They did this twice more before she was able to sit quietly, the stink and sweat and shit and death and fear and corruption of years finally scraped from her skin. She hadn't seen her normal skin for so long she almost didn't recognize herself. By the time she emerged from the water, she was wrinkled and shivering. He wrapped her in a blanket and set her in front of the fire where she remained unmoving for more than an hour.

"Are you hungry?" he asked. "I've got lots of stuff to eat. I have cans and I have dried meat and stuff like that. And lots of MREs. Want a can of peaches?"

She continued to stare at the fire as if she hadn't heard.

Finally he opened a can of peaches and brought it over to her. He put it down on the stone beside her and she glanced at it and then looked back at the fire.

"I drug the peaches here in two trips. I carried them in seventy-pound loads. That's fifty cans. So I had a hundred cans when I started but now I've only got about 20 left. I think they're all right. I mean I ain't died from eating them that I know of...You want another blanket? I wish this was bear country and I could get a bearskin, you know? But there haven't been any bears in Indiana for a while. Now cats, that's different. There were plenty of big cats around...well, not plenty, more like some big cats...but I won't shoot a cat unless I have to. Now a bear, you can eat. I ate bear meat once and it ain't too bad but you don't want to undercook it because it is very stringy. If we could shoot a bear I'd make a coat out of it or maybe just a big blanket. It got pretty cold here a while back. Now it's going back the other way again and warming up..."

She took the can of peaches and tilted it into her mouth. Some of the juice ran down and she wicked it away with her hand. Then she let the peach slices slide down her throat.

"You better take it easy, maybe," he warned her. "If it's been a while since you had anything like that you might-."

She exploded with laughter.

"Yes, it's been a while," she said, tears running down her cheeks. She couldn't stop laughing and he just sat and watched, knowing the hysteria would pass and she'd probably lurch back in the other direction and start crying a lot. He'd seen it all before, in both men and women; first they laugh like crazy and then they start to sob.

But her laughter subsided and she went back to a calm state. It took about five minutes before the peaches and the juice came back up. She tried to stand but didn't make it and threw up into the fire where chunks of peach and the syrup sizzled.

"I'm sorry," she moaned. "I am so sorry…"

"Don't you worry about it," he said. "I'm the one should be sorry for making you eat peaches before you were ready. Anyways, I threw up plenty of times. I've thrown up even when there wasn't a good reason to. One time I was just walking and all of a sudden I get this crunching feeling in my gut and before you know it: Splot! And I threw up all over the place. Never did figure out why but I guess it must have been something I ate."

He handed her a cup of water.

She accepted it and sipped at it more judiciously.

"Do you mind wearing some men's clothing?" he asked her after a few minutes. "I threw your stuff out because, well, there wasn't much there and it was pretty stiff. If you don't mind I got some extra trousers and shirts and so forth. You are pretty skinny but I think we could pin it up or something. And I can sew pretty good so if you want, I'll cut them down to fit. But then after a while when you get some meat on your bones, they might be too small. It's not as easy putting something back together like it is taking it apart. That's true about a lot of things, now isn't it? I mean that's your old toothpaste and the tube story. That is something I didn't think of when I started filling this place up. Toothpaste. People were always saying how it's toilette paper that you will miss but it's toothpaste, I think. Just about any leaf will do for toilette paper if you know I mean? As long as you don't grab some poison ivy or something. I knew of a woman once who used poison ivy like that by accident. Whooeee, did she ever have a time of it. Can't imagine. Scratched herself bloody, from what I heard. Course you never know with people. They tell you things but they always change the story a little bit. Did you ever do that when you were a kid, you know all sitting in a circle and someone starts a story and by the time it gets around the circle, why it's a different story altogether. You might not even recognize it…

228

Chapter Three

They were able to block off a reasonable paddock for the horse using some rudimentary fence and the walls of the gully so that he didn't have to live inside with them. They still took him every day to the pasture and he anticipated the walk like a dog.

Over the summer, the land returned to some recognizable form faster than Valerie did. After a month, she had regained some weight and much of the exaggerated weathering on her face had moderated, but she would never look her age, not after almost ten years wandering through the nightmare that had settled over a land that once upon a time had a name and an identity and supported a third of a billion souls.

They were walking back to the pasture with Brutus when Albert broke the rule about asking questions, almost by accident, but more likely because she gave him the excuse when she poked fun at him for getting winded so easily.

"Well how old are you?" he said and she quickly shut up and pretended to be looking at the scenery and not throwing him sideways glances.

"Twenty-four – I think," she muttered.

He took this in with a slow breath and his face darkened a bit.

"I know, I don't look a day over sixty, right?"

"Well, I was just thinking that you are twenty four and I am fifty seven – more or less – which means I am-."

"So what?" she interrupted. "What possible difference could that make?"

"I dunno. It's just I always disliked it when I saw an old man with a young girl."

"Well, you can relax," she said. "I am not a young girl. Never have been."

And then after several minutes of uncomfortable silence she stabbed him with her eyes and said, "You are stupid sometimes, you know that?"

"Yes mam," he muttered.

"Oh shut up," she snapped and stopped to stroke the horse who could smell the grass now and was prancing like a colt.

Then she decided to just let him go and not hobble him. She took the halter off and rubbed his nose and he realized instantly that he was free. He danced sideways a few yards and then tossed his head and took off running. He had a long, black mane that flew back and fluttered like a cape as he galloped and she watched him go without any weeping or self-indulgent remarks. Albert watched him go with dismay; he had already started to count on the horse for all kinds of work.

They followed his path, but he vanished over a hill at full speed.

The grass was a foot high almost ready for a first cutting of hay. Albert pulled up a few heads and examined them closely. He thought it was wheat at first. The little, ovals hugging the head looked like wheat berries until you looked closer and saw that they were deformed. They should have been uniform, all tucked against the head like good babies. Some were twisted, some were round and some were empty, just hollow like little bubbles.

"Jesus Christ," he said.

"What?" she looked around expecting some sort of attack. "What is it, dogs?"

"No," he said. "Look at this."

He spread the kernels out on his palm and she looked at them and shrugged.

"So?"

"So this wheat field, it's...there's something wrong with it. I think maybe the radioactivity has affected it or something."

When he put together the strange deer head and the squirrel with five rear digits and the abnormal wheat berries, there was no way to avoid it; some form of radioactivity from the bombs had settled right on top of them. It had been enough to cause mutations.

"Don't you think we'd be dead by now if there was a problem?" she said.

"I don't know," he answered. "Maybe it's just enough to give you cancer in a few years. I don't know."

"Well what do you want to do about it?"

"Do? Hell, there's nothing to do. I've been drinking the water and eating the meat...so have you for that matter. Besides, there's nowhere to run."

They topped the hill and saw Brutus yanking tufts of fresh wheat grass out of the ground and chewing with a slow, determined enjoyment. He raised his head periodically to look around but the land them seemed empty.

How long could they expect that to continue?

Valerie showed up here and so would others, some of them just passing through, wandering; but not all.

He dropped the handful of seeds and started walking again. Wherever he stopped to check it was the same; every head had abnormal growth, and then another thought occurred to him. It was too early to have fully developed heads. The wheat was a month ahead of itself. They continued walking around the edge of the field and everywhere he stopped it was the same.

"Let's get out of here," she said, slipping her hand into his. It startled him and he almost jerked his arm.

"What's the matter? If we're dead, we're dead, right? You can't do anything about it now; you said so yourself."

They started back and as they crested the hill, Brutus was peacefully grazing. He looked up occasionally, but never back at them.

It was only a few days later that the first travellers came through, passing no more than a quarter mile from the den. Valerie was looking for edible legumes when she heard men's voices; they were roughhousing and laughing. She watched them pass from a thicket of bramble, her hand firmly wrapped around a small-frame .45. She didn't need any lessons. Albert could tell right away that with some coaching and practice she'd outshoot him and just about anyone in no time. Her gaze was very cold; she controlled breathing without a lot of effort. She always pictured the target as one of the gentlemen she had run into over the years.

There were four of them, all young, probably in their twenties. It meant they had spent almost half their lives after the Catastrophe. They had essentially grown up in a state of unrestrained freedom, if that was really the right word. They only had one rifle among them. It was a bolt-action hunting rifle. But they all carried weapons, including knives and clubs and one of them was packing a crossbow, though she couldn't see if he had any bolts for it or not.

Valerie was a little older, maybe by five years but she had spent the same decade under the same conditions. Her wariness was not emotional or based on fear as much as it was a simple survival tool. In that respect she was no different from any prey, anywhere. She had developed an extra sense just as the animals did. All energy passed through the air and it might be out of the range of hearing or seeing and it might not excite the tactile senses but it was discoverable, nonetheless. The first time she had been fooled in several years was when Albert had caught her off guard that first night. But Albert wasn't really a person, anymore. Albert was a creature who lived in the woods and looked like a man and read books. But he was not a person and no one could sneak past Albert.

And just like her, these four boys had developed the extra senses necessary to survive and they stopped at once as they came level with her position. They did not speak, but each listened and sniffed and tried to reach out to the disturbance in the air. Then, without speaking, they split up and disappeared into the foliage all around her. She had to decide whether to stay or flee. Each had its advantages and obvious disadvantages. But the fact was, she really couldn't run for it because they would catch her. It didn't matter who was fastest; when four chase one, the one is almost always caught. Besides, she wasn't prepared to lead them right back to Albert. They were good at the task of stalking. She heard only a few branches break and leaves rasp against something and she wasn't even sure where the noise had come from. She had the pistol with 13 shots in it. The first crack of doom would bring Albert running. If she could stay alive until he showed up, the odds would be turned around. She closed her eyes for a moment to calm her breathing. She counted, slowly, exhaling silently, careful not to hyperventilate. She concentrated on the air, trying to apprehend the vibration they were making but they were somehow moving just outside the effective area. The ripples died before they reached her.

But not the hand.

The hand gripped her hair and yanked it back with a savage jerk that nearly broke her neck.

"Here!" he screamed, "Bitch! Bitch!"

She smashed into the bramble and the spikes entered her arms and side, jabbing half an inch deep. Blood ran. She let him yank her half way through the spike tree and then she pushed the little .45 against his stomach and fired a single shot. It threw him backwards, howling, blood squirting between his fingers. She had nicked the liver. He had less than an hour to live.

She scrambled back under cover, blood running from half a dozen holes in her arm and flank and crouched down low. She squeezed into a little ring of cedar trees where deer often camped for the night. She wouldn't be invisible, but the stockade might keep her from being taken alive, at least for a while.

The other three had located her and were closing in. She had to keep the pistol close until she spotted one and then she could shove it out between the trunks and fire. She heard them when the discovered their friend. He was howling and crying. Then he stopped and there was silence. They had abandoned him and run off; she was sure of it; but she did not move until Albert arrived.

The three had taken everything from their dying friend except his clothes, which were not worth stealing. They had taken his belt and his boots. Just like wild dogs; stub your toe and you're dinner.

He was crying when Albert and Valerie squatted down to talk to him, tears merely smudged in the filth on his cheeks.

"Fuckin bitch!" he shouted at her. "Fuckin bitch!"

Albert moved his head from a root that was keeping it an odd angle and it seemed to give him some relief.

"Where are your friends?" Albert asked, gently. "Maybe we can help them."

"Fuck them and fuck you," the boy screamed. He couldn't be twenty yet.

"Where were you going?" Albert tried again, but the boy refused to answer. He looked at Albert and Valerie with a child's hateful glare.

Valerie had moved off and was searching the ground for some indication when she found a bolt from the crossbow.

"They ran east," she said.

Albert stood up. The boy's eyes followed him.

"There's dogs around here," Albert said. "They'll be on you before long."

The boy started to cry.

Valerie walked over and without a word, shot him through the forehead. Then she looked at Albert, expecting some recrimination and he looked disappointed and frowned.

"Next time use a rock," he said.

Albert had his AK and a pocketful of clips as well as his usual battle gear. He handed Valerie her AR15 and two magazines.

The trail was easy to follow and several times he made them pull back and wait until the three men had gotten a little farther away. When they got to the wheat field, they had stopped and gone around the perimeter rather than cross the green sea and leave a permanent wake.

Albert squatted down and methodically worked the edge of the woods with his field glasses but they either had doubled back into the woods or had struck off in a new direction.

"There," she said.

Valerie had been scanning with her riflescope and had spotted a flash of clothing at about two o'clock.

Albert switched his view and found them. They had stopped just inside the tree line about a mile away.

"You want to let them go?" she asked.

"I don't think so," Albert said. "They are just going to keep on acting like this."

"You can't kill them all, Albert."

He shrugged and went back to scanning the field.

"That's true," he said quietly.

They waited for dark and Albert flipped on the infrared but quickly found it was unnecessary. The men had built a fire and he could see at least one of them silhouetted against the backdrop of trees and foliage. They heard a single shot just before moonrise but it could have been anything and they paid it no mind.

They had decided to come at them from both flanks. Albert would follow their trail along the edge of the woods while Valerie would take the other two sides of the diamond. They'd meet at the top point and kill everybody, have something to eat and go home.

She had the longer route so Albert waited about a hundred feet from the fire, watching them as they roasted a large piece of some kind of meat. It smelled wonderful, he thought and he fully intended to have a good meal on their tab. That must have been the shot they'd heard earlier. Somehow they'd gotten hold of a feral cow or perhaps a really big deer. Every day it seemed animal life was returning to the area.

It took her the better part of an hour to get into position. He couldn't see her but she signaled by throwing something into the bush and raising the alarm. The three men jumped to their feet but after a few minutes of prodding the very edge darkness, they sat down again. They would figure it was an animal, and to a large extent they were right.

She fired first, hitting one of the men in the gut while he stood up in front of the fire. He toppled backwards and Albert turned the hose on the other two, walking in as he did so. One of them caught a full burst and died on the spot; the fourth man was wounded and tried to drag himself out of the penumbra of the fire. Valerie shot him through the head from 50 feet.

There was the usual complete and utter silence that rushed to fill the vacuum created by the gunfire. Then the sound of the fire crackling broke in and then forest sounds and as they got closer, the spatter of fat dripping onto the flames.

Albert probed the woods with a flashlight looking for the rest of the animal and he spotted the carcass under some bushes.

He walked up and pulled away the cover.

Brutus still had his eyes open.

Valerie was standing by the fire looking at the spit. She didn't look up right away when Albert joined her. Albert took the nearest corpse by the leg and dragged it onto the fire. The clothes caught and the smell of burning human flesh rose almost immediately.

"Leave them for the dogs," Valerie said.

"Not much else to do, I s'ppose," Albert replied.

That was their entire conversation about how Brutus died, though over the years she occasionally remembered something the big horse had done or "said" with his body language or his catalogue of sounds. She was near starved to death herself, when she found him with a piece of fence wrapped around his leg. He couldn't walk any further. She debated whether to kill him and eat him or set him loose. Back then she was still a bit foolish and made decisions that were not always practical, so she cut his leg loose and he still couldn't move very well. His head drooped and he whinnied softly from the pain. She did the best she could with it for a few days and in the meanwhile they wandered together until she found a barn that was still half full of hay. Then she found some canned food in the farmhouse. When she came out of the house a few days later, he was standing there, waiting for her.

"Sounds like bull shit to me," Albert said, as he dozed off.

"What would you know?" she snapped.

"Not too much," he said.

"Well shut up, then."

"Yes mam."

"Oh do shut up, please."

"Yes, mam."

From that day on, they knew that tourists would be coming this way. Even if no one ever mentioned the area, somehow the information went out through the synchronized ether. And after the first few transits the trail would be visible, anyway. And then, eventually someone would find the cave, just as he had.

All they could do was watch and patrol and if necessary, eliminate people who declined to move on. But it was a losing battle and they knew it. It wasn't just the numbers that would eventually overwhelm, but the inability to control anything larger than where you were standing at any given moment.

"I'm starting to feel more like a Sioux Indian every day," he said.

The four men they had killed had come the closest to the cave. Most everyone else came through the area by following the old Emit River, which was more than three miles away and did not make a return until it hit the big oxbow. But it would only take an errant gunshot or a careless fire to announce their presence and the constant vigilance was tiring.

The poisoned wheat field where they used to take the horse turned out to be the draw. It was here the first settlers decided to stop. Albert and Valerie watched them from behind the tree line as they pulled up in a big, rubber tire farm wagon pulled by two horses. The team was mismatched, one being a full three hands higher than the other, but the driver managed to keep the wagon moving. It was three men and two women, one of whom was pregnant. The wagon was overloaded with equipment and the horses had a hard time dragging it through the high wheat. When they finally crossed the field, they dismounted and walked back through the waves of wheat, stopping occasionally to pull a head an examine it. It was over ripe and no longer worth harvesting but it indicated good growing land.

Albert watched them for a long time before he dropped the field glasses and sat with his back against a tree.

"Want to go say hello?" she asked him.

He didn't answer. He was thinking about the others who would follow. It was how planets are formed. Particles accrete over time until their mass and subsequent gravity is large enough to attract large pieces and pretty soon you've got yourself an asteroid and that becomes a planetoid and so forth. And then it sweeps out its orbit without regard for anything in its path. And anything that comes within its grasp is dragged in.

"I was thinking just to run 'em off," he said.

"That'll work," she commented sarcastically.

"Nest thing you know they'll be staking claims."

"Well, isn't that what you've done?"

He put the glasses back on them again. Two of them men talked while the third, younger and taller, had started to unload the wagon. One of the men had a pistol on his hip and the boy carried two long guns from the wagon and leaned them against a tree.

"Well I won't have it," Albert said finally, standing up.

He strode right out in the open and headed across the field towards them. They saw him coming right away and the boy brought the two long guns over. The women stood back, but they were armed with blade weapons and were making a clear statement about their intentions.

"Don't come no closer," one of them said.

Albert kept walking as if he hadn't heard.

"I'm telling you-"

"You are telling me shit," Albert barked, as he came within a few feet of them. They stared back at him, faces tight and eyes wobbling a little with fear.

"There's enough firepower on you right now to kill everybody in about three seconds," Albert said. "You pack up and get out of here. There's plenty of territory around for everyone."

"Who the hell are you?" the boy said.

"Never mind who I am," Albert told him severely. "If you are here in the morning, I will kill all of you; the women, too."

He turned and headed along the wake he'd cut through the grain and in a few minutes was back behind the tree line.

Valerie had watched the whole event through her scope, ready to start shooting the instant things went south and she kept her eye on them until Albert had joined her.

"You can't do this," she said.

"Why not?"

"You know why not."

He knew he was being irrational and he shut right up.

She watched them through the scope.

"Well they are leaving, it looks like," she said. But Albert wasn't listening. He was thinking about the next traveler, the one who came by and wouldn't scare off.

He brooded all the way back, unable to come to terms with the loss of his secrecy. It wasn't privacy he wanted; that just meant people left you alone. He wanted them not to even know he existed.

They had several more encounters over the summer, but these were encounters at a distance. A few shots fired into the undergrowth and the travelers moved on, having neither the inclination nor the need to fight. There really was a surfeit of land available for settlement; all anyone had to do was keep walking for a while. But the pace picked up in the fall and it seemed they were running into someone new every few days. Most were on foot, single men and women carrying what they could. Some were on horseback. A few had wagons, including several that had no tires and just plodded along on the rims. Others pulled crude, hand made carts or hasty travois lashed down with ropes of torn cloth. They weren't stopping, any longer, just blazing through whether it be night or day, rain or shine.

"I guess the word finally got out," Valerie said, filling his plate with chunks of dried venison that had been simmering for several hours in a stew pot of roots and berries and flower heads and anything else that seemed edible.

"It's the last can of tomatoes," she said, ladling the juice into his bowl.

He had made large, flat breads with the remains of the flower.

"What's got into you?" she demanded.

"I saw smoke today."

She waited for him to continue and decided she'd be damned if she'd start sending leading questions.

"I was up on the ridge and I looked over and seen the smoke rising. Maybe fifteen, twenty miles away to the north."

"Forest fire?"

"I don't think so," he said slowly. "It was rising straight up like a chimley and when I put the glasses on it I seen a few others, too."

"People fifteen or twenty miles away...you can't-."

238

"I know, I know…I'm not thinking that," he conceded. "I think they must have a settlement or something over there and that's why all these people coming through just go right on without stopping."

"A settlement? You mean…?"

"I mean a settlement. Millions and millions of people crowded up together, getting in each other's face all the time. Screaming in the middle of the night, teenagers, drunks. The whole fucking crock of shit."

She started to laugh and then it caught her full force and she couldn't eat. She covered her mouth and jiggled and rattled. Tears sprouted and ran down her cheeks. She couldn't stop and he watched her, eyes wide like an owl wondering if she had finally, suddenly, irrevocably cracked and all the crazy was leaking out. Finally he folded his arms and watched her while she danced around the cave, howling with laughter and bending over.

"My stomach…" she screeched. "It hurts…"

"Well cut out the laughing, then," he said, which just sent her off into paroxysms.

She came around to his side of the table and sat down in his lap. She still didn't weigh quite 115 pounds. Her face was soaked with tears and he started to grin at her in spite of himself. She kissed his forehead and then she kissed him on the mouth and in the middle she started laughing again and they choked together. Now he was laughing too. He pushed his hand up under her shirt and pressed her smooth, warm back and felt her laughing. He buried his face in her neck and listened to the sounds emanating from her throat.

"Oh my," she gasped, "I can't stand it," and then off it started again. He held her for quite a while. He tried to push his hand down her pants and she slapped him and told him to wait. He tried again and she pulled his ears.

"Okay," he yelled.

Then he slipped his hand down the back of her pants and squeezed her ass and she stopped laughing and they went to bed.

After a few days of brooding about it, they decided to drop in for a visit. At least a hundred people had passed through over the summer but another two hundred had come from other directions and when they arrived at the settlement, they were stunned by the size of the "town." Buildings had been crafted from salvaged materials, logs, stone and even earth, creating an odd collection of dwellings, some of which clearly would not make it through the winter if things got bad.

They had reclaimed about three acres of farmland and planted it with vegetables and grains, but the planting was haphazard and the weeds were taking over. The smoke he had seen was from a central fire pit that seemed to be running night and day without any real purpose. The smell of human waste hit them as they came closer and the wind shifted. Apparently they were using open slit trenches and the clouds of flies over the sewers looked like screen on a storm door.

There did not seem to be any guards or sentries and they walked in unchallenged, though a few people turned to stare at them. The chunk-chunk of an axe slamming into the side of a tree came from the forest. The spot they had selected was five hundred feet from the "new" Emit, really just a tributary of the river that had opened up when the land had shifted, either from natural causes or otherwise. They were a few feet about the bank, but a serious rain of even a few days would flood them out and fill their toilettes.

"Jesus," Valerie muttered. "What a dump."

Albert was watching some men raise a wall constructed from salvaged timber and a few skinny tree trunks. They had failed to brace it properly and as they tugged on the ropes, the wall wobbled and collapsed sideways. Everyone got out of the way, but arguments immediately broke out.

For the first time in years, there were children. For the number of people, it was an extraordinarily low ratio. Among three hundred, approximately a hundred and ten men and a hundred and fifty women, there were half-a-dozen toddlers. And that was it. There was nothing between them and the adults, who ranged from about twenty-years-old to maybe, fifty.

The mood changed perceptibly when four men emerged from the woods dragging a she-wolf on the end of several ropes. She snarled and snapped at them as they nearly choked her to death. A man on each side of her with a rope kept her from getting away. The other two each carried a dead pup, no more than six months old. They tied the snarling animal up between two posts and left her there jerking and yanking to get loose.

Several people came around to look at the dead pups and one of the men slit the belly of the smaller one and dumped the guts on the ground. Then he kneeled down and tore the skin off, ripping it several times. They tossed the carcass into the fire. The she-wolf finally lay down in the dust, panting, having pulled the ropes so tight around her

240

own throat she could barely breathe. Albert waited to see what the man would do. He had gutted the other pup and was in the process of skinning it when Albert decided to go over to the wolf.

He approached slowly, a piece of heavy cord in his hand.

"What the fuck d'you think yer doin?" the man called at him.

He left the half-skinned corpse on the ground and strutted over to Albert, his face twisted with anger.

"She's going to choke to death," Albert said. "I was just going to loosen her up a bit."

"Oh you were, were you?" the man said. "Why don't you get the fuck outta here before I loosen you up?"

Valerie came up beside Albert and looked at the man calmly. The man squinted at her and then pushed Albert's shoulder.

"Oh Christ," she whispered.

"Fuck off and take this cunt with ya or I might loosen her up too," the man said.

"Hey," Albert said, quietly. "I just want to...the wolf is choking!"

The man swung a roundhouse at Albert and lunged towards him. The Emerson sliced into his abdomen just above the belly button and Albert jerked it straight up until it glanced off one of the ribs.

No one knew what happened until the man fell on the ground, bleeding almost like the wolf pups he had so roughly skinned.

The she-wolf was unconscious when he got to her and he didn't need to tie her jaws. He cut the ropes and yanked them from her neck, but she didn't come around. Her eyes rolled back and her tongue lolled.

The man's companions had watched the proceedings from a distance and had been caught off guard by the swift slaying of their friend. One of them pointed an old colt revolver at Albert and walked towards him.

"You fuckin little cock-."

Valerie's shot entered his ear and came out at a slight angle. He tumbled to the ground, Albert jerking the old gun out of his hand before he fell.

Now they were surrounded and at least half the community fenced them in, staring at them. There were not a few weapons among them, but they were typically bolt-action hunting rifles. He saw a number of .22s and a few .30 caliber weapons. He couldn't tell what kind of handguns they might have.

"You gonna kill us all, mister?" someone said. "We know your type."

Albert swung the AK off his shoulder and released the safety. Valerie just watched them coldly, scanning the crowd, back and forth, looking for a movement or a gesture or someone breathing slightly out of rhythm.

"Albert, is that really you?" came a voice.

Pat Kingston stepped out from the semi-circle and strode towards him. His right ear was missing and he limped. Albert hardly recognized him. His hair was snow white and his face was broken out in blisters or maybe a rash. He extended his hand but Albert didn't accept it. They looked at each other for a full minute.

"Ya, it's really me," Kingston said. Then he turned to the crowd. "Better go about your business," he told them. "This here is Albert Smythe."

The crowd did start to disintegrate, albeit slowly and several took an eccentric path on their way out so they could pass by and look at him. He paid no attention, but somehow kept his eye on all of them. Valerie kept looking at Pat Kingston in between scans.

"What the fuck is this place?" Albert asked him.

Kingston looked hollowed out, somehow, ill, degraded. He had a weak stare.

"What's it look like?" he said, attempting to be the man Albert had known years ago; the man who had led the raid on Provost, for whatever it was worth.

"What are you doing with shit like this?" Albert asked, indicating the two dead men. No one had even stopped to check the bodies, never mind remove them.

"I got cancer," he said.

"That doesn't explain this," he said.

"I don't need to explain it. It's obvious," Kingston said.

A woman emerged from the crowd and walked up to them. She was about Albert's height. She touched Kingston's shoulder and he glanced at her.

"Mai, this is Albert, the guy I told you about," Kingston said.

The woman's age was hard to pin down. Like most Asians, she seemed to reach a certain point in her thirties or forties and stayed that way until she was about a hundred. She looked Albert over carefully, glanced at Valerie and then took Kingston's arm.

"He's got to lie down," she said. "You want to talk, follow me."

She led Kingston towards a small hut and after a few moments, Albert and Valerie decided to follow.

"What was all that?" she asked him as they crossed the dirt campus, but he didn't answer.

Mai helped Kingston lie back on a small cot and took up a chair nearby. She didn't offer the visitors a place to sit.

Albert sat down on the bed.

"Good to see you, man," Kingston said. "I knew you'd make it. Everybody said you were dead – again."

He grinned and held his hand up to Albert. This time he took it.

"Radiation?" Albert said.

"I guess," he answered. "Don't know what else it could be."

"What are you doing here?"

"Just ended up here, is all, like most. Heard there was something starting up and I figured maybe I could…I don't really know."

"These assholes won't make it through the winter," Albert said. "This is the biggest cluster fuck I have seen in a long time."

Mai looked up at this and glared at him.

"We don't need you telling us what to do," she said.

"While I am talking to my friend here, you better keep shut," he said.

She looked from Albert to Valerie and then she got up.

"I'll come back when your company is gone," she said.

"You going to give us a hand?" Kingston asked, his eyebrows knitting seriously.

Albert looked away.

"Not a fucking chance," he said after a moment. "You knew that before you asked me."

"Those guys with the wolf. Everybody hated them, but they don't know how to do anything," Kingston said, closing his eyes and breathing hard for a moment.

"They're not all like him, believe me. If you would just help them out a bit, they could really have something here."

"I don't want them here," Albert said.

Kingston had closed his eyes and was no longer listening.

Albert looked at him for a few moments and then stood up.

As they walked away, Valerie was silent but he knew what she was thinking.

They scanned the grounds but no one seemed to be paying any attention to them. The two bodies were gone, at least.

"Let's go," he said.

Once they had cleared the area and were back in familiar territory, she stopped and sat down on the ground.

"Not now," he said. "It's getting dark."

"You afraid of the dark?"

"Damn rights."

"What was all that back there?"

"It was just the war, Val, that's all. People love to talk shit about war and I don't."

She stood up and they started out again.

"What did you do in the war, daddy?" she teased him.

"I stayed alive. That's about it."

Like everything Albert said, it was only partly true. Yes, he had stayed alive, somehow, but she doubted very much if that was "about it."

***

Chapter Four

It would be the mildest winter since the end of the interglacial, 12,000 years ago. The growing season, which had effectively been five years in coming, seemed to be making up for lost time. Trees were so heavy with leaves the sun could not get to the forest floor. Grasses, grains, and legumes – everything was racing ahead of itself. They saw flocks of birds whirling in the air in that synchronized flight that could only be attributed to some form of telepathy. How did they know how to act in concert like that? It wasn't just Starlings performing these wild acrobatics; now there were huge flocks of multi-colored birds hanging in the trees and swarming like flies over the fields. Grass shot up everywhere, including the stony shoulders of the limestone bluffs and even in the wash that ran past their front door; a gully about twelve feet deep and twice as wide with a gravel bed that had been impregnated with every type of seed that could be washed away in a storm. Johnson Grass, fescue, clover - wheat - the whole gamut of forage surged up through the stone in exactly the same way grass will split a concrete sidewalk given enough time.

In November Albert found new growth in the woods, long after everything should have departed. He picked a leaf and examined it closely. It might be hemp, he thought. He'd look it up later. The serrations at the edge of the leaves were too deeply incised. Then he found sassafras where the cutouts had fused or failed to form. There were oaks that had produced Siamese acorns.

He followed a rabbit track for about an hour, catching sight of the beast only once. It was definitely offspring of the population he'd observed years ago. Feral rabbits had bred with local stock and produced a kind of Holstein-colored hare; but twice the size he'd expected to find.

He caught up with it on the edge of field by a thick, overgrown fence. He waited to see if the big bunny would carry on or duck under cover. When it vanished, he moved in. He pulled away the overgrowth and eventually exposed a warren with a dozen kits, all different colors. They couldn't be six weeks old. They were dead; but more remarkably, half of them had radical birth defects. One had no mouth; another lacked appendages. Some were eyeless; one was nothing but a ball, not even half formed. Several looked normal but had large growths on the back. The mother stood about twenty feet away, trying to lure him away from the warren. He let her go.

By December, new growth had sprouted wherever there was soil to hold it. He shot several squirrels and they all appeared normal. He had not encountered the maker of the odd print he'd seen before. Scraping a small trench for tomato seeds they decided to experiment with, Valerie pulled an earthworm from the soil covered with tiny blisters or lumps. At the edge of the Emit River, Albert spotted a pure white fish he'd never seen before. There was only one of them and it vanished as quickly as it had appeared. Albinism was possible in anything, he supposed, but there was little doubt in his mind that the fish was just another example of what was happening all around them.

Near what would have been Christmas, deer came back to the woods in unusually large numbers and he took half a dozen before the end of January. They were all fat and healthy and he could find nothing unusual in their anatomy. He did not encounter another buck with the extra antlers growing out of its head. February should have been an unpredictable mélange of snow and thaw, but instead, the temperature reached seventy- five degrees and stayed that way.

Valerie had expressed an interest in visiting the settlement several times and Albert had to admit he was curious. So long as they stayed out of his reach, twenty miles away, he didn't care what happened to them, but it was just good tactics to know what they were up to.

Albert knew that she was drawn to the company of others, women especially. Holding out in a cave with a mildly schizoid recluse old enough to be her grandfather probably had its charms; they just didn't have a long shelf life. He couldn't expect her to adopt his misanthropy, a condition he had been cultivating for many years more than she had lived.

She created the opening one March morning as he was cleaning several fat trout he had dragged from the river.

"Aren't you even curious?" she asked him.

"A little bit," he said.

The next morning they left early for the twenty-mile walk, carrying enough food and water for three days. They could have made the journey in seven hours but they were still wary of open spaces and took many diversions by following the edges between forest and field.

About half way there, they came to the edge of a large former cornfield, now overgrown with weeds and interspersed with tall, volunteer stalks, some of them green and some rust colored. Some carried cobs in the normal fashion. Some were barren. Several displayed the same deformities he had found in everything else: Unaccounted for lumps or blisters; shriveled, deformed kernels or nothing at all. On one cob, half the kernels had fused.

But it was here they saw the herd of feral horses grazing out in the open. There were two-dozen of them led by a husky stallion that wouldn't win any sort of beauty contest. He might be a bigger-than-average Halflinger or perhaps a Belgian cross, something like Brutus. But where Brutus had all the traditional lines of a horse, this fellow almost looked like he had a bit of rhinoceros in his genes.

"He sure is ugly," she observed.

Albert was thinking of one thing only; he had to devise a plan to catch some of them. They appeared to be almost all mares. He saw two adolescent colts among them who looked a lot like their sire. The memory of Brutus' untimely death pressed on Valerie as she watched them.

"How could we get them?" she asked.

Albert scanned the herd slowly through the glasses.

"I was thinking the same thing."

"Aren't you some kind of horse whisperer," she said.

"No," he answered before he realized she was teasing him.

"Me neither," she said. "That stallion will kill you if you bother him.

"I know it."

The problem was timing. They were half way to the settlement. If they kept going, the horses would surely move on. If they went back for rope, the horses would surely move on.

They sat down and unpacked some food and watched the animals while they ate and then rested in the grass.

In the end, they left the herd and carried on towards the settlement.

Several miles out, they spotted the familiar column of black smoke and when they emerged from the woods at the edge of the last field, Valerie happened to notice movement on the other side. It appeared to be sentries posted along the tree line.

"I guess they wised up," Valerie said, after scoping them for a moment.

Albert wasn't so sure. The men were too close together and they were not watching the prairie for intruders. They were armed, but once again it looked like simple bolt-action long guns. Albert became certain when they lit a small fire and dropped green foliage on it to make smoke; they were waiting for someone.

It didn't take long before a troop of about thirty men, half-a-dozen on horseback came across the field from the south, heading straight for the two in the woods. The scouts spotted them and emerged, waving their arms.

"Oh," was all Valerie said.

They could probably get into the settlement with a warning before the raiders, so they ducked back into the woods and started running. By the time the first shacks were in sight, it was obvious that the settlers had no idea what was about to happen. They entered the commons area and heads turned their way. Some people ducked inside; others just stared.

Albert spotted Mai preparing a meal. She glared when she saw him coming.

"Where's Pat?" he demanded.

"Died last month," she said.

Albert caught his breath.

"Shit. Is there somebody in charge?"

Mai ignored him and went back to stirring a pot bubbling over a wood fire. Albert looked at her with a mixture of pity and contempt.

"Hey," he said. "You are about to get raided."

She shook her head slowly and refused to look at him.

"Go away," she told him.

They approached several others, but no one wanted to talk to them. They came to a circle of bedraggled and underfed worshippers gathered around some kind of alter.

"The lord is my shepherd..." they chanted in unison.

They were following the instructions of a man in their circle who was reading from a bible.

"He leadeth me beside the still waters..." he shouted, and they echoed it back in a haphazard way.

Then his voice boomed out with that forced, unctuous theatricality of the make-believe preacher: "He restoreth my soul..."

Albert walked up and yanked the book out of the man's hands. He startled as if he'd been slapped and everyone went silent. Many remembered Albert from his first visit and they began to move off.

"There's a mob at the edge of that big field to the west of you. I think they're coming this way."

"Well, they are most welcome," he said. "We bear no one ill will."

"I don't think they feel the same," Albert said. "They look like raiders, to me. You need to get your shit together-."

"We are not going to fight," the man interrupted him. "Why should they bother us? We only want to live peacefully and serve the Lord."

"Jesus Christ," Valerie snapped at him. "Haven't you assholes learned anything?"

The man barely noticed her. He was glaring back at Albert now.

"We don't want you here," someone shouted.

"You come in here and killed our men," a woman screeched, tears welling up in her face. "Jody never hurt nobody in his entire life."

Who the fuck is Jody? Jody the wolf skinner? Too bad you can't die more than once.

Albert handed the book back to the man who accepted it without a word and resumed reading.

"Yea, though I walk through the valley of the shadow of death..."

Albert marched back to the center of the settlement and stood near the fire. He noticed that the population of the village had already decreased by half in the few months since he'd first seen it. The children were gone.

He took out the .45 and fired a shot into the air, forcing everyone within hearing to stop and look at him.

"There's a raiding party coming this way," he announced. "They are not coming here to plant tomatoes, understand?"

Nobody moved at first and Albert thought that maybe they were in some kind of trance.

"We know who you are, Mister Smythe," an older man said, coming out of a nearby shack. "We aren't interested in fighting anybody," he said.

"They are going to-."

"Get out of here," a woman interrupted him. "We don't want your type here."

Albert looked at them and frowned. Then he shrugged and put the pistol away.

"Suit yourself," he said.

Albert and Valerie made it out of the settlement and back into the woods by a roundabout route, striking deep into the forest to avoid any possible contact with the raiding party. Before long, they were out of sight and hearing.

It added another two hours to their forced march back to the cave during which they did not speak. Albert didn't even stop for his usual breaks every hour. He ploughed through the bramble and clinging foliage without altering his pace until he saw the familiar shoulders of limestone. Only then did he seem to relax.

Normally he would have scouted the area for half an hour before entering to make sure it had been undisturbed, but this time he just barreled through, almost slipping on the gravel bed of the wash before he climbed up to the cave entrance. He disappeared without waiting for her.

She arrived a few minutes later, her face tight with anxiety.

"What's the matter?" he asked her.

"Don't you play innocent with me," she said. "Do you really think we should have just left them there?" She turned away and hung her pack and weapons up against the wall.

"I hate to state the obvious, but-."

"We should have stayed and helped them anyway," she insisted.

"You can't help people who won't help themselves," he replied. "I've tried it."

That was it for a few days until Albert thought of the horses again.

"I've got plenty of rope, but I don't know how to lasso or anything light that," he said.

Valerie was morose and joined in the conversation half-heartedly.

"I don't see how you can do it with only two people. We need a whole bunch to surround one or two of the young ones and cut them out of the herd...then maybe. What makes you think they are still there, anyway?"

"They'll stay as long as the grass is good."

But there was no way to do it without some form of assistance, either another horse that could keep up, mounted by a rider who could rope, or some kind of moveable corral where they could be directed. A horse has about exactly one blind spot; directly behind his behind; otherwise, he can see almost 180 degrees looking forward and with a slight turn of his head in either direction he can complete the circle. Nobody sneaks up on a horse. It can see you coming a mile away – literally. Eventually, they abandoned the idea and concentrated on restoring their food supply that was now down to about half a year's worth. For Albert that was dangerously low.

"We are out of flour," he said, pounding his fist down on a ball of dough.

"There's that field," she said, glumly.

He was tormented by her unhappiness and it terrified him.

"Why don't we go look," he suggested.

The next morning they set out early, and walked into the sunrise. By the time they got to the wheat field, the sun had burned off the dew and the field waved gently. The grain was high, as he expected it to be and the heads were studded with twisted and deformed berries and to his mild astonishment, ready for harvest. It had been growing all winter without any rest. Somehow, it had vernalized and flowered in a matter of weeks despite the high temperatures. At this rate, he figured the field would produce three or four crops a year.

"Aren't you worried about eating it?" Valerie asked tentatively, as she examined the strange little beads.

Unable to mask the sarcasm, he said, "Eat it and die of cancer or don't eat and starve to death. I report, you decide."

"Huh?" she said, staring at him.

"Never mind. Bad joke."

They had not expected to find a harvestable crop here so they had nothing in which to carry the grain back to the cave.

"There's still time to make a trip and collect some," he suggested, but it was clear that she had her mind on something else.

"I want to go see how they are doing," she told him.

Albert never argued with her or contradicted her except when she was in danger. He did not care what she said or did or thought as long as she stayed with him.

"Okay," was all he said.

It was another fifteen miles to the settlement.

Once again they stood at the edge of the field where they had spotted the scouts several days before. There was no smoke rising from the settlement, an ominous omission from the scene. It could have only a few explanations, none of them good.

They entered the commons and were greeted by the burnt skeletons of houses and shacks leaning unhappily towards the earth, some still smoking. A pack of dogs saw them and immediately formed up to attack. They were well coordinated and came at them from several sides at once.

"Easy," he said, as she raised her rifle.

She shot the first inbound canine, a large German shepherd right between the eyes. It didn't even make a sound. Several of the smaller ones tried circling and she shot them one after the other with a cold, methodical deliberation. When the fourth dog yelped in mid-air and slammed into the dirt, the others stopped and crouched. They were snarling and barking but they were no longer interested in the dangerous two-legged prey that had just provided them with a fine dinner.

They were able to walk right past the dogs as they feasted on their brethren, tearing, snarling and shrieking as they ripped the flesh off the bones and threw it back.

They came across a number of human skeletons variously sized and dozens of long bones and skulls scattered around the buildings. Not a soul had survived; at least no one was here to tell the story of what really happened.

*

They camped in a stone ruins with their fire banked in a corner.

"We couldn't have stopped this," he said. "We'd just be dead, too."

252

"I know, Albert." Valerie answered. "I'm not blaming anybody."

He handed her a bowl of Albert Smythe Special and she looked at it warily.

"No bugs," he said. "Just meat and berries and smoked oysters."

"What?"

"I found this can of smoked oysters, so I put it in. Can you imagine what kind of an idjit would store smoked oysters for an emergency food supply?"

"Oh, I can imagine," she said.

"Now sardines, I can understand; but oysters? Shit. I must've been plumb outta my mind."

"Tastes alright," she observed. I don't think I ever ate an oyster. Is it that squishy thing in there that looks like a big brown curled up maggot?"

"Ya."

"Tastes kinda like a maggot," she said.

"Lot better, I'd say," he replied. "I have ate a lot of maggots and I like oysters better; but I sure wouldn't waste space on them again. Rather have a sardine."

They had to spell each other on sentry duty because of the dogs. He watched her sleeping and let her run right through her first shift. It made her angry when she woke.

"I've told you before that I don't need anybody to look after me," she scolded him. "I do my share."

"I know."

"And I take what I'm owed."

"I know."

She took the cup of sugared warm water he handed her and sipped it while he lay into the bedding and closed his eyes. She heard the dogs prowling the perimeter for the rest of the night but they daren't come in.

When he woke she was not there and he was stung with a momentary panic. But reason told him there was no way they would take her and leave him. She had wandered off and would be back. It wasn't up to him to tell her what to do. The woman had been looking after herself since she was about 15 years old in circumstances he didn't even want to imagine.

He heard her coming and feigned sleep.

"C'mon, I know you're awake," she said. "Look."

He opened his eyes and she showed him half a dozen chicken eggs.

"What?" he said.

"They had chickens and I guess one old hen has outwitted the dogs so far. I found her nest."

Albert took one of the eggs and gently sawed the end off with his knife. The gluey albumin wobbled and the yolk shone through like a tiny sun. He tilted it back and sucked the contents down, yolk and white sticking to his beard and running from the edges of his mouth. She followed suit and in a few minutes they finished them, washing it down with warm water. Trying to pack them for later was just plain stupid.

"Come on," she said and took off for the woods.

At the edge of the settlement in a path seeming to head due north, they picked up a trail of horses and people on foot. It was no longer possible to tell how many of anything but it seemed that there had to be a lot more than the thirty raiders. The only logical conclusion was that the raiders had taken prisoners.

"Same ol' same ol'," Albert muttered.

"Where would they be going?"

"Hell."

"Hell?"

"How you going to know? I don't know what's going on out there anymore. You probably know more than I do. I been locked up, remember?"

"It's only been four days," she said. "That many people…they'll be traveling slow…You don't think they are worth it."

"That's a fact. A whole hundred of them ain't worth your finger to me."

That was as close as Albert had ever come to uttering that terrible phrase and it shocked him deeply as soon as he said it. He knew his face had turned red and his stomach was churning. He couldn't speak. He couldn't even look at her. He was already trying to figure a way out of it if she said something he didn't want to hear. His brain was echoing like a subway tunnel: Asshole…Moron…Fuckhead…Schmuck…"

"We can't just look after each other, Albert. Not when there are so many people out there who, well they are so helpless."

She said 'look after each other.' 'Look after each other.' Look after-.'

"Okay," he said, and that was that.

They would be out of provisions in a few days, but that wasn't really an issue for either of them. They had both survived the woods for years and improvising came naturally. They'd eat a rabbit or a deer or a squirrel; or, maybe a dog or a rat or a hat full of wood lice. They knew that water was the crucial element. The problem was Albert's hypoglycemia, something he had never revealed to her. He had been tested repeatedly for diabetes and had always come up negative, but the condition persisted. If he failed to eat, to consume sugar or some carbohydrate at regular intervals, he could almost lose consciousness. His eyes would swim; his joints would turn to jelly; his breathing might even become erratic. He was never far from a carbohydrate source, whether it be the small amounts in other foods or the massive dose he could get from a sugar cube. But it was the reason he was prepared to transport five hundred pounds of sugar on his back across the growing wilderness of southern Indiana when he was stocking his cave. Sugar, to Albert could easily be the difference between life and death.

They were moving at more than twice the speed of their quary, but even so, it would take days to catch them and there was no way of knowing what they might encounter along the way that would add to their travel time. They knew only that the longer they delayed, the less likely they would come upon the slavers. Neither questioned the notion that the raiding party was a gang of slavers. You don't force people to join a kibbutz. If there were slavers, there were slave buyers. If there were slave buyers, there must be a location, a market, a place to do business.

"Let's go back and mount up proper," Albert suggested.

"They'll get away, Albert. They already got a big head start and you being such a slowpoke, we have to go now."

In their favor was the fact that a large mass of people and horses create trail as they go, beating down bushes, flattening roadways, removing obstacles or identifying traps. The slowest speed they would tolerate was always slower than their pursuer. They didn't know they were being followed and their vigilance would be compromised by hubris. They would want to spend plenty of time raping the women before they sold them. They had no idea who they were dealing with.

Two hours in, they came across the first bodies. They had been shot or beaten to death and left for the dogs. He couldn't tell if they were male or female as everyone pretty well wore the same clothing, these days and there was not a scrap of flesh left.

By the end of the day, they had come across another dozen at various intervals and it made Albert think that the captives were resisting; why else would the raiders shoot their profit? They kept going until dusk and then decided to stop for a few hours. Even in the near absolute darkness of a moonless night, Albert could pick out the trail; but they needed rest. She was anxious to keep going but he insisted. Valerie's face was drawn and dark and her eyes seemed overlarge as they collapsed onto the ground. He offered her the canteen and she took a sip and handed it back. She watched him to make sure he swallowed his share and then capped the bottle and set it aside.

They did not make a fire, but ate the jerky and dried berries cold, washed down with water that was beginning to take on the flavor of the canteen. They would have to take some time in the morning to collect dew or they would dehydrate within twenty four hours. They more than doubled the speed of the column but it was still two full days ahead of them.

Albert was experiencing the beginning rush of the sugar deficit and knew he had to find something pretty soon or he could simply faint like a coed. Sleep might help.

At midnight, he shook her awake.

It was slow going, but they emerged from the woods onto an old, overgrow road. The group had split, with three horses going north and everyone else going south. That was at least two days ago, Albert thought. He headed south. Wherever the three horsemen were going, he had a feeling they'd be coming back. By sunrise they had come across two more bodies, one still being worked on by a young coyote. The animal hunkered down and snarled as they passed, but didn't run. They must be closing on the group.

Albert surreptitiously took a sugar packet from his pocket and filled his mouth as he trotted. He had two left.

They came to a crossroads and followed the trail east again, closing on them much sooner than they had expected. This new road was much better traveled and most of the pavement had been cleared of vegetation and debris. There were wagon tracks and even tire tracks in the gravel.

Albert stopped to catch his breath and Valerie dropped down on the ground and held her head.

"You run pretty good for an old guy," she gasped.

Albert paid her little attention. He had switched into attack mode, banishing everything from his mind except the task. Then they heard a shot over the rise in the road. It was the familiar snap of a .22 caliber.

"My guess is we're here," he said and struck out across a field cutting a diagonal to the next wood lot from where he expected to be able to see what was going on. She followed without question. They heard a car engine without a muffler before they got half way across and dove into weeds. A pickup truck raced along the road, past the turn and kept going. Albert waited until it was out of sight before he stood up and started jogging again. They arrived at the wood lot, breathless.

"Stay back and to my left," he ordered. The look on her face told him she would do exactly as he asked, but she didn't know what was happening.

"You're a lefty...you cover my left flank...I'll go in ahead of you and over about twenty feet or so...understand?"

They separated and struck into the trees, struggling with the creeper and the Walking Stick and the bramble that had taken over. He stopped to listen and found himself in a berry patch. As quickly as he could, he stripped the fruit and ate it. It wasn't quite ripe but it was better than nothing.

They began to hear voices and smell the cooking fires.

They heard shouting and a woman wailed and then screamed.

They began to move towards the camp, trying to time their movements to outbursts of noise. Dogs began a frenzied barking and Albert froze, but the sound stopped with a dog's whimpering followed by a single yelp.

The undergrowth between the trees was so thick it was almost impossible to see through. He crept within a hundred feet of the edge and managed to part enough of the foliage to see into the campsite.

There were people in a wire compound and men walking around, some of them armed. He counted 27 guns of varying calibers and actions. A couple of trailers stood at one end and there were tents and other rough shelters. He saw the horses tied up at the far end. A door opened on one of the trailers and a naked woman was thrown down the steps onto the dirt. She cried when two men grabbed her by

257

the hair and dragged her back to the wire. There, two others opened the gate and they threw her inside. Then they grabbed another woman who began to scream and fight until one of the men swung a wooden club against the back of her leg and she buckled. She was crying and begging as they jerked her to her feet and began dragging her to the trailer. But she continued to resist and finally one of the men punched her in the stomach. She buckled, unable to breathe and they dragged her the rest of the way to the trailer without any trouble.

Albert sat back against a tree and closed his eyes.

He felt Valerie's approach and turned his head her way.

"There sure is a lot of them," she whispered.

"Too many," he said.

"What does that mean?"

"It means we can't just go in there and start something."

He could see the rage and the hatred in her face and it was a little worrisome. People who make rash decisions in cases like this usually get killed.

"Well what then?"

"We watch for the rest of the day, try and figure out what they're doing. Then maybe we hit them at night, somehow."

"And meanwhile-!"

"And meanwhile you don't get caught."

The sound of another woman screaming as she flew out the door of the trailer punctuated his comment.

"Look. I've been doing this for a long time. There is no way I am going up against twenty-seven armed men just like that. I am not prepared to throw my life away on a bet. Are you?"

She stared at him and then fell back against the tree.

"You come to a river and there's five hundred people drowning and you try to save them all at once, you're all going to die. You try and save them one at a time, maybe you might do something."

"I just keep thinking if it was me in there."

"It wouldn't be, though, would it?"

She didn't answer.

"You have first watch," he mumbled, the sugar-fugue shutting down his brain.

*

258

She woke him at dusk and he dragged himself to the surface but it felt like a stone was tied to his legs. He pulled a sugar pack from his pocket and didn't even bother to hide it this time. He poured every granule into his mouth and held it there until it dissolved.

When he opened his eyes, she was looking at him.

"I saved mine for you," she said, passing him five little paper sacks of sugar that used to be displayed at every coffee bar in the world for free. Now they could easily be traded for five pounds of jerky.

"My brother was diabetic," she said by way of explanation.

That was the first piece of personal information she had revealed to him. He nodded and accepted the packets. He put four in his pocket and ate the fifth one right away. In a matter of five minutes his head cleared and his joints stopped wobbling.

"Someone just showed up," she said.

As it got darker, they could get closer and he crawled across the dirt and seedlings until he was barely 50 feet from the edge of the camp.

A short man with a wide-brimmed hat emerged from an old Ford car and walked over to several of the raiders who were gathered around what seemed to be their leader.

Then a woman got out of the car and she walked over to the wire compound and looked in, hands on hips. She was wearing a fancy dress of some kind that flowed out at the bottom. It would have been antiquated even before the Catastrophe. She must have taken it from a museum display or something similar.

There were about 100 people left in the enclosure and they clung to the wire and stared out at her.

She walked back and forth along the cage and stopped occasionally. She would gesture and someone would get out of the way or someone would come forward.

She walked back to the two men and Albert could see her laughing. They seemed to come to some agreement and the two visitors returned to their vehicle. He had trouble starting it at first but it coughed to life and blue smoke flowed from the muffler. The headlights blazed across the compound.

"Buyers?" Valerie asked, quietly.

Albert nodded.

"I figure they are going to move them or something," he said.

Valerie was almost too enraged to speak.

"You better get your head straight," he told her sternly. "You go in there like that and you'll come out dead."

She knew he was right but it didn't help. Her heart was pounding so hard it hurt and she had broken out into a heavy sweat.

Then he explained his plan to her and she seemed to calm down a bit. He made her repeat it back, simple as it was and looked into her face.

Getting close to the wire was not a problem. Even opening it up and letting people loose probably wouldn't even be noticed for a minute or so. They had four guards walking back and forth, one on each side of the wire compound. Sometimes they stopped and chatted or exchanged cigarettes. He could hear them laughing. The balance of the raiders were hanging around a large fire pit, "off duty" or eating or waiting for orders. He had seen only two military weapons among them, a pair of AR15s, but he couldn't know if they were capable of fully automatic fire or not. It was much more likely that each man had been given a magazine or maybe two and warned about wasting ammunition. He had three clips of 30 rounds each for his AK; two magazines of 13 rounds each for his .45; and five .22 magnum bullets in his pocket revolver. Valerie had two magazines, but one had been partially emptied to kill the dogs. If they started a firefight they'd be surrounded and wiped out in twenty minutes.

Albert and Valerie remained at the edge of the cage. It seemed the raiders had provided sufficient water to their prisoners but very little food. Many of them had started out in poor condition and were already skeletons. They sat on the ground, back against the fence, waiting to die.

As the night wore on, the fire died and the guards were relieved. They were standing four-hour shifts. By midnight, a few sentries posted near the road and the guards were the only ones awake.

The guard pacing the fence nearest Albert stopped once to light a cigarette. He drew hard on it and seemed to be looking right at him. But in a few minutes he resumed his monotonous routine. Another hour passed and he stopped for a conversation with the guard from the next leg of the compound. They met at a corner and talked briefly before separating. Albert's guard started back and decided he had to urinate. He walked up to the edge of the bush and leaned his rifle against a tree. Once he had begun to relive himself, Albert came at him from the side.

The man managed a croaked noise as the Emerson split his trachea and then ripped out the front of his throat. The blood spurted and he lowered the man quietly to the ground. Valerie dragged him into the trees. Albert checked the rifle and grunted, derisively. It was an old lever action 30.30 with a 6-shot tube magazine. If it didn't jam it wasn't bad for close range work. Even the best of them were finicky and could let you down at any time.

Albert picked up where the man left off and started pacing the fence. When he got to the corner, the man on the next leg was coming towards him. He stepped out and then crouched down pretending to be examining the ground close up. The other man came towards him and then slowed for a moment.

"What is it?" he said, suspiciously.

Albert muttered and the man came closer; but he had half-raised his rifle. He was looking quizzically at Albert, trying to get a look at Albert's face.

"Shit!" Albert said. "Look at this!"

The man came forward and bent down to see what Albert was pointing at.

Albert shoved the Emerson as hard as he could straight up under the man's chin. The blood spurted and drenched his arm as he forced the blade through the roof of his mouth and finally with a last violent, twisting shove, tore through his sinus cavity and rammed straight into his brain. He ripped the knife back out and let the man hit the ground. Blood was dripping from his face and he tried to wipe it from his eyes but it just smeared.

The guard carried a single barrel shotgun and Albert took it and quickly searched his pockets for shells. He had none.

When he looked up, a dozen prisoners were standing at the wire, staring at him.

The enclosure was a very rough affair, a mixture of boards and rusted farm fencing and even a few strands of barbwire. It wouldn't take much to topple it. The people behind the fence for some reason refused to move. They just stood there and stared at him.

"Push the fence down," he whispered harshly at them. "Push the fucking thing over and get outta here."

While they stared at him, the front gate guard discovered the attack and sounded the alarm.

The camp burst like an anthill as the two-dozen armed men ran for the cage.

Screaming could be heard over the shouting as the men began to surround the cage, moving towards the back wall where Albert was trying to tear boards off the fence and loosen the wire.

"Come on you fuckers!" he screamed at them, but they didn't move. They didn't seem to know what to do.

Then he heard a shot from Valerie's rifle and a raider went down with a hole in his throat. There was a five second pause and then another shot.

Albert looked into the compound as the guards and the other raiders swarmed the prisoners, heading towards him.

He could wait no longer and had to repair to the tree line fifty feet away where he would become the other leg of the crossfire. The prisoners were supposed to have broken the fence by now and be streaming into the woods with Albert and Valerie covering them.

But the first people at the fence were the raiders who began spraying the woods with rifle fire. Albert narrowed himself behind a tree and waited until the shooting stopped. The prisoners had started to scream and shout and the guards had to turn their attention to them instead.

Every few seconds Valerie's unerring rifle would select a target and a head would explode or a gut-shot raider would crumple screaming to the ground. She had killed six with six shots by the time the inmates turned on their captors.

Completely unarmed and debilitated by hunger and the mistreatment of the march, they had trouble coordinating their counterattack. But when the first raider fell to their flailing arms it seemed to ignite the others and they turned on their jailers with a typical ferocity.

Albert watched as a dozen women cornered one man who swung his rifle at them. He struck one across the temple and she fell. Another rushed him and he jammed the barrel into her throat. She staggered, gasping. Two more rushed in, screaming at him and finally managed to push the rifle down. The remaining women moved in and dragged him by his hair to the dirt. A young woman, no more than twenty jumped on his back and jabbed her thumbs repeatedly into his eyes until one of them split open and fluid ran down his cheek. He screamed wildly as they tore at him, ripping his ears off before he collapsed. He rolled back and forth on the ground holding his head. They began to kick his sides and groin. He tried to squeeze his legs together

262

but they yanked them apart and several women stood in front of him, kicking him repeatedly until he just sagged.

The dozen raiders who had rushed into the compound were being pressed against the fences. Two prisoners grabbed a bearded man and held him down while others stomped on his throat. They moved with the screaming pack to a pair of younger men who were swinging their weapons at the crowd but were soon bowled over. He could hear the men screaming above the shrieking fury of the prisoners as their bodies were ripped open and strips of skin were torn off like wallpaper.

This massacre continued for an hour until all twelve of the men in the compound had been literally ripped to shreds. Blood soaked into the dirt and the crowd, possessed now by the insurgent madness of its own behavior simply went looking for more victims. Albert could see them heading towards him and he stepped out with his .45 and pointed it at the first man in the group. But he never had a chance to fire. Valerie's rifle cracked three times and the spearhead of the mob collapsed on the ground. It stopped them, cold.

There was complete silence.

Albert could hear his feet on the stones as he flanked them, his .45 pointed directly their way.

"You all better snap out of it," he said calmly.

They continued to stare at him, making no sound. He heard Valerie's familiar step behind him and he glanced her way for a second. A man rushed towards them and Valerie fired, catching him in the forehead.

Now Albert was infusing with rage and hatred and he could feel his hand tightening on the pistol.

"Last chance," he snarled. 'Back the fuck off."

*

At dawn the full extent of the carnage became evident. Besides the dead in the compound itself, a portion of the mob had flung itself against the trailers. There was at least a dozen dead prisoners on the ground. Both trailers had been smashed open and dead lay across the doorsteps.

They seemed to have run out of enthusiasm and the living sat in the dirt or stood in small groups, while the dead looked at them blankly.

Albert dragged a dead man from the steps of the first trailer and looked inside. Four bodies had been ripped open and eviscerated. Organs hung partially out of torn abdomens and blood was an inch deep. Two of the individuals were faceless. The other trailer was basically the same. The best count he could come up with was twenty four and when he saw the empty hitching post he knew the remaining three had escaped on horseback. No doubt they were heading directly for the short, chubby man in the hat and his girlfriend with the flowing dress.

Albert watched a group of five men and two women approaching him slowly. He raised the AK and took off the safety.

They stopped and one of the women came forward.

"I guess we should thank you," she said.

Albert looked at her indifferently. He didn't care whether she lived or died or became Queen of England or was raped to death in a trailer. He didn't want her thanks, either.

"Far enough," he told her as she took another step.

"We had no idea…" she started to say, clearly bewildered.

Albert walked away and joined Valerie who had stayed on the perimeter while he searched the grounds. She kept the rifle on the woman until Albert was beside her.

"The horses are gone," he told her.

"You think they just lit out?"

"No. I figure they have run to wherever that man in the hat is. They are going to come back, is my guess."

"Are we going to wait here?"

He glanced at her and shrugged.

"I'm not leaving without those horses," he said.

When they had collected all the hardware, they had nineteen rifles, two shotguns and 167 rounds of ammunition.

Valerie found a storage shed with several hundred MREs and she detailed several of the prisoners to hand them out.

"Apparently this man in the hat has a place about ten miles from here straight down that road. It's a relocation center."

"And that's where the horses are," she finished for him.

"I figure we hike down there and steal them horses and get the hell out of here," he said.

"What about them?" she asked.

"What about 'em?"

"Are we just going to leave them here?"

Albert looked at her curiously.

"What exactly am I supposed to do with them?"

"I don't know," she fretted, "but we should try and help them, somehow."

For the first time since he'd found her, Albert felt anger rising in his craw. He glanced past her to the seventy-five or so people wandering around in a daze or sitting and staring at the ground. Not one of them had left the scene since being liberated. Not a one had taken a rifle and disappeared or gone after the men behind what had happened. They just sat there, waiting for the next official they could obey. She couldn't have missed it; there's no way she didn't see what they were. He looked at her again.

"I know," she said. "I know..."

The woman who had tried to approach Albert earlier came towards them and Albert straightened up and unhitched his rifle.

"Please," she begged from twenty feet away. "I need to talk to you."

"So talk," Albert replied.

"We want to go with you," she said.

"Fuck you," he snapped and then colored deeply, sorry he had slashed at her so roughly.

"We'll do whatever you say," she continued.

"Oh, I am sure you will," Albert said. "That's the problem with you people."

"Are you going to go after the man in charge of this, the one who set it all up? We want to come with you and fight. We're all prepared to die."

Albert couldn't help a savage grin and shook his head as if to try and clear it.

"I don't do business with people who are looking to die. Sorry."

Valerie approached the woman and steered her away. Albert began packing the dozen MREs they had confiscated and getting ready to move. Albert watched her out of the corner of his eye as he prepared their kit. He saw the people surrounding her, gathering together like bits of space debris caught in a planet's gravity. He dropped what he was doing and started over.

"Can any of you use a gun?" she asked them.

Hands went up and some were retracted immediately.

"We have 17 rifles with a little bit of ammunition," she said. "The rest of you, well, I don't know what to say."

She turned as he came up beside her. He looked hard at her and then away.

Fifteen men and two women rummaged through the pathetic arsenal, selecting a firearm and taking the handful of shells that went with it.

"What about the rest of us?" someone called. "What the hell are we supposed to do?"

Albert clamped his mouth shut to keep the fury inside and turned away.

"Okay, let's go," he shouted, sergeant-style.

He started walking, certain that the majority of the prisoners would end up prisoners again, in no time. He could hear marching behind him and then Valerie came up alongside.

"I think you better take a look," she said.

Albert turned and his stomach clenched.

"Oh Jesus, sweet Jesus," he lamented as he watched all seventy-five of them falling in behind in ones and twos, each carrying a stick or shovel handle and two, green, military MREs.

He looked at Valerie who raised her eyebrows and shrugged.

Everyone stared at him in silence.

"Do you all understand that you are walking into almost certain death?" he yelled.

There was no response.

"You are unarmed, untrained and basically unfit. The only thing you will find at the end of this road is a bullet – or worse!"

No response.

They stood still, listening with that infuriatingly obedient mien that had directed them almost from birth.

Albert closed his eyes and thought for a moment.

"One last thing," he said with sad resignation: "I personally will shoot anyone who starts singing, "It's a long way to Tipperary."

A laugh rippled through the column and their faces opened with relief, almost joy. Everything would be all right now.

They were saved.

***

Chapter Five

The column stopped after about two hours of steady walking, during which they covered almost eight miles. Albert drew them off the road across a wide, overgrown field into a wood lot. The field would give them a kill zone if they were discovered and a decent place to run and/or hide when they ran out of ammunition after 30 seconds of fighting.

"No fires!" Valerie yelled at three men collecting wood.

Albert took Valerie aside and insisted she take the AK. She shook her head and patted her AR15.

"You can keep your damn water pistol. I don't care. Just take this until I get back," he insisted.

"Where are you going?"

"I figured out where we are. I thought I recognized it but it's overgrown so much. This is a state road we're on and it runs all the way across to The Nine Nine.

"What's the nine nine?"

"Interstate Ninety-nine!"

When she stared at him blankly, he just shook his head.

"Okay. So what?"

"What I am saying is, up here about two miles, we got a little town called Ashton. They had a big yard, the Crawley Docks and I bet it's still there and-."

"Are you going to make your point?" she demanded.

"It's a place to transport…anything. I mean they got a huge holding area inside and plenty of room for any kind of vehicle…my guess is, that fellah in the hat is selling people. He's got himself an auction house or a shipping dock or something like that. There could be hundreds of people up there."

"Well you aren't superman, in spite of what you've been told."

"Just going to have a look…then we'll decide what to do."

He offered her the AK again but she refused. It was clumsy and inaccurate over about three hundred feet and she wasn't used to it, anyway.

They went behind a large oak tree and embraced for a few minutes and then he left.

Valerie watched him until he disappeared between the trees, as silent as any deer. She began organizing the troop as best she could, posting sentries all around and advising the others to stay spread out and ready to bolt without any notice at all.

"If you fire a shot, you better be damn sure you have a reason," she told them. "We have no ammo and you're sure to bring someone in after us."

"What if we see somebody?" a woman asked.

"You peel back silently, without being seen and you get me."

"Well what if they start shooting?" a man asked.

"Shoot back, what do you think?"

"But you just said-."

"I know what I said."

She paused and looked at them.

"You'll figure it out," she told them, quietly. "Either that or you're dead."

*

Albert was quickly recalling the neighborhood, despite the changes of the last five years, which had led not only to actual geo- logical dislocations, but massive, uncontrolled overgrowth. He hugged the edges of the woodlots for about a mile-and-a-half before he was forced to cut across open ground. The old hay field had three feet of weed growth that would give him some protection if he needed it.

The ground sloped gently upwards over the 30-acre field and Albert found himself on a wide ridge overlooking the Crawley Transport property. It comprised about five acres of pavement with a warehouse and docking facility that occupied more than an acre. The building was almost sixty thousand square feet of racks; columns; secure cargo cages that would be the envy of any zoo; small, cramped offices; and free space enough for a decent game of football. There were more than forty loading docks for semi-trucks. It was built of concrete block with steel trusses covered by a flat roof. Strikingly, it had survived everything, in tact. There didn't seem to be a scrape on the paint.

He didn't need the field glasses to see what was going on. A military transport truck was pulling onto the lot. It stopped and a couple of officers jumped down. Albert watched as the main office door opened and the short man with the hat came out. Several other men joined them and they conversed for a while. Albert saw them point down the road towards the holding camp. The soldiers got back into the truck, turned it around and headed straight towards the camp. Albert followed the truck with the glasses. The rear flaps were pinned open and he could see about thirty heavily armed troops in the back. They had called in a military unit to round up the escaped prisoners and return them to their rightful owners. That's why they weren't using a helicopter, he decided. And then right on cue, he saw the Apache appear suddenly out of the sky and head towards the camp. Whether they were using it for spotting or they intended to kill everybody, its presence changed the equation.

The truck might run past the woodlot where he'd left them but the helicopter could and would wander in a wide radius. It would spot them immediately unless Valerie had somehow managed to get them under cover. All it would take is the glint of sunlight off a rifle barrel and they'd be wiped out in minutes. And he also knew that in the time he had considered this, the helicopter and truck were already coming parallel with the woodlot and either they would be discovered or not. It was out of his hands.

*

She saw the truck and heard the helicopter at the same time. The land vehicle was streaming up the highway and would arrive at the ruined holding camp in ten minutes. The helicopter dropped down to about 1000 feet and skimmed along behind the truck. It deked off course and surveyed a small woodlot and then swung across the road to the other side and headed straight for them.

"Anybody moves and we're all dead," she called out. Then she pulled herself back against a fallen log and slid a few cut branches over herself.

269

She had given up patrolling after a few minutes, realizing that it was not only hopeless, but the wrong action. The likeliest possibility, Albert had explained before he left, was that they would send a recovery team of some sort back to the site of the massacre. They might have vehicles, they might be on foot; they might even have a helicopter. There was no way to know. Their only hope of surviving the reconnaissance was to stay completely hidden until Albert got back or enough time had elapsed for them to realize he wasn't coming back. In that case, they would be on their own. What that meant, was anybody's guess.

The truck passed without pause. With no ability to investigate every possible hiding place or escape route, the foot soldiers would have to start at the scene and work their way out. The helicopter was another matter.

It descended to about five hundred feet as it approached, close enough to see the facial features on the side-gunner. She had bedded them all down as best she could. Some were rolled under hedge, some under trees. Most simply lay flat on the ground and pulled as much forest detritus over themselves as they could.

She had seen many times what a .50 caliber machine gun could do. A short burst was enough to obliterate a civilian vehicle or annihilate a dozen individuals in a few seconds. The helicopter's electric machine guns could level the entire two-acre plot in a couple of passes. The sheer volume of mixed hardball and incendiary ammunition was enough to penetrate any forest cover. They might kill everybody hidden under leaves and branches and not even know it; throw in a few Hellfire missiles and no one was going to get out of here.

She lay against the log as the machine approached, the womp-womp getting louder and faster as it cruised towards them. Even at five hundred feet they could feel its passage and leaves were scattered and whirled in its wake. They would have no trouble whatsoever spotting anybody who broke cover and that was her worst fear; some fool would panic at the sound and proximity of the machine and make a run for it. Then their only hope would be to take off in a hundred different directions but there was so much open ground around this little island of trees and Kudzu, the helicopter could simply start cruising an ever-widening circle, dispensing a lead hail that made escape highly unlikely. All it would take was one fool, one coward who could not

270

hold himself together for the five seconds while the Apache traversed their patch and that would be it for all of them.

It filled the sky as it hovered directly above her. She could just see through a break in the leaves as the Apache descended to about two hundred feet. The rotor downwash whipped the debris into a expanding cloud, a loose colloid of sticks and leaves, insects and even a small mouse that got caught in the draught. The machine drifted slowly sideways until it had surveyed the entire length of the wood lot.

Valerie was remembering a camp-out when she was ten years old. She remembered her father and mother hastily drawing down the tent and packing everything helter skelter into the van as the wind picked up. The vehicle rocked and jittered in the wind and hail stones smacked into the roof and bounced off the windshield. And it got very dark, like dusk just before the night falls. The trees whipped back and forth and branches snapped off and went flying. She remembered their laughter as they waited inside until the freak storm had moved on. And she remembered her disappointment when it had and the sun followed in behind and they set everything back up again. She hadn't thought of either of her parents or her two brothers since finding them dead from the Red Plague eleven, or twelve, or was it thirteen years now? No one could tell any more.

She sat up once the helicopter had moved on and watched as the blanket of leaves and debris moved and heads popped out from under cover like wary groundhogs. She closed her eyes and lay back, wanting to return to that blissful moment of hiding when you know they won't find you. This time it was their cheering that roused her.

"Shut the fuck up," she hissed at them. "Shut up! Shut up!"

They fell silent and looked at her, not sure why she was angry.

"Sound carries. Don't get into the habit of making noise, understand? Ever. You drop your guard like that and you'll get us all wiped out. Now get back under cover until I tell you different, understand? If you have to piss, piss your pants. But don't move and don't make a sound!"

Valerie emerged from her camouflage about every hour. It would take her five minutes before she was standing. She would make a small movement and then stop to listen. She repeated this until she was clinging to a thick tree trunk, surveying the road. She knew they'd be back. Would they come racing down that highway in their truck again, or would they fan out and beat the bush all the way back, searching for their prey?

To the group's advantage, they were walking towards the enemy stronghold and not away from it. It might not occur to the search team that these people would turn and fight. Maybe these gentlemen would make a big Warsaw Ghetto mistake and dismiss the notion of the prisoners fighting back. It would be a reasonable assumption. The sixty men in this group had stood by without saying a word while every one of these women was gang raped. They had stood in silence while their fellows were taken out and shot or delivered into some unknown hell down the road. They didn't even try to get away. The problem was that if the team knew how to track, they would discover almost immediately that no one had retreated through the woods.

She was standing at the edge behind a trunk when the helicopter suddenly appeared on the horizon. It was making larger and larger sweeps. The prisoners had been missing only a short time; they could not have gotten very far. Somebody was going to put it together. They had to. The helicopter had passed over them once, but it would likely come snooping around again. If they moved at the wrong moment, they were almost certain to be sighted. If they stayed, they were likely to be discovered. If they were on the move, some of them might get away. If they were all clustered together hiding behind the trees, they were doomed.

"Don't move until I tell you," she said quietly.

She moved carefully through the woods to the first man.

"When I say, you get up, take your gun and run into that big field. You get down on your belly and you crawl...the weeds are pretty high. If they don't pass right over you, they might miss you. Don't stop. Don't look back. If you hear the helicopter: Freeze, face in the dirt. When you get to the next woods, get under cover."

The last person to go was the woman who had approached them at the camp.

"What's your name," Valerie asked.

"Mary-Louise."

"Mary-Louise, huh? Okay, Mary-Louise: Keep them under cover and silent. If they find you...well, you do whatever you want. I'm going to get Albert and bring him back. If I'm not back by this time tomorrow, you are on your own.

"Don't move until pitch dark," she added as an afterthought. "Then eat your MREs and shit or whatever you have to do and get back under cover. Stay hydrated. Water is more important than food."

272

Mary-Louise had a sad, grave expression when Valerie disappeared into the foliage.

She heard the helicopter periodically as it headed in their direction and then passed. There was no sign yet of the troops. She didn't know if that was good news or bad. They might be looking in the wrong place or they might have fanned out and are right now pushing a long front towards the prisoners in the woods with their seventeen guns and their hundred and sixty seven bullets. All she knew was that Albert had been gone too long and she wasn't prepared to just accept that. She would see his body, one way or the other.

*

At that moment, Albert was completing a long, wide tour of the landscape so that he could approach the building from the side closest to the tree line. Even so, he would have to cross a quarter mile of open pavement to get up to the docks. There were tall parking lot lights on thick concrete bases that might hide him for a few seconds at night while a searchlight passed, but were useless in daylight. There were two sentries who walked the three hundred feet of the docks together. He saw others posted in the woods, away from the property and a heavy concentration around the front where a twelve-foot fence topped with razor wire enclosed the entrance. They had a sort of guardhouse out front of that with three men carrying M16s.

As dusk fell, he was surprised to see the floodlights turn on. Where were these people getting electricity? He couldn't hear a generator, which meant that someone had hooked up the grid.

He had no way in. There was no way to breach their defenses and he had accidentally happened to fall into a blind spot between two pickets. If either of them moved fifty feet, he could be in their field of view. He couldn't get across the lot. He decided the only thing he could do was go back, sans horses, sans revenge - *sans everything.*[12]

"You gave yourself away when you crossed the road," he said, quietly.

Valerie spun around, the rifle on her hip, her face bright with fear. Her eyes closed as Albert stepped out from the trees and looked at her. Then he put his arms around her and she sagged into him, burying her face in his jacket. She wouldn't let go for a few minutes. He pressed his lips against her neck and inhaled deeply.

"That was foolish, wasn't it," she stated, pushing away finally.

He looked at the ground.

"Well, if we make a plan and somebody doesn't come through...I mean, I understand but...I mean...it doesn't work that way," he replied. "I'm really glad...to see you," he fumbled. "I-"

"It's all right, Albert," she said, regaining her composure. "Don't try and talk."

Above them the helicopter returning to base beat the air above them and vanished. A few moments later, they saw the headlights from the troop transport as it raced down the road back to the Crawley docks.

"You got them stashed somewhere good?" he asked.

"I moved them across the field to a bigger forest area. I figured-"

He took her hand and started pulling her towards him.

"No!" she protested. "It's too cold. Are you crazy?"

He held her firmly and they collapsed into the soft bed of the forest floor.

Later, she led him roundabout to the new location and they made it into cover by dawn.

Seeing the lost platoon emerge from the leaves and sticks and branches, Albert confirmed in his mind the only plan he thought would work. They had one MRE left each and he told them to eat it, first thing. No fires: Cold water and flavor crystals only.

He waited until they had finished and then he bade them sit and listen. He explained the near-invulnerability of the docks, describing as accurately as he could and without embellishment the layout, the positions of sentries, the manpower at the front gate and various other details.

"We'd need a fully-armed company, maybe two hundred men, with the right equipment and the experience to get in there...and even then...we don't know what they've got inside. We don't know how far away the military base is. We don't know fuck all about their strength or even who they are. What I am trying to say here is, we cannot attack this place. There is no way."

They looked at him and each other, glumly, picking at the leaves like a troop of bored apes.

"Well, I guess we just get the hell out of here then," someone said.

"I'm not sticking around to get killed, that's for sure."

"I hear there's settlements to the south..."

"I heard it was north..."

274

It was about what he expected and he let them run it out.

"What are you going to do?" Mister Smythe.

"Who told you to call me Mister Smythe," he said, irritated.

"Pat told us about you."

"I heard of you," someone piped up.

"Ya, me too. I thought you were dead."

"Well Pat was delirious by the end, I'm sure," Albert commented

"No, he died quiet - asking if you had come back," a woman said, standing up and walking towards him.

It was Mai. She hand an ancient, five-shot Ivor-Johnson .38 revolver tucked into her waistband like a Mexican bandit.

"I guess I owe you an-" she started to say, but Albert cut her off.

"Forget it. There's no point and no time."

She nodded and went silent for a moment and then looked straight at him.

"We want to do something," she said.

"Well, save your own life. Get the hell out of here as fast as you can and…I don't know…join up with some other folks…something…I don't know."

Valerie observed the interactions without comment, but she was becoming increasingly curious about Albert. He had said nothing about himself to her. He treated her better than anyone ever had. She felt completely at ease in his presence. He never even criticized her. It was unusual. Even the best of friends have disagreements, but she and Albert had never had a cross word between them. They had never argued about anything except in fun. She knew there was something unusual about him by the way the cave had been provisioned. But why was he so well known?

"There's one possibility I can see that might get us inside…at least get me and maybe a few others inside," he said.

"Let's hear it."

"You aren't going to like it," he warned them.

"Just try me," Mai said evenly. "We don't have much left to lose, Mister Smythe."

When he had finished, a heavy, almost dead silence hung over the grove. Albert turned and walked out of range of their voices and lay down under a big poplar tree. He had given them time to work it out.

Valerie lay down beside him and in a few moments they were asleep.

Albert never remembered dreams. He knew he had dreamed but that was it. He had a feeling when he finally woke, that indicated what kind of dream it was. He might feel good. He might feel bad. That was it. There might be a flash of something in his memory, like the moment a fish breaks through the water and then instantly vanishes leaving only a series of expanding rings; but there was no story to tell.

For Valerie it was different. She dreamed every night and remembered much of the detail for hours, sometimes for days. She never had pleasant dreams. She wondered if anyone did anymore. She never recognized anyone in her dreams but they were always in trouble. She never had a dream about someone who was enjoying life. She woke in a terrified state, her hands usually clenched tightly around the rifle. She was often afraid to move at first because she didn't know if she was dreaming or if it was really happening.

But this time, they shared a dream. They were separated by a chasm too wide to leap over, so Albert felled two large trees and laid them down over the gap. Before he could walk across, the chasm filled with water and carried the logs away. Then the water subsided and they were back to the beginning, staring at each other across this deep gorge. Albert cut two more logs and laid them over the chasm but just as he was about to walk across, the gorge exploded with fire and flames shot fifty feet in the air. Smoke poured over them until they were both blind. And then a wind came and cleared the air and the chasm was sewed back together. But when Valerie looked, Albert was gone. And when Albert looked, Valerie was gone, though each believed him/herself to be standing there.

They told each other what they had dreamt and were suitably surprised and puzzled, but neither managed any sort of satisfactory explanation. They thought it must have been about the fear of separation. Then they thought it might have been about the fear of being together. Then they concluded that those conditions begat each other. Albert said it was about the difference in their ages. Valerie called him a moron and said it was about the differences in their willingness to be part of a society. Albert said he had proof that she was the moron and he was the genius. "I chose you," he said, "but you chose me."

"I love you, Albert," she said.

He felt his heart leap and adrenalin rushed into his system. What was he going to do? He couldn't walk away from this. He couldn't make a joke or say something stupid. He had to respond. He had to. There was no choice. It was either that, or-

"I love you," he said, hearing the sound of his own voice for the first time in years.

They talked it through a dozen times, but all they could agree on was the fact that the plan "really sucked."

"I'm open to suggestions," he said. "But you better make it quick. I'm not sticking around here any longer than I have to. Every minute we sit here, we risk being detected. We don't even know if they have operating drones."

The choice was theirs. No one was going to make it for them. They would be taking a terrible risk and there would be no one to blame if it went wrong – which it most likely would. Regardless of what they said now, they were untested. Faced with the reality of combat, half of them would turn and run; the rest would probably surrender. And he told them so straight up.

"This plan is insane," he said, one more time.

"That's good enough for me," a man called out and laughter rippled through the crowd.

***

Chapter Six

Albert had followed the rider's progress through field glasses, anticipating where he would come out of the bush, back to open ground and where he would likely take a break. Valerie had taken up a position 50 yards away from the edge of the Emit in a heavily over-grown Sycamore. The extravagant growth patterns over the last months had made it ideal for snipers, if nothing else.

As Albert had imagined, the cool, rushing water and the bank overhung with heavily draped limbs was too tempting to pass up. The scout, who had been riding since morning on a wide patrol extending almost a mile radius from the Crawley warehouse, pulled the horse up and looked around. He carried an old M1 Garand rifle, packed with great difficulty into a rifle scabbard designed for a Winchester and a 1911 strapped to his leg. He dismounted, holding the horse with one hand and inexpertly dragging the M1 out at the same time.

The horse whinnied and its ears went back, alerting the rider. He tied the lead to a branch and loaded the rifle. After a few minutes, the horse seemed to relax and he followed suit. He leaned the rifle against a trunk and then kneeled down over the river. He splashed his face and slurped handfuls of the cold water.

When he stood up, Albert tripped him and was on him in a split second. He punched the man in the jaw, twice, hearing the bone crack from the second blow. The Emerson was placed against the man's throat. He was staring at Albert with a look of complete surprise. He wanted to speak, but his jaw screamed with pain so he just tried to keep it still while tears sprouted and ran down his cheeks. Albert took the 1911 and quickly searched the man for any other weapons. He had a paratrooper's knife, a sort of butterfly affair popular with ghetto gangs but entirely useless in circumstances like this. He threw it into the river.

He jerked the man to his feet, keeping the point of the knife touching his Adam's apple.

"Don't speak," he said, "just listen."

The man nodded and tried to move his jaw. Pain shot through to his eye and he gasped.

"You' be all right in a couple of weeks if you can keep your jaw closed," Albert said. "Try not to move it. Keep it straight and just drink. It will probably heal okay if you do that..."

The man stared at Albert, terrified now because he was obviously insane.

"Anyway," Albert continued in a friendly tone. "You get back on your horse...nice animal, by the way. Cinch strap is too loose; that's how come the saddle keeps slipping when you dismount. You need to put another hole in the leather."

The man just stared, waiting for Albert to sprout wings or start breathing fire.

"You all are missing something," Albert said. "I got 'em. Most of them, I figure, anw ays."

The man started to speak and Albert backhanded him so hard he knocked him down. He picked the man up and jerked him to his feet.

"I do not like repeating myself," he said.

The man's jaw was trembling in spite of his efforts to control it and the pain was hitting him like a grease gun.

"You go back and tell your man, there, the little fellah with the big hat...you tell him just what I said. You tell him if he wants to negotiate, well by God I will negotiate," Albert said cheerfully.

"You tell him I got about sixty of 'em holed up where they can't get away and he can come and see 'em if he wants. He can bring a few boys along too. I understand how it works. You tell him if I even smell army or hear a helicopter I'll just kill 'em all. I don't give a fuck, understand? Good!

"You tell him to drive out and head back towards that camp where you boys lost 'em all. You tell him I got the people that done that, too, but that will be extra. You tell him to drive slow and we'll pick him up wherever we decide, understand?"

The man barely nodded.

"You go back and tell him he's got two hours to show up in that car without no soldiers, now, ya hear? We are just looking to make some trade, just like him. You tell him to bring that girl with him, too. Two hours. Now it's going to take you twenty-five minutes minimum to get back to your little headquarters there, so you better git to going. Two hours from now, we're gone with his cargo."

Albert smiled broadly and extended his hand.

The man took it, in a daze and they shook.

"I'll get this hardware back to you, don't you worry," Albert chimed.

The man got up on the horse after two tries and didn't even look back. He urged the mount to a trot and was absorbed by the foliage in half a minute.

Valerie came down from her perch and looked at him, quizzically.

"Now what was that all about?" she asked, some kind of a grin on her face.

He shrugged and looked after the place where the rider had disappeared.

"Sure hope it works," he said.

When they got back to their camp, the group was silent and Albert was already having doubts. He looked around at them, wondering what had compelled to stay and take such obvious risk when they could just as easily have lit out for the woods and maybe gotten away.

But that was their problem. They had all tried that, probably more than once. They had no food, no woodland skills, and no survival instincts. It was actually safer for them to stay. Albert Smythe and his plan was a better bet than being out there on your own where they wouldn't last a day.

"Last chance to back out," he said. "Anybody wants out now, just make a run for it. Anybody that turns chicken once this thing gets going, well, let me tell you. It's not just your ass you will be risking. You do what you are supposed to do no matter what. No matter what!"

The three armed 'prisoners' who had been chosen to accompany Albert and Valerie, fell in behind them.

Albert looked for a long moment at Mai who looked back without expression. It had been explained to him, that in many Asian cultures facial expressions that betrayed feelings were discouraged. That spawned "the inscrutable" label. Well, here was a perfect case of it. Her eyes were very dark and looked back at him without fear.

"You're in charge," he said, and she gave a brief nod, and then turned to the group. Fourteen "guards" stood while sixty or seventy captives sat on the ground, waiting to be sold down the river.

Albert picked the only decent site for an ambush at a bend in the road where a clump of cedars blocked the view around the corner. The other side of the road was an empty field with deep drainage ditch still functional near the shoulder. The next cover was three hundred yards away where the edge of a woodlot began.

Valerie placed herself in the arms of a tree and watched them deploy through her scope. Then they dragged enough loose timber from the lot to make a barricade across the asphalt. It wasn't much but it would force the vehicle to stop.

Those inside would not be surprised; they would know that contact was about to be made. Now all they could do was wait.

And not for long.

The car came into view a few minutes early, followed by a pickup truck carrying eight armed guards. As the car grew, he could hear the breathing of the man beside him.

"Easy," he said. "Calm is what it's all about."

The car was travelling about 25 M.P.H. when it rounded the bend and stopped abruptly in front of the barricade, not much more than a transported beaver damn by the looks of it.

The pickup arrived within seconds and the eight men were on the ground, fanning out in a circle towards the cedar bush. The first man there emptied a clip into the little patch of trees, severing limbs and kicking up a lot of leaves and forest debris.

But his disappointment was obvious when he looked inside and shook his head negatively.

The guards stood around, their weapons ready but they didn't know where to look. There was no cover nearby. There would be no point in hiding out in that wood lot. It was too far away. The lead guard walked slowly towards the barricade and kicked at it. It flew apart, easily, but it hid nothing.

Finally, the passenger window of the car rolled down and Valerie could see a woman sitting in the seat. It looked like the woman from the other night. The rear doors of the car opened and two more men carrying heavy, automatic weapons emerged. They looked around, scanning 360 degrees but had to admit they could detect nothing. One of them looked at the overgrown field and ordered the troop across the road.

The first few stumbled at the ditch and others leapt over. They fanned out and started to beat the grass, but after a few minutes, they abandoned that, as well.

"Must have changed his mind; the leader said, shouldering his weapon. The others took their cue from him to stand down and leaned their rifles against the vehicles. Several began to roll cigarettes. The woman got out of the car and put her hands on her hips and glared over the field.

"This is bull shit," she said, and turned to climb back into the car.

Valerie's first bullet struck the leader in the philitrum, sliced through his sinuses and exited his midbrain. The guards grabbed their weapons and ran behind the vehicles as Valerie's next shot crashed through the pickup windshield and entered the driver's right eye.

They began returning fire from behind the truck and the car and were concentrating it in a heavy rain at the point they saw the muzzle flash.

But now Albert and his three companions sprung out of the ditch and immediately killed four of the guards. The others were in the process of turning around but Albert stayed them with a short burst from his AK that killed one of the remaining men and persuaded the others to abandon their weapons.

Albert's companions were breathing hard and their eyes were lit. They stared at their prisoners, unable to hold in their smiles.

Albert meanwhile had walked to the driver's door and knocked on the window.

It came down and a rifle barrel poked out, pointed directly at his solar plexus.

"Don't be hasty, now," Albert said. "I could have killed you already and I think you know it."

The beefy little man with the shaved, bullet head and pale blue eyes watched him with a concentrated hatred.

He pushed open the door and fought his way out of the car.

"Your friend, too," Albert said.

The woman was glaring at him, already preparing her threats and promises of retribution.

She had barely uttered a single word when the man with the hat told her to, "shut up."

"Good idea," Albert said cheerfully. "Just shut your hole and spoke when you are spoken to," he said.

She paled and came around the front of the car, staring at him. It wasn't feminine anger he was seeing. This woman was psychotic. She believed her own press about her authority and Albert had sensed it right away. She wasn't playing along; she was deeply involved, probably more influential than people thought. She folded her arms and leaned back against the fender.

"I figure you are going to take me seriously, now," Albert said.

"You figure whatever you like," the man with the hat replied.

Albert frowned and looked hard at both of them. The man's eyes darted back and forth trying to scan him but the woman stared without blinking or showing any fear at all.

Albert walked a few feet and took one of the men under guard and dragged him over to Mr. and Mrs. Hat. The man smirked sideways at Albert, probably a show for his boss and the woman.

The guard's face exploded right into them, spattering brains and blood over a wide area. It stuck to her face and clothing and Mr. Hat, who had been closer was holding his ear. He spit a piece of skull onto the ground and began to wretch. Mrs. Hat was frozen in place, unable even to scream at him.

Albert dropped the dead man on the ground at their feet and stepped back a few paces. The other two captives had lost their bravado and tried to bow, their hands laced behind the head, eyes kissing the ground.

"Okay," Albert said. "I understand. I mean why should you take me seriously? I would probably be skeptical in your place as well, so don't feel bad."

Mr. Hat had lost his nerve and his eyes were on the run. He glanced at Mrs. Hat who was trying to pick bits of bone and skin from her hair. She spit out a glob of brain matter that had dribbled down her cheek.

"What in hell?" Mr. Hat said.

"Oh, come on," Albert chided him. "What did you go and bring ten guys with you for? I said a couple or didn't that fellah explain it right? A couple is two."

The man nodded and exhaled. He had trouble focusing because blood was already drying and hardening on his eyelashes.

"Well, what now?" Hat said. "It's your show."

Albert smiled broadly.

"Well, there you have it. Now we can all be friends, right missy?" he said, his eyes drilling into Mrs. Hat. She refused to speak and he left it that way.

"How do you know the army isn't on its way?" Hat said.

"I can kill you whenever I want," Albert replied, pushing them across the road and into the field. I told you no army; now am I going to have to impress you again?"

"No," Mr. Hat said quickly. "I haven't called anyone but if we're gone too long…"

"Ya, ya, ya," Albert said, giving him a shove. "You better hope they don't."

The prisoners trudged across the field, sometimes having to move around orphan corn stocks twelve feet high. No one had ever seen anything like it. The base was three inches thick and the cob at the top looked like a watermelon. As they broke into the woods, they went single file, with the three armed prisoners (who now called themselves soldiers) in front and Albert behind.

A half-hour of walking and they were forced to stop while Mr. Hat caught his breath. His face was bulging with high blood pressure and ands covered with sweat.

Albert allowed them a five minutes and a sip of water. He was waiting for one of Hat's men to break.

They walked a meandering roundabout trail that finally led them to a clearing. They had never been more than half a mile from the road. There sat the escaped prisoners, hands on head, legs crossed, and around them, thirteen armed guards.

The Hat's were startled by the discovery and Mr. Hat looked at Albert with some admiration.

"Son of a bitch," he said.

"Ya," Albert replied.

The prisoners stared at the Hats and the Hats stared at the prisoners. One man tried to get up and make a run at them and the guard hit him across the head with a rifle butt.

"Get back in there, you fuck," the guard shouted. The other guards were suddenly alert and prisoners sat immobilized, trying not to attract any attention.

284

"Will you get these folks some water so they can clean up?" Albert told his soldiers. They took his order silently and went immediately about finding a bowl and some clean water and towels.

"Sit down if you like," Albert said, indicating a couple of large stumps.

Mr. Hat gratefully plopped down. Mrs. Hat continued to stand for a while and then sat down, making sure he saw that it was her choice.

Albert remained silent while the men brought water and towels. The Hats washed their faces off as best they could. There were still bits of grey brain matter and pale skull bone tangled in Mrs. Hat's hair.

"Okay. So this is how it's going to be," Albert said.

"Mr. Hat here and me, we are going to get back into that car and turn around and drive into your compound. I, of course, am going to have a pistol up against that little fat belly of yours. You are going to introduce me as your new catcher."

"Do you want the job?" Mrs. Hat asked archly. "We have a vacancy."

Albert smiled and nodded vigorously.

"I was hoping that's what you would say. But let's not get ahead of ourselves, okay? Believe it or not, all I really want from you is trade for these...whatever you want to call them."

"What trade?" Hat asked.

"Well, what ya got?" he said.

The Hat's exchanged looks and Mrs. Hat took over the conversation.

"We've got more than you can imagine," she said boastfully.

"That's what I figured," Albert said. "So Mr. Hat here is going to take me to his warehouse and show me around and I am going to tell you what you are going to give me for these folks over here. And while Mr. Hat and I are gone, you, kind lady and your two champions over here will stay as my guests."

For the first time, he saw a flicker of doubt in her eyes. She knew something wasn't right. Mr. Hat didn't seem to get it.

Albert helped Mr. Hat to his feet and they set off down the trail, the three soldiers now guarding Mrs. Hat and her two companions.

At the edge of the field, they saw that the car was still there but had blown a tire somehow in the brief firefight. The pickup truck windshield was broken but the vehicle had four good wheels. Albert dragged out the dead driver and threw him into the ditch. He got in the shotgun seat and with a few maneuvers, they were headed back to the Crawley Docks.

"You think the gate isn't going to know?" Hat asked him. It was a real question, not an attempt to unnerve him.

"They better," Albert said. "Not only will I kill you and probably quite a few of your buddies before it's over, my men had orders to rape that girl of yours to death, first sign anything goes wrong."

The man's blood pressure mounted suddenly again as he stared out the window.

"On the other hand, Albert said with some congeniality, "if you do the right thing here, you can have those people and I'll even show you the bunch that over-run your holding cage.

"Why would you do that?"

"Just getting rid of the competition," Albert said.

Hat nodded, seeming to understand. Really, what else could there be? This fool knows as soon as he steps inside there he will be facing fifty armed guards. Maybe I'll just tell him to go ahead and kill Melba. Melba. He would hate to lose her for no good reason. That girl was the only one who could get him up anymore. She'd start working those lips and tongue of hers down where it counted and before you know it, "Bob's your uncle." He'd tried a dozen of the slaves but it wasn't any good. She was the only one could get him up. You don't throw that away on a bet, he thought. If this really was a job application, he was very impressed so far.

"How do I know you are going to turn them over?"

"What the hell do I want with them?" Albert said, looking at him. "What the hell do you want with them, for that matter? Are you a cannibal?"

Hat burst out laughing.

"No, no," he chortled. "Cannibal, by God….Ha, Ha, Ha…"

Albert shrugged.

"You don't know!" Hat said.

"So tell me."

"We sell them to the new administration for this Culture Zone."

"Never heard of that," Albert replied casually, his blood vessels starting to pound.

"The government has opened all the old coal fields along the Indiana/Illinois border. You know, surface mining. You scrape away some rock and dirt and there it is: Millions and millions of tons of good bituminous coal. They are using it to run the electric plant."

Albert tried to show no reaction, but Hat could see that he was getting through to him.

You mean-?"

"Slavery," Hat replied. "Only this time it isn't just blacks. It's everybody. They are working the coalfields and the crops and…lots of other stuff. I buy job lots and hold them here until I get an order. They send a couple trucks down, pick what they want and Bob's your uncle."

Albert looked across at Mr. Hat who was looking back at him with a curious smile on his face.

"If you know what's good for you, boy, you'll get that cargo back to me double-damn quick before this goes any farther."

Albert stared out the window.

"I got to get something for all my trouble," Albert whined.

Hat nodded confidently and cheered up.

"You'll do all right. I'll make sure of that. We'll figure this mess out."

The relief on Hat's face was evident and he smiled the whole way to the front gate.

"Just in case," Albert said, pushing the barrel of the .45 against his back.

"There's no need for that," Hat protested.

"Good," Albert said.

They drove up to the front gate that was manned by four guards, all carrying automatic weapons.

Everything was becoming clear. The coal was generating electricity and the electricity was bringing back some machinery, though maybe not the gas-powered kind - yet. There would be an insatiable hunger for coal. They couldn't get enough coal or enough slaves to scrape it up. That's what accounted for all these weapons and ammunition…this army group had managed to reform and was now starting to expand, looking for territory and treasure.

"Everything okay there, Mr. Beale?" the guard said, staring at the bullet shattered windshield.

"Thanks to this fellow right here," he said cheerfully. "He pulled me right out of harm's way…This here is my friend," Beale said.

"Where's everybody else? Where's Miss Melba and Jake?"

"Jake got killed right in this seat," Beale said sadly. "And we're going to have to get something together so we can bring her home...so don't you boys be wasting any time now. You, Arnie, you get a group together and wait for me."

Beale had played to his ego and the guard suddenly forgot his suspicions as he assumed the role, of posse leader for the great rescue operation.

Beale parked the truck and got out, Albert right beside him.

They walked up a short set of concrete steps through a steel door and into the vast universe of Crawley Transport. Albert had forgotten just how big it was. And just as if nothing had gone wrong, as if they were all in a time warp, men in shirtsleeves raced past with forklifts and others moved crates and equipment around on hand dollies.

"Something, ain't it?" Beale said, proudly.

Albert nodded.

He led Beal down a long corridor to another section of the warehouse. It was brightly lit and had a heavy odor.

"Oh, that's just the product," Beale said.

Albert stopped.

"Wanna see?" Beale said.

He followed Beal through a heavily secured door into the compound where the high-value cargo used to be stored. The cages went from floor to ceiling, all quarter-inch steel mesh. Albert blinked.

Behind the wire he saw hundreds of people. They paced back and forth or clung to the cages staring out or sat, nearly comatose on the ground. The men and women were separated and there was a special section where children were kept. They ranged in age from about eight to about twelve. Anyone older than that was classed as an adult and thrown into the big cages.

"We got two thousand four hundred on hand right now," Beale said. "We can hold about four thousand if we pack 'em tight, but you get too many problems, that way.

"You think it's cruel?" he said, glancing at Albert.

Albert shrugged.

"These kids haven't got a prayer out there," Beale said. "Ain't one of them got a living parent. We feed 'em and clothe 'em and give them something to do. It's no different for the adults. Most of them are glad to be in here."

Albert nodded and looked at Beale.

288

"Okay," he said, controlling his breathing. "Now how about that trade, huh?"

*

Melba was getting anxious. The two men with her had their hands bound behind their backs with some nylon cord and were sitting on the ground. They looked pale and uninterested in their surroundings. She found them disgusting and vowed to have them slaughtered in public if they got out of this.

The woman guarding her, the big chink, kept her eyes on Melba the whole time.

"Could I have some water to drink?" Melba asked.

Mai shook her head, no and resumed her unblinking stare.

Melba was going to deal with her as well. But she was also starting to feel uncomfortable. She knew there was something wrong here, something that fat idiot Beale never guessed. And telling her to shut up like that! Mr. Beal's days were numbered. She had already received indications from the main Peace and Tranquility Center, that Beale was not in much favor. They had almost suggested she arrange an accident for him. But this would be much better. She would emerge from this as the only one with the guts – and the brains - to deal with an operation of this size.

"Why are you smiling," Mai asked her.

It was the first words Mai had said since the woman had arrived.

"Oh, just thinking," she said softly. "About my children."

Mai nodded slowly.

"You have children?" she said, friendliness and female solidarity melting away the iron mask.

"Brantford, you get the lady some water," Mai called.

Melba smiled gratefully.

"You seem to have a lot of responsibility here," Melba said and Mai smiled proudly.

"Oh yes," she said, Mister Smythe put me in charge while he's away."

Brantford brought Melba a skin of water. She drank some and choked and spit it out.

"What in God's name?" she cried.

"That's the taste of the sac," Mai said. "Made from a bladder. I don't know what kind. Maybe deer. Ain't seen a hog in a long while."

Melba handed the skin back and closed her eyes tightly to force the images and the taste out of her mind.

"How old are your children?" Mai asked.

"My daughter, Gracie is seventeen and Leon is four."

"Ah…" Mai commented and Melba laughed with her.

"Most definitely unexpected," Melba said.

Mai was impressed with the woman, with her poise in the face of such danger.

"And to have kept your children, somehow. Everyone's children died so young and it was getting so people couldn't even get pregnant anymore."

Melba acknowledged the admiration with a smile.

Then Melba seemed to catch herself and she looked directly at Mai, her friendly, inviting countenance replaced by a dark, penetrating glare.

"Did you say Mister Smythe?" she asked. "Albert Smythe?"

"Ya. That's him, all right, Mai said. "He's the big boss around here. I'm just a little mouse," she said, laughing.

Melba glanced furtively around the clearing from guard to guard and prisoner to prisoner. She suddenly realized what was happening.

Even her two compatriots had perked up at the sound of that name.

"What's taking them so long?" Melba asked.

Mai shrugged.

"Who knows? Probably they are getting drunk and laughing, I don't know."

She had been studying Melba's reaction to this sudden piece of knowledge and it confirmed what she already suspected.

A loud whistle came across the top of the trees and everybody stood up. Mai indicated to Melba that it was time to go.

"Where are we going?" she demanded.

"We're taking you home," she said. "We just got the signal that the deal is done and we're going to deliver all these prisoners to your boss."

Melba's heart was racing and she was finding it difficult to think clearly. She saw so-called prisoners and so-called guards all talking and laughing together as they formed up.

"Awright, cut the shit," Mary-Louise barked. "You better look like prisoners, let me tell ya," she yelled at them.

Melba's face went blank.

Mai was smiling as she came in behind her and tightened a noose around her neck.

"What are you doing?" Melba screamed.

"Calm down," Mai soothed her. It's just a precaution...you know. Did you think I was going to strangle you? Why would I do that?" she cooed. She tied Melba's arms behind her back, giving the rope an extra cinch.

"Jesus," Melba complained.

"Too tight? Oh don't worry," Mai said. "You will be home with your children in no time. What were their names again?"

Melba closed her eyes and started to walk.

The train of prisoners slogged single-file down the road with Melba and her two comrades out front.

The armed guards repeatedly cuffed and slapped the prisoners to hurry them along. Some prisoners cried out in anguish; others remained silent. Then everyone would giggle.

"Don't!" Mary-Louise shouted. "You are going to blow this," she said. "Is that what you want?"

"You're not fooling me," Melba hissed at Mai.

"Whatever do you mean, dear?" she asked.

"I know what you are up to."

Mai let it go but Melba couldn't and after a few minutes she yelled out as loudly as she could: "Trojan Horse! Trojan Horse!"

Mai gave the noose a little jerk and Melba was silent.

"It won't do you any good," Melba said. "There's a hundred armed soldiers in there and they are going to kill every one of you."

"That would be terrible," Mai conceded.

"I can help you," Melba said. "I can speak up for you."

Mai smiled.

"Thank you, my dear," she said. "I am counting on it."

A mile from the docks, the front gate was coming into view. Instead of four guards, now there were twenty-four, all armed and ready for a fight.

Arnie's Army, he called them. The twenty-three best fighters in the warehouse had joined his posse. He was just waiting for the chance to get at these bastards. He watched them coming up the road through field glasses.

"Get ready," he said.

From a bared window above, Beale and Albert watched the soldiers preparing and the column of prisoners walking towards them.

"Are you sure those boys are under control?" Albert asked.

"Don't worry," Beale said. "Their lives depend on me."

He pressed a button and suddenly they could hear everything outside.

Beale pressed another button and there was a loud squawk.

"Arnie? This is Beale, Do you hear me."

"Yes sir Mr. Beal Arnie came back almost immediately. They are on their way in sir...looks like there must be near fifty or sixty at least...Mr. Beale?

"Go ahead."

"I think I see Miss Melba out front and she's...she's...why those Godamned---...she's tied up sir!"

Beale nodded, as if Arnie was right in the room with him.

"I know. Don't you worry about that. When they get to the gate, you just let them in. No rough stuff, Arnie, okay?"

"But sir, they got Miss Melba tied up!"

"I know it," Beale said. "You just do what I tell you, right?"

"Yes sir," Arnie said. "Over."

"Well, it seems you are a man of your word," Beale said, turning to Albert.

"I've been told that before," Albert answered. "The question is, are you?"

This brought a hard, penetrating look from Beale but he couldn't quite figure out what it was that troubled him about this man. He had done everything he said he would do. He was a serious player and probably one hell of a catcher. They could make a good team. He needed people like this.

They watched as the prisoners were marched through the gates under the eyes of Arnie's Army. Arnie was determined he was going to shoot somebody this day and he watched intently, staring at every face that passed him.

Once everyone was inside the compound, the prisoners were seated and the guards were posted. Beale ordered Arnie to back off and leave the guests alone.

Albert saw Mai standing very close to Melba, pressing something in her back and he smiled.

"Do you really have to keep Melba?" Beale asked. "Don't you trust me, yet? I could have every one of you killed in five seconds flat. I mean, let her go, man. She's the best blow job I ever had!"

Albert busted a laugh and shook his head like a Mississippi hawg farmer.

"That's a good one, Beale," he said. "I like that. But maybe that's the only thing keeping you back, right?"

Beale nodded and pursed his lips.

"But you still haven't told me what you want," Beale said.

"I'm looking to the future here, Mr. Beale," Albert said. "I'm trying to get myself some security, something that will allow me and my men to live decent."

Beale smiled and nodded.

"I understand," he said. "I understand completely."

"So I ain't going to ask for nothing," Albert said. "I'm giving you this bunch free gratis. Sort of like a gift, you know what I mean?"

This man was incredible. He was like anybody's dream of a consigliore.

"Why would you do that?" Beale asked.

"Because I want to work with you. I can bring you in a couple of hundred people a month. I know this area, good. I been all over. You just give us some decent weapons like your boys have got and we'd be able to do just about anything. And you pay good. I know that."

"That's quite a proposition," Beale said.

"Those men of yours that I took out. They weren't worth shit, Mr. Beale. I did you a favor."

Beale glared for a moment and then laughed.

"You may be right."

"And I'll tell you. Me and my boys are the ones that raided that camp."

"Oh, I already figured that," Beale said. "You gimme my suction machine back and we'll make a deal."

Albert looked at him skeptically and then thought for a moment.

"Okay, you tell Mai – just, Mai now – to bring her up here. No one else."

Beale was already on the COM.

"Arnie, you let Miss Melba and that chink behind her come on in."

"Yes sir," Arnie replied, sadly.

They watched them speak and then Mai pushed Melba towards the steps, the Ivor Johnson jammed tight against her back.

"I'm just itching to kill you," Mai said. "So don't do anything stupid."

Melba didn't answer but she had suddenly perked up. In a few minutes, this Chinese matron would be groveling at her feet.

They climbed the stairs and entered the vast concourse, which had been cleared of all personnel.

Melba led her along various corridors until they got to the last hallway. Beale's big office was here and the special door that led to the cages.

Beale heard them coming and stuck his head into the hallway.

"This way," he said.

Mai and Melba walked into the room, Melba's face a concentrated beam of hatred and outrage, her little close-set eyes shining. She stared at Beale, expecting him to order her release but he stood there without speaking.

"Mister Beale," she snapped at him. "Tell this bitch to let-."

Mai jerked on the rope, cutting off her sentence.

"What are you doing, Mai?" Albert asked. "Let that woman go this minute. I told you to look after her, not mistreat her."

But Mai smiled; not with her whole face, just with her eyes.

"Mister. Beale...this is a setup," Melba said, half-choking as Mai tightened her grip.

"I ordered you to let her go," Albert said, staring at Mai, his hand tightening around the .45, but Mai was transfixed.

"They're going to-." Melba shrieked, but she never finished the sentence. Mai pulled the trigger on the Ivor Johnson and sent a .38 wad-cutter into her lung. Then she pulled the trigger again and again. The fourth bullet found Melba's heart and she collapsed like a rag doll, blood spewing from her mouth. Albert and Beale stared at Mai in disbelief.

"You fucking idiot," Albert shouted, as he raised the .45. He pushed the barrel against her solar plexus and stared into her face.

"Why did you do that?" he shouted, but Mai said nothing. She stared back, her face calm, her eyes smiling.

Albert pulled the trigger and she pitched back, her eyes still frozen in a secret smile.

294

The COM was going crazy and Albert could see Arnie's men running towards the building from their stand-off.

Beale was shaken, staring at the dead women with a confused mixture of suspicion and disappointment.

"You better get on the COM."

Beale looked at Albert and nodded.

He picked up the mic and seemed to forget what he was going to say.

"Come on," Albert urged.

"Stand down, Arnie," he finally croaked. "Everything's fine up here. I repeat, stand down. Do you copy?"

There was a moment's silence and then Arnie's voice came back, clearly unhappy.

"Are you sure, Mister Beale? I-."

"Are you questioning my orders?" Beale snapped.

"No sir," Arnie replied.

"Then stand the hell down. Don't do anything without my say-so."

"Yes sir...over."

Albert seemed badly shaken, his face contorted and his breath coming quickly.

"I'm really sorry about all this, Mr. Beale," he said. "This isn't how it was supposed to go."

Beale hardly heard him. He was staring at Melba's shattered body, those wonderful, acrobatic lips all smeared with blood.

"Jesus H. Christ," he said, disgustedly. "You better learn to choose your people," he told Albert.

"Yes sir," Albert replied meekly. "I never would have imagined-."

"Well you need imagination in this line," Beale said.

He was already wondering about a replacement for Melba. It wasn't all bad, he reasoned. He knew that she was working behind his back. She was getting a little too confident.

"We all need to clean house once in a while," Beale sighed.

***

Chapter Seven

Albert knew that time was running out. With Melba dead, his last real piece of leverage was gone. The fact that he had shot and killed Mai, his most trusted lieutenant, right in front of Beale bought him a few hours at most. If Beale had time to reflect on the events, he'd likely conclude that this fellow and his gang were not worth the trouble.

From Beale's perspective, all Albert wanted, it seemed, was a chance to prove himself. He was thinking long term. He was showing the necessary obeisance, offering the entire group of prisoners in exchange for a few weapons. The deal was going all Beale's way, so far. If Albert was up to something else, he couldn't imagine what it was.

"I guess I am going to give you a chance," Beale said finally, sitting back in his big chair like a banker and staring down his nose at Albert. Albert sat forward, elbows on his knees, eager for anything Beale might offer.

"I really appreciate that, mister Beale," he said. "I can tell you right now, we will make it worth your while...of course, you have to make it worth our while, too."

Beale nodded agreeably. The fact was, Beale faced other difficulties. The demand for slave labor was increasing all the time and his ability to provide it would be the only matter considered when they reviewed his performance. He had seen things falling off a bit, lately, which had encouraged Melba's ambitions and put him in an unpleasant light at Peace and Harmony headquarters. That had been the real reason he did not call for assistance from headquarters. They were looking for an excuse to find him wanting and this would have been a beaut. This man could be a real asset under the circumstances. He had never liked Prescott, the dead leader of the now-defunct band of catchers, anyway. Clean House, he thought.

"Able-bodied fetch about ten silver, depending," Beale said. "But they have to be able to work. I'm not paying for wards of the state to look after."

Albert nodded.

"Women, if they're…you know…worthwhile, fetch about eight. Now I have paid a full gold ounce for a girl. But I mean she was something else, you know? And I knew I could move her for twice that. They don't come along very often, anymore."

"That's for damn sure," Albert agreed. "Pretty well got to boil 'em first these days," he said.

Beale burst out laughing.

"I like that," he said. "It's mostly coal workers, farm labor…anything like that," he said. "We don't really need that many women, you know? One can do for five or six men in the field and they are easy enough to replace."

Albert leaned back and smiled.

"Now kids…well, they can a fetch a price if they aren't all crippled up or something. There's a whole different market for them and we can discuss that at the time."

Albert was getting anxious and he shifted in his seat. Beale seemed not to notice.

"Now about these guns you are looking for…"

"Just some good weaponry," Albert said. "I mean if we all had the same rifle we wouldn't be scrounging around looking for ammo all the time. I was thinking a rifle and maybe five magazines per man and we'd be hell on wheels out there."

Beale frowned into his double chin and closed his eyes for a moment.

"Exactly how are we going to do this?" Beale asked.

There was still a wall of mistrust between them. Beale especially, couldn't kick the notion that Albert was up to something. On the other hand, Beale had 50 armed guards on call and half of them were deployed against Morgan's group right now. One word from him and they'd all be dead.

"I'll march them prisoner's in myself," Albert offered.

"Okay," Beale said with finality.

He depressed the COM and instructed Arnie to come to the office. While they waited, Beale took out a bottle of brown liquor of some sort and a couple of glasses.

"Sorry, I don't drink," Albert said.

Beale shrugged and poured himself one.

"Do enjoy it myself," he replied.

"Son of alcoholics, you know?" Albert said.

Beale stared at him for a moment and turned away.

Arnie came into the room, dressed for combat and carrying his rifle.

Word had gotten out about the firefight and there were still blood stains on the floor and wall. He stared at them momentarily.

"Arnie, this here is Morgan," Beale said.

The two men eyed each other without comment.

"I want you to take him down to the armory and let him have whatever he wants," Beale said.

Arnie stared at the two men, unable to speak.

"It's all right, Arnie, Beale said. "This man has saved my ass twice today."

Arnie wasn't convinced. He was in deep turmoil. Melba had performed her oral gymnastics on him as well and he was profoundly disappointed at the loss. The rumor that she was plotting against Beale had already begun to circulate and Arnie had a queasy sensation that he too might be under some sort of suspicion.

"Right away," he said. "You want to come with me."

Albert left Beale and followed Arnie down the corridor and back out into the main campus. Things were almost back to normal, with forklift trucks and dollies and stackers moving back and forth, beeping and flashing yellow lights at anyone in the way.

"I'll get my guys," Albert said.

"How's that?" Arnie demanded.

"Well do you expect me to carry all this shit out there, myself?" he asked, with some humor.

When Arnie didn't budge he shook his head.

"Put your guys on my prisoners and send my guys in. Where's the problem?"

"Have we ever met?" Arnie asked Albert suddenly?

"I doubt it," Albert said, with a grin. "You aren't my type."

Arnie stiffened and turned back to the task at hand.

Albert left him at the door and went outside.

It was a cool night and some of the prisoners were shivering.

Arnie's second in command was already waiting.

"Come on boys," Albert said. "We're done with this bunch."

The men hesitated and Albert grew suddenly impatient.

"We're upgrading. We made the deal, now come on."

Slowly at first and then without much more coercion, the guards followed Albert inside and Arnie's men replaced them around the huddled refugees.

They walked in single file down the hallway, Arnie in front and Albert next. Many of them had not seen electric light for years and stared at the bulbs. Some had not been inside a weatherproof building for 10 years.

The armory was past a double-lock steel fire door with an electronically controlled bolt.

They filed in quietly and he led them down the isles past rows of AR152; M16s; a number of P5s and handguns and other rifles too numerous to mention. It was the largest collection of guns and ammunition any of them had ever seen and they looked around like illiterates in a library.

Albert pulled an AR from the rack, yanked the bolt, fired it, checked it out and handed it to the first man. A blank-faced Arnie shoved five full magazines across the table. The man tried to install one and it jammed. He looked up sheepishly and Albert yanked the clip, shoved it in correctly and handed it back.

"Put the safety on, asshole," he barked.

The man dropped the rifle, to find the safety, pointing it right at Arnie who smacked it our of the way and quick drew a 9 mm. on the man's head.

"Easy," Albert said.

Arnie dropped his weapon and holstered it.

"What the fuck is going on here?" he asked. "These guys don't know shit."

"They're just a little rusty from having to use that old stuff," Albert smiled, but Arnie was having none of it.

He gripped the COM on his shoulder and pressed the button to speak, but he never got the chance.

Albert drove the Emerson straight into the side of his neck, severing the carotid, which hosed blood in a wild, red shower over the room.

Arnie fell, twitching and gulping involuntarily as the blood pulsed out of his neck and ran back into his throat. His eyes fluttered and his arms twitched as he died.

The men were silent.

"That wasn't exactly what I had in mind," Albert said, glaring at the fool who had fumbled the magazine.

"I'm sorry, Mister Smythe, I really am," he blubbered.

"Sorry doesn't count," Albert said. "Why are you apologizing to me? You have maybe killed us all. There's no apologizing. You do it right or you die. Now we are probably going to die."

The men turned their anger on the culprit and he glared back defiantly.

"You wouldn't have done no better,' he sneered.

"I never would have tried until I was sure," someone said.

Albert looked at the man and motioned him forward.

"This is my second in command. What's your name?"

"Kyle," he said.

"Pass out guns and clips, Kyle. Take as many clips as you can carry. Forget the handguns. Clips and rifles," he said.

Kyle began distributing the weapons, sliding around in Arnie's blood.

Albert was rifling through the storage room for hand grenades or some kind of explosives but there didn't seem to be any.

Everyone was armed in a few minutes and he led them out and back down the corridor to the double-lock steel door. But it wouldn't open.

He slammed against the door and turned the handle several times, but it didn't budge.

"That fucker," he swore.

Arnie had allowed the door to lock behind them, forcing them to call for someone else to let them out.

"Get his COM," Albert ordered the last man in line.

He ran back down the hallway and disappeared into the gunroom.

Albert felt his chest constricting.

Arnie had suspected and now that they had killed him, they had no way of knowing the code to open the door.

The men looked at Albert, waiting for a command and he found their gaze intolerable.

The runner came back with Arnie's com and Albert pressed the button and listened. He could hear sounds of the prisoners and their guards.

"Come in," he said, slurring the words a little.

"Go ahead," a voice came back.

"Can you send some boys down here…I need a hand," he said.

There was a long silence and finally a voice came back: "On the way. Over."

"Get back into the gun room," Albert ordered them. "Make noise. Laugh. Joke around. We're all friends, here, get it?"

They nodded and shuffled back down the hallway and disappeared into the room.

Albert waited tensely at the door.

"I can't hear you," he shouted at them.

The noise level suddenly increased as the men in the gunroom laughed and joked. It almost sounded natural.

The COM buzzed and a voice came on: "Zulu-one this is Zulu-six," he said.

Albert stared at the COM for a few seconds and pushed the transmit button.

"Cut the crap," he said. "I need a couple of guys to carry ammunition."

There was a long silence and then the voice came back: "Two on the way. Over."

Albert did not reply. He pressed his ear to the door and heard the clatter of many boots in the next hallway. They were sending an assault team.

He ran back to the gunroom and everyone went silent.

"No," he said. "Keep it up; but I gotta tell you; they're coming in hard."

The men looked at each other but no one seemed to know what to do.

"I'll meet them when the door opens," he said. "When you hear me shout the word 'Quiet,' or you hear the first shot, you will have about two seconds to get into this hallway and star firing. I will fall to the floor. Don't shoot me. I'm the good looking one."

A nervous laugh.

He saw hands shaking and eyes darting around in fear.

"It's better than the alternative," he told them. "If they get down this hallway with you inside, I promise you they will use grenades. You won't have a chance. You've got to stop them."

Albert was halfway back to the door, his hands empty, when he heard the electronics kick open the bolts.

"The door opened slowly and an M16 pointed at him. He raised his hands immediately.

"Whoa," he laughed. The noise coming from the back room was cheerful and loud.

"Against the wall," the voice said. The soldier was outfitted for combat with body armor and a Kevlar helmet but his face was still vulnerable and Albert knew he would have to shoot him in the mouth. There was no time for the knife.

"I said against the wall," he commanded again, threatening Albert with the gun.

"Hey, man, what's the problem?" he said.

The noise and laughter from down the hall was distracting the man and he stepped into the hallway and pinned the door open. There were five others behind him, all crouching combat stance as they moved through the door and down the hallway.

"Jesus Christ," Albert shouted. "Quiet, will ya?"

The soldier's eyes lanced at him and Albert pushed the barrel of the .45 into his mouth and pulled the trigger. The helmet jounced but caught the brains and skull as he pushed him away. The last man through was in the process turning around when Albert began unloading the.45 into his head. The noise from the firing snapped against eardrums and he fell down and began shooting the legs of the intruders. They had killed the first two of his men out the door and were wheeling around when a half dozen of them broke out and emptied their entire magazines into the three remaining guards. Blood leaked out from under helmets and spilled onto the floor. The door was jammed open with the body of the man Albert had killed.

They piled out of the gunroom and ran straight down the hall. Albert left the body holding the door and picked up his M16 and grabbed magazines from the others. Then he followed his own troops who were heading straight for the main concourse with instructions to kill anybody and everybody who was not behind a cage door.

He heard the firing immediately and when he emerged into the big room, a dozen warehouse workers were sprawled on the floor.

The test would be when they ran into Arnie's trained soldiers who had been left outside to guard the prisoners.

Albert let them go. They either did it or they didn't.

The firing had alerted the entire warehouse and off-duty guards were running into the fight. The second in command of Arnie's group turned and shouted but the sound never came.

Valerie's bullet went right out the back of his head. The man next to him fell and then another and then the sixty prisoners rose up as one wave of rage and hatred and overpowered the remaining guards.

They fired their automatics directly in to the horde, but nothing could hold them back. The dispossessed climbed over the bodies of their dead comrades just for the opportunity to tear one of their guards to pieces.

More guards emerged from the building, but without some leadership they didn't even know who they were fighting. And every few seconds another one would wheel and fall, a bullet through his head or his throat.

Albert listened to the firing as he made his way back down the corridors and up to the level where Beale had locked himself in.

He shot the lock off and entered the room, gun forward like a prow and marched right over to the blubbering man seated in the banker's chair.

"The army will be here," he squealed as Albert grabbed his ear and dragged him to his feet.

He pushed the fat man out of the room and down the hallway. When he stumbled, he kicked him in the ribs, which made him scream and bend over. So Albert kicked him harder and he got up.

He half slid, half stumbled down the stairs and through the hallway into the secure area. The prisoners had all started to shake their cages and scream and shout. The wire was bending and cracking but the bolts held true.

Albert went to the first cage where at least five hundred men were imprisoned. The smell was overwhelming and he saw why. Open buckets covered with boards had been set for their use and they hadn't even been emptied for so long that the slop was splashing over the edges.

He fired twice, breaking the lock and then opened the door. The men backed away from him and made a circle.

"Here," Albert said, and he grabbed Beale by the scruff of his neck and threw him into the crowd.

Beale couldn't even speak. He stood up, trembling, urine running down his leg.

He heard Beale's scream as half a dozen men grabbed him and dragged him towards the slop pails.

"I can pay!" Beale shouted but his words were drowned – literally - as they pushed his head deep into a half-barrel of human waste. They held him under for a minute and then jerked him out, his face running with slime and his mouth open as he gasped and tried to breathe and spit out the waste at the same time.

Then they did it again.

Beale was crying and screaming like a baby the second time they pulled his head out and he began to vomit.

Then they pushed his head under again and his body bounced and kicked as his lungs filled with the slop.

They left him hanging over the barrel like a man in prayer.

Albert moved from cage to cage, shooting off the bolts and releasing the prisoners. They rushed into the vast area, grabbing anything they could lay their hands on. Their screaming and shouting came in waves and echoed in the huge rooms.

Finally he came to the children's cage. They had moved to the back of the room, about twenty of them, and did not move when he shot the door open. No one spoke or cried or made a gesture. He pointed at the door and waved them towards it.

"Get out," he said. "Run."

But they didn't move.

The sound of firing and screaming rose and fell as the enraged crowd happened upon a guard or a dockworker. They began to tear the building apart from the inside, pushing over racks which exploded on the floor spilling contents.

Albert put his gun away and walked towards the group. He saw them prepare for something, but he didn't understand it. Then they closed their eyes and put their arms up, as if to be handcuffed.

Albert stopped and turned back. He closed the cage door and jammed the bolt.

"I will be back with someone," he said. "Don't worry."

One by one they dropped their arms but still, no one said a word.

Albert moved towards the sound of the battle, not sure what he would find. Groups of released prisoners continued to rip and tear anything they could find. In their mania, they opened MREs and threw the contents in the air. They discovered a forklift operator cowering behind a stack of medical supplies and they dragged her out onto the floor. She screamed at them, wild eyed, trying to force them back with her hands. Two men moved on her and others soon joined. They ripped her clothes off and carried her struggling and screaming to a steel post sticking up about six feet from the floor. She fought back, but it wasn't enough and they lifted her onto the post and pushed until it had ripped her open. She was still screaming as they pressed her down and then backed off. Blood squirted from her insides as she struggled, trying to remove herself, but the more she fought, the less strength she had.

The men watched in silence as she impaled herself on the steel post and finally pitched forward in one last agonizing wail.

It had taken her fifteen minutes to die.

Then they spotted Albert and made a move towards him but one of them shouted: "No."

They stopped, their eyes bulging and their veins popped out of their arms and necks like steel cords.

"He's the one," the man said.

Then they turned and headed for the front gate, where their fellow prisoners had surrounded the last dozen or so living members of the warehouse guard.

The twelve men had formed a defensive perimeter and they had enough ammunition to kill a lot of people before they were overwhelmed.

With their initial lust sated, the prisoners were not so eager to die and they surrounded the twelve men and stared at them.

Albert came out the front door and found what was left of his squad: Three men had survived. They looked at him and two of them began to cry. Albert looked away.

"You did good," he told them quietly. "You did what you were supposed to."

A shout exploded from the gathered crowd and Albert watched them rush the guards, who managed to kill twenty or thirty before they were overwhelmed.

The mob dragged them into the light. The men were terrified and the best they could hope for was a merciful death. They pleaded and shrieked as their limbs were disjointed or ears were torn off.

But this crowd showed no mercy and one by one, each of the men was tied to a lamppost and doused with fuel they had taken from the parked vehicles. And one by one, they were lit on fire. The screaming went on for some time, for the crowd would immolate a man before his friends and then pass around food and drink they had liberated from the warehouse. They would smash bottles across the head of the next victim and gouge out his eyes and in one case, they sliced off genitals and shoved them down his throat – before they burned him.

There were about three hundred female prisoners among the released and Albert wanted to talk to them; but they were equally enflamed by the rights of revenge. These women were no longer women or even people, in some cases. They had become demons, succubae that would roam the earth for eternity killing every man they could find.

Many of them smiled as the men howled down the angel of death; many, but not all.

Albert had to find the "not all."

He approached a group sitting on a curb watching the rites without the slightest emotion. As he approached they rose as one, many holding clubs or broken bottles; several had shards of glass wrapped in cloth and dripping with blood.

"I need some help with these children," he said.

The women looked at him and then one by one, they turned away and sat down. The next sacrifice was starting to scream as they pulled his eye out with a pair of pliers and they didn't want to miss any of it.

It took him half a dozen tries before he found someone who would talk to him, but she shook her head, said "not me," and wandered off.

He sat down and hung his head between his arms, exhausted.

What had happened to Valerie? He had seen the flash of her gun barrel and the effects it had in the compound. He counted seven headshots before he was drawn away by one of his own men caught in the frenzy.

"Can I help, maybe?" she said.

He thought he had imagined it but when he looked up, Valerie was sitting beside him, her face calm.

She put her arm over his shoulders and he pushed his face against her neck.

"That was some good shootin'," he said.

"Ya," she said.

She pressed her lips against his face and he tried to fight back the tears. He would be good God damned to hell if he would ever let her, or anybody else, see him cry.

"Come on," he said, standing up.

They wound their way through the crowds and fires and the debris until they were back at the children's cage. Everything was exactly as he had left it. She looked in and got a sense of what was going on.

"You wait here," she said. "I will try and find somebody, but I gotta tell you, Albert: This is way beyond me."

He debated whether to open the door or wait outside. He didn't want to frighten them or trigger any responses they had learned from Beale.

"I'll just stay here," he said. "Ain't nobody coming in there while I am alive," he promised. "I will just sit here until Val gets back. She knows what to do. She will get somebody here to help you all out..." his voice trailed off.

It took her several hours to find three women who were willing to follow her back into the building. She had to promise she would kill them all rather than let them get caught again.

When they arrived, Albert saw that they were old. At least they looked old.

Albert pulled the bolt on the door and let them in.

"Leave that open," one of them said, as she passed.

The children reacted exactly the same to them as they had to Albert.

"What the...?"

"They'll be alright," Valerie said, but he could hear the lack of confidence in her voice. They were probably beyond rescue at this point.

"The army's on the way," he stressed. "They gotta get them the hell out of here."

"And go where? Do what?" Valerie asked.

"Well what are we doing here, then?" Albert said.

Valerie watched the three women moving amongst the children who obeyed without a moment's hesitation, anything they were told to do. There were no tears.

"I guess we should get out of here," she said.

"I can't look after a kid," Albert said, reading her mind. "Not with what's coming."

She agreed.

She led him back through the crowds and the fires and drunken orgy of murder to a small stable where two chestnut horses stood, ears perked at the strange sounds outside. They whinnied softly. Their hayracks were empty. The stable was well apportioned, with all the tack necessary.

They saddled them quickly and in a few minutes were walking along the perimeter fence, heading the burning guardhouse at the front gate. They passed two men who had been strangled and were hanging on the steel mesh. As they got closer, they saw the ripped abdomens and the piles of blood and entrails on the ground, exactly as if they were being bled and butchered for the freezer.

The horses reared as they got too close to the fire, but they found a more acceptable exit where the fence had been torn down.

Albert was imagining what would happen about an hour or so from now, when Centre for Peace and Tranquility troops arrived with their Apache gunship. Excepting a few who seemed to understand what had really happened, the liberated prisoners had succumbed to the opportunity, rather than subordinate the opportunity to some cause. There was no reason left among them. They slaughtered the living and then they dismembered the dead. Fueled by liberated alcohol, the ululations of rage expanded through the ether of an expanding universe. The more they killed, the more they wanted to kill. He wondered how many among them would take what they could from that unlocked armory and make a run for it where they might regroup in preparation for what must come next.

Don't turn around, he told himself. Don't look back.

***

Part Four

*I am Alpha and Omega, the beginning and the
end, the first and the last.*

Revelations: 22, 13

Chapter One

For the balance of the year, rumblings of war came and went, almost with each week. The familiar sound of distant explosions that could only be from aerial bombardment, carried for fifty miles; but nothing came close to their refuge. At least, nothing came close enough to cause alarm.

Occasionally, while hunting or gathering, they came across travelers heading east in groups of five to sometimes fifty. There was some great migration taking place and the refugees were mostly packed for travel, not settlement. They were often armed, albeit with antique weapons and more often than not with simple bows and spears. The availability of military grade guns and ammunition had declined rapidly after the slave revolt that had begun at Crawley's warehouse. News of the rebellion spread from the Ohio Valley to the Mississippi River, and from the thumb of Michigan to the rapidly vanishing Alabama shoreline.

The talk was always war; a new war, the travelers claimed; one that would "finish this business once and for all."

When Albert overheard remarks like this, it convinced him more than ever that men were incapable of learning from their mistakes. It didn't seem to matter that everything new was old. There was no genetic memory. There was no new war, coming; it was just the same war, interrupted for a while; it was the same people, doing the same things, that all the people before them had done; only now, Einstein was slowly being proven right. This war, would likely be fought with clubs and stones. Albert intended to sit this one out.

Now where have I heard that before?

He marveled at his own inability to learn as well.

They had rebuilt the corral originally devised to contain Brutus, expanding it enough to allow their two horses exercise room and protection. They even had crude hayracks they kept filled with grasses cut from the fields when they couldn't attend the animals while they grazed.

He rode the mare, called Lucile and Valerie took the stallion, whom she named Turk. She was the better rider and had a keener horse sense than Albert. Turk was always glad to see her and seldom acted up, while Lucile snorted at him and stamped her foot occasionally, outraged by something he was doing, though he was never quite sure what it was that bothered her.

He had noticed the same problem with Valerie at times. She seemed to be scolding him somehow with her attitude and he could not figure out why. When he asked her, she got even madder. Albert thought about this quite a bit and wondered if there was something wrong with him, but he didn't ask her about it because she would probably get mad again; so he wandered around, wondering why all the females in his life were always upset with him. He took solace from the fact that they did not run away. Of course, Lucile was, chained up.

He decided that he would not ask any questions or make any comments that might be seen as provocative by either of them. He made a point of being always cheerful and smiling whenever either of them looked his way. That worked for a while, at least with the horse; but Valerie asked him if he was retarded or something and why did he go around smiling all the time? Was he trying to make her crazy? Ah, he thought. For a while, he did not smile and she demanded to know why he was so unhappy. Was it her fault, somehow that he couldn't enjoy life? So he went fishing, hoping things would clear up. That was the wrong thing to do. When he got back and showed her the trout she demanded to know why he was out fishing while she was stuck here in the cave all day. After that, Albert decided to make moonshine.

Over the summer, they hauled wheat back from the near field in travois they constructed from poles and skins and threshed it on the floor of the cave. He packed the berries in tight, plastic containers that were both mouse and moisture proof but some sort of desiccant would have gone a long way in their preserving. It was something he had never considered in his preparations all those years ago, mainly because he wasn't thinking about surviving the end of civilization. He had always believed he could stay clear of the social consequences of a temporary breakdown for a few months, until things righted themselves. Nothing would be right again around here for a long time.

By the start of winter, they had almost three hundred pounds of dried wheat in storage and Albert made bread every day. He liked to make bread. It was a contemplative activity. He thought about the things that he liked to do, while he was making bread. He liked to go fishing and hunting and he liked to kill his enemies. He liked to lie in bed with Valerie. He liked to sneak up on people and listen in on their conversations without them knowing.

That is how he learned about the gatherings taking place all over the country. By the country, he meant the land and villages in a radius of about a hundred and fifty miles from his lair. That is what he had gathered, eves dropping on the campsites of travelers.

"They pretty well give up after Crawley's fell," he heard one night. "The bastards didn't know what to do, so they pulled back. Then, a group from up north a-ways-."

"You mean that old dyke, Ramsey's crew?" someone interrupted.

"You call her what you like. She gets it done, by gawd. Blew that power plant all to hell."

"I heard they near got wiped out doin it," someone said.

The speaker was silent for a moment.

"Well, that's about right," I expect.

Then there was silence for a while and they stared at the fire and poked it with sticks.

That is how Albert learned that Viola Ramsey had survived. He smiled, thinking about her. She was no dyke, though. Just ask Pat.

Somewhere east of Provost, an army was gathering. It was not so much an army of citizens as an army of the dispossessed. And their intention – at least for the time being – was to secure a defensible area and make a settlement, not start a revolution. How large an area and how it would be administered, had not been discussed because few believed they would survive the onslaught of raiders, rogue military units, criminal gangs and other assorted miscreants who now wandered the landscape.

Albert told Valerie what he had learned and she absorbed the information without much comment; but he could tell that she was

312

thinking about it. She was not pulling away from him, exactly; she was being drawn away and she wanted him to come with her.

"I hear they are getting together maybe a thousand people, so far," he said. "Won't do them any good to throw rocks at tanks and machine guns," he said.

"Well why don't you tell them?" she asked.

He knew that was coming and he had given her the opening on purpose.

"I don't see myself leading anybody," he said.

"Well how about just tell them what to do?"

"And when they all get killed, then what?"

Valerie looked at him earnestly and handed him a cup of hot water with sugar.

"They're pretty well dead, anyway," she said.

The same old conversation with the same old arguments, he mused. Just like him and everybody, Valerie didn't learn, either. This time it was going to work. This time they would miraculously become battlefield-savy soldiers who understand what fighting was about. They would know that you fought to stay alive, to kill the other guy and take his stuff and to protect your friends so that they would protect you. There was nothing more to it. The only cause was "self."

That was the end of August – maybe – and they didn't discuss it again for a while.

The streams of refugees continued and he watched them closely, but from a distance, more concerned about somebody accidentally discovering his cave than he was about any danger they may have posed as individuals.

The news changed constantly.

One day he would hear that an entire platoon of two hundred soldiers had crossed over and joined up with remnants of American Free Forces. The next day he would hear they had all been killed and a week later, someone would report that they had gone rogue on their own and owed allegiance to nobody.

It wasn't a matter of what you believed. Believe whatever you want; just realize none of it is true.

And inevitably, word of a rendezvous began circulating, where strategies would be discussed and plans for a perfect future were developed.

"I guess I will attend," Albert said, one evening. "You are coming, I presume?"

They set off the next morning, early, the horses eager to be on the move after several weeks' confinement in the corral while Albert and Valerie secured their food supply. It was about sixty miles to the town of Provost. They fell in with a gaggle of twenty-five or thirty travelers, all of who were on foot. They seemed to appreciate the company of the two riders and Albert and Valerie closed up the rear of the column, content to follow it wherever it was going.

A twenty-mile day was about it for people in this condition. They had some food and water, but they had been scrabbling around for sustenance, in some cases for years and their hollow-eyed stare and sallow complexion was indicative the privation. They made a rough camp and many fell right to sleep, wrapping themselves in no more than they carried.

Albert and Valerie stayed some distance off by themselves and hobbled the horses so they could browse.

"I might just be one of them, you know that?" Valerie said after a while.

Their fire rumbled happily in a depression surrounded by stones and it reflected off their faces. Albert didn't know what to say. He looked at her and wanted to tell her that she had nothing to worry about so long as he lived, but he didn't think she wanted to hear that.

"What if I hadn't captured you sneaking around in the woods?" she said. "I might be just like them – or worse.

"I tell you, Albert, I can't stand it being up like this with everyone else all ruined like they are. I'm no better than any of them!"

"You ain't worse for doing alright by yerself, neither," he said.

She curled up tight against him and went to sleep and Albert was afraid to move because she might wake up and change her position. He liked the way it felt when she pressed on him like that.

The conversation had unnerved him a bit, not because he didn't feel sorry for many of those people. He felt sorry, he supposed, for anyone who couldn't look after himself. But then if someone doesn't look after himself, is that proof that he can't? Is everyone entitled to the same sympathy?

Here we go again, he thought.

But that wasn't the only thing on his mind.

About half through the day, he had detected someone following them about a mile back in the woods. He lost them again when the group crossed a field and found an old county road heading due east.

They had followed the road for a while until it dead-ended and then they cut through the forest again and he had seen the flash in the distance. It was nothing anyone would have ordinarily noticed. But Albert noticed it. When he saw it a third time, he was certain. Whoever it was, they were staying way back, out of sight and out of rifle range.

Night was the best time to make a move and he expected it sometime in the hour or two before sunrise. He unhooked himself from Valerie and put out the fire. Then he dragged her to a large oak that had a hollowed out base. He sat down in the opening and pulled her to him again. His hand rested on her shoulder, a tight grip on the .45.

His eyes flicked open for a moment and he listened. He listened the way an animal listens, knowing how the woods should sound. Whoever it was, they had stopped well outside the camp and seemed to have no intention of coming in from the cold. Eventually the forest recovered and the balance of insects and wind returned. They were waiting for a better opportunity. He closed his eyes.

The next day they found many old roads that were still usable – more usable than rough woods, at any rate – and made a lot better progress.

A younger man fell back with them after a few hours and asked if he could walk between the horses. Valerie told him no and he moved to her side.

"What do you want?" she asked, suspiciously

"I used to have a horse," he said. "I just wanted to smell 'em."

Valerie tried not to look at him too closely. He was about thirty, taller than average but malnourished and his teeth had just about rotted out. When a horse loses its teeth, you shoot him, she thought.

"You joining up with Mr. Armitage?" he asked.

Valerie looked at him and studied his face for a moment. His eyes were like glowing spirals.

"Who is that?" she asked.

"He's putting together this revolutionary army and we're going to take back what's ourn," the man said.

"Take back," Valerie repeated.

"They took everything, right? So now we are going to take it back. Mr. Armitage has a plan all ready just as soon as he gets enough men."

Albert listened intently to the conversation but resisted the urge to start asking questions. It could easily throw the man off and it was obvious he wanted to talk to Valerie.

Albert did not know if this pleased him or annoyed him and then he decided quite definitely in favor of annoyed.

"We ain't looking to take over nobody's land or anything like that," the man said.

"We are just going to stake our claim and then everyone will just live there. Why you might be a baker and that one there would look after horses and such. Just like it used to be.

"Everybody going to have their own place and a few acres and a garden and so forth. And then every Sunday we are all going to go into town and there will be a big market where everyone will trade...ain't going to be no more money. No sir. That is the end of that," he said.

"We are all going to help each other. Like I will help you build your house and then we will build mine. I don't mind not being first. I will help plenty before I ask to get a place of my own. I want to get a real good spot, somewhere I can just have a nice view and a good garden patch and so forth.

"Mr. Armitage says everybody going to have what they need and ain't nobody going to be without.

"I know what you are thinking: This sounds like Commonism. But it ain't, see, because there ain't going to be no government. Everybody going to own his own place and do whatever he likes and if he don't want to join in with something, well he don't have to.

"Like he could just sit in his house and nobody would say nothing because there won't be no government and no cops and no politicians. And no money...I already said, that didn't I...

"Like if you got a basket of chicken eggs and I got a side of bacon, why maybe I will trade you, half and half and that way we both will have breakfast."

He was beaming at this point, wound up in his fantasy to the point that he almost stepped in front of Val's horse and she had to pull up.

Valerie looked down at him and was afraid to meet his open, haunted gaze. He was nothing more than a rattling skeleton, draped in yellow, peeling skin, wandering through the forest in a demented state.

316

"I'd sure like to meet this Mr. Armitage," Valerie said.

Albert had caught a glimpse of their tail and he was starting to experience an unusual anxiety about it. He first attributed it to Valerie being there with him; sometimes he would torment himself with scenarios in which she was abducted or taken from him somehow.

But after a while, that settled and he was left with a simple sense of dread, knowing instinctively that the pursuer was after him and no one else.

At mid-day they broke by a pond and most of the travelers flopped down in the high grass and slept. One man tried to fish, but he didn't catch anything; not even a bite.

Albert tied Lucile to a tree rather than set her loose to graze and told Valerie he would be back shortly. If the column decided to move on, she should go with them and he would catch up. She noticed his anxiety but she knew better than to argue. If Albert wanted her to stay behind, there was a reason. As far as moving on with the column, that was another matter.

Albert had a pretty good idea where the tail was and he decided to come in from behind. It meant cutting a wide detour around the suspect's location and guessing, with some precision, where he was holed up. In the haphazard organization of the column, there was no way to tell when they would decide to move on. He guessed he had about an hour to make contact and get back to the bivouac.

The normal difficulties of tracking through woodlands had been exacerbated by the intense growth rate of the foliage over the last few years. Even for Albert, it was slow going and he found himself cornered on more than one occasion by fallen trunks, wildly overgrown Walking Stick and bramble and was forced to backtrack and star again. After an hour in which he did not make contact with his quarry, he decided to turn back.

He sat down to catch his breath and drink some water.

The sound of breathing was coming from behind him and he made no move to alarm the intruder. He continued to drink as though detecting nothing whatsoever and even coughed a few times to make it seem realistic.

He was assessing his rest spot, criticizing himself for having chosen badly. He could roll to the ground and probably turn and fire in about two or three seconds, but the damn log would be partly obscuring his kill zone.

The breathing continued and Albert ostentatiously closed his

317

canteen and hung it back on his utility belt. Then he leaned forward and extracted the pistol. It was locked and loaded. All he had to do was flip the safety, which he did as he fell.

He looked up directly into a pair of very dark eyes staring back at him. The creature used its large, prehensile lips to grab the kudzu and chew it. Albert sat up slowly and lowered the weapon. A hand reached out of the foliage towards him and then drew back.

Albert was looking at a chimpanzee, an older female it seemed. She watched him closely as he got back up, all the while pulling at the kudzu, chewing it up, and then spitting it out. She was hungry.

Albert had dried fruit and jerky in his pouch and he took it all out and laid it on the trunk. She looked at it and made faces at him but she would not come any closer to get it. Then he noticed an identification band on her leg.

He backed slowly away and folded into the trees without any attempt at contacting her.

As he suspected she would be, Valerie was waiting at the pond campsite while the others had continued on. She tried not to show too much relief at seeing him.

"Did you find whatever you were looking for?" she asked.

"I really don't know," he said, swinging into the saddle.

They found the company by their fires, having come within two day's walk of their destination.

Albert had kept an eye on the trail behind, all day long as they rode to catch up and had not seen his purser again. The image of the chimp with its identification bracelet dangling from an ankle, would not leave his mind, but he did not want to discuss it with anyone; not even Valerie. But she could tell he was not entirely present and finally pressed him into an explanation and he told her he thought they were being followed. But he gave no details. She was not alarmed by the news. She said she had suspected the same, a few hours after they had joined the troop but had dismissed it as an artifact of the light. They had both seen what appeared to be a white flash.

***

Chapter Two

With the militias effectively destroyed, the regular forces worried more about their competitors in uniform than a group of wasted vagabonds and the gangs of raiders and marauders still unorganized, the reestablishment of Provost was able to proceed fairly easily.

Albert and Valerie had volunteered to scout the surrounding area on a more or less permanent basis. They set off for the southern end of the county and began a long slow, meandering circuit across the fields and through bush. They often traveled on the old roads for miles at a time.

They were drawing down for the night in a hollow that had ground cover so thick it was like a mattress. Albert scraped away a small depression and lay in a fire with necklace of sandstone chunks.

"Look here," he called Valerie.

He was holding a large round chunk.

"Who would have thought it," she said.

"What?"

"I guess cavemen played bowling."

Albert frowned and slammed the orb against an exposed shoulder of limestone, cracking it open in one smack.

"Hey," she said and then looked.

It was a large, sparkling geode, about the size of a cantaloupe. The inside was ringed with ridges and quadrants of calcite and quartz, but what startled them both was the large, perfect quartz crystal nested in the hoary center.

"Is it a diamond?" she squealed

Albert frowned again.

"Course not," he said. "It's a quartz crystal. About three hundred million, I figure."

Valerie's eyes widened and she reached for it.

"Are you kidding me?"

"What?" he said. He looked her and laughed.

"Three hundred million years old," he said.

She was obviously disappointed and he kept laughing for quite a while.

"What would you do with that much money?" he asked, playing along.

"Very funny."

"Well now, just suppose," he said.

"What for? Money isn't worth anything anymore. Three hundred million wouldn't buy a cup of coffee."

"No."

"I remember there was a woman in our town who won the lottery when I was about twelve…you remember them, right? She won fifteen million, I think it was and everybody was just so jealous you wouldn't believe it. They were calling her names and asking her for money. I saw her downtown once and she couldn't even go into the drug store without somebody coming on to her. She finally moved away. I wonder what happened to her."

"She's dead or aught to be, just like the rest of us," he said. "Hell, I think I'd pay three hundred million right now for a good bottle of Earl Haig and a big beef steak like I used to make. Damn, they were good. I can't remember last time I had a piece of beef," he said.

He looked down and she was asleep. The fire was well-banked in the depression he made but he decided to let it die.

He couldn't sleep as easily as she seemed to. She would lie down and close her eyes and be asleep so fast, it didn't seem possible. Never made a sound or moved until the next morning and she'd awaken up the same way. She'd open her eyes and sit up and be doing 60 MPH by the time she was on her feet.

Whenever they were in the woods, they slept the same way. He would back up against a tree and she would put her head in his lap. He would rest the .45 on her shoulder and cat-nap in twenty-minute spells until morning.

He was not five minutes into his first doze when he heard a

voice somewhere in the bush, maybe a hundred yards out. It was a female voice. Then a man answered. He could clearly hear them talking now, thought the words were unclear.

He placed a hand over Valerie's mouth and tapped her awake. She knew what it meant and rose slowly, as silently as she could. She looked at him and then she too heard the voices. Then the voices stopped and there was nothing for quite a while until they heard some rough movement in the bush to their right. This was much closer. It was only one person, someone moving slowly, but not stealthily, through the briars and stick grass. A flashlight beam jumped out and deflected in the foliage.

Valerie rolled left, taking her rifle and Albert moved the other way so that the intruder was between them. He seemed to be looking for something, the flashlight playing along the ground, back and forth and then trying to pierce the foliage at eye level.

A man's voice called from farther away and the intruder stopped and replied with a loud whistle. Was it the woman? She was standing no more than twenty feet from Albert when she turned the flashlight back on and held to her wrist.

Albert caught his breath and then exhaled slowly.

Greta looked up and the light shone against her face, creating shadows under her eyes. It was hard to tell what condition she was in, but there was no doubt who it was. She hesitated for a moment, almost as if she suspected she was being watched and then clicked the flashlight off.

Albert closed his eyes and concentrated his hearing, trying to pick up the slightest motion in the air that would give away her position. Then the flashlight blinked on again and he watched it disappear as she walked away.

There was no sleeping now for either of them and they quickly broke camp and located both hobbled horses. Fortunately, the animals had wandered far enough that they hadn't been disturbed by the intrusion, or at least hadn't reacted to it.

They waited until dawn before they moved. They found the faint trail left by Greta and her companion and followed it to a large campsite that had been abandoned very recently. The coals were not warm but there was still heat in the ground from the fire. There had to have been at least fifteen riders here. They found the picket line and Albert felt the dung. It was cold, but not dry. They had left their garbage all over the site, including wrappings from MREs and plenty of unburied human waste.

Valerie picked up several MRE bags, flattened them and stuffed them in her pack.

"Why would they just throw away something like that?" she asked.

The heavy plastic bag each meal came in, had a hundred different uses, from preserving food to holding water in a pinch. No survivor was without his collection of sturdy, green plastic bags.

Albert thought he knew the answer but he did not offer it. Greta wasn't worried about survival in that sense. She was being bankrolled, so to speak, by some military authority with a huge supply of anything she might require. She was leading a troop of government agents. What kind of government was open to question; but it was some larger authority that she had attached herself to. Greta was an acolyte. She needed to follow someone who would appreciate her skills.

They decided to split up and follow the band from both flanks; she would move along the north, staying at least half a mile from them at all times. Albert would come at them from the south and get as close to them as he could.

"Come night, you will be on your own," he warned her.

"Well it won't be the first time, Albert."

"I know…it's just, well, I kinda…"

"I'll miss you too," she said.

There wasn't time for a proper goodbye.

"Stay alive, no matter what happens," he told her. "I will get to you."

Valerie cut into the woods about a hundred yards outside of the camp and set out on the north trail. It was easy to see where they were headed. The group was well mounted and probably well armed. Her northern route was the less obstructed, Turk picking his way along the rock ledges and wending through the sparser tree growth with relative ease. Periodically, she would dismount, tie him up and then scout due south until she picked up their trail again. They were not even trying to hide it. She would get a line on their general direction and then recover Turk and head that way. She never rode closer than a mile to them, but even that was a risk. This bunch obviously had some bush skills and if she let herself be seen even once, they would run her down.

Albert had a tougher time of it, the southern side of this east-west highway completely overgrown with every irritating, aggravating, insulting and ornery vegetable ever conceived. Ground cover tripped the horse and over-reaching branches clutched at him as he bulled his way along. He had to walk Lucile through the undergrowth more than he rode her. He was traveling much closer to the band, but without much increased risk. They would be worried about Provost scouts or sentries spotting them from the north. Their southern flank, as far as they were concerned, was no threat.

The arrogance of the grandiose. What did Sun Tzu say?: *Know yourself or know defeat.* In the minds of these conquerors, half-starved refugees could never mount a pincer attack against a lobster, never mind fifteen determined outriders, who among them couldn't come up with one complete conscience and were willing - and able – to commit any atrocity in order to achieve their goals. Well. Albert knew himself and his charges and he knew his enemy equally. Hubris would defeat them. But he'd have to set them up for it.

More than likely, they were there to probe the defenses of this group and report back to a larger force that had designs on Provost. The more work the settlers accomplished, the more attractive the property became. Greta's masters would wait until all the hard labor had been completed and then, just like criminals have always done, they would move in and claim it. They wouldn't have to fire a shot. Threat alone would convince the population to surrender – like it always had.

There was a time, most certainly, when this would have worked. But the refugees who had streamed into Provost over the last many months were almost all veterans of relocation centers or slave camps or had seen the futility of paying tribute to thugs, whether uniformed or not, whether official or otherwise. Many, if not all, were prepared to die here rather than surrender again and he doubted they would fall for any negotiated settlement, either. It was going to be all or nothing this time.

Greta's band finally made camp near sundown in a clearing below a rock outcrop. It was a good choice. The rock wall protected them from a northern attack and banked their fires while a southern attack would have to mount up hill.

Albert tied Lucile to a tree a mile from the camp and then moved back in slowly, until he could see the glow of their cooking fire through the leaves. Surely, they would mount sentries, and he remained in position for an hour, hardly even breathing, just like he hunted for deer. The crack of underbrush reached him while he was in a kind of trance. It is not enough to remain still. Information is transmitted subliminally through the air between animals even when they are silent and they are much attuned to receiving it from manbeasts as well, though manbeasts do not hear them. Albert had discovered the Zen of total fusion with the environment and he could almost feel the disturbance in the air when something changed. The walker was still out of sight and for all intents out of sound when Albert picked up his movements.

It was not long before he heard the sentry walking through the bush, ostensibly on duty, but much more concerned about the bramble and nettle catching on his clothes.

The man was tugging at the vines that seemed to be grabbing at his ankles when Albert came from behind and encircled his throat. The man gagged and dropped his equipment. He jumped and shook trying to lever Albert's forearm from his throat but anoxia soon overtook his brain and he sagged.

Albert began searching his equipment, finding an M16 with five full clips and a full compliment of military accouterments, everything from watch to morphine. The man was starting to come around and Albert pressed the Emerson against his throat and covered his mouth. His eyes fluttered open and he instinctively tried to resist until Albert allowed the point of the blade to cut an eighth of an inch into the Adam's apple. The man's eyes bulged with terror.

"I will take my hand away," Albert whispered. "If you make a sound, any sound at all without my permission, I will slit your throat. Is that understood?"

The man nodded and Albert removed his hand and the man started gasping.

"Stop," Albert commanded him. "Slow down."

The man nodded again and started to breathe normally.

"How many are you?"

The man did not answer. He looked at Albert with pursed lips.

"Jesus," Albert said. "You are not really going to do this, are you?"

The man still refused to speak. Albert cocked his head and looked at the man as if he were some strange fish just pulled from the sea.

"One more time," Albert said, leaning very close.

The man looked away.

"Look at me," Albert said. He refused and Albert grabbed his jaw and yanked his head.

"Are you sure?" he said.

The man stared, but did not speak.

Albert shook his head regretfully and then pushed the blade into the man's throat, severing the windpipe and the main artery. The man spasmed and choked, his eyes rolling wildly until the knife found the spinal cord and severed it, snapping the third cervical vertebra and poking out the other side.

Albert wiped the knife off on the man's shirt and sheathed it.

He would have to try again.

They had posted three sentries on the southern flank and they were probably meant to communicate on a regular basis. Albert had no time to waste.

He moved rapidly through the bush until he caught moonlight glinting off a rifle barrel. The guard was walking towards him, probably expecting to meet the dead man.

Albert took the M16, slung it like he was on duty and walked out.

The other man slowed when he saw him coming and Albert waved.

The man tensed and tried to make out Albert's face, but he could not quite see it.

"Mike?" he called.

Albert thought for a split second and then replied, "Ya, man, wazup?"

The sentry allowed a burst of fire from the gun and Albert took a slug in the chest that ricocheted off a rib and sunk deep into the muscle of his side. A second pair slammed into his right bicep, the tumbling bullets ripping the muscle and shattering the humerous. Albert fired back but missed and the man dove into the night.

Albert fell back on the ground, blood oozing from his side and arm. The arm was already useless. He couldn't raise it and he had to leave the AK on the ground as he scrambled for cover.

The rest of the troop had doused the campfires and were running towards the firefight. He could hear their shouts and the clatter of their boots on the stone.

Albert knew he would not make it back to the horse before they got him. He would have to lead them way out and lose them but his arm was screaming with pain. It would go numb in a few moments when enough adrenalin kicked in, but right now, he had to hold it still while he crashed through the undergrowth.

He had to stay out of the swarm of flashlights streaking everywhere around him, moving a few feet when he heard them move and stopping when they stopped to listen. They gave each other directions and sometimes they would be drawn away from him and sometimes it seemed like they were right on him.

He had no idea where he was or if the location provided any cover at all in daylight. They would not stop looking for him, especially once they found the dead sentry. He heard boots on the ground nearby and a flashlight beam swept back and forth, passing right over him once while he buried his face in the dirt. The clothing might pass a cursory glance at a distance, but once light hits a human face and human eyes, there was no hiding.

The walker stopped and Albert held his breath and began counting. He could hold his breath for two minutes. The boots kicked away some leaves and sticks and then turned abruptly. The man walked back in the direction he'd come.

Albert exhaled slowly and tried to regulate his breathing.

There was surprisingly little blood from the wound, though it throbbed painfully with each pulse of his heart. He really had no choice but to move. They were setting up a noose of shooters all around his suspected position and come daylight they would simply pull it closed. They stationed themselves about fifty feet apart, repeatedly sweeping the ground with flashlights.

He crawled along the ground, eking out distance a foot at a time. He would slowly draw a leg up, then push, and draw the other leg. Instead of heading for the greatest distance between the two sentries nearest his position, he aimed directly for the man on his left. They were coordinating their searchlights in the center, leaving a five-foot space around each man, unchecked. Albert timed his crawl and twice buried his face in the grass as the beam of light shot straight at him.

Valerie would have heard all the noise by now and realize what was happening. They had not planned for this.

Hubris, Albert. Hubris.

He was certain she would be moving in on them, fully aware that they were now alert and ready and no doubt expecting more infil-

326

trators at any moment. Albert was no more than ten feet from the nearest guard, his body nestled in the high weed growth, but perfectly visible if the man happened to look his way. He had never trained himself to shoot left-handed. He could not bring his arm up to get the .45 out of his holster, anyway.

"You will think of everything and then find out what you missed," Lenny says. *"You will fuck up. You will, fuck up. The point is to be able to deal with your own fuckups."*

There is Lenny, sitting on a cowboy chair out in the New Mexican desert, drinking a beer and lecturing. And there is Albert, listening, but not hearing the information – until now.

If he tries any harder to retrieve the pistol, he will give himself away. He manages to get the Emerson out but again; he is no good with his left hand.

And then the shot.

On the other side of the circle, a man hit the ground and Albert froze. Automatic fire immediately flew towards the muzzle flash. The man nearest him knelt down and turned his full attention to the firefight, adding his swarm to the cloud of deadly bees striking the woods above them.

Albert crawled, widening the distance between himself and the shooter and pulled up parallel with him. The man had emptied his clip and was replacing it. Albert waited for Valerie's next shot. He counted slowly. She knew the rules. He could not teach her much about shooting but he could show her some tactics. One shot and then you have to move. One shot. In thirty seconds, they can locate your position and send a missile down the trajectory of your shot that will blow a hole fifty feet wide where you were standing. One shot and then you have to move. Is the best cover to your right? Move left. What is he looking at? You just killed the man beside him and he is looking straight into the trajectory of the bullet. They sweep a hundred and eighty degrees with automatic fire. Where are you? High? Low. Flat? Behind a rock? Did you think about this before you pulled the trigger?

Her next shot came from almost two hundred feet to the east and caught one of them in the chest. She had aimed for his muzzle flash. This time the automatic fire was almost instantaneous. The tracers streaked in a wide swath like meteorites all racing to one spot.

Albert was now past the man and behind him. One chance.

He rose, fell forward and slammed the Emerson as hard as he could into the man's neck, severing the cord and dropping him silently. His neighbor was too busy to notice and Albert started running, hunched over, holding his bad arm so it wouldn't flop around. He scrambled over the lichen and was torn by the Devil's Stick and bramble caught on his clothes and tripped him. He finally escaped the enfilade and crashed through the bush towards Lucile.

"Don't go!" the foliage begged, reaching out and trying to grip his shoulders and slapping his face. "Stay!" the trees whispered as he crashed through the maze, tripping again and again as the spiked vines and the thorn bushes tripped him up. The trees were laughing. "Fool," they chided and tripped him again...

Lucile was angry with him when he arrived and stomped the ground and snorted.

"Not now," he said, yanking her lede rope loose.

He tried mounting her from the right side and she balked. He went around to her left flank and twisted himself like a rope until he could get his left boot in the stirrup and then he grabbed her mane and heaved himself into the saddle.

She danced and resisted for a moment and he just leaned forward until she calmed down. Once he had the reins, he turned south and then west, tracing a wide loop around the fight scene. The forest was so dense, sound was absorbed in short order and if there was firing going on still, he could not hear it. She would continue to take them out, one at a time until it became untenable.

Run. Always run. Whenever you can; run.

He had followed a meandering trail for about a mile when he detected someone on his tail.

He saw the shadow of movement on a ridge and urged Lucile on. She was hungry and pissed off and nickered at him and tossed her head. He jerked the bit several times until she reared and got the message. He kicked her flanks and she began to trot.

They had established their first fallback in a dense cedar copse, that had an almost hidden trail entrance. The area was no more than half an acre, but there was plenty of cover. He coaxed her in and then dismounted.

Lucile stared at him, outraged by the treatment she had received and she rolled her upper lip at him and showed her teeth.

"Ya, ya," he said, as he pulled the bit out.

He tried to unbuckle the saddle but he couldn't do it with one arm so he cut the synch strap with the knife and pushed the saddle and blanket onto the ground. Then he pulled off the halter and she backed up and looked at him. As if she understood, she turned and scrambled out of the redoubt, crashing noisily through the woods. He heard her call once and then she was gone. It might buy him some time.

He would wait until one hour after dawn, which was only minutes off. If Valerie didn't show by then, he'd go to their next fallback and wait there. After that...

"Just one more," Valerie whispered to herself.

She had moved closer to them, rather than try to escape and now she was pinned behind a dead trunk. They had stopped firing and were rearranging themselves to repel an attack. One of them turned his flashlight on for a split second, long enough for her to focus on the darker shadow that must be a body. She squeezed the trigger and heard a shout as the bullet creased the man's head.

They were firing wildly again as she backed out of her position and got far enough from the ridge to stand up and run.

She found Turk waiting patiently where she had left him, bored, possibly, but not angry.

She mounted and urged the animal to a trot, counting on his night vision to save them from disaster.

She had decided to follow their plan, exactly. Her instincts were to stay and kill as many people as she could, but that was not the plan. She headed west and south towards the fallback, stopping occasionally to listen; no one was following her.

Dawn broke a half-hour later and she steered the big stallion around rocks and along ledges at speeds, much against his better judgment. But she talked to him the whole time and he obeyed, his eyes shiny and alert.

An hour later, she was too far from the fallback to believe he would still be there and she changed direction and headed west to their last stand. If Albert wasn't there...if...if...

It was another two hours through the bush to this last fallback and she knew as she arrived that he wasn't there.

She looked north towards Provost. That was part three. She was to return directly to Provost if he didn't meet her at the last point.

The permutations began tumbling in her mind and she tried to reason herself into a satisfactory state.

In the end, she pointed the horse back towards their first fallback station, though it made no sense. He always followed the plan, which was to wait until one-hour after dawn and then move to the next station. Well, one hour after dawn was three hours ago and the stations were only about two hours apart.

What if he were alive and injured? What if she would more effective going back to Provost and trying to find him with a full compliment of...idiots? What if...

He was on the trail when she found him, exhausted from running all night with the bad arm and bleeding side. He had pulled himself up against a tree and held the .45 in his good hand.

He was seeing double when he looked at her and his head was thumping. The bullet had not only ripped his bicep to shreds, it had cracked the humerous and bone splinters were digging into the flesh.

"Where's Lucile?" she asked, bending down and taking the gun from his hand.

"Run her off," he said. "Get moving, They'll be onto us again in no time."

With Albert in the saddle, bobbing and weaving like a punch clown, she led them back through the long stretches of woods and cross numerous fields.

They took an extra day getting back as they set up ambushes on three occasions and waited for visitors. When they were sure it was clear, she headed them due north and without considering it too much, took the main road into Provost for the last twenty miles.

On the ridge they had left behind, Greta watched them through binoculars. She had Lucile in tow, who complained about being so close to another horse.

Greta slashed her three or four times across the muzzle with her whip until the horse was screaming and bucking. Lucile's eyes were wild and blood was leaking from a laceration on her soft muzzle.

And then, without another thought, Greta put the glasses back up to her eyes and watched until Albert and Valerie had blinked out of existence.

***

Chapter Three

Forewarned was not forearmed in the case of Richard Armitage and his cohort of the dispossessed. They counted thirteen hundred souls, more or less on any given day, of whom fewer than two hundred had any fighting skills or experience. Of those, their exposure to battle amounted to hit-and-run raids on storehouses and army patrols and the occasional woodland shoot-out with other groups of equally untrained adversaries.

When Albert and Valerie had offered to take over outland patrols, they had dropped any preparations for defense, in the belief that these two would know what to do.

So when they saw Valerie leading the wounded Albert into town, the shock ran through the entire community.

He was taken down from the horse and bedded on a cot in a back room at Lee Baker's old hardware store. Baker was long gone, as was the hardware, but the building had managed to withstand several incarnations and was now the official town infirmary.

They even had a physician, of sorts.

He went by the name of Granby and he seemed to know what he was talking about. He had helped a few convalesce through various viral infections that periodically swept through the community over the last few months and he had mended some broken limbs.

When he saw Albert's arm, he could see that there was little time to repair it.

The wound was deep and damaging, just as it was meant to be, with flesh and bone torn off and splintered and mixed together in a bath of blood and infection, already starting fester. The skin all around the hole was red, swollen and hot.

Albert lay back on the cot and Granby stretched his arm out as gently as possible. Albert gritted his teeth and yelled.

Valerie was sitting beside him, her face ashen, one hand holding Albert's inert paw.

Granby finally had to ask her to get out of the way.

"Just get it out," Albert breathed heavily.

"Well, it's not that simple," Granby explained. "You've got a lot of muscle damage and that bone...Jesus, I can see it and it's cracked."

"So?" Albert demanded. "Are you saying you can't do it?"

Granby looked sadly at Albert and nodded.

"I can do it, but...but there's no telling if I am going to make it worse or better," he said.

"Anything's better than this," Val interjected.

"There's no anesthetic, no drugs, not even a decent knife," Granby said.

"So what? Just let him lie here?"

"Knock him out and cut the arm off," Granby advised. "Cauterize the stump with a torch. That's the only way I can see to stop the infection."

The side wound wasn't so bad. The bullet was deeply imbedded but it had missed anything vital.

Albert heard this and closed his eyes.

"And what if you go ahead and dig it out?" she asked.

"He'll probably die. Did you hear me, Albert? You'll probably die if I try and get in there."

"Don't want to die," he breathed heavily."

"Are you saying if you cut his arm off he'll *live*?"

Granby shook his head slowly.

"Not at all. As a matter of fact, the shock without anesthetic could kill him."

He stood up and looked around the room.

"I'll be back in a few minutes," he said."

Albert heard him leave. His eyes closed and he was imagining himself with one arm. He couldn't ride, couldn't shoot...couldn't work. Valerie guessed his thoughts.

"There's lots of people with one arm," she said, her voice trembling a bit.

"I know it," he grunted. "I don't think I'd be very much use, though."

332

"Yes you would," she cried. "You know so many things...you could teach people what you know. They need your knowledge more than your arm."

Albert listened to her, but her voice seemed far away. Loss of blood, shock and fatigue were working overtime.

"Why couldn't he have shot my other arm?" he mumbled. He thought he said it, anyway. She kept calling him and he answered her repeatedly, but she never got the message.

A shimmering specter of Dr. Granby loomed over him and he felt them tying his arm down to a chair. Then they strapped his other arm and both legs so he couldn't twist around.

"Forget that crap about alcohol," Granby said. "You don't want to give him any alcohol, not even water. We'll use it to clean the outside of the wound, but I wouldn't put much stock in it. It's only about 30 percent."

Granby had returned with an oil lamp, a hack saw, a dirty-looking pair of long-nosed electrician's pliers, a strip of rubber tubing and a freshly honed hunting knife.

"Are you up for this?" he asked her.

She nodded but her face was white. She had seen a lot of blood and many dead people over the years but she had deliberately banished from her thoughts any ideas about losing Albert. Albert couldn't ride a horse very well and he wasn't a great shot, but he was otherwise indestructible. He was-

"Are you sure?" Granby demanded and she nodded more confidently.

"I'm going to cut open the wound a little, just enough to see in there better. I'll try to get the bits out...the bullets and the bone fragments. He's going to be screaming the entire time. He's going to screaming like nothing you have ever heard," Granby finished.

"Okay," she said quietly.

"If he's lucky, he'll pass out."

"Okay," she said again.

"Then I am going to take a red hot butter knife and slide it around inside the wound to try and kill the infection, stop the bleeding...you understand?"

"Then I will sew it up and bandage it and we will watch to see what happens. If the infection persists, we will have to do it all again and take the arm off. Are you hearing me Albert?"

Albert's eyes were closed and he was shaking with fear, antici-

333

pating the pain about to be visited upon him. He looked briefly at Valerie and their eyes collided and veered away from each other.

"Bite on this," Granby said, putting a piece of soft wood in his mouth. "You will break your own teeth off or bite your tongue in half if you don't do it."

Albert chomped down on the stick and then closed his eyes again.

"Damn," was all he said.

He felt the rubber tubing synch around his arm just below the shoulder. It was very tight and it began to hurt, adding to his misery.

"Okay," Granby said.

The first cut of the knife was not too bad. The flesh had already been battered and much of the nerve tissue was damaged. But then he felt Granby's fingers spreading the wound and his hand touched something deep.

Albert howled. He arched his back and screamed as Granby pushed the heated pliers into his arm muscle and plucked a piece of bone fragment from the tangle of blood and flesh. He heard himself crying in pain, sobbing like a child, he thought. There would be a moment of respite and then the near-red hot tip of the pliers would penetrate some piece of tissue, grip the splinter, and remove it. And each time, he screamed and cried, begging them to stop.

He heard Granby say: "There's one," and the pliers plunged into his flesh again, but this time he didn't scream at all.

His mind went completely dark and he fell into a well. He was floating in black space, unable to move, or see or affect his condition in any way. But it was no longer scary. He thought he could feel the cool ether of outer space as he drifted around. He saw lights streaking past far in the distance. He saw shadows moving around and coming close and then disappearing. And then there was just floating...slowly, quietly, through an endless dark inanition where he did not have to feel anything at all. He did not wake up as Granby sliced open his side and plunged the pliers deep into the muscle where they grabbed the little lead slug.

Valerie was silent as Albert dove deeper and deeper into unconsciousness.

Granby pulled the last stich through and looked at her soberly.

"It's less than fifty-fifty," he said.

She nodded.

Albert woke suddenly, three days after his surgery, his arm bandaged and stiffened with a pair of boards and some rope and his right side bandaged and enflamed.

"The infection has not spread that I can see," Granby told him.

The surgery had been crude and incomplete. The cracked bone had merely been pressed together and the arm taped to hold it that way. Perhaps in two or three months, Albert might try to bend it. Perhaps.

"You might be able to move the arm some," Granby told him, "but the muscle was shredded...I'd say a quarter of it is gone and the bone might heal right...and it might not. My guess is, you'll have some movement. That's about all I could say."

Valerie changed his bandages and reset the splint twice a day. He did not complain.

"Did I make a lot of noise?" he asked her finally.

"Sure did," she said. "Screamed like a twelve-year-old girl."

Albert didn't laugh.

"I'm just kidding for Chrissakes," she said.

"I know," Albert replied.

There was nothing anyone could do about the pain; the throbbing, searing pain that never stopped, that kept him awake at night and made him want to sleep during the day. He found a new respect for old Lonny Pickens who had managed without complaining for so long under worse conditions than this. It made Albert feel ashamed.

He learned of Lonny's fate shortly after arriving in Provost. A compatriot of Lonny's explained that he was killed in battle by short-range nuclear artillery that struck the last operating Free Forces unit three miles north of Provost about six months after the Legion had been wiped out. Two thousand were killed outright and another three thousand died of wounds and radiation poisoning. Some lasted a few hours...some lasted years. Pat Kingston had been among the latter group.

The battle ground was now called "the dead zone" because no one had dared enter it since the last pulsing, mushroom cloud had dissipated. The dead were left along with all the abandoned cars and trucks and junk carried by the Free Forces as they readied for an attack on Indianapolis.

"It was the last big disaster in a string of disasters," the man said.

At the mention of Pat Kingston, the imagine of Mai loomed in his mind.

"I've got it bad...here," she says, pressing on her midsection. "All through. I'm done for, just like Pat."

"How do you know?"

"How do you think I know? I been looking after cancer patients for thirty years. I'm done for, Mister Smythe. And this is better than dying in a bed screaming because there's no morphine. Everybody has a part to play, right? Might as well die for something as nothing."

He still didn't know if she was telling the truth or not. He looked into her eyes just before he pulled the trigger, hoping to see the truth, hoping to see something that would exonerate him for what he was about to do. She looked back at him with those dark, expressionless eyes, her face as serene as an alabaster bust.

Ever since returning to the town, Albert had thought about going to visit the Legion compound where the terrible battle had been fought those years ago, but he hadn't been able to make himself do it.

The only point would be to visit the cemetery they had established just before they had to run for it. And then what? Flowers? And then what? Tears? Speeches? I don't need anything to remind me about what happened there, he thought.

"Fuck it," he spat.

"What," Valerie said, looking at him.

"What what?" he said.

She didn't want to play. Instead, she took his good hand and held it tightly before letting it go.

When it was known that Albert would live – at least for a while, Richard Armitage called a general meeting to discuss the whole problem of self-defense.

A furniture store on the town square was the largest building available, the high-school having been bombed and destroyed during the Big War.

There were perhaps three hundred residents there, many of them representing small cooperatives within the community. They all knew Albert and Valerie and made way when they entered, a fact that annoyed Albert.

"Never mind," she said to him. "Just sit down and shut up."

Richard Armitage and half a dozen others, including Granby, sat at a table in front. Behind them was a giant map of the county that had been commissioned by the owner of the furniture store in celebration of the two hundredth anniversary of the town's founding.

There was very little conversation and Armitage stood up without a lot of ceremony. He had been a businessman in his other life. That term didn't mean much anymore and it didn't explain what he really did, either. For all anyone knew, he might have been on the inside of this fiasco up until last year, living for profit before he decided to become a prophet and lead his children through the wilderness.

Albert despised charisma and he was well on his way to despising Armitage who seemed to have a hypnotic hold on the crowd. Like every good salesman, Armitage knew when to shut up and when to speak.

"We're all glad to see you up and around, Albert," he said and everybody turned and stared at the two of them and started to applaud. Albert glared with the disapproving face of an angry rooster.

"And thank you Dr. Granby," Armitage continued. There was sporadic applause for Granby who smiled to himself.

"We have been discussing what to do about this situation and quite frankly, none of us here feels confident in making any suggestions.

"Obviously, the arrival of these raiders, or whatever they were, can only be the start of something. We cannot believe that this was an accident or they will just disappear. We have to plan for…whatever is coming."

Albert disliked Armitage a whole bunch less, all of a sudden.

"I'm going to ask Mister Smythe if he would come up here and talk to us all."

They started to applaud again and Albert turned red, then white, and then black before he could get to his feet.

"I'm here to listen, just like everyone else," he said and sat down.

"Come on, Albert," someone called "You can do it."

He turned around to spot the caller, but he was met by a bouquet of earnest faces.

"At lease give us your thoughts," Armitage said.

Albert realized there was no way out of it at this point and, hanging his head, he thought for a moment and then looked up, aware of the expectation laid on him."

"I don't think they've got air or satellite," he said.

The people in the room were silent.

"They wouldn't send horse-mounted scouts in like that if the had air. And my guess is the satellites are pretty well screwed anyway. Anyway, that's what I think," he said and sat down.

"What are we supposed to do about it?" someone called.

"What *do* they have, then?" someone else asked and then someone called out: "Who the hell are *they*?"

"Well, I know who one of them is," he said, rising again, trying to ignore Valerie's puzzled gaze.

"Her name is Greta and she is a trained spy or whatever you call them now. She is an agent who can do just about anything. If the rest of them are anything like her, we are probably all screwed."

This brought gasps and chatter from everywhere and Armitage quickly quieted the crowd.

"Please," he said…

Albert looked at him and shrugged.

"There was twenty of them, well mounted and well armed. Most of them had military issue M16s though I seen one guy with a Winchester. I guess they are not a hundred percent. They seem to know what they are doing, though and that is a lot more than I could say for any of you."

Albert regretted the remark, instantly and red flooded his face and his eyes flashed with embarrassment. Valerie shook her head and looked away.

"My guess is they will be back after they get themselves a whole bunch more people," he continued, trying to move on.

"They'll attack from the south and the east and maybe they will try to push us back down to the west end of town where there's no place to run except straight down the road for a while. It's all open land either side of the highway for about ten miles. They might even have some back there waiting for when we break. That is what I would do, anyway," he finished, almost out of breath.

"That's it?" someone said.

"What?" Albert responded to the belligerence. "You think you are going to stand off a bunch like that with some baseball bats and a few rocks?"

"Well what do you suggest?"

"Pick up the babies and grab the old ladies…get the hell out of here before they come back."

This released a barrage of questions and accusations, statements and announcements that rolled over him in a confused mass. He

338

looked around the room, stunned. He didn't know what to do.

"Albert...Albert," Armitage shouted and the crowd calmed.

"Can't we do anything?" Armitage asked.

"Not in my opinion you can't."

"Is there anyone else?" Armitage sighed.

"I say let's build barricades and when they come in here, we just shoot them down," someone called out.

Albert looked around to see who it was. He pointed at the man and everyone became quiet.

"Now right there, you see it. That's what's wrong. That's the dumbest thing I ever heard," Albert said.

"You haven't got fifty serviceable weapons in this place and most of them got almost no ammunition. You are up against troops with automatic weapons, don't you understand? They will overrun you in five minutes."

"Well I'm not leaving," someone said and once again, the conversation bubbled up over the top.

"Suppose you are right about them," Armitage began. "Suppose everything you say is true about how they will attack and so forth. What would you do if you just couldn't run?"

Albert shook his head slowly.

"I don't do 'if'," he said.

"Albert, somebody has to organize this. At least if we are all going to die here, let's make it hard for them."

Albert was struck by the comment. For the first time in years, these people were prepared to stand up for themselves and here he was abandoning them. He stood there for a while without speaking and then seemed to come up with an idea.

"Well, they will not use bombardment in my opinion," he stated.

"They want this place in tact now that you've done all the work. This would be a great place to have as a headquarters for all kinds of reasons...but anyways...they will be looking to take over...they'll take slaves and they'll round up any resistance they find and kill them, you can bet on that...Usually what they do is grab anybody who is anybody and hang them right away and then they...well...you all know it's like, one way or the other."

He frowned and thought some more and then looked at Armitage

"But if they come at us from three sides like you said..."

"I know it," Albert nodded. "I guess I will have to think on it and get back to you."

Valerie walked him back to their quarters, a room in a bungalow that had been stripped of everything down to the wood lath that held the old plaster.

They had blankets and whatever they carried with them, but that was all. There was no furniture. The glass windows had long ago been smashed and rough boards covered the hole to keep out the rain.

Valerie opened two MREs and he reached over and took his away.

"I ain't crippled," he grumped. He held the heater bag open with his teeth and dropped in the entre.

"I can't imagine living like this," he said, looking around. It was dark and stank from human filth that had dried and hardened in corners. People had likely died in this room and lain there for weeks or even months. Animals had nested here, whelped and moved on.

"It's better than some places I've lived in," she said.

Albert didn't understand. The cave was a palace compared to this shit-hole. What were they doing here?

"Not everybody is lucky like you," she said, petulantly.

Albert felt his face rushing with heat and blood and his eyes crackled when he looked at her. He was afraid to speak for fear of the bile that might pour from his mouth.

"You don't think it's luck?" she said.

"Well you are wrong. It's pure luck that you found that place and you know it. You've done better than almost everyone, Albert, because you worked; I know that. What I am saying is, you were lucky enough to be born who you are. And you should be a little grateful for that, not just full of yourself…"

The words seemed to cut him and he felt sick, like he might vomit. The hamburger steak was ready and he took it out of the pouch.

She grabbed it from him and cut it open and then laid out his meal for him, using the MRE bag for a plate.

Lucky! Godamn. Lucky! I spent every cent I had on my own life. I worked for wages, goddamn it. I didn't make money in the goddamned stock market. I traded my sweat for cash and you call me lucky. God damn. You are missing the point. No one is taking that away from you. You did exactly what you said. So what? You're lucky to have been able to do it. What about the next guy that just cannot put it together. Can't? How about won't? It's the same thing. He doesn't. Whatever you need to be able to do it, he doesn't have it. That's luck. But I made choices...Yes. And all I am saying Albert is that you should be grateful to someone...something, some...being. The universe. I don't know. Be aware, that's all. No one ever does it all himself.

He finished the meal and she took their plastic bags and anything washable and spilled water on it into a pail. Then she wiped it all down and packed it away. She saw him watching her.

"I'm only doing this because of your arm," she said.

"I know it. I guess I'm lucky," he said.

*

Luck my ass, he mused as he wandered around the town, looking into each building, checking out basements, and testing back doors. He wandered down the residential streets as well, poking his nose into every house along the way.

He called on Armitage who was on hands and knees pulling weeds from a vegetable patch. What the hell is he trying to prove? the ungenerous Albert wondered.

Valerie was leading horseback patrols a few miles out on three sides of the community as a kind of early warning system, but other than a collection of mismatched weapons, idiotic ideas and a whole pile of inexperience, they did not have much of a defense set up.

"What's on your mind," Armitage asked without looking up.

"You better come along with me," Albert said. "I don't expect we've got more than a day or so before they're back in force."

Armitage invited him inside and Albert was immediately struck by the difference between Armitage's residence and the rest. He had a table and several wood chairs. Someone had found an old sofa that had missed bullets, burnings, rainstorms, nuclear bombs and a hundred forms of death and set it up for him.

The room had two oil lamps and a five-gallon water jug with two cracked porcelain mugs.

"Nice," Albert commented, forcing an ironic smile from Armitage.

"Necessary," he countered.

"Ya? I guess," Albert replied.

"I doubt if you'd understand," Armitage said, pouring them each a cup of water.

"Talking down to me like that might get you killed," Albert said

341

with a smile.

"You think, 'do as I do, not as I say.' Am I right?"

Albert did not reply.

"You're not a leader, Albert. Fortunately, you know it. That's what makes you so important, so vital."

"Cut the foreplay..."

"I'm serious. Most men – people, if you prefer – are not leaders and they are not independents. Most people belong to something and they need to be led just the way a baby needs to be fed.

"Remember back in the old days when unemployment was going through the roof...first it was nine percent and then ten percent and then we found out – well, you found out; people like me already knew – the government was fudging the numbers. Real unemployment was actually nineteen percent and twenty-one percent...?"

"Ya, so?"

"And all those people screaming 'we want jobs! Give us jobs. A job is a right! We have a right to work. You have to make jobs for us...'"

"Ya, I remember," Albert conceded.

"We couldn't just leave those people on their own, could we?"

"I managed."

"Wrong answer, Albert and I think you know it. You take a thousand people, one of them will be like you and one of them will be like me and the rest will be like them," he said, pointing dramatically.

"You leave them on their own...well, you see what happens. They can't manage it."

"And here's where I say, "they won't manage it," and you say, 'it's the same,' right? Already had that conversation. Now tell me what a lucky bastard I am."

"I won't do that. It's your luck, I guess to be who you are. My luck, you might say, to be who I am. I know how to make these people calm down and cooperate with each other and therefore preserve the species..."

"Aren't you a wonderful guy."

"Well, they have to think so if they are going to do what I tell them. They have to believe that I am, in front because I am better than they are and one of the ways we do that is to dress up the king in purple. There was a time when only royalty could wear purple. If a commoner wore purple, he was executed. Do you know why?"

"Same old shit…terrify them into obedience."

"If they let anyone wear purple, the whole thing could collapse. The organization falls because the mystique of the leader dissolves. You pull the curtain back…you know what I mean?"

"Thanks for the history lecture."

"You know why I'm different?" Armitage asked.

"I think I'm going to hear why."

"Because I know where this leads and I do not want it. Until then…"

"You get the big house and the table."

"That is right, and they have belief, which is the only thing that keeps them alive. Now, what did you want to talk to me about?"

They spoke for several hours, Albert outlining the only reasonable defense he could come up with and Armitage poking holes in it here and there, but otherwise agreeing to it.

As he rose from to the table, Albert thought: "Someday I am going to have to slit your throat," and Armitage thought: "Someday I am going to have to slit your throat…"

Until then, Armitage seemed to understand the plan for what it was: Necessary insanity.

***

Chapter Four

Albert stood in front of the furniture store map, tracing the various access routes into Provost.

Behind him, about a hundred volunteers, some with some experience laid out seventy-three different projectile weapons, which included everything from a .50 caliber muzzleloader to an operational M16. In between there were five-shot .38s with five bullets; various shotguns, including a Cosmi eight-shot autoloader worth about $10,000 in the old days. Albert took it from the "owner" and looked it over carefully.

"Where did you get this?" he asked.

"I found it," he said.

Albert handed it back.

Numerous 9 mm. pistols, a handful of .357s, four Mosin Nagant rifles from the Crimean war or something, each with a hundred rounds still wrapped in wax paper; numerous .308 hunting rifles and one Garand 30.06. Among them, three thousand five hundred rounds, more or less. In a typical firefight lasting an hour, say, it would be nothing to expend seven or eight thirty-round magazines per man.

"You'll have to work it out among yourselves," Albert instructed them. "I don't know who can shoot and who can't and who is lying. You need to break up into groups.

"If you really can shoot, go over there," he said, pointing to a corner. "If it's just so-so, you stand somewhere else...you get me?"

He went to the big display window that looked out onto the square. More than a thousand people were falling into line, each carrying something of value and something he believed was of value and would end up throwing away. They trudged with that deliberate, methodical clomping down the main street, heading north out of town,

The road from Provost had become impassible to vehicles a long time ago and hundreds of burned out and rusted hulks were scattered across fields, along ditches and crammed together like sculpture in the middle of the road.

There had apparently been a significant fight here after the Legion was defeated and there were plenty of skeletons around to testify.

The area had been scavenged so many times there was nothing moveable, never mind anything even remotely useful, left to take.

Its great value was to make an attack from the North unlikely. The debris field was four miles deep and eleven miles across. Albert remembered seeing similar pictures from the Iraq wars of the end of the Century, back in that other time, but this was the first he had seen of mass extermination by low-yield nuclear artillery shells.

No one knew if the ground was radioactive or not. The plant growth in the fields was as immoderate here as everywhere else and there was no apparent dead zone. The refugees streaming north knew the chances they took, but it was the only possible escape from Provost, that did not lead directly into an enemy force.

Albert left the group to divide themselves and walked around the square to the southern spoke of the wheel.

He panned across 180^0 out twelve miles to the beginnings of the southern bluff. There was no sign of anyone yet. The replacement scouts had already vanished from sight. Valerie and her crew should be visible by now. He ground his teeth and cursed the arm tied to his body.

He returned to the furniture store and found they had divided themselves into respective groups. About half the hundred claimed to be shooters; half of the rest claimed familiarity and the balance made no claims at all.

Ten men with high-powered rifles were the first to leave. There was no bravado and no excitement as they filed out the front door, each man clutching a bag of ammunition, a few MREs and some drinking water.

Everyone watched them as the disappeared into the town.

The next forty took their weapons and seemed to disappear, as well.

Albert led the balance of his force down the main street to

Firth's Service Centre, a burned out, gutted garage. Around back, they uncovered various drums and tanks that had somehow escaped the carnage.

They were filled with a stinking, rancid, mix of waste oil, dead animals, rainwater and anything else that might have fallen into the soup.

Albert showed them how to separate the oil and the water but setting pans and cans and pots to boil on wood fires. In many of the drums there was more water than oil, but over the next hours they would extract enough to make cocktails, composed of a bottle or jar containing two cups of oil and three ounces of the last known stock of gasoline anyone knew about. It wasn't enough to run an engine, but it was enough to make the waste oil flammable – maybe.

Albert took one of the first jars and they watched as he dipped a piece of cloth into the mixture and then stuffed the rag into the bottle. He lit it let the fuse get fully engaged before he threw it against the old block wall of the garage. The glass shattered but they didn't get the explosion they were looking for. The fuel was not volatile enough. The fuse dropped out and sluggish oil ran down the wall but stopped before it hit the ground.

They made a second one with twice the amount of gasoline, but it still did not ignite the viscous, contaminated dross. They tried again, with nine ounces of gasoline poured into the mix and shaken, rather than stirred.

This time the bomb exploded against the wall, sending off a cloud of black smoke. The mixture of gas and oil crackled as it burned. It was not Napalm but it was better than just pure gasoline. The oil adhered to everything it touched and continued to burn long after the gasoline was used up.

Then Albert wanted to try one more experiment.

They shredded an old tire, cutting off a pile of the smallest, thinnest slices they could manage. When he had a good handful, he dumped the rubber into the mix and added another ounce of gasoline.

The resulting explosion was powerful enough to be felt twenty or thirty feet away and the swelling heat ball burned black. The tiny pieces of tire rubber snapped, crackled and popped as they glued themselves to anything they touched and burned.

They made thirty-seven cocktails and then the gasoline supply was gone. It was the last gasoline any of them would ever see.

Albert kept glancing southward, though he couldn't see over the buildings. These weren't clockwork schedules but she was overdue now by at least an hour.

He went over the procedures with them all again. Each man carried one cocktail. He was responsible for it. If he dropped it or spilled it, he was killing his friends and neighbors as well as himself.

They broke up into eight teams of five. Albert looked at them looking at him and felt the pain in his arm. He felt a deep nausea at the prospect that something had happened to Valerie.

"Listen..." he demanded, but then nothing came out.

Then he watched them slowly break up and shuffle off into the town.

He waited for a while and then walked down the main street. It was empty and silent. There was nothing sinister or challenging about any of it. The buildings were burnt and crippled and the pavement was cracked and had separated from the sidewalks. The storefronts were all boarded up.

He walked through the residential streets and found carcass after carcass caving in on its foundations or eaten away by weather.

Essentially, he was the last man on earth.

He would give it one more hour he thought, dropping the field glasses. They hung on his neck with a piece of thin rope that cut into the skin.

He placed them again and swept the highway and then across the fields, back and forth, raising the level each time.

"Ah," he said, as they pulled into view, maybe two miles out and just visible in the glasses.

There were four of them and they did not seem to be in any hurry.

Albert sat down on the curb and pressed his temples. His head hurt all the time, now. It never seemed to stop and there was no medicine. And his arm ached with a dull constancy that was not bad enough to incapacitate him and not mild enough to ignore.

After a few minutes, he stood up and walked to the edge of town where he could greet the incoming scouts.

He sipped some water and looked at the sun falling rapidly and dying the undersides of the clouds.

It might be a normal day, if you didn't know any different.

He placed the binoculars again and focused on Valerie who led

347

the troop. She seemed unharmed, but she kept looking back at the man behind her.

Albert focused on him but he couldn't see anything at first and then she moved and he was looking at a large black body of some kind laid across the man's saddle. He couldn't make out detail. He watched it getting closer in the glasses and after a few moments the head of a large, black panther came into view. It's tongue hung out and its eyes were green.

He watched them grow in the field glasses until they entered the town limits.

The man named Kincaid pushed the dead animal onto the street in front of Albert and climbed down from his horse.

Albert was looking at Valerie and she seemed as relieved to see him, as he was to see her.

"You bleeve this?" Kincaid bragged.

"I shot this sonofabitch sneaking around our camp this afternoon."

Albert knelt down and touched the animal's thick coat.

Kincaid was grinning and looking at everyone for the praise and approval he felt he had earned.

Albert looked at Kincaid and nodded.

"I knew it," Kincaid claimed broadly. "Ever since I was a kid they said there was black lions in the woods around here."

He looked from one to the next but no one, including the other two scouts offered him anything but blank looks.

Albert turned to Valerie who was staring at the dead cat.

"Anything doing out there?" he asked her finally.

The two men left to put their horses away and Valerie and Albert sat down on the curb. Valerie's big stallion leaned forward and nibbled her hat.

"Okay, in a minute," she said.

Kincaid looked around and shrugged with exaggerated indifference. He lifted the dead cat back across the saddle and led his horse to the stable.

"There wasn't anything except that cat," she said and Albert put an arm around her.

"I always thought they were just stories, a myth," Albert said. "Like the abysmal snow woman…"

She grinned at him involuntarily.

348

"Why in hell would anybody want to kill a myth like that?" Valerie asked.

"Can't help himself, I expect," he answered. "The idea of that fellow wandering around the woods just don't sit with him. When he thinks of the woods, he wants to think of all the animals dead so's he can have it to himself."

Albert snorted a laugh and she looked at him, pained.

"Oh, I was just thinking. After he has killed off all the wildlife, he'll stand there and tell you how much better everything when he first arrived. Somebody has gone and ruined it. You mark my words."

*

The four scouts who had replaced Valerie and Kincaid and the others, were taken down before they even knew what was happening. A designated, trained killer followed each man on his rounds and in a matter of fifteen minutes all four were dead and their horses taken. As well as losing four fighters, the colony lost four guns and the chance of a first early warning, when the flare gun with its single, green rocket fell in the struggle.

Albert had never really imagined they would manage to catch sight of the enemy forces and ring the alarm. He knew they would attack at night and he was certain and advance party would clear the ridge before hand. He would deny that he arranged the scouting to keep Valerie off the ridge at night. But it would be a lie. She would never have stood for it had she known. He didn't care. He expected they would all die, this time and he was going to have her with him. What difference did it make if one of the scouts was killed here or on the ridge?

One of the night scouts, Bartlett, he thought; or was it Barrett? He had a watch and Albert had a watch. Every thirty minutes, Bartlett was to turn a small LED flashlight on and direct it at a certain spot on the highway. He was ten minutes late and Albert's image intensifiers could not pick up anything much after about three hundred yards. When ten more minutes passed without a signal, Albert felt his chest tighten and his stomach clench down hard.

He scanned the incoming roads and the fields that bordered them and picked up a small dog pack.

At thirty minutes, he knew what had happened. There was no flare, no LED signal and very little moonlight.

He had to move now. If he waited until they were within visual range of the uncomfortable night scope strapped to his head, they would overtake him before he got back.

"Shit," he cursed, banging his arm against the tree as he stood up.

Then he turned and started to jog. It was almost two miles back to the town and he believed he could make it in twenty minutes.

The sound of his heavy footfall and his labored breathing reminded him how old and smashed up he was. Every footstep jogged his arm and he was off balance by having it taped to his side.

"Won't matter if you are dead," he said and ripped the tape off.

He grimaced and lifted his forearm until it was pumping properly. The pain had been replaced by a profound numbness. He couldn't tell where is arm was, but he was running straight.

One mile out from town, he stopped and listened.

Then he turned and started running again.

Now he was closing the gap. He could see the town approaching and each meter of travel really started to have meaning.

He stopped again and this time he heard it. It was the low grumble of a Humvee diesel. It couldn't be half a mile out from him. They were closing fast.

He was a quarter mile out and he could see the outline of the building against the sky. The motor was gaining on him.

He started to run again and then realized he wouldn't be able to outrun the vehicle.

He stopped, took out the only other flare they had and aimed it 45 degrees towards the oncoming Humvee.

The 12-gauge shell popped and the flare streaked out over the road. It burst almost immediately, bathing the whole area in a Christmas green light. The Humvee was out front, fully armed and riders and foot infantry spread out across both fields.

Albert turned and started to run again as the .50 caliber bullets smacked into the ground around him. He was running so hard now his face was molded into a sardonic grimace and he seemed to have stopped breathing.

But he got there and headed for his position.

Two minutes later, the first lead hail rained down on the sleeping town.

Albert squeezed through the basement window that looked out onto the street and replaced the plywood cover.

"Your arm," she said.

"It's all right," Albert told her.

Valerie was waiting at the foot of the stairwell that used to rise to the barbershop on ground level. Albert had instructed two men to remove the stairs so now there was an eight-foot open drop to the basement floor. Then they had ripped up two barber chairs and pushed them into the basement. The skeletal remains of a family were scattered over the broken chairs and then the basement door was torn off and dumped on top of it all.

Valerie and Albert now huddled in a corner, camouflaged by the debris. To anyone looking down, it was a tomb, long ago abandoned, even by rats.

"What happened?" Valerie asked.

"They must have sent in an SF unit to take out our sentries," he said.

He could feel her looking at him.

"Oh, Albert…" she said, dismayed, realizing what he had done.

He didn't respond. He closed his eyes and concentrated on the pain in his arm. He could feel blood running down from the torn stitches.

The roar of the Humvee as it entered the town square grew louder and then it diminished as it passed. Every few seconds, the gunner would loose a burst from the .50 caliber.

The horses were next and they clattered on the asphalt and neighed wildly whenever the machinegun opened up.

In a matter of minutes, the bulk of the attacking force had occupied the town – so far without a shot being returned.

They could hear boots running and the clank and clatter of equipment as the infantry moved in and began its house-to-house search.

They heard a loud burst of static and then a voice hailed them through an electric bullhorn.

"People of Provost: Throw down your weapons and surrender. We mean you no harm! I repeat, you must surrender your weapons immediately and no harm will come to you. We are your friends!"

Silence followed in on the announcement, interrupted only by the clatter of Humvee engine and the sound of troop movements.

The bullhorn switched on again and the message was repeated.

Albert had moved to the street-level basement window he'd used for an entrance and removed a slot in the wood. He was able to insert the night goggles just enough to give him a view of the street.

There appeared to be about a hundred troops, including about thirty riders. The man with the bullhorn was using the Humvee for cover. The troops were all crouched against walls, behind old planters or otherwise arraigned behind what ever cover they could find.

Without warning, a flare exploded overhead, bathing the town square in a pinkish hue. Albert could see the troops more clearly now and it was a bit more heartening than he had expected. They were not all as well armed as he'd thought. Most carried civilian long-guns rather than military assault weapons and most were without body armor.

He finally caught sight of Greta at the head of a small cavalry unit making its way around the square.

The Humvee gunner swapped his .50 caliber for a searchlight and began a methodical sweep of every building.

A few seconds later, the sound of incoming cavalry drew everyone's attention. Another twenty riders appeared from the west spoke.

"There's plenty of them," he whispered. "Looks like maybe a hundred and fifty plus the Humvee."

"Can you see her?" Valerie asked.

"Ya," Albert replied. "She's there."

"Let me see," Valerie demanded.

"No!" he said.

Albert focused on the man with the bullhorn who was preparing to make another speech.

"People of Provost. This is Lieutenant Colonel George Griggson…"

Albert felt his heart pounding again. So that's what happened to Griggson. Albert thought he had been killed at the Legion battle. So these were "Grigsson's Boys," as he liked to call them.

The impulse to let Valerie kill Griggson right then was pushing on him and he glanced down at her.

"Just wait," he cautioned her. "It's not time."

She sat back against the cold, damp wall of the basement and closed her eyes.

Griggson stepped back from the Humvee and two other men joined him. They gesticulated and talked at each other for about ten minutes and then separated; one man rejoined the infantry group and the other collected the cavalry and headed straight up the north spoke. Greta and her small cohort remained behind.

Griggson was back on the horn in a few minutes, his impatience starting to show.

"People of Provost, you have nothing – I repeat – nothing to fear. We are here to help you. For the protection of our soldiers, we ask that you surrender all weapons immediately. You have my word you will not be harmed..."

Griggson continued to huddle up against the Humvee, though the streets remained completely silent.

Albert had drummed it into their heads that they had to to stay hidden, but he knew they would break before long. Someone would be unable to resist the opportunity to take a shot and they would loose the only advantage they had.

The sky was lightening and that would reset the schedule for everyone.

Griggson stood back from the Humvee and scouted every building in the square. He lingered on every chimney and at every window, as did three other sub-commanders. They did not believe the town was empty. Someone had set off the green flare.

They remained in place well after sunrise and Albert was beginning to wonder what was keeping them.

"They probably think we booby-trapped the place," Valerie suggested.

Albert nodded. Even so, they would have to start a search before long.

Griggson was back behind the Humvee when news came that the mounted troop that had headed north was returning.

The cordon opened to let them in and the commander dismounted near Griggson. Once again, they conferred and all the command staff looked northward. Their discussion continued for quite a while and then Griggson walked out into the open.

"Please," Albert prayed. "Please...hold your fire...hold your fire."

Valerie was pinned against the wall, her face ashen and fear sparking in her eyes. If they even suspected there was anyone down here, a hand grenade would come through the window and that would be it.

Griggson strutted, grinning in front of the company and climbed up onto the Humvee.

"It appears we have run them off," Griggson said, to cheers and hoots.

"Now I don't want you men to let your guard down…we have to check every building in this town. The cavalry under Captain Lambert will pursue these terrorists and find out exactly where they are headed and bring them back here to face justice."

Lambert saluted ostentatiously and mounted his horse. Albert almost laughed aloud.

"What is it?" Valerie pestered him.

"It's just George Griggson…he knows how to get it out of some people."

"What are they doing?"

"They're going to do exactly what we hoped they would do," Albert said, surprise evident in his voice.

Almost immediately, boots hit the pavement and squads of four or five began a building-by-building search.

The barbershop was one of the first and Albert and Valerie huddled under the pile of junk, holding onto each other in a tight embrace, expecting the bullets to arrive at any moment.

"Over here," someone said and they knew he was standing at the top of the stairwell, looking down.

They saw the flashlight beams poking around in the corners, straying here and there into shadow and then focusing on a pair of human skulls.

Then without a word, they turned and left.

Albert grimaced as he sat up, his arm, dripping blood.

"Here," she said. "Let me."

He remained still, eyes closed while she rebandaged his wound, pulling the cloth tight to try and suppress the bleeding.

The colony fighters deployed in and around the town, were supposed to remain hidden for another twenty four hours, enough time for the invaders to convince themselves that the town was truly empty.

Albert knew it wasn't going to happen. But every moment they were able to remain undiscovered had an inverse relationship with the vigilance of the invaders. Every house they cleared, added to their sense of victory. The discovery of a single hidden cell would erupt in an uncontrolled firefight with the odds overwhelmingly against the defenders.

Albert and Valerie shared a silent meal of powdered sugar, spam and flavored water. Since the first probe, no one had entered the barbershop but they had to remain were they were, cramped, almost immobilized behind the pile of garbage and human bones.

Albert tried to kiss her and she turned away from him.

"No," she whispered. "Don't."

He was stung and felt his breath catch in his throat.

"It's too much like the end," she said.

"But-."

He never got to finish the sentence.

The first rattle of machinegun fire since the invasion shook them both out of their stupor and they could hear the yelling and counterfire outside.

Albert went to his window and could see horses rearing and men shouting. Several of them fell as Albert's snipers began picking them off from the roof tops.

"The Humvee gunner swung his barrel around and focusing on an old red brick chimney sticking out of the drugstore roof, he released a long burst. The bricks exploded and flew in every direction as the heavy slugs tore the chimney apart and Albert saw the body of the sniper fly off the roof, carried in a colloid of lead and brick.

"Okay," he said to Valerie. "Get the gunner."

Finally able to do something, she replaced him at the window. The Humvee was at the end of the street and the gunner was protected by a steel barrier, but his head was visible.

She had to hit him in the side of the head just at his eye to bypass the armor he wore as well as the material surrounding him.

It was not a long shot, but the rise was enough to make her nervous. She knew that the bullet would travel a straight line from her to the target. She had to aim lower; exactly the right amount to hit him in the one spot he was vulnerable.

By the time she had sighted him, he had turned the gun away from her and was firing at another rooftop.

"He moved," she said.

The Humvee rolled forward about fifty feet, forcing her once again to adjust her sight line.

"If he doesn't turn his head this way-"

And then she fired.

She watched his head jerk in the scope and he collapsed over the gun.

"Got him," she cried.

"Keep going," he said. "Kill everyone you can see. We are not taking prisoners."

The first firebomb explosion occurred in a residence, when the five-man raider squad entered an old house that appeared to be completely abandoned. There was nowhere for anyone to hide. They made a cursory examination of the two others rooms and then as they turned to leave, a cocktail hit the floor in front of them with a tremendous whoosh and fire blew up around them.

Two of the soldiers were burning and they others were firing wildly. A second firebomb hit them from an open window and the building went up in flames. One of the burning soldiers expired as flames melted his face, the tiny bits of shredded rubber sticking to his skin and blistering it off, then sinking into the muscle tissue where it continued to jump and burn. The fifth man fell off the front porch, his clothes like a torch, as three bullets smacked into his body.

The five colony fighters had taken out an entire invading squad and had not suffered a scratch. The men looked at each other, amazed and delighted. They grinned and laughed at the burning bodies.

The scene was repeated many times as the invading troops were surprised again and again, either by cocktails or bullets that flew from nowhere. They had concentrated themselves in the town and were now surrounded. They couldn't fight their way out and they couldn't see their enemy.

Albert slumped against the wall. He watched Valerie methodically picking off invaders with the quiet determination that always seemed to take her over when she was killing people.

The Humvee was the prime target now, with the gunner dead and no one among them willing to risk taking the position. The driver raced towards the east end of town hoping to escape and almost made it before a meteor shower of burning bottles exploded against the hull, cracking the bulletproof windshield. The attackers heard the men screaming inside the burning vehicle and waiting until the started to make a break. They shot them one buy one. The vehicle was now destroyed.

Greta's cavalry troop was having much better luck and had killed three cocktail squads before they could throw their ordnance. She preferred to kill close up, but in this case, she was just as happy to take out every defender she saw with her 9 mm. Her horse was shot from under her and she tumbled to the ground with it but escaped, almost unscathed.

Pursed by a pack of six colony defenders, she vanished into a house that was still burning and leapt right through the flames and out the back door.

Someone said her hair was on fire as she ran.

Valerie had shot eleven men when they discovered her position.

A wild burst of M16 fire, slashed the wooden board with its peephole to ribbons, bullets streaking past her ear. She whirled away as a sustained burst came through the opening and smashed into the wall on the other side of the room.

"We have to get out of here," she cried at Albert.

He was delirious from blood loss and his right arm hung uselessly once again at his side.

"Go," he said.

"Fuck you," she answered. "Get up, asshole!"

She dragged him to his feet and pushed him towards the stairwell. She moved enough debris under the opening so that he could stand on it and pull himself up over the edge. He started to slip back and she grabbed his legs and pushed until he was able to squirm onto the barber shop floor.

She followed him, swinging over the edge and rolling to his side.

Bullets wacked into the room, sliced through the plaster walls and hammered the brick exterior.

The last gasp of the invading force was a standoff in the old furniture store. About thirty men were inside, all heavily armed and delivering a withering fire on the defenders-turned attackers.

Albert watched helplessly as they charged into the machineguns, just like the Chinese had during the Korean War. Albert watched them fall in the street, carried into the guns by the adrenalin of battle.

Somehow, they got control of themselves and fell back, leaving more than twenty men dead in the street who had been alive only moments before.

Someone took charge of them and they began moving sideways towards the building, out of the enfilade. They were carrying the last of the cocktails.

They lit them one after another and tossed them into the building.

The fire started slowly but grew exponentially as they added the remaining bombs and the sizzling rubber latched onto anything it touched.

A roar went up from inside the furniture store and bullets started flying out again, but the men inside had no targets. They were firing blind, panicked by the roiling flames.

Smoke completely enveloped the building and the first escapees made a break for the street where they were gunned down, one after the other. The screaming in the building rose to a siren-like wail and then a dozen men broke loose, some firing weapons and others just running. The colony defenders tracked them down one by one and executed them on the spot. They eventually found ten bodies in the ruins.

The fires continued all day as various buildings on the square and houses on the side-streets burned to the ground. Smoke hung over the town once again.

The colony had lost half its force, but Griggson's Boys were no more. All of their horses had been killed or were shot later. They found one hundred and nineteen bodies of the enemy and fifty of their own scattered across town. Several had been decapitated.

By nightfall, there was one outstanding question: What had happened to the refugees and corps that had followed them to set up a backfire attack in the staggered ruins of the northern dead zone?

Watch was kept all night and finally, just after three a.m., torches were seen coming over the northern rise and descending into the valley. The line went back for more than a mile.

They staggered back into Provost, some of them wounded, but most simply, exhausted. Their faces told the story.

The forty men who had positioned themselves among the wrecks and broken boulders to defend the fleeing refugees, had been killed to the last man. Six of Griggson's riders had escaped to fight another day – among them; George Griggson.

***

Chapter Five

It was their great fortune that winter no longer visited these latitudes (though it would take another ten years to confirm it), otherwise the colony would most certainly have perished that first winter after routing the invaders.

They had made little preparation in the face of impending destruction and when all the living had returned to the settlement or moved on and the dead were burned and buried, there wasn't enough food for a month.

It was also true that few of them had any notion of gardening or hunting or even simple scavenging. Add to that even a mild winter, just enough to cause dormancy in the plants and starvation would have completed what Griggson's Boys had been unable to.

The first thing they did was to start butchering the dead horses and preserving the meat. That alone probably saved them the first two or three months. After that, their food stocks diminished at an increasing rate and severe rationing was imposed.

In the aftermath of the battle, they had managed to collect more than a hundred rifles and handguns and a few thousand rounds of ammunition but Albert convinced them that it must be seconded for defense rather than hunting.

Each day, horse patrols roamed a wide radius and Albert had some difficulty preventing the population from butchering their remaining animals.

"I don't even want to think about where this could end up," Armitage said.

Albert looked up from the table and then returned to his inspection of the rifle. He had taken it apart and dried mud crumbled from the action.

"That isn't my department," Albert said.

"We're going to need some kind of enforcement system to keep order," Armitage stated.

"I'm not a policeman," Albert said. "The first person – you, anybody – tries to tell me what I can or can't do will find his head blown clean off," he said matter-of-factly.

"I'm not worried about you," Armitage said, coloring.

"Well you should be," Albert replied, "because I am sure worried about you."

That evening, a patrol returned with news that a herd of feral cattle had been spotted about twenty miles southwest.

"There must've been a thousand of them," the scout said. "I've never seen anything like it."

Albert frowned at him. He was about thirty years old and had grown up in Vermont. How he ended up here was anybody's guess, but there was little doubt he hadn't seen many cows in his short life.

"It wasn't just cattle, either," he continued, excitedly. "There was elephants, too," he said.

Albert looked at him for a long moment.

"It's true," another man said. "I seen them. There was three or four elephants wandering around with them."

"Elephants," Albert repeated. "You seen many elephants in your life?" he asked.

"Enough to know one when I'm looking at it," he said.

Word spread rapidly that herds of wild elephants were roaming the prairie south-west of Provost and by the time the story got back to Albert, the herd had grown to the hundreds and lions and Zulu warriors with nose bones and poison spears were loose in the woods as well.

Albert was actually much less surprised by the report than he appeared. He had never told anyone about the chimpanzee he'd run into the previous summer, but he had not forgotten it, either. Zoo animals had escaped or been let loose and maybe research labs had released their captives as well. In the latter case, it could mean the makings of a new plague. Who knew what they had been infected with? Hadn't government manipulation of one of the bird flu strains wiped out most of the population already? The totalitarian mind possesses no conscience and therefore no limits.

Armitage was still the nominal head of the colony. He occupied the "governor's mansion" and always sat at the head of the table. But it was Albert who effectively ran the settlement and kept the population from starvation.

They were just now harvesting a wild wheat crop and for the first time in months – years – the smell of fresh bread wafted in the air.

He had shown them how to thresh and how to grind and how to collect clay from the banks of the Emit to make wood-fired ovens. For the majority, these esoteric skills were a revelation; they had never eaten anything they hadn't paid for in their entire lives.

Now they had a corn crop growing in a three-acre field that was only a few weeks from harvest. It was like nothing anyone had ever seen before.

The stalks were ten and twelve feet high, thick as small trees at the base and carried a burden of cobs two feet long and six inches in diameter. Very often, the kernels would be fused into a mass of yellow, marbled with streaks of white and sometimes rusty red. Occasionally a normal cob would appear halfway up the stalk.

Volunteer tomato seeds had been carefully dried and planted with little success. The shoots appeared quickly but withered after a day or so. The few plants that made it to flower did not produce fruit. All they needed was one, of course and they could probably propagate a viable crop over time. So far, it had not appeared.

Human propagation was facing its own difficulties as well. The colony now stood at about eight hundred, of whom seventy percent were women. But only ten percent of those – fewer than 60 adult females – were pregnant. So far, spontaneous abortions in the first trimester had resulted in zero population growth.

Valerie and Albert had never discussed the idea of children. It seemed too unlikely considering their age difference and neither seemed drawn or even very interested in children except as an academic issue.

"Would you want to bring a kid into this world?" he asked her.

She didn't answer right away. She was scratching at the dirt around half a dozen experimental plants, something that had taken more and more of her interest, lately.

"You think I'm nesting, is that it?" she asked.

"I don't know," he said. "I didn't know you liked plants so much."

"That's your fault," she said. "I never used to."

Albert got down beside her and started yanking weeds from around a raspberry bush. The one thing he had noticed about rhizomes was there seeming ability to withstand just about any kind of mistreatment and still keep producing.

"You're the best shot around here," he said.

She looked at him, puzzled.

"What's that got to do with anything?"

"I don't know," he admitted.

"Can't a person like plants and shooting, too?"

"I guess…"

"Do you need me to shoot somebody, is that it?"

"No. I just…hell, I don't know."

But she did. He didn't want anything to change. He was a surprisingly insecure man, she thought, considering how much power he held. He was afraid if she changed one thing about herself, she'd change other things.

Then he told her about the cattle.

"We need riders who can help round up those beeves," he told her.

"That's fine," she said, cheerfully. "When do we leave?"

There were plenty of volunteers for the cattle drive, but Albert selected seven of the best riders to go along with Valerie and him. None of them had ever worked cattle on horseback, but there didn't seem to be any other way to move the animals back to Provost.

"Not to mention the elephants," she said pointedly.

"We're not going after elephants," he said.

"That's not what Kincaid thinks," she said, indicating the man riding ahead of them.

Albert glanced at him and then trotted up beside him.

"Ever move cattle?" Albert asked.

"We had cattle when I was a boy, before dad sold the farm. Used to help get them into the trucks," he said.

"This is different," Albert said. "We're trying to keep them moving and quiet."

"What's your point?" Kincaid demanded.

"We're not going after any elephants, is my point," Albert said.

"Oh, ya? Says who? You?"

Albert swung his good arm across Kincaid's face, smashing his nose in a bloody spurt and sending the man toppling backwards off his horse. The animal neighed and reared and then took off. One of the others raced after it as Albert climbed down. Kincaid was lying on his back, his face a contortion of hatred.

"Don't get up," Albert said, but Kincaid ignored him and started to scramble to his feet. Albert's boot caught him in the gut and he yelped and hit the ground, curled up like a fetus.

"You crazy mother fucker!" Kincaid gasped.

"I said stay down," Albert reminded him.

The runaway horse had been recaptured and a man was leading it back.

Albert took the reins and walked over to Kincaid who was still holding his gut.

"You head back," Albert said. "I asked you along because I've seen you ride. But you don't want to do like I say – which is fine. I'm somewhat the same. Difference is, if you don't do what I tell you, then you don't ride with me. Unless of course you really want to try and make an issue of it."

Kincaid got to his feet and took the reins angrily.

"Be careful with that animal," Albert warned him. "I will hold you personally responsible if anything happens to it. Now get the fuck outta here."

They stood on the prairie and watched Kincaid as he trotted back towards Provost.

Albert looked at the others one by one.

"Any man shoots an elephant or tries to shoot an elephant or does anything except what I tell him from here on...well, I am now completely out of patience and forgiveness. We're going to round up some cattle and drive 'em back to Provost. Anybody here got a problem with that?"

Valerie walked beside him, more comfortable in the saddle than on a dining room chair. Albert always seemed to doze.

"You can't just beat people up when they disagree with you," she said.

"Why not?"

"You know why not."

"No I don't. You tell me."

"Because they have rights just like you."

"Nope."

"No? Did you just say no?"

"Yes."

"Jesus Albert…"

"It's Jesus Christ. I am Albert Smythe. The one and the only."

"My God, I think you've finally lost it."

"I think I've finally found it."

She peeled away angrily and loped on ahead of the group until she was out front by a quarter mile and then she resumed a walking pace.

He had never realized before how it actually worked. He had seen men lead and men follow and he didn't understand either of them. No matter how many times the "people" were fooled, the very next fellow that showed up and told them the right lie would get the purple robe. Every time. Every time someone came along, he claimed he was acting in the best interests of "the people." And every time, they would believe him and every time, he'd rob them blind and abuse them and lie to them. And then it would happen again. And keep happening.

Where's Frodo when you really need him.

The thing is, there is no Frodo in this world. There is no one who can resist. And you don't have to give them much to get away with it, either. Just let a bit of the gravy slop down over the edge of your plate and they will lick it off the floor and be grateful for it. And then he realized why he had never been able to get along. He understood why authority always seemed to converge on him even when he wasn't doing anything to attract their attention. He understood in a flash why they hated him. They hated him because they were afraid of him. And they were afraid of him because he didn't want anything they had. If they let one person get away with not participating…well, it might catch on. And if it catches on, then what?!

From there it was an easy stroll to the idea that he would simply act as he pleased. He wasn't rounding up these cattle because people were hungry. He was rounding up the cattle because he liked to fix things. Did he want recognition? No. Did he want praise? No. Did he want some compensation? No. What did he want? He wanted to control his world. And his world was wherever he chose to be.

He had decided that the area on the big county map was his world and the other people were simply visitors. If they wanted to live here, they were going to do what he told them to do. Just like all the other big shots from Armitage to George Griggson. He was going to decide how things happened around here. Period. And if people didn't like it, he would abandon them.

He had devised an imaginary ring around his cave, extending in every direction for an unknown distance. It seemed very simple. If someone upstream from him poisoned the water, he would go and kill them. If anyone shot an elephant, he would hunt them down and kill them too. How far did his realm stretch? As far as he decided. It was only by this method, he realized, that he would be left alone. Ignoring them had not worked. Now it was time to get involved, as they so quaintly put it. Okay, he thought. I am involved.

They were able to follow the old highway south all the way to the southern prairies that used to rush with grain and now were overgrown with untold numbers and species.

They spotted the cattle grazing quietly on the eastern edge of a three or four hundred acre plot.

Albert swept the field glasses across the range and smiled.

"Looks like maybe three or four hundred," he said.

The troop was eager to get started and he explained the method as clearly as he could, considering he had never done it himself.

"Herds will move as you move them," he said. "That is why we will have to go all the way around and come in from behind."

"Shit," Valerie said, scoping the herd with field glasses.

Everyone turned.

"That's not just cattle," she said. "I see some buffalo and...shit...there is an elephant standing there eating the trees."

They passed the glasses around and everyone got a chance to see the huge gray beast yanking tree limbs down with his trunk. His tusks were four feet long.

It took them an hour to cut around behind the herd and they had to come back through thick bush before they got to the edge of the field. The animals had moved little and the majority lay in the sun, quietly chewing.

Three riders moved into position on each side, with Valerie and Albert pushing from behind. The cattle alerted quickly and started bawling and bunching up.

They were a strange mixture of varieties, including half a dozen bulls who stood their ground without twitching an ear.

The elephant had disappeared.

They slowly closed the circle up and the cattle began an orderly march north. At least it seemed that way.

They had gone a few hundred feet and were feeling very accomplished when the bugle came from the bush to the west and the elephant ran out of the woods.

The cattle spooked instantly and began a wild stampede in every direction, some running directly towards the eight ton monster howling in a rage, its ears flapping like the wings on a pterodactyl.

The riders were barely able to stay mounted and were of no use in trying to control the direction of the herd.

The elephant stopped and blew its nose at them and they watched as the cattle flowed around the beast and took off running behind it. Within a few minutes, all but a handful had disappeared into the bush, and the stragglers soon trotted after them.

It had taken about fifteen minutes to clear the field entirely.

The elephant watched them for a few minutes and then turned and followed his friends back to the cool shelter of the woods.

"Nobody is killing any elephants," Albert said again.

The argument had been ongoing for about an hour. The crew did not want to return empty-handed and the cattle could mean the difference between survival and failure for the eight hundred people left in the colony.

"We'll find a way to get some of them loose; but I swear, I will kill any man who shoots that elephant," Albert said.

The strange trumpeting of the big bull and the answer of coyotes punctuated the night.

"I remember reading once about them bringing back all kinds of extinct animals to the west," a man said. "First there was going to be lions and then...I don't know what else."

"I always figured those animals for needing the tropics," said another.

"Well, used be there was big cats all around here," Beecham said.

Albert stared at the coals, his mind blank. Valerie hugged his arm, half asleep.

"We just cut some of them out and run the others off," Albert said finally. "They're all holed up in the bush right now but they'll have to come out to feed. Cattle can't live on browse."

The next morning they split up and began beating the woodlot where the animals had taken refuge for the night.

It wasn't long before they attracted the elephant who charged them repeatedly and blew his trumpet. The herd was apparently his and like some kind of giant grey shepherd, he was protecting his flock.

"Damn," Albert said after the fourth charge.

They finally set on a plan of running the cattle instead of herding them.

Half the drovers came at them from behind, causing a moderate stampede out of the woods and into the field. The remainder drew up alongside the running heard and encouraged them with whoops and other noises they had seen on television westerns.

At the last minute, two of the men cut through the herd, effectively splitting it. The front fifty or so cattle continued to run north and the rest turned about and headed straight back to the woodlot where their mighty champion bellowed and stamped the earth, raising clouds of brown dust.

The riders kept the cattle at an almost dead run until they stopped on their own, exhausted and the rest of the team caught up.

A quick survey showed they had taken two of the bulls.

"Can't have two bulls," someone observed.

"Let them work it out," Albert said, climbing down off his horse.

The cattle were nervous but they had crowded up behind their two bulls and stared at the humans. It was their first contact, most of them having been born wild over the last dozen years.

The bulls snorted and stared at them, but eventually became much more interested in each other.

"Watch out," someone yelled, as three tons of furious jealousy crashed head on, shaking the ground.

The cows were unimpressed and resumed grazing as if nothing unusual was happening.

The bulls rammed each other repeatedly until the smaller of the two suddenly turned and ran.

Then the winner turned on the drovers and charged at them until they were scattered haphazardly around the herd.

"Someone has to stay with them for a few days," Albert said. "Get them used to us."

It was only ten miles back to the town where a temporary corral had been set up but the animals could decide to bolt at any moment. They needed to get some control over them before they tried moving them again.

Albert lay his head down on the saddle and Valerie curled up beside him. The horses grazed nearby.

"What is on your mind?" she asked him.

He didn't want to play the usual guessing game but he was hesitant to start the conversation.

"I guess I am not comfortable here," he said finally.

"You want to go back."

"Yes."

She felt stung and her breath came in gasps.

"No!"

"I don't expect you to-" he started to explain, but it caught in his throat.

There was nothing to say.

*

Albert woke before dawn, as he had for years and drank a cup of flavored hot water.

The men on watch were just silhouettes against a dark blue sky.

Valerie kept her eyes closed and her back to him as she listened to him pack up his kit. She heard every footstep. She knew when he stopped that he was looking at her, but she did not move or speak.

The leather creaked as he climbed aboard and the horse snorted. Its hooves slapped against the soft ground

***

Epilogue

Several hours after departing the prairie camp, Albert turned due west towards his cave. From there it was a three- or four-day easy ride.

Just as he entered a woodlot, something caught his attention. He wasn't even sure if he'd seen it. He pondered whether to head directly "home" or to lead his companion astray and force him to reveal himself.

The horse perked up its ears.

Then he caught sight of it again.

A pair of eyes *were* focused on him.

Greta...

The End

Author's Note:

The story of Albert Smythe's conflict with Greta cannot reasonably be told in a few pages and this tale is long enough. Suffice to say, the adventures of Albert Smythe ranged across the former lands of The United States from the cool forests of Indiana to the beckoning waters of the Pacific Ocean. In that time, he was to encounter strange beasts of every persuasion, landforms and flora not seen for a million years and genetic transformations beyond the temporal imaginings of man.

But that is a story for another day.

HGL

Annotation

1. Albert Einstein

2. W.S., *Macbeth*

3. The Council of Governors is a group composed of 10 state governors of the United States. It was established in January, 2010 in order to strengthen the partnership between federal and state governments in protecting the nation against all manner of threats, including terrorism and natural disasters. The Council was created by Executive Order 13528, signed by President Barack Obama on January 11, 2010, as recommended by the National Defense Authorization Act for Fiscal Year 2008 which was passed by the 110th Congress and signed by President George W. Bush on January 28, 2008.

4. Rabbi Hillel, 110 BCE - 10CE

5. Vietnam War (1962–1975): Malaria felled more combatants during the war than bullets. The disease reduced the combat strength of some units by half.
    (http://www.malariasite.com)

6. Description of starvation according to Justice Lynch of the Supreme Court of Massachusetts in his opinion in 1986.

7. Napoleon Bonaparte.

8. Pre-1965 U.S. dimes and quarters contained approximately 93% pure silver.

9. Kahil Gibran

10. JOB 5:22 (King James bible)

11. Hindu verse: "Now, I am become Death, the destroyer of worlds."

12. W.S., As You Like It...

Made in the USA
Charleston, SC
14 March 2012